# Duplicity

ELODIE HART

*This one's for my dear friends*

*Susie Tate & Rosa Lucas.*

*THANK YOU*
*for workshopping the heck out of this one with me.*

*Brendan's betrayal and grovelling are all the better for your help and wisdom!*

*Xxx*

# *British Lingo*

**A&E** = Accident & Emergency = ER

**Bellend** = the head of a penis = excellent British insult!

**Council estate** = housing project

**Fly tipping** = illegal dumping of rubbish on the street

**Fringe** = bangs

**GOSH** = Great Ormond Street Hospital, a famous children's hospital in London

**GP** = general practitioner = medical doctor (same as an MD)

**MP** =Member of Parliament

**NHS** = National Health Service

**Plait** = braid

**Stag party** = bachelor party

**"The dole"** = unemployment benefit

# CHAPTER 1

# Marlowe

The skin around her little rosebud mouth is tinged with blue.

It's visible even on my phone screen, as are the tear tracks and the ominous pallor of her cheeks, and it makes my stomach lurch.

'It's going to be okay, my love, I promise.' That's all the reassurance I have time for. In this moment, getting my daughter to the hospital is more urgent than talking her through this. 'Have you called an ambulance?' I bark at the unlucky teaching assistant who placed the video call to me. Miss Lewis, her name is. She's new to the school, which means she's new to dealing with Tabby's condition, and nothing about that is good. The phone screen jerks back to the TA's face: young and terrified.

I get it. Believe me.

'Yes. Miss Conway told me to—'

I cut her off. 'Good. Will you go with her to the hospital?'

She blinks. It's clear she hasn't thought this far ahead, but it's not really a request she can decline. Sending an eight-year-old girl off in an ambulance by herself is not an option. 'Yes. Yes, of course.'

As long as an ambulance is en route, I can talk this woman through the rest of our well-practised protocol. Tabby's class teacher, Miss Conway, has far more experience of dealing with her condition, but I'm all too aware that she's responsible for twenty-nine other kids, too. 'Listen to me. Get her to the school office as quickly as you can. Mrs Hopkins knows the score. Put Tabs back on, can you?'

As I talk, I push back my chair and get on my knees, pulling my tote bag from beneath my desk before reaching further back for Tabby's A&E backpack. I have one at home and one at the office, both permanently packed and ready to go for whenever we have a spontaneous visit to Accident & Emergency. They contain the bare minimum: books and colouring paraphernalia; healthy snacks; a phone charger; toothbrushes; PJs for Tabs and clean underwear for both of us in case they end up admitting her overnight, plus the oblig-atory earplugs. There is nowhere on the planet less conducive to a night's sleep than a paediatrics ward in a busy London hospital.

We're old hands at this routine by now.

'Yes. Okay, I'll—hang on.' The TA sounds even more out of breath than the little girl currently suffering from oxygen deprivation.

My daughter's face reappears, and I force my expression into a smile I hope is confident, competent, and reassuring in equal measure. 'Hi again, my love. The ambulance is going to come and get you, and Miss, er, Lewis is going to go with you. But you need to get to the office so Mrs Hopkins can take your sats, okay? Do you think you can walk there? Are you feeling dizzy?'

I already know the answer to that. Her deathly pale complexion is evidence enough that she'll be feeling light-headed, but she nods. 'Yeah, but I can walk.' Her voice is so quiet.

'That's my brave girl.' I kick off my heels and push my feet one by one into a pair of trainers, slamming my laptop shut as I do and then shoving it into the tote.

'Will you come in the ambulance too, Mummy?'

'I can't, angel. I'm at work. I'll have to get the tube straight to the hospital and meet you there. But I'll stay on the line until the paramedics turn up, I promise.'

No way in hell am I risking going underground until I know Tabby's in the hands of professionals. I tug my long hair over one shoulder so I can toss both bags over the other. 'Hang on a sec,' I tell my daughter, and I clamp the phone to my boob for a little privacy. My boss, Dean, is preemptively glaring at me.

'Tabby needs to go to hospital. I'm sorry. I'll log in when I get there.'

He stands up and crosses his arms over his chest. 'We've talked about this, Marlowe. You know you're on your last strike here.'

I widen my eyes in disbelief and hold the phone tighter against my body, hoping Tabs can't hear any of this. 'Tabby's heart didn't get the last strike memo, I'm afraid. I'm sorry to leave you in the lurch, but this is actual life or death. You *know* that.'

He flinches slightly at the *D* word but recovers his inner arsehole pretty quickly. 'That's unfortunate, but I'm not running a charity here.'

I can't help a small scoff, because the Royal Academy of Arts, for whom I'm a strategist, is *literally* a registered charity.

He picks up what I'm putting down. 'You know what I mean. I have a business to run. If you walk out that door, don't bother coming back. Got it?'

'Jesus Christ, Dean,' someone says behind me. I point the

index finger of my free hand at him. My body started pumping adrenaline out as soon as Miss Lewis called me, and now it has me in a dangerous haze of laser focus. If this prick thinks his ultimatum will slow me down for a single second in my singular mission to get my daughter to A&E and meet her there, then he is fucking deluded.

Yes, I take the piss in terms of scarpering every time I get an emergency call from the school, but I'm also that employee feverishly answering emails from a plastic chair in the bowels of our local hospital at 2 am, and he bloody well knows it.

'That you think you're giving me a choice here tells me everything I need to know,' I spit out. I don't spare him or his threat a second glance. In this second, I'm not the usual eager-to-please employee who is horribly aware of how crucial this salary is. I'm a mama bear harnessing the full power of every maternal instinct I've honed over eight years of managing a child with a congenital heart defect, and woe betide anyone who tries to get in my way.

With what I hope is some devastating side-eye, I sweep towards the exit and unplug my phone from my boob. 'Have you got to the office yet?'

'Yeah,' Tabs pants.

'Excellent. Great.' Adrenaline is a dangerous drug. I'm not panicked—I'm invincible. I've got this. 'Put me onto Mrs Hopkins.'

Mrs Hopkins, the receptionist, is first-aid trained and a huge fan of Tabs.

'She's here,' Tabby tells me faintly.

'Mrs Hopkins?' I sprint, unseeing, through the stunning foyer of Burlington House, where the Royal Academy is housed, and emerge out into the spectacular courtyard. 'Do you have the oximeter?'

'Yup.' Her confident tone is music to my ears. 'Hold tight, Miss Winters.'

Tabby is still holding onto her teacher's phone, though she's not doing a great job of keeping it still. My current view as I cross the courtyard and take a left on Piccadilly is of the school crest on her royal blue sweatshirt and a segment of her plaited hair, long and blonde like mine.

'Seventy-nine,' Mrs Hopkins announces.

Fuck, fuck, fuck. Those oxygen levels are way too low. 'Knees to your chest, sweetie. What were you doing when you started to feel bad?' I ask Tabs as I speed-walk along Piccadilly. I'll duck underground as soon as I've handed her over, but we'll need to give the paramedics as much context as possible.

I get a shaky image of her pulling her bare knees up to her chest. By curtailing blood flow to the lower half of her body, her heart can focus on directing more of its limited supply to her lungs.

The TA's voice sounds through my phone. 'We were just rehearsing for the class assembly. The kids were doing a dance routine, and Tabby said she felt dizzy.'

Tabby's condition, Tetralogy of Fallot, sounds like something from the Legend of King Arthur but is, in fact, a congenital heart defect. The pulmonary valve sending blood from her heart to her lungs was too narrow at birth, constraining her oxygen supply. She's endured two open-heart surgeries to replace the valve, one at birth and one aged three, but she's once again outgrown her current valve. Right now, it only takes a small amount of physical exertion to bring on what Tabs and I call a "blue spell", where blood flow to the lungs decreases and oxygen levels plummet.

'Got it. Mrs Hopkins, can you grab a fact sheet, please?'

'Absolutely,' I hear. 'Don't you worry. We've got this little pixie, don't we, Tabs?'

Thank God for people like Mrs Hopkins, who treat everyone else's kids with as much love and attention as their own. She keeps a stack of printed sheets that I've put together and filled with all of Tabby's salient information—contact details for me, an overview of her condition and surgical history, her meds, and contact details for her cardiac team at Great Ormond Street Hospital, or GOSH, London's preeminent and wildly under-resourced children's hospital.

If my maths is right, we've handed over eight fact sheets since January, and it never gets easier.

The hours following my arrival at the hospital are the usual blur of doctors and machines and beeping. Tabby was given beta blockers and an oxygen mask when she was admitted, and both her oxygen saturation and heart rate have normalised, thank fuck. She's had a chest X-ray as well as an ECG to assess the functionality of her pulmonary valve.

Between treatments, I've sung to her softly, and we've read from the *Anne of Green Gables* paperback we keep in her hospital backpack. We've been given a bed in one of the main A&E wards so that the doctors can observe Tabby before discharging her.

As I read to her, my gaze keeps drifting to a little girl in one of the bays across from us. She's probably a couple of years younger than Tabby. I'm not sure what's wrong with her, but she was vomiting and crying in pain earlier. She's happier now, thank God, but the thing that grabs my attention over and over is the two parents flanking her. Her mother and father sit on plastic chairs on either side of her bed like two adoring guardian angels. They haven't left her side. As I watch, they interlace their fingers on her lap, and the gesture is so tender, so natural, that I have to look away. Those three are thick as thieves, and it couldn't be any more obvious.

It's not that I want someone here for *me*. I'm an A&E expert by now, and I'm used to being the grown-up, to acting like I'm not falling apart without having anyone to rub *my* back and tell me it's all going to be okay. But it's not fair that a little girl as brave and amazing as Tabs should have to make do without a father figure in her tough little life.

It's not fucking fair.

Fucking Joe.

The only silver lining is that I've had no time at all to ruminate over being fired. I had a text from my colleague Jake —*You can appeal this, you know*—but I'm too damn exhausted, as the adrenaline vacates my nervous system, to even consider that option. I'm too overwhelmed with emotion to have any capacity for the financial worries that I know are waiting to flood my brain.

Right now, my only focus is the frail little girl on the bed next to me. The colour has returned to her cheeks, and that terrifying blue tinge has faded for now. Miss Lewis told me when I arrived that the dance they'd been rehearsing for their assembly wasn't even particularly high energy, and the knowledge terrifies me.

I don't need a doctor to tell me what I already know, but a paediatric cardiologist swings by and pulls me aside just to ram home the incontrovertible truth anyway.

'The ECG has shown a further deterioration in her pulmonary valve,' she tells me gently. 'We spoke to her cardiac team at GOSH. I understand she's waitlisted for a valve replacement surgery, but not until November?'

'That's right.'

November is six months from now, and the doctor's grimace says it all.

It's too far away.

'If this pattern continues, I'd expect she may be in need of an emergency replacement sooner than that. So far, the right ventricle is holding up remarkably well, but I'd expect to start seeing a thickening of the wall given the strain it's under. If you find that her tolerance for exertion declines further, or the tet spells become more severe or frequent, or her sats start to worsen when she's resting, we'd conclude that the heart is struggling to cope.

'An emergency surgery is far from ideal for many reasons that I'm happy to expand on, but I'm afraid Tabby's heart may not be equipped to last another six months with a profoundly inadequate valve.'

Each sentence is a blow to the stomach. I have never in my life felt so powerless. So sickened. Every single day, I watch my daughter, so small and frail for her age, navigate the art of surviving life rather than thriving on it because one of her body's most basic functions is compromised. I'm forced to decline her pleas for gym classes and ballet classes. I'm the mother who hands over medical fact sheets to any parent who hosts her for a playdate.

She needs a new fucking pulmonary valve, and she needs it now, and I don't have the hundreds of thousands of pounds required to get it for her privately. So I'm stuck here, hopelessly dependent on our overstretched National Health Service to shuffle us along in its never-ending queue of equally deserving, equally sick children until we one day reach the front.

'I know how frustrating it is,' the doctor tells me softly. 'Perhaps this is something you and your partner can discuss, so that if emergency surgery is the only option, you feel better prepared for—'

'There is no partner,' I say quickly. 'I mean, Tabby's father's not in the picture. It's just me and her.'

I swear the compassion on her face ratchets up a notch. 'Of course. I apologise. This is a lot to bear alone. We have support services available to the parents of children with these conditions. I can give you a leaflet...' She trails off.

I don't need a leaflet.

I need a Hail Mary.

Such an unfortunate turn of phrase when the only possible *Hail Mary* available to me is to sell my soul to some guy who may as well be the Devil himself for the price he'll demand.

But God knows, I'll pay it.

I pull out my phone and shoot off a few texts.

> At the hospital

> Tabs had another blue spell

> And Dean fired me for leaving early

> Looks like Seraph is the only card I have left to play

# CHAPTER 2

# *Marlowe*

Six months ago, my best friend and part-time fairy godmother, and Tabby's *actual* godmother, handed me a brochure whose contents felt more forbidden than that godforsaken apple in the Garden of Eden.

Because that brochure contained *hope* within its glossy pages.

Hope in the form of non-invasive, laparoscopic heart surgeries by the most experienced paediatric cardiothoracic surgeons in the world.

Hope that can only be a reality for the lucky children whose parents have six figures to drop on the noble cause of making their kids' medical worries go away, just like that.

I was pissed off when Athena showed it to me, and I was even more pissed off when she offered to pay for the whole shebang with money she'd earned in the hardest way possible up until last month: by having sex with rich, powerful dickheads whenever they wanted a piece of her.

No fucking way. I don't know how she's done it all these years, even if she's a nympho to my nun on the sexuality scale.

Besides, if I let her fix this for me, then I honestly don't know what would be left of me.

Mum. Carer. Provider. Those roles consumed the rest of me years ago. They're all I am these days, and I'm damn well not going to let anyone else do my job for me.

It wasn't until a few weeks ago that a friend and fellow escort of hers, Sophia, casually suggested that *I* do a stint with their agency in order to fund a US-based valve replacement for Tabs. It was a solution so improbable, so unhinged, and so outrageously pragmatic that I haven't been able to stop thinking about it since.

The women on Seraph's books are full-service executive assistants who get paid seven figures a year by their bosses for the privilege of fucking them whenever they (their bosses, that is) want. And while I'm the first to admit that for the past four years the merest thought of my best friend enduring that career has given me hives, the concept of *me* enduring it, for a few months, anyway, has grown less outlandish the more I let it percolate.

If you remove the following small details—that I haven't actually had sex since my married music professor seduced me, knocked me up, and dumped me at university, or that my sexy skills would barely warrant someone slipping me fifty quid afterwards, or that Athena is so fiercely protective that she won't even discuss it with me—then the dilemma I have is so achingly simple that, really, there's no dilemma at all.

My daughter needs her pulmonary valve replaced yesterday.

And it is technically within my power to take action and fund that replacement in the safest, most expedient, and least invasive way possible.

I say *technically*, because the chances of Seraph taking me on its books are borderline zero. Without Athena's magical powers of persuasion, anyway.

'Over my dead body.' She takes a sip of the excellent white wine she's brought along and flicks her perfect, glossy waves over her shoulder.

'No. Over your goddaughter's dead body.'

Even Athena, the chronic under-reactor, flinches at that. 'That's unnecessary. And overly dramatic.'

'I'm serious. If you distil this situation to its barest bones, Tabby's best chance of survival is an operation as soon as possible, especially if it avoids open-heart surgery. You know it and I know it.'

We were discharged from the hospital a couple of hours ago, thank God. It's only eight o'clock, but Tabby fell asleep after a couple of lullabies, her tiny body exhausted from the day's events. She insisted on sleeping in her sleeping bag inside the stunning (and ludicrously expensive) tent she got a few months ago when Athena insisted on playing Father Christmas. It came from Harrods and isn't something I could ever, ever have afforded, but Athena suggested that Tabby treat it as her safe space between "battles". So tonight, another battle bravely fought and won, my little warrior princess slumbers in her magical refuge.

Athena responded to my text messages like the goddess she is, by showing up at my flat with wine, chocolate, and yummy Whole Foods microwave meals, even though I told her not to and even though she has a huge new job and a disgustingly handsome, disgustingly rich, and disgustingly adoring boss-slash-boyfriend waiting for her to get home and warm up his bed, because that's the kind of human being she is. Our deal is that she always brings the wine. She refuses to drink the "cheap shit" that's within my budget.

I take her in and marvel, like I always do. Not only is she

stunningly beautiful, with her huge hazel eyes and auburn tresses, but she's put together in a way I can't even dream of being. She's in some sparkly tweed dress with big diamanté buttons that I suspect is Chanel and she could not look less at home among my IKEA furniture.

She's also the singularly most fearsome and most impressive individual I've ever, ever met. I couldn't ask for a better person to have in my corner.

'I agree,' she says in response to my assessment of Tabs's health status. 'And we both know this goes away tomorrow if you let me pay for it.'

'Categorically not.' I don't need to expand on my argument. She knows my views. I'm not taking money she's earned in such a brutal way. Especially not as she's just taken a hefty pay cut. She's no longer her boss, Gabe's EA with benefits but his official girlfriend and the new CEO of his multi-billion-pound foundation.

The Audacity Foundation.

She told me he named it after her, his audacious girlfriend.

I can't even.

With Athena, you have to be direct. It's what she values and understands. So I set down my delicious box of sesame salmon and I lean forward so I can look her in the eye.

'Babes. I appreciate your offer more than you will ever, ever know. But it has to be me. If I have the option to save my own daughter, then I have to do it. Do you understand?'

She nods once, matter-of-factly, displeasure written all over her face.

'In theory, I could do this. Right? I mean, I have an MBA and I'm hopefully not entirely unfuckable.' It's been so long since I've put myself out there that I can't quite be sure on that front, but men are pretty basic creatures, aren't they? Hopefully one of them will find the clueless born-again virgin vibe hot.

And while Athena's friend Sophia told me that Seraph usually hires candidates with MBAs from the top schools—the Whartons and INSEADs and Sorbonnes of this world—the Open University one that I completed remotely while working for the Royal Academy gives me the only three letters I need after my name to make me technically eligible.

Technically.

She snorts at that. 'You're one of the most exquisite creatures I've ever had the pleasure of knowing, and those dirty bastards would be queuing around the block for you. But that's not the issue, and you know it.'

I scrunch up my face as I pick up my salmon and wild rice. 'You could refresh me on how to give a blow job. We could put condoms on courgettes and practise.' I wasn't half bad at blow jobs, back in the day. Joe, my professor and Tabby's biological father, was always beside himself when I used my mouth on him. Surely it's just like riding a bike?

'Stop being disingenuous. Of course you could handle a blow job. They're not exactly rocket science. The issue is that you've been celibate for most of your adult life, and you're making a case for becoming a whore and letting a random guy for whom you have no feelings do whatever the fuck he wants to your body, day after day after day.'

She glares at me, and a wave of nausea swirls through my stomach. I set the salmon down next to me again.

'When they're paying out this kind of money, they don't fuck around. You think they're going to pay out close to a hundred grand a month to kiss you and play with your tits every now and again? Whoever hires you will work you hard as fuck, and you are not cut out for it. It would be entirely too overwhelming for your nervous system. I can't even imagine the toll it would take on your mental health. What good will it do Tabby if her sole caregiver has a nervous breakdown because she's so traumatised?'

I stare at her in horror. Her tone is cold, and her words have their desired effect because I know she's right. When it comes to a normal, healthy sex life, I haven't even been playing in the paddling pool in recent years. What I'm proposing would be the equivalent of cliff-diving into treacherous, shark-filled waters.

I'd be so out of my depth it would be laughable if it weren't so utterly terrifying.

Except that I'm all out of options, and if prostituting myself is the sole remaining solution left to me, then I'm sure as hell going to take it. And every time I have to put out, I'll close my eyes and think of my daughter's right ventricle pumping lots and lots of juicy blood into her little lungs to get beautifully oxygenated.

'I understand what you're saying,' I tell my best friend. 'But you're the smartest person I know and the most practical. This has to happen. For God's sake, tell me how we do it in the least painful way possible.'

There's silence as we glare at each other, and I see the moment she accepts that I'm not backing down. Her breath leaves her body with a loud, defeated whoosh, and she stands. She's still in sky-high ivory-coloured heels and glossy nude stockings, and it strikes me that I'd have to seriously up my work attire game from the floaty, cheap sundresses I've favoured while working at the Royal Academy.

'Getting you in would be the first hurdle,' she muses aloud, strumming her fingers on the top of my TV. 'But I could speak to Camille and try to pave the way. She won't like it, but if I assure her that you can handle it, I suspect she'll do it as a favour to me.'

Camille runs the Seraph team and is responsible for the hiring. From everything Athena's told me about her over the years, she sounds both fair and sensible. I nod. 'Okay. Good. I suppose you'll have to tell her about Tabs, but I wouldn't want any of the guys knowing.'

'Agreed. No offence, but a single mum wouldn't be top of their list for an easy-fuck assistant. We could get away without disclosing that on any of your materials. Right, the best way to do this would be to set up a prospective employer before you even go in to interview with Camille. That way, it saves you from unnecessary photos and things.'

I freeze. 'What photos?'

'Everyone on their books has a portfolio.' I can tell by her delivery that she's choosing her words carefully. 'There are photos that the guys can look at before they ask you to interview. Facial portraits, full body, clothed and unclothed. They do a seated open-legged one as standard so the guys can see what they're getting.'

I can't help it. My face floods with heat. Oh my fucking God, this is horrific. I'm sure my horror is written all over my face, but I can't openly freak out at the first hurdle. If the prospect of being photographed nude is too much for me, I'll never make it in this job. That said, the last guy I trusted enough to see me naked for any extended period was Joe—the man who promised me the world but disappeared when I needed him most.

Athena, of course, doesn't miss a thing. 'Oh, Jesus,' she groans. 'This is a total non-starter, honestly.'

'No, go on. Please. I promise you I can handle it.'

She sighs heavily. 'I hate to say this, because Camille is a friend and I'd hate to shaft her, but in theory we could get you employed for just a few months and then you can quit once Tabby's had her op and you've put some money aside for private follow-up care. Once someone interviews you and wants to take things forward to the audition stage, he has to fork out twenty-five grand before he fucks you. Then you get around a hundred grand sign-on bonus.'

*A hundred grand.*
*A hundred grand.*
*Don't focus on the word* audition.
*Don't think for a second about what that might entail.*
*Getting yourself worked up is unhelpful right now.*
*Just focus on the operation.*
*On what it costs and what you need to earn before you run for the hills.*

'Okay,' I say shakily. 'That sounds good.'

'Nothing about this is good. The key is to find you someone who's horny enough to fork out for a Seraph EA but decent enough to treat you with respect. Let me see, let me see. *Fuck.*'

She whirls around, wineglass in hand, her mouth open and her expression triumphant. 'I think I've got someone.'

'Who?' I ask with trepidation, because if she has a man in mind, that means that this outrageous plan is gathering mass and may actually become something real as opposed to a crazy scheme hatched from the mind of a desperate mother.

'Remember Gabe's brother Brendan?'

Brendan.

I met him at an exhibition at the Royal Academy a few months ago, the first night I met Gabe.

Stupidly attractive.

The kind of guy who looks like he has a different woman in his bed every night.

Swagger for days, or so you'd think... But he was extremely weird with me that night. All stuttering and awkward. It made me feel so uncomfortable, in fact, that I excused myself soon after and went back to schmoozing our patrons.

'Yeah?' I say cautiously.

'He was so into you that night. He was completely tongue-tied—I've never seen him like that since. And he's asked about you a few times, but he's a total fuckboy.' She takes a few steps towards me and cocks her head, surveying me thoughtfully. 'He's still got a massive bee in his bonnet about the fact that his brother, who used to be a *priest*, hooked himself up with a Seraph EA and he was totally oblivious to the entire concept. It really pissed him off.'

She sucks the inside of her cheek before continuing. 'How about I have a little chat with our Brendan? He may be a player, but he's a good guy at heart. I bet he'd jump at the chance to have someone like you at his beck and call.

'And, most importantly, I know where he lives, so if he hurts you, I can get to him and hurt *him*.'

# CHAPTER 3

# *Brendan*

I n the arse end of the London Docklands lies a jewel: an absolutely massive former aircraft hangar that's now a showroom for Lagoon, one of the world's highest-end brands of catamaran.

Others may favour yachts, but I don't have the patience for sailing. Why the fuck would I want to fanny around with the wind when I can rely on sheer horsepower instead? And, given that I'm low-key claustrophobic and not mad about the concept of spending millions to sleep in a glorified bunk room, I'm partial to the twin-hull design and extra space a catamaran affords me.

After my last two-week holiday in the Maldives, I swore I'd never base myself in one vacation spot again. I nearly died of boredom. The same view, every day. By day three I wanted to bang my head against a palm tree, over and over. I'd far rather take one of these babies to the Greek Islands or BVIs and island hop whenever I get itchy feet.

I know in my bones that the Lagoon SEVENTY 8 is the one. She's fucking gorgeous—a seventy-eight-foot masterclass in nautical design with lightweight carbon fibre hulls and an owner's suite so luxurious I swear it gives me a semi. While my mates increasingly choose to spend their time swapping their fuck-me cologne for regurgitated breast milk, I'll be cruising around the Caribbean with my on-deck jacuzzi and rainfall shower, living the dream with a different woman in every island harbour.

Commissioning my very own SEVENTY 8 is a straightforward decision made even easier now that my brother has persuaded our family to appoint his indecently hot new girlfriend as the head of our foundation. She, in turn, has us pledging to reduce our joint wealth by seventy-five per cent over the next two decades.

That's around six billion pounds, a sum so vast it makes me want to curl up into a ball and weep like a baby when I think about it. While none of us will ever find ourselves near the breadline, collecting shiny toys like this may become less of a no-brainer going forward. I may as well go crazy with the toy acquisitions while the golden times are still upon us.

Besides, if Gabe can spend millions on a *five-hundred-year-old prayer book* from Sotheby's—I kid you not—I can sure as fuck spend the same on an honest-to-God piece of kit.

The icing on the cake is Vanessa, the leggy honey-blonde salesperson currently doing a stellar job of looking after me. She's even valiantly pretending not to be repulsed by my dog, Mark. He may be my favourite sentient creature on this planet, but, God bless him, with his mismatched eyes and weirdly short legs, his looks won't be flooding anyone's Instagram feed in the near future. Vanessa's commission on a sale like this must be eye-watering, but I'd like to think that's real attraction in her big blue eyes.

Attraction to me, that is.

Not Mark.

She's just as sleek and pretty and, I bet, high maintenance, as my glorious carbon fibre buddy here. Mark, however, is having none of it. He shunned her attempt at petting him by trundling pointedly off to lie in front of the reception desk.

'Let's get you a cold beer while we go over your bespoke specifications,' she purrs, batting her long eyelashes at me. 'There's a lot to go through.'

I shoot her the playboy grin I know she's expecting before surreptitiously glancing at my watch. My research ahead of this showroom visit was a rabbit hole of feverish hyper-focus, but the biochemical thrill of deciding on such a sizeable purchase is already dissipating at the prospect of being cornered with pages and pages of questions around leather finish and carpet colour and cabin layouts.

Kill me now.

My fingers seek out the fidget toy on the keychain in my pocket, rolling the little spinner thingy around and around. I don't usually take my Ritalin on the weekends, but I should have known better than to embark on a project like this without my study buddies. I wonder if I can get my interior designer to take on the kit-out. She has a great eye and I frankly don't give a fuck which shade of ivory my on-deck sun loungers end up. Mark's bored too; he just does a worse job of showing it. He's still sprawled out near the reception desk, head on his paws and eyes doleful.

Once Vanessa and her pert little arse have disappeared around the corner in search of beer, I go to him and hike up the legs of my jeans so I can squat and pet his broad head, which is a legacy of the twenty-eight per cent American Staffy in his lineage. The DNA test I commissioned after I rescued him also showed six other breeds, all clues to his bizarrely perfect appearance.

As I stroke Mark's sleek fur, I become aware of the woman behind the desk lowering her voice as she speaks on the phone. She's probably a decade older than me, and I've seen her sneak at least two dog biscuits to Mark from the glass jar on the desk.

I assume she's responsible for the bowl of water that's appeared beside him, too.

'No, Will, I can't—how am I supposed to get there?' Her voice is a low hiss. 'You'll have to see if your mum can grab him. I don't know—can she take a bus over there and Uber him to the doctor's?'

I keep my head discreetly bent until she hangs up with a whispered *keep me posted*.

'Everything okay?' I ask, getting to my feet. My quads complain as I rise, thanks to a punishing weights session yesterday with my PT, Si the Sadist.

'I'm so sorry about that.' She blushes. I've flustered her on top of everything else.

'I'm the one who should apologise for eavesdropping,' I say easily. 'Terrible habit. But it sounds like you've got a bit of an emergency going on there.'

'My son's twisted his ankle at football,' she admits. 'The coach called my husband, but he's in the middle of a shift. He can't leave, and he's got the car. He dropped me here on his way earlier. I'll have to sneak out and find a bus, I think.'

The words are out before I can take them back, though, for once, my impulsivity feels justified. 'Sorry to hear that. My driver's sitting outside, twiddling his thumbs. He can take you to pick up your son and drop you at a walk-in centre or something?'

She stares at me like I've grown an extra head. 'I can't do that! You're very, very kind but it's not an option. I'll get the bus.'

'Where's the football pitch?' I ask her in my CEO Voice.

'Um, Poplar.'

This hangar is in the middle of fucking nowhere. There's no way she's going to find an easy bus route to Poplar. 'Yeah, the bus thing isn't going to happen. Let Yan drive you. Honestly. Call your husband back.' I give her what I hope is a reassuring smile. 'Vanessa has made it very clear that I have hours of decision-making in my near future. Mark and I are good here for the afternoon.'

I brush off her effusive, teary thanks as I escort her out to my Defender.

Back inside, Vanessa's leaning against the twin of my soon-to-be catamaran, a cold Peroni in her hand and her skirt hiked just enough to make me forget about the receptionist's problem almost instantly. Here's hoping she'll make the next couple of hours worthwhile... and I'm not talking about linen swatches.

Mark gives me a judgmental look before flopping back down with a huff.

'Don't give me that,' I mutter to him. 'Unlike boats, blondes are easily replaceable.'

The hot ones always think they're special. But they all blur together eventually: this month's diversion until something shinier comes along. Just like the SEVENTY 8 will be this year's toy until next year's model catches my eye.

At least the catamaran won't expect a phone call the next day.

CHAPTER 4

*Brendan*

The bank of glass walls behind my desk and the expanse of space and light beyond it are both luxuries of having our headquarters based in the London Docklands, where square footage comes at less of a premium than in the city centre.

When my grandfather dragged his eldest son—my father —over from their home in the Dublin docks to forge a name for the Sullivan family within the London construction industry, neither of them could have conceived of the success they would go on to achieve, the wealth they would build. Wealth that was crystallised when we took Sullivan Construction public on the stock market a few years ago, netting our family billions of pounds, which my brother Gabe now manages under the umbrella of our in-house investment firm, Rath Mor.

Billions that we've recently pledged to give away.

While our sister Mairead spends most of her time managing stallions with boners—she runs our family's stud farm—Gabe and I stand at the helms of our asset management and construction businesses respectively. Gabe's still a little green behind the ears, having left his calling as a priest after a decade to take up the reins at Rath Mor, but I've grown up in Sullivan Construction and I've earned the top job.

I may be less academically inclined than my little brother, who's always reading ancient philosophers and studying the fucking Bible, but I'm a doer. A grafter. I'm no nepo baby, no matter what the press likes to say about me.

Construction suits me. It suits my attention span (short) and my energy levels (high). Every single day there's a different fight to have, a different fire to put out, and when the toiling has ceased, you have a building at the end of it. A building that shelters humans, allows them to live and work and dream.

If that's not job satisfaction, I don't know what is.

My favourite workdays are those where I'm out of the office, walking our sites. Even with this dazzling bank of glass behind me, I get antsy pretty quickly staring at my monitor. Today has been a desk day, which is why I'm particularly intrigued by the next appointment in my diary.

My brother's girlfriend and the new CEO of our foundation, Athena, has requested a meeting. Even if she's most likely only here to charm me into handing over some land earmarked for Sullivan Construction so she can turn it into a fucking equestrian centre or public library, I'll find it entertaining. First, she's stupid levels of hot, and second, I've quickly learnt that any conversation with her is like a particularly strenuous game of squash—athletic and exhausting.

I'm sure today's not the day she'll disappoint on either front.

'I have a proposition for you,' Athena announces, running her hand over Mark's head. He's sitting to attention at her side as if she's dangling a roast chicken leg in front of him. Clearly, even dogs aren't immune to her charms. Once again, I'm half tickled, half pissed off that my holier-than-thou brother hired himself a full-service executive assistant. Tickled because I can't believe he had the initiative, let alone the balls, and pissed off because the Angel Gabriel has landed his perfect girlfriend.

I bet he hasn't had a boring day in the office since he met this bombshell.

And I'd put money on their workdays being just as 'fruitful' since she switched from being his fuck toy to the head of his philanthropic mission.

'Of course you do.'

I bet she gets everything she asks for. It would be a stupid man who goes up against her fierce intellect and her total lack of fucks given. Still, I won't roll over without a fight.

She licks her lips and leans forward, offering her palm to Mark, who proceeds to slobber all over it. I'm absolutely *not* expecting the next word out of her mouth.

'Seraph.'

I grin, intrigued. 'What about it?'

'Don't tell me you haven't been entertaining the idea of hiring a Seraph EA since you found out the capacity in which Gabe hired me.'

I have many charms, but clearly an air of mystery is not one of them. 'And if I have?'

'Not only can I get you on their books.' She pauses for effect. 'But I have the perfect candidate for you. She's just in the process of joining them, and I thought I'd do you the courtesy of giving you first refusal.'

'Playing pimp now, are you? Did my brother slash your salary by that much?'

She shakes her head as if to say *you foolish, foolish man.* 'No one's twisting your arm. Are you interested or not?'

'Why are you being nice?' I demand. 'Is this about sequestering some of my land?'

'I'm never nice. I'm disappointed you haven't worked that out already. And no, this isn't about your land. I'll let Mairead wear you down about the equestrian centre all on her own. This is because there are a handful of people in this world whom I care about—literally one hand's worth—and your brother is one, but my friend Marlowe is another.' She arches an eyebrow, cool as you like. 'You remember her, don't you?'

'You know I do,' I say mulishly, because not only did I make a gigantic tit of myself the night I met the celestial Marlowe, but I've submitted some inelegant requests to Athena since then to put in a good word for me with her mate, and she's refused point blank.

'Thought so. Well, Marlowe is joining Seraph, and I thought you might be a good fit for her. From a hiring perspective, I mean.'

She smiles innocently, as if she hasn't just intentionally dropped a double entendre that goes straight to my groin, because her friend is nothing short of delectable, and I know very fucking well that she'd be a *stellar* "fit" for me.

But *joining Seraph?* That's a concept I can't begin to wrap my head around. The Marlowe I met was all wispy blonde hair and long, floaty dress and bohemian elegance. The vibe she projected before I scared her off with my creepy nerves was very much that of the wholesome, unwittingly hot primary school teacher you'd try to fuck if you had a kid in her class. Like Miss Honey from *Matilda* but with that virginal sexuality thing ramped up to porno levels, if that makes sense.

It doesn't make sense.

But neither does her being a professional whore.

'She has a job, doesn't she?' I ask, performing a mental

scramble. 'At the RA? Why the fuck would she want to join Seraph?'

'Like most people who prostitute themselves, she needs the money,' Athena says crisply. Clear subtext: *Don't for a single second dare to think that women actually want to be in these roles, you entitled dickhead.*

'What does she need it for?'

She frowns, hesitating before she answers me. 'Let's just say she's been hit with some... unforeseen expenses recently.'

That sentence is brimming with subtext, but the unspoken has never been my strong point. I'm a guy who takes things at face value. So Marlowe's got greedy, has she? Either that or she's in some kind of debt. Well, I can get on board with funding her shopping addiction.

'And you want me to hire her? Why the hell would you be okay with me hiring her but not okay with helping me date her?'

'Oh, please.' She gives me a look that's beyond disdainful while massaging Mark's jowls. 'Firstly, you don't want to date her, you want to fuck her. I'm under no illusions about guys like you, Brendan, so don't waste my time or insult my intelligence by trying to pretend otherwise. And secondly, she needs this job. Do you really want to date someone who's fucking another guy during office hours, Monday to Friday?'

My face, I assume, provides its own answer. On second thought, my brother is welcome to this woman. Smoking she may be, but she's a piece of work.

'I thought not. And thirdly, I may not think you're anywhere near worthy of being dating material for Marlowe, but I suspect you're a semi-decent guy behind this fuckboy-slash-alphahole exterior you have going on.' Her expression grows more serious. 'And, after four years of working for Seraph, I'm all too aware of what kind of clients it attracts. I'm just looking out for my friend, and I trust you, as far as I can trust any man, not to behave like a gigantic twat. I'm trusting that you'd abide by the spirit of the contract and treat her with decency.'

I'm half listening. I think she just said something that, by her standards, could be construed as almost touching. But, honestly, my chimp brain is racing away with me, because *fuuuuuuuuuuck.*

Marlowe in my office every day, where Plain Elaine currently sits? Marlowe sucking my dick *under* my desk and bending *over* my desk whenever the fuck I like?

*Jesus Christ.*

'If you get so much as a semi right now, then I'm out of here,' Athena warns, pointing her free hand at me.

'Give me a fucking break,' I grumble, but I scoot my chair closer towards my desk just in case.

'Here's the score, Brendan, just in case you were too busy fantasising about banging my friend to absorb what I've been telling you.' *Damn it, how does she do that?* 'This is the only way you're going to get your hands on Marlowe. She has a lot going on right now. I won't let you dick her around, but I *will* let you dick her down if you play by my rules and the Seraph rules.

'You don't even need to be exclusive—she's your employee. You can have your fun with her at work and then get your end away in whatever wanky nightclubs you like to frequent out of work.'

She literally had me at *Marlowe:* beautiful, classy, and cultured. Having a woman like her decorate my office would be the ultimate win, but there's no way I'm caving so easily. For some reason, Athena really wants this. I can tell by the steeliness in her voice and the intensity in her demeanour. I cock my head and chew on my lower lip as I pretend to appraise her offer.

'I want you to throw in an Alchemy membership.'

'Done,' she says immediately.

'There's no way you'll get my brother to budge on that front.' Gabe's been dragging his feet on proposing me for the exclusive sex club he joined before he met Athena. Selfish little dog in the manger. I thought former priests were supposed to be more charitable.

'I don't need to. I have plenty of ways in. My former boss's wife, Genevieve, owns the place, and my new friend's boyfriend has a stake. Adam Wright. I've got you covered. If that's your price, consider it done.'

I sit back and allow myself a smirk. Marlowe, Marlowe, Marlowe. Five minutes in her presence and I knew she served up that ladylike, classy thing I love with aplomb.

I bet she'd be all doe-eyed and tremulous and shy if I fed her my dick. I've thought about it since; I'm not going to lie.

Thought about how her eyelashes would flutter, and how she'd protest that it wouldn't fit.

How incredibly fucking gratifying it would be to watch as ecstasy took over that beautiful face and her outward breeding gave way to her inner prurience.

How tiny she'd feel as I caged her beneath my body.

No wonder I've been hounding Athena about putting in a good word for me.

And here she is, telling me in so many words that I'm not fit to wipe the dog shit off Marlowe's shoe but that, for the right price, I can have her anyway, in the most salacious ways possible.

It should sicken me, fill me with guilt, but it doesn't.

Quite the opposite. It flips a switch that has an ill-earned sense of power and entitlement coursing through my veins. If I'm completely honest with myself, a sense of *ownership*.

'You're on.'

Athena nods once, as if she expected nothing less, and

caresses Mark's head one more time before elegantly getting to her feet.

'I'll speak to the Alchemy team and I'll get Camille from Seraph to email over a questionnaire and application form today. With me as a character reference, you can skip some of the due diligence. The paperwork is more about assessing your needs rather than your eligibility.'

My needs.

I began this meeting preparing to do battle with Athena.

I'm ending it wondering if this little firecracker is, in fact, my sexual fairy godmother.

She takes a step forward and slams her palms down on my desk, and I find myself cowering instinctively.

'One more thing. You harm my friend, physically or emotionally, and I will take great pleasure in skinning your balls with a rusty butter knife. Do I make myself clear?'

I have no doubt she means every word.

Just as I have no plans to harm a hair on her beautiful friend's head.

But if the lovely Marlowe wants to sell herself to me, body and soul, to fund her penchant for self-indulgence, she should understand that I expect my pound of flesh.

I'll take exquisite pleasure in breaking her in and working her as hard as I can.

I hope she knows what she's signing up for.

# CHAPTER 5

# *Marlowe*

I t's been five years since I've had to brave a job interview. While I wanted the job at the RA—badly, in fact—the stakes have never been this high.

I'm so close to taking Tabby's health into my own hands and funding an operation that will change her life. I even have a potential new boss lined up. And while I'm nowhere near ready to let myself entertain what the daily reality of being a Seraph EA will entail, I'm damned if I'm going to fail at this final hurdle of getting past the gatekeeper.

Camille.

The worst of it is that, from what Athena's told me, she's far more likely to block my way because she perceives me to be ill-equipped to handle the role emotionally rather than due to any inadequacies—professional or aesthetic—on my part.

Which is why this has to be the performance of a lifetime.

On Athena's instructions, I've borrowed a pair of her horrifyingly expensive heels and rented a sleek black shift dress that "shows off the goods" (her words) and makes me feel like an extra from *Suits*. She blow-dried my hair into long, sleek waves this morning and made me put on far more eye makeup than I ever would myself.

The result is vampish and, like all good theatrical costumes, it's doing its job, wrapping around the real Marlowe like the best kind of armour.

I just hope it arms me enough to convince Camille that I am capable of handling the very specific challenges that come with this role.

Camille is everything Athena said she would be: groomed in a glossy, borderline severe kind of way; raven-black hair parted in the centre and scraped back; red lips immaculate. She's no-nonsense, with a warmth that's faint but enough to take the slightest edge off my nerves.

*Tabby, Tabby, Tabby,* I chant to myself.

Nothing else matters.

I have a job to do.

I will not let my daughter down.

I am willing to do whatever it takes.

And no one, particularly not this woman sitting across from me, will rob me of my opportunity to give Tabby the dazzling, healthy, *normal* future she so thoroughly deserves.

We start with the business stuff. Camille asks me about my CV, most notably the fact that my three-year degree took four years.

'I took a year out when my daughter was born,' I explain. 'Kings let me rejoin the course a year later.'

'I understand. And you've been working and single parenting ever since?'

There's something shining in her eyes: something, I think,

between pity and admiration. Usually, it would bother me, because Tabby is the best thing that's ever happened to me. The idea that anyone could think otherwise would make me baulk. But today, I'll take whatever emotions my circumstances throw up for her, if only to get her to root for me hard enough to take a chance on me.

We move through my CV, even though my success in this job will depend on a set of skills about which I'm waaay less confident. After fifteen minutes of shooting work-related questions at me, Camille sits back in her chair in this sleek glass-walled office we're in and surveys me through eyes that I think are narrowed more in thought and less in judgement.

'I'll be honest with you. Your qualifications are fine. More than fine—I'm sure you'd do an admirable job. It's clear to me that you're level-headed, efficient and resilient. And, apropos the requirements of this particular agency, your looks are stellar. You're an incredibly beautiful woman, Marlowe. I could get you a dozen interviews just like that.'

She pauses to blow out a breath, and it's the most ruffled I've seen her. 'Here's the thing, though. Nothing I've seen or heard tells me you're truly ready—or emotionally equipped— for the rigours this job entails, and that's a major, major problem for me.'

Our eyes are locked, and my ability to take anything but the most shallow breaths evades me.

'Make no mistake about it, Marlowe. This is sex work. High value, high stakes sex work for men who are used to getting whatever the hell they want. You are a classically trained musician who, from what I can tell, has led a reasonably sheltered life. For you to accept a role as a Seraph EA would be like never having climbed before and deciding to tackle the North Face of the Eiger. In a nutshell: foolhardy and dangerous.'

I force another tiny inhale, rubbing my newly clammy

palms together in my lap. My spine pricks with sweat. Persuading Camille that I'm some secret sex addict for whom this will be child's play seems pointless, so I take another tack.

'Believe me, I know how high the stakes are. They're literally life and death for my daughter. I promise you I've thought this through and I'm willing to do whatever it takes.'

She says nothing but taps her stylus against her sleek iPad as she continues to survey me.

I clear my throat. 'May I ask you a question?'

'Of course.'

'Are you just worried about my wellbeing, or are you concerned about Seraph's reputation if you place someone who's not up to the task?'

'Both. The latter only because the owner of this agency depends on me to uphold it. But I'm far more concerned about how irresponsible it would be to let one of our clients loose on you without you having the experience and the toughness to go the distance emotionally.'

'I appreciate that. But if Brendan Sullivan hired me... well, Athena has vouched for him,' I conclude lamely.

She frowns. 'His application, and my initial checks, tell me he's far from being an angel.'

Something of which I'm painfully aware and require no reminder. The most cursory internet search pours forth an obscene amount of images of him with model-types draped over him.

The good news for me? It seems he has a thing for long blonde hair.

'But he's not a rapist or a psychopathic killer, at least,' I say with a bravado I do not feel.

'That bar is far, far too low for my liking. Let me ask you, Marlowe. How many sexual partners have you had in the past?'

It's time for my other tactic. The one Athena coached me on extensively in preparation for this particular moment.

*Lie through my teeth.*

'I think twelve or thirteen,' I muse. 'Or fourteen, maybe?'

She's not buying it. 'Really. With a child?'

I shrug. 'I started young.' *Untrue.* 'And my daughter's father wasn't in the picture after he found out I was pregnant. He was my professor.'

That has her elegantly raising an eyebrow. 'Your professor?'

'I have a thing for older guys. What can I say? I wanted him, so I seduced him.'

*Untrue.*

'I didn't date much when Tabby was a toddler—I was finishing up my degree, for one—but my parents have been very hands-on. They moved to London so they could help me with childcare, and it's meant I've been able to have a pretty active dating life.'

One truth, one lie.

I hope she buys it.

'So how would you rate your level of sexual expertise?'

'As you know, I'm not a professional. But I'd like to think I'm pretty experienced.'

She doesn't answer. I'm getting desperate now. 'How about this?' I propose as nonchalantly as possible. 'Let me interview with Brendan. If he doesn't offer me the job, then we can recalibrate.'

'How about *this*?' she counters. 'You take a look at his questionnaire and *then* we'll see if you feel ready to consider this role. If you do, I'll set up the interview.'

'Perfect,' I say with far more bravado than I feel. This is the crunch point: the first chance I have to see inside this guy's brain. To know what terrors may await me.

Camille hits something that has her iPad streaming to the

large screen in front of us in the middle of the table. The questionnaire is topped with the distinctive angel wings that comprise the Seraph logo. I see *BRENDAN SULLIVAN* typed in large letters across the top of the form, and I swear the pinpricks of sweat along my spine multiply. In my lap, I dig the nails of one hand into the palm of the other, a reminder to hold myself the fuck together.

She scrolls through the initial information—Brendan is thirty-seven—ten years older than me, has never been married, and identifies as a heterosexual male. So far, so manageable.

He cites his main reasons for signing up to Seraph as in-office entertainment, convenience and stress relief, in that order.

*Breathe, Marlowe. None of this is remotely salacious.*

But it's about to be.

He's looking to have sex every day, at least once a day. Not a huge surprise, given the amount of money he'd be forking out for the pleasure, but the thought of having actual sex with an actual man *every single workday* when I haven't had it at all in nine years makes me want to laugh in a totally humourless way.

'What happens when I'm on my period?' I ask Camille.

'Depends on the guy,' she says. 'Some guys like it, and some of our seraphim are happy to have sex on their periods. Some opt to run their pills together to avoid the issue altogether, and others just get creative. You have three working holes, after all,' she adds drily.

*Oh. My. God.*

I swear my body thinks I've just dropped ten storeys in a lift, and what little breakfast I got down before I came here threatens to make a reappearance. Giving head I can handle, but—

Camille must notice something's up because her expression softens. 'This is precisely why you get to submit a questionnaire, too. This isn't a one-way street. Like any kind of working *or* sexual relationship, there's compromise. Just because a client has expressed certain preferences, it absolutely does not mean you have to roll over and say yes to everything. Quite the contrary. And you can always negotiate and renegotiate terms depending on what you're comfortable with.'

Because sitting down with some billionaire and calmly discussing whether he can put his dick in my arse is something I have the wherewithal to endure. Nevertheless, her qualification is reassuring, I suppose.

His favourite position is doggy-style. This should be music to my ears, because every mafia boss in every dark romance I read has a penchant for getting his girl on all fours. When I'm on my sofa under a soft blanket, I'm so onboard it's not funny, but if I imagine *myself* as the doggy in some oversexed guy's office, I could honestly vomit from nerves.

Brendan, it seems, is a big fan of oral sex, both ways. 'It's usually a good sign when they're into cunnilingus,' Camille confides. 'Makes it more likely they're a considerate lover.'

There is not one single thing about that statement I can handle processing right now, so I squeak *mmm hmm* and attempt, unsuccessfully, to arrest the tide of red I know is creeping up my neck at the images of Brendan's handsome face dipping between my legs.

I can't do this. I can't. I'll die of mortification and terror. Is a vulnerability-driven stroke a thing? I want to push back my chair and bolt for that door, but the sensation only lasts a second, replaced with the heart-splitting image of Tabby's face when she's having a blue spell.

*I have to do this.*

*I'll deal with it when it comes to it.*

'Ready to see his kinks?' Camille asks, then, 'Breathe, Marlowe.'

I suck in a breath and read what he's written.

*I love it when they pretend to be inexperienced. Gets me every time. It really, really turns me on to imagine that I'm the one teaching them how good it can be.*

There's a sudden slackening of the tension in my chest. Well, that won't be a problem. He should be careful what he wishes for. I imagine I'll excel at seeming experienced.

I recall the takeaways from my three-or-four-minute interaction with him. Hot. Looked like a playboy. Was weirdly tongue-tied. That I'm now browsing his sexual proclivities is surreal, and that any of this may pertain to *me* is off-the-charts bizarre.

We read on.

*I like to have fun. I like to mix it up. I fucking LOVE to watch, so I'll make her fuck and suck off other guys while I sit back and enjoy the show. She has to remember that she's my fuck toy. She's there to entertain, and to take what we give her. I won't go easy on her.*

Oh my God. Oh my God. My face is aflame, my entire body so taut I could puke from the tension. It's nearly impossible for me to equate the filthy, depraved things he's saying with the concept that he could be talking about *me*.

He could be doing those things to *me*.

But beneath it all, beneath the blushing and the nausea and the tension and the ringing in my ears is the oddest pulse between my legs. It's the kind of cavalier, fatalistic thrill you get when you strap yourself into a death-defying rollercoaster. The kind of thrill parachutists must feel in that moment as they stare at the earth thousands of feet below, right before they throw themselves out of a plane door.

It's some kind of fucked-up life force that welcomes existential threats, that thinks *bring it on*. And it's the only thing that saves me from running from this room and the prospect of putting myself in this man's hands.

Because, God knows, this is the mother of all rollercoasters. And if I'm going to survive a day in this role then I'll have to buckle the hell up.

# CHAPTER 6

# *Brendan*

I was wrong-footed last time I met Marlowe; that's why I behaved like such a fucking loser. I was prepared for a boring night of "culture" at the Royal Academy, prepared to suck it up for the sake of the family name, to drink champagne, and give my brother a hard time about how he should fuck his hot assistant, and possibly flirt with a few attractive women.

I was most definitely *not* prepared to come face to face with a woman who had the face of an angel. Neither could I have ever expected that my well-trodden autopilot functions of sexy smile and flirty one-liners would malfunction to the point of non-existence and leave me gaping and stuttering and barely able to shake her hand.

It had never happened to me before, and it hasn't happened since, and it's sure as fuck not happening today. Because I am a CEO of a FTSE 100 company, not to mention one of the most eligible—and accomplished—players in London, and I won't tolerate being a tongue-tied schoolboy in front of my prospective EA with benefits.

I just won't.

When Plain Elaine, who is more of a general PA than a dedicated EA anyway, calls through to say that Marlowe has arrived, I force myself to sit tight for a few minutes. First impressions are important, especially when they're actually second impressions and you've already fucked up the first round. So I'm intent on portraying to Miss Winters from the offset that I'm a busy, powerful guy juggling a million Very Important Balls.

I hastily pop a mint in my mouth, take out my keyring with its fidget spinner, and watch three recent TikToks from my favourite creator and owner of a barrel-shaped Staffy called Tinkerbell. Fuck, she's cute. Not as cute as Mark, obviously. If the owner didn't live somewhere in Scotland, I'd be tempted to cyber-stalk him and suggest a doggy play date. I can just tell Mark and Tinks would get on famously.

When I arbitrarily judge that I've kept Marlowe waiting long enough, I press the intercom for reception.

'Send her in.'

I open my office door before standing in front of my desk to greet her. Mark trundles to the doorframe. My office takes up one corner of the executive floor and is a showcase for the quality Sullivan Construction is known for, with its double-height ceilings, floor-to-ceiling windows, acres of plush white carpet, and impeccable finish. I've purposely kept the furnishings minimal to emphasise the sense of spaciousness. It's really very Zen, especially for a guy like me. Nothing about me is Zen.

I roll my shoulders back to improve my posture, widening my legs to assume a victory stance as I stick my hands in my pockets. I've got this. I am a strong, capable man, the head of a business empire, and a respected leader. I have women coming out of my ears, smoke coming off my Raya app, and so many options for pussy that I don't need Alchemy or Seraph or— wait. Did I remember to send back those contracts, or...?

Focus, Sullivan. Woman. Job. Interview. Respected leader. Where was I? Right.

Oh, fuck.

Jesus fucking Christ.

She's just so damn *beautiful*, in a way that's ethereal and natural. Wholesome and sexy at the same time. She appears in the doorframe, bending to greet Mark. He's lodged himself squarely in her path, giving her no choice but to acknowledge him. Her long blonde hair falls in a sleek curtain over her face, and I shamelessly ogle the silhouette of her body in heels and a pale pink fitted dress that might just be my downfall. She hasn't seen me yet.

Mark, the little tart, is wiggling his ample arse at her as he laps up her attention. I issue myself a stern reminder that the scope of today's interview is strictly limited to the executive part of the role and that I can't overtly drool over her, make any innuendos, or shove her to her knees to commence her "audition". All that is shelved until I decide whether she's qualified to be my EA and she decides if she's up for moving forward to the next stage, which really means that this afternoon is my audition, if you think about it.

I have to attract her and impress her and make her trust me and desist from freaking her out, and as I stare at her, that all seems like a pretty tall order.

I clear my throat in preparation for taking my voice as low as it'll go. 'Marlowe. Thanks so much for coming.'

She stops cooing over my dog and straightens up with a snap, her eyes going wide as her hair flies about her face. 'Oh, hi,' she says, clearly flustered. 'I'm—it's good to see you again, Mr Sullivan.'

I shoot her my well-proven smile. 'It's Brendan, please.' *Except when you're sucking my cock.* 'Mark. *Sit.*'

My stupid dog does no such thing, and instead rubs his head against Marlowe's thigh, something that should be my move. The little traitor has completely abandoned our 'bros before hoes' pact. We're going to have a serious talk about loyalty later, preferably when I'm not busy imagining what Marlowe looks like under that dress.

She manoeuvres herself gracefully around him so she can approach me. She moves like she's completely unaware of her effect on men, which either makes her the most convincing actress I've ever met or dangerously naïve. I'm going to enjoy finding out which it is.

We extend our hands and shake.

'It's good to see you again, Brendan.'

This time, I'm prepared. This time, the shock of her skin against mine doesn't turn me into a spineless, voiceless wanker. Because this time, I'm a big swinging dick in my big swinging dick office, and she is not my acquaintance's stupidly hot friend but instead a candidate for the most big-swinging-dick hire I've ever made.

'Thanks for coming in. This is Mark, my one-man welcoming committee.'

She turns to beam at him, and I'm instantly jealous.

'He's very sweet.'

'He likes you. He doesn't like everyone.' *Clever doggy.* Mark is exquisitely discerning when it comes to humans, and Marlowe has passed his test with flying colours. My dog, who regularly snubs supermodels and once growled at a Victoria's Secret Angel, is acting like Marlowe has slipped him a steak. Between his silent if enthusiastic approval and the glorious fucking sight in front of me, I may as well hire her on the spot. It's not like I give a shit what her qualifications are like. The only skills of hers I'm interested in are the ones I won't get to test out until the next round.

Fuck, I wish it was the next round.

As I usher her over to the huge white L-shaped sofa in the

corner and Plain Elaine appears to take our coffee orders, I eye-fuck her as hard as I can.

Marlowe, that is. Not Elaine.

She looks far more groomed than at our ill-fated meeting at the RA. I was too busy spinning out to lock down a concrete memory of her, but my memory is of a messy bun and lots of blonde wisps and a floaty dress. Now her hair is a shiny golden curtain, and I'm a far bigger fan of the fitted sleeveless dress she's wearing today. It's demure but sexy, and it definitely says *bend me over your desk and spank me, Mr Sullivan.* So there's that. Still, it's not screaming for attention, unlike the packaging most of the women I date present themselves in. It's just framing what's already worth looking at. It's classy.

And I'd forgotten her eyes were brown. How the hell could I have forgotten that? Blonde hair—it looks natural—and brown eyes and creamy, lightly tanned skin are an intoxicating combination. They're a clear coffee colour and they bring so much warmth to her appearance. She's tall and willowy and her bare legs are, from the clear view I got as she was petting Mark, knockout.

Between the legs and the face, she's a solid ten, and she'll hold that rank as long as she knows how to use her little pink mouth properly. The fact that I'll soon be paying to find out feels almost criminal—kind of like getting a brand new Aston Martin at a police auction.

She's everything I remembered from that first sucker punch but all wrapped up in some *sexy secretary* package, which is so compelling that it feels like Christmas. She could play some kind of sleek receptionist to a Bond villain.

The logical conclusion to that train of thought is that *I'm* the Bond villain in this scenario.

Elaine scurries off, shutting the door behind her—*good*—and I realise I've been staring at Marlowe's mouth for an uncomfortably long time while my brain took a trip to Fantasy Island. This is why I take Ritalin on weekdays, for fuck's sake. Not that any amount of brain food could keep me focused on spreadsheets with *her* in the room.

Shiny new catamarans be damned, because she's undoubtedly going to be my new favourite toy.

I can't wait to take her for a ride.

# CHAPTER 7

# Marlowe

Okay.

Brendan Sullivan is ridiculous. Like, the kind of ridiculous that would make women more at ease than me with their sexuality (read: anyone) drop their panties just like that but makes me want to let out some kind of high-pitched, nervous titter, because I'm here to interview with some kind of bad boy, alpha-hole romance hero come to life *for the well-paid honour of sleeping with him.*

If I allow myself to think about it like that, even for a second, I will probably faint.

Or pee myself.

I mean, I realised he was extremely attractive that night at the exhibition, but I was more focused on meeting Athena's new boss-with-benefits, if I'm honest. And Brendan seemed shy that night, so I didn't really give him much of a second thought.

But now that I'm in his crazy corner office that's conservatively three times bigger than my entire flat, and I'm alone with him, and he's in CEO mode, and he's found his voice—

and his swagger—it's absolutely impossible not to be affected by him.

First of all, he's big. Bigger than I realised, and bigger than his brother. *I used to play rugby and now lift serious weights* big. The breadth of his shoulders and the heft of those arms under his beautiful navy suit are unmistakable. I'm tall, and I'm in Athena's four-inch pale-pink suede Gianvito Rossi's, but he still towers over me. He must be six-three or six-four. I find myself wondering if he's built proportionally all over and have to talk myself down with a blush.

*Stop it.*

Second, he totally has a playboy tan. I bet he works his way all around the women of the Med over the summer, and I bet he's disgustingly successful at it—so successful, in fact, that I wonder why the hell he needs a Seraph EA. If it wasn't for those sky-blue eyes, the tan and almost black beard would be giving serious Mob vibes.

Third, I may have googled him far too extensively in the days since Athena suggested this gig, and I can't conclude that I did myself any favours. I told myself it was purely for interview research purposes, but there's context and there's *context*.

The penchant-for-blondes thing? Helpful.

The penchant-for-blonde actual, literal *supermodels* thing? Unhelpful.

Acquainting myself with his career history and his rise through the ranks at Sullivan Construction? Helpful.

Acquainting myself with his net worth? Unhelpful.

As was happening upon a *Tatler* article citing him as the second most eligible bachelor in London last year (the current Duke of Oxford pipped him to the post), and reading a tell-all in the *Daily Mail* by a—platinum blonde, obviously—reality TV star he'd dated and allegedly dumped.

The article reeked of sour grapes while also being a blatant plug for her new line of planet-friendly yoga mats, but she didn't hold back on slagging off his bedroom behaviour ("demanding bordering on aggressive") or his maturity levels ("a spoilt five-year-old on a good day").

A bratty kid by day and a wannabe porn star by night?

Fucking excellent.

From what I can tell, having done far too much of this "research", I have two advantages over all the other women who cross his path and throw themselves at him.

One. I will do anything to make him happy and keep him satisfied. *Anything.*

Two. My only agenda is saving my daughter's life. Unlike the rest of them, I have no interest in trying to become Mrs Brendan Sullivan, so he can rest easy that I'll fuck him to his heart's content without angling for a proposal.

Which brings me to the other elephant in the room—our questionnaires. I will fully admit to having completed mine while being half a bottle of wine down, a move that was as necessary as it was ill-judged. I answered *yes* to far too many things, even if Athena, who guided me through it over a video call, seconded Camille's words: that I absolutely did not have to roll over and say yes to everything.

The problem is that neither Athena nor Camille have a daughter who needs hundreds of thousands of pounds' worth of medical care *yesterday.* So they can discern all they want, but I know that the more boxes I tick *yes* to, the more likely Brendan will offer me this job.

Is it irresponsible to opt in to potentially indulge in sex acts I may not be comfortable with?

Are you crazy?! Of course it is!!!!!!

But when you have purposely put the glossy Duke Children's Hospital brochure directly in your line of sight as you fill out a sexy questionnaire, you will damn well complete said questionnaire in the way that has the best chance of getting you through the doors of that hospital.

Also, I was at home in my flat at the time. I was in my little sanctuary. It was a not dissimilar experience to watching *365 Days* and idly wishing someone hot would bundle you up and kidnap you. It felt safe, like a distant fantasy that your nervous system is so confident is impossible that it's happy to stand down and let you fantasise about.

But now? Now my pulse is skittering all over the place and my breakfast is reconsidering its home in my stomach right as my nervous system reconsiders the *is impossible* part of this situation. I'm watching the curves of Brendan's moving lips as he gives Elaine his coffee order, and I'm noticing the muscles flexing right beneath that expensive wool jacket, and every part of me is sensing his bulk, his strength, his proximity, and all those filthy things I glibly signed up for suddenly feel shockingly real. Terrifyingly imminent.

I won't even get started on all the things *he* mentioned, because I absolutely will not be able to focus on selling my tenuous assistant skillset in a pleasant and convincing manner if I think about the fact that he wrote *ANAL* in capital letters on his questionnaire.

*Capital letters.*

I have strong and easily digested—haha—views on anal. In a nutshell, that hole back there is an exit hole, not an entry hole. I value my digestive health, thank you very much. In fact, it's the one sodding area of my life where everything is ship-shape. It all runs like clockwork. Never will a man get back there, and *definitely* not a man of this guy's size. No, sir.

Ten bottles of wine wouldn't have been enough to make me tick that box. If Mr Brendan Sullivan wants to stick it up the wrong 'un, he'll have to do so out of office hours with someone who categorically isn't me.

'So, Marlowe,' he says, settling into the opposite end of the couch with casual confidence after Elaine's left us, 'tell me what brings you to Seraph after your time at the Royal Academy.'

His tone is conversational, but those blue eyes are assessing me with an intensity that makes my skin prickle, because the way he's checking me out is most definitely outside of the remit of this interview. He's not playing fair, and I have to remind myself that nothing about this situation is fair. If I'm going to get flustered the second my potential future boss eye-fucks me, I won't last a day in this job.

'I was there for five years,' I say as steadily as I can. 'It felt stagnant. It's a wonderful place to work, but it's quite set in its ways. I'm looking for a new challenge.' This may be my first job interview in years, but even I know that *I'm looking for a new challenge* is as desperately cliché as it gets. I clear my throat and channel my inner Athena.

'I got tired of not learning new things. I know that an executive assistant position will give me so much access, and I imagine the work is different every day. I love the idea of that. I may not be the most experienced EA you'll ever meet, but I'm really hardworking and seriously focused. I'd just love the opportunity to show you.'

Okay, I might have gone in a little hot and heavy with the pitch right then, but I'm not leaving anything to chance here. I'd rather he thought I was an embarrassingly keen "pick me" than someone who was apathetic. I wait for him to say something, but he's staring at my mouth like a man on drugs.

The realisation hits me that this part of the interview may just be a technicality. While it stings, it's also a relief. Today I'm not the good girl who wants goodwill and validation and gold stars, who wants her every effort recognised. I'm a grown woman who has a clear goal and a *very* compelling motivation for that goal and who, most importantly, is not above using every trick in the book to reach it.

I lick my lips. Not in an overt, porno way; just in a subtle way, but his eyes track the flicker of my tongue, and the first surge of power hits me in the gut like a shot of tequila.

*He wants me.*

Of course he does.

Athena's told me so over and over. I'm so stupid. I've been so stressed about how high the stakes are, and how much I need this guy to take a chance on me, and I've let that freak me the hell out. I've let it make me feel completely disenfranchised, but perhaps my looks, something I can't take credit for and something I've deliberately underplayed since Joe chewed me up and spat me out, give me far more agency here than I've accepted up until now.

Sometimes, catching a man's eye is a bad thing. Joe told me so in as many words, over and over again.

*My little prize.*

*My gorgeous little secret.*

*If my colleagues could see me now, buried inside the most beautiful student on campus.*

Being the woman whom men want to conquer, to claim, is a liability. I learned that the hard way.

But it's dawning on me that sometimes, in the right circumstances, it's a breathtakingly powerful currency.

At the end of the day, Brendan is just a guy. A stupidly hot, stupidly rich guy who's clearly very smart and successful but is probably also quite straightforward. If he's interested in taking this forward, then all I have to do in this interview is ensure I give him zero reasons not to.

This approach goes against every feminist bone in my body. My and Athena's former headmistress would die if she knew I was using my physical attributes to land a job—but then she'd die if she knew that two of her most studious alumni were selling their bodies in the first place.

I cross my legs in as ladylike a fashion as I can, and Brendan's gaze drops to linger on my bare knees. It's been so long since I've entertained the slightest bit of interest from a guy that this feels completely alien to me, but the feeling is not unpleasant.

'You asked why Seraph in particular,' I continue softly, and his eyes flash up to my face. God, they're striking. Being the focus of his attention is really full on. 'I realise it's not the most conventional agency.' I give him a little smile that I really hope is coquettish, because I'm far too rusty at this flirting business. It's a relief when the sight of it has his eyes widening a fraction. 'But I love their philosophy. I love the idea of working alongside a man who's as insanely busy and stressed and prevailed upon as you and being the person who can make some of it go away. Not all of it, obviously. But I think it's the full-service element that appeals to me, and by that I mean the holistic nature. I want to help you.'

I spread my hands wide. 'I'm a natural-born helper. So if there are stressors or headaches or obstacles that stand in your way, whatever they are, I'm going to make it my mission to make them go away. I'm scrappy and resourceful and fierce and really, really hardworking, and I promise you I'll do my utmost in every situation to give you every last thing you need and want.'

*Except anal, you know.*

I'm not sure where all this stuff is coming from, but I mean it. I may not be Athena-level smart, but I'm like a dog with a bone when it comes to fighting for the people in my corner. If there's a pit bull element to this job, I'll excel. Every CEO should think about hiring the mother of a sick child— we're resilient as fuck and tough as old boots and we don't take no for an answer, because we've fought every fight and challenged every *no* and hustled every single medical body with laser focus and indefatigable commitment to a single cause.

He leans forward. 'Elaine's been doing a joint PA-slash-EA role for a while now, and it's become clear that I need dedicated personnel for both of those roles. I won't insult your intelligence by pretending that's the only reason I signed up with Seraph. But while the role is complex and ever-changing, the ideology behind it is pretty simple—and you've just nailed it.'

He allows himself a leisurely peruse of my body, and I force myself to relax as he mentally undresses me.

'I'm tired, you know? I work hard and play hard. Sometimes it feels like everyone's an idiot. I'm looking for someone who can protect me from the idiots and make my life easier. Someone who can anticipate problems and make them go away, and help me work through the stress when they can't.'

He licks his lips after the last part in a not unsexy way, and there's no denying that he's referencing both sides of the job. I nod with what I hope is an understanding smile, though I'm rolling my eyes internally. Oh, please. I'm sure this guy doesn't lift a finger. He probably has chefs and drivers and minions galore. I bet he hasn't put a wash on or stepped foot into a dry cleaner or opened his own mail for years and years.

Sure, he has a huge job, and I'm sure he works his arse off at it. But we all work hard, and some of us come home from our jobs and cook and clean and then find ourselves in A&E at all hours of the night.

For most of us, *playing hard* is unfathomable. But I'll suck it up, because him needing a glorified nanny equates to the biggest opportunity I've ever had. This overprivileged playboy is Tabby's lifeline, and I won't forget it.

'I can be all those things for you,' I tell him. 'I'll make it all go away. If you hired me, your wellbeing would be my sole focus, I promise.' During office hours only, pal. I have someone whose wellbeing is far more worthy of my attention in real life. There's an eight-year-old girl with insufficient oxygen circulating in her body, and she's known stress and pain the likes of which you can never, ever imagine.

Stress is your body shutting down because your lungs are being slowly suffocated.

It is *not* fending off unwanted attention from society gold-diggers.

He closes his eyes briefly and presses his lips together in a weirdly earnest way, as if he's carrying the weight of the world but is trying to be a big brave boy. If you remove the sex, this gig is sounding more and more like a nannying role. And I may not be an experienced EA, but I *have* raised a child, albeit one with more problems and more resilience than this guy will ever have. Placating and enduring tantrums and making the pain go away are second nature to me. And if that's what Brendan essentially wants, I'll deliver it in spades.

I flick my hair back over my shoulder, and it jolts him out of his spontaneous little pity party. His handsome face turns predatory again as his gaze lingers on my hair.

'You know,' he says, his voice gruff, 'you're making it very difficult for me to keep this professional. If I had my way, we'd be moving onto Round Two right now.'

My smile turns coquettish, and my insides dance at his tone as much as his words.

*Bring it.*

It seems the terrified clutcher of pearls in Camille's office is on her way out.

In her place?

A mama bear who's just caught her first whiff of victory.

And boy, is it heady.

# CHAPTER 8

# Marlowe

'I think I'm loving High Class Hooker Barbie even more than Sexy Secretary Barbie,' Athena muses from somewhere near my knee as she rubs moisturiser with a hint of light-reflecting highlighter into my legs. Apparently, the trick is to use enough leg makeup to be alluring but not so much that it comes off on the bed in revolting pinky streaks.

*On the bed.*

Oh my sweet Jesus.

I'm at her palatial flat getting ready for Interview Round Two, AKA The Audition, AKA I Need To Actually Put Out For The First Time in Eight Years. It's a relief in a whole host of ways. Not only is my "date" with Brendan over this side of town, but I definitely need Athena's particular brand of moral support right now, and I didn't want Tabs to see me getting tarted up.

I've left her with a sitter she loves—a young woman called Hattie from a specialist babysitting agency that only takes on paediatric nurses. There was no way I was leaving her with my parents, who'd smell a hell of a rat if I went out on a "date", nor would I risk leaving her with a random sixteen-year-old who wouldn't know how to call nine-nine-nine if anything happened.

Paediatric nurses as sitters don't come cheap, but God knows no one would begrudge them making a few extra quid on the side of their relentless and underpaid day job. Besides, a cool twenty-five grand from Brendan is currently sitting in Seraph's corporate bank account and will become mine tomorrow, as long as I put out tonight. The first thing I'll do with my leisure time—after calling Athena to give her a lengthy and probably graphic debrief—will be to contact Duke Children's Hospital and request an initial consultation. The enormity of the sum sends actual shivers down my spine. Even without the challenge of the months that lie ahead *if* I land this job, that money represents the single biggest stride I've made in years towards securing Tabby's health for the future. *Years.*

I already know that I won't lie back and think of England tonight, when this sexy, scary man is doing untold things to my body.

I'll lie back and think of that particular corner of North Carolina. I just hope he's into it enough not to notice when I go into full dissociation mode. Guys are pretty basic when it comes to sex, aren't they? I'm fully aware that my success in this role—and this "audition"—will come down to more than spreading my legs for him.

I'll have to feign enthusiasm and arousal and all the other shit. I'll have to feed his ego, persuade him that the power of his mighty dick has shattered me into a million pieces. The performance of a lifetime awaits, because I promised him in yesterday's interview that I'd fulfil all his needs.

I really hope he buys it.

At least I won't have to fake the whole *inexperienced almost-virgin* thing I know he likes so much.

'High Class Hooker Barbie had better not be all talk and

no trousers,' I mutter, more to myself than to her. There's a very large part of me that worries I'll totally freeze when Brendan gets his hands on me later. That I won't be able to come up with the goods, or worse, that I'll completely freak out and run for the door.

'She won't be,' Athena assures me, rising elegantly to her feet so she can shoot me what should be a trademarked Athena Davenport Glare. 'I know you, Marls. You'll do anything for that little girl. Besides.' She drops the glare and winks. 'Don't underestimate the mind-melting power of a good fuck. God knows, you need it. And Brendan may be the billionaire equivalent of a basic bitch, but you can't deny he's attractive.' She sighs. 'Those Sullivan boys have seriously excellent Irish genes. If they were studs, Mairead would breed the hell out of them and make a fortune.'

I giggle. Mairead is Gabe and Brendan's sister and, by all accounts, not to be messed with. Apparently, she runs the stud farm attached to their parents' stables. 'Well, I will definitely *not* be breeding him. I love my daughter dearly, but a little Sullivan baby is not part of the plan.' I cough meaningfully and give my friend a look. 'For me, anyway.'

She rolls her eyes, which is an excellent sign that I've flustered the unflappable ice queen. I know my friend, and she so wants Gabe's little dark-haired, blue-eyed babies it's not even funny. 'You are attracted to him, correct?' she demands instead of gracing my little jibe with a reply.

'He's gorgeous, obviously. I mean, it's not like he's an acquired taste. I'm sure he's everybody's type. But that doesn't mean I want to just show up and shag him. I'm terrified,' I add softly, and she sighs and folds me into a hug.

'I know you are, sweetie. I hope you know how proud I am of you. This is an amazing, amazing thing you're doing for Tabs. Remember that. Now, let's look at you.'

She gives me one last squeeze and releases me before

turning me around to face the full-length freestanding mirror in the corner of her beautiful, neutral bedroom. This is undoubtedly a more uplifting and glamorous location to prep for my weird rendezvous. There isn't room to swing a cat in my bedroom. I gave Tabby the big room, so mine just about fits a double bed, even if I can't open the wardrobe doors next to it a full ninety degrees.

I force myself to take in my reflection: the finished product. The woman looking back at me is not an exhausted single mother, nor is she the usual boho, shabby-chic working version of me who favours air-dried hair and long, cheapo sundresses in the summer or fleece-lined yoga pants made from crappy petroleum-based fabrics in the winter.

Nope. I can confirm that this woman is categorically neither of those things. Instead, she looks like the kind of person I might see on Instagram, if I'm honest. The kind of person I have never, ever presumed to be. You always assume you either are or aren't a certain type of person, and I've always assumed that I'm not the woman who treats making her oat milk matcha latte as a "sacred ritual" or goes out on the town looking like she's about to step onto a red carpet or would ever insert a hashtag before the word *blessed*.

There may not be any ceremonial-grade matcha in sight, but, to my shock, High Class Hooker Barbie looks a lot like a red-carpet-walking, Instagram-posting socialite.

I'm wearing a dress that I would deem downright slutty but which my socialite Insta-woman would probably class as normal night-out attire. Like the dresses for my interviews with both Camille and Brendan, I've rented this designer dress for the evening, giving me a thousand-pound dress for just over a hundred pounds.

Unlike my interview dresses, this one is made from stretchy pale gold lamé, stops at mid-thigh, clings *everywhere*, and has tiny straps and some sort of clever mesh architecture that serves my boobs up on a platter. One of the benefits of having a kid pretty young is that my boobs held up nicely in the face of breastfeeding and my figure reappeared relatively easily, something I didn't care much about until now, because *I've borne and birthed a child* is absolutely not the message I want to lead with this evening.

I smooth my hands over my hips, appreciating the luxurious drape of the fabric as well as the crazily flattering cut. I just hope no dodgy bodily fluids get spilt on this dress. I have a sudden flashback to that eternally cringey dry-cleaners scene in the movie *The Sweetest Thing*.

I'm even wearing a very tiny, sexily pointless lace thong that Athena made me buy from Harrods. Between the thong and the dress length, I scream *easy access*. Once again, I've borrowed her shoes—strappy gold Jimmy Choos this time. They make my legs look endless. I jiggle my left foot to admire the faint sheen of highlighter and the radiant effect it gives my leg.

The biggest transformation, though, has to be my hair and makeup. I'm a bit-of-cream-blush kind of girl, but Athena has worked her magic with flawless makeup, including some sort of bold and smoky eye makeup that accentuates my brown eyes. My hair hangs over my shoulders in beachy waves that look effortless rather than "done", and I decide I wouldn't mind having my hair like this every single day.

I look like a magical, sexy creature. When I twist my mouth, a nervous tic I'm well used to seeing in the mirror, I have the most surreal out-of-body experience—a flash of dissonance that feels like someone's just walked over my grave. Because that's *me* in there, under this glossy shell of expensive, attention-grabbing clothes and perfect hair and makeup that looks like the end of a YouTube tutorial.

It's me... but it's not.

Even if I can catch glimpses of myself behind the veneer, I

definitely don't *feel* like myself. Maybe that's a good thing—a protective measure. Maybe it's a way of reeling Brendan in and snagging this job and compartmentalising the woman who then has to *deliver* on this job.

Maybe it's apt that the Marlowe who will shortly walk out of this bedroom and put herself into a cab to go and intentionally seduce a rich, powerful, gorgeous man for her own ends doesn't look or feel familiar at all. I'm the woman who dresses up out of obligation, for family celebrations or when Athena drags me out for girls' drinks.

I used to dress up back at uni, when lectures were few and far between and I had so much spare time on my hands that I could spend hours trying dupes of designer face masks or giving myself a mani-pedi. I even dressed up for lectures and tutorials, because every class with Joe was essentially foreplay and every foray into the Music Department was a chance to bump into him.

I was young and romantic and naïve as *fuck*. I just wish the reminder of how deluded I was would make me feel less cynical and more righteous about my reasons for dressing up to the nines tonight.

But it doesn't. It just makes me feel sad.

'God,' I whisper. 'I feel like I'm tricking him, or something. This isn't me.'

It's a relief when she meets my eyes in the mirror and whispers, 'This is you. It's just a particularly glamorous, seductive part of you that doesn't get to come out and play very often because you're so busy being an amazing mother and taking care of Tabs.'

I nod, only partially convinced, and she ploughs on.

'Just remember, he's a big boy. You may be scared shitless, and this may all feel really fucking weird, but you're going to do what you need to do, and Brendan will love every minute of it. Don't feel remotely bad taking his money.' She leans in and whispers in my ear. 'I promise you, he's going to think you're worth every penny.'

'You're good,' I tell her, nudging her with my bare shoulder. 'That was almost as good as the sexy pep talk Nick gives Kat in *The Wedding Date.*' I shoot her a smile that's far brighter and braver than how I'm feeling.

She shrugs in her cute, French-chic way. 'I know. But also —do me a favour and just take a look at yourself. Forget what you know. If you saw this woman on the street, you would be *wowed*. There's no question. You're a fucking knockout, and it's a travesty that you've been celibate for so long. Go let Brendan clean out those vaginal cobwebs with his big Sullivan dick and remember to *have fun.*'

I take a deep breath and study the girl in the mirror again. This time, I allow myself to stare objectively. She may not look or feel quite like me, but my friend is right.

She looks fantastic.

Maybe it won't kill me to cut loose and let the old, fun Marlowe out from her daily grind. Because, while my life is full of love, it's also pretty heavy on the drudgery and worry and that relentless grind of putting one foot in front of the other.

I force a smile at myself.

Looks like Cinders is going to the ball.

I just hope Prince Charming behaves himself.

# CHAPTER 9

# *Brendan*

When that Camille person told me it was customary to kick the next round of the interview process off over dinner, I was like *yep, nope.* Hard fucking pass.

Sit-down meals are still my least favourite thing in the world. For years and years before my diagnosis—which didn't happen until I was fifteen—family dinner was an excruciating hour where I had to exert unbelievable mental effort to glue my arse to my chair when my entire nervous system was literally *screaming* at me to spring up and jump around the room.

I can still remember how scratchy the seat of the chairs at our dining table felt in the summer or after games when I was wearing shorts.

If mealtimes were excruciating for me, they were equally painful for my parents, who were constantly stressed out by my inability to sit still. I inevitably caved to my impulses to get rid of all that nervous energy and jumped up, so I could spin or walk around and around and around the table or—the thing that pissed my parents off the most—bent myself over the backs of whatever fucking Chippendale chairs they had so I could lift my feet off and swing back and forth.

And, just as inevitably, Mum and Dad would go fucking nuclear. I'll admit that, twenty years or more on from my diagnosis, I'm still smug AF that they had to eat humble pie after the psychiatrist explained to them that forcing me to resist my body's impulse to move and expend energy was both unhealthy and cruel. They felt terrible about it, of course, but I still haven't quite forgiven them for the yelling and the shaming and the punishments when I couldn't "behave" at the dinner table like my brother and sister.

So no, I'm not partial to sit-down meals these days, funnily enough. No amount of meds can get me over that life-long trauma. I have enough work dinners to attend, thanks very much. I have no intention of ruining a perfectly good evening of sexy negotiations by sticking my arse down at a dinner table, no matter how attractive the view across from me.

Instead, I hook myself and Marlowe up with a private space at a new lounge bar and nightclub located, conveniently, in the basement of a hotel in Knightsbridge. The hotel is the brand-new baby of one of my nemeses, Sovereign Structures, who are guilty of more than just wanky alliteration. I don't like them, and I've been dying for a hate-snoop. This way, I can check them out *and* check Marlowe out before we move upstairs later.

If we move upstairs, that is. The private room may be up to the job if it has a working lock and a sturdy sofa.

I make sure I get to the bar half an hour early. I have to admit, it's fucking gorgeous, with a black-and-bronze colour palette and plenty of marble and onyx. The finish is impeccable, and they certainly haven't skimped on the materials. The layout is cool too. They've dug out a double basement, allowing for a double-height main bar and club area with the

VIP spaces dotted around on a mezzanine reachable via a show-stopping circular staircase. These range from open-plan areas with couches and stools to more luxurious suites separated from the dance floor and main bar by a one-way mirror. Their inhabitants get a clear view of the action below while being concealed from sight.

It is my intention to make *full* use of the fact that no one can see into our suite this evening.

When the time approaches for Marlowe to show up, I'm pacing like a caged tiger, all edgy anticipation and raging sex hormones, and trying to make my very long G&T last while I watch the bar below us fill up. It's a Thursday night, and plenty of finance bros are making their way over from the City so they can live it up tonight and nurse their hangovers on company time tomorrow. Where the finance bros go, the hot gold-diggers follow. The eye candy is excellent, the champagne corks are popping, and the DJ is cutting loose on sexy, sundowner-style beats.

None of those douchebags down there have as high a chance of scoring tonight as I do. If I don't fuck it up and scare her off, that is.

Apparently, the hiring process for her is unusual by Seraph's standards. My brother admitted to me over drinks recently that he viewed some *very* salacious photos of Athena at the agency's offices before he moved forward with her. As Marlowe is brand new to the agency, I haven't had that luxury. Camille has explained that she hasn't had her photo shoot yet, but that I'm welcome to view other candidates' "portfolios" if I decide not to hire her.

Whatever. I don't need some porno photos to tell me what I already know. Between what I've seen of Marlowe so far and the helpful assistance of my overactive imagination to fill in the gaps, I'm in no doubt as to the quality of what I'm buying.

Bang on time, a server ushers Marlowe into the suite, and holy fucking shit.

The woman is a *knockout.*

It seems even my imagination has its limits, because I've filled the spank bank this week with fantasies of taking that little pink work dress off her, but here she is, already half naked. She's my type on steroids.

Or maybe it's that she's my type with a bit of soul. She has all the admittedly pretty stereotypical physical attributes I love —long blonde hair, perky tits, fantastic legs—but she's classy. Soulful. Interesting. It's in her delicate bone structure and her big brown eyes, and—

She makes her way towards me, and my brain short-circuits. While she doesn't seem to be a natural on heels that high, the way that little gold dress clings to her willowy frame is spectacular. I can feel the grin spreading across my face.

My evening just got a thousand times better.

'Hi,' she says, slightly breathlessly.

'Evening.' I flash that grin at her one more time as I stoop to kiss her on both cheeks. She smells incredible—something floral and feminine, which suits her. Her fragrant hair tickles my nose as I kiss her, and her skin is soft where I've laid my palm against her upper arm as we greet each other.

The hovering server takes our drink orders—a glass of Chablis for her and another long G&T for me.

'Actually,' I tell her. 'Bring a bottle of Chablis and one of gin. I want ice buckets and tonic, too. Some still water, and a big mezze platter. That should do us.'

While I have no intention of drinking anywhere near a bottle of gin, I don't want to give the server any reason to disturb us again. I'm hoping Marlowe isn't a flight risk, but I don't want her getting skittish, either during what could (for her) be a sensitive conversation or once I finally get my hands on her.

Particularly the latter.

I stick my spare hand in my pocket, my fingers reaching out of habit for the spinner on my fidget toy. 'I'm glad you said yes.'

I really am. I thought the work-oriented interview went well, but Camille had previously made it very clear that if the candidate didn't feel adequate chemistry, she was under no obligation to proceed to the next round. As it turned out, she called me the following morning with a big fat yes from Marlowe, and I wasted no time setting up tonight's rendezvous.

That gets me a smile. 'Of course,' she says, then blows out a shuddery breath that strikes me as involuntary.

'You nervous?' I ask, scrutinising her face. She really is an extraordinarily beautiful woman, but she doesn't give much away.

That's okay.

If she wants me to work for it, I will.

Even if I'm paying through the nose for the privilege.

'No, not at all,' she says, far too quickly.

I raise a sceptical eyebrow. 'If it helps, just think of it as a first date. A *really slutty* first date.' I wink. 'My absolute favourite kind.'

She presses her lips together like she's trying not to laugh and blushes a little. How a woman who's intent on embarking on a career as a sex worker can have the whole bashful, virginal vibe going quite so effectively, I have zero clue, but clearly the universe is really into me, and I'm not going to question it.

Our drinks and mezze arrive quickly on a bar cart, our

server making brisk work of setting the food up on the low table in the middle of the long, curved sofa and the drinks on the marble-topped bar area to one side of the space. I go to hold the door open for her as she wheels the bar cart back out and subtly take a few hundred quid in cash from my pocket.

'What's your name?'

'Anastasia, sir.'

'Thanks for all your help, Anastasia. I'd appreciate it if you made sure we weren't disturbed for the rest of the night.'

Her eyes widen at the sight of the money. 'Of course not, sir. Have a good evening.'

I shut and lock the door behind her. That the owners of this place fitted their private suites with locks tells me they anticipated *exactly* the kinds of shenanigans that would go down in here. Once that's taken care of, I pour Marlowe a glass of perfectly chilled wine and take it over to her, openly looking her up and down as I do.

'God, I can't wait to touch you.'

My meds may have worn off by this time of day—if I take them too late, it really affects my sleep—but I'm not sure all the Ritalin in the world could stop me from blurting that out. It's true. I'm a starving lion attempting to hold off while a juicy T-bone is dangled in front of me. Not going to happen, mate.

She hesitates. She looks taken aback by my admission. After all, she's only been here a few minutes.

'You can touch me if you want,' she says, which doesn't exactly smack of the enthusiastic consent I'm hoping for.

I tilt my head as I consider. 'Maybe I'll get to know you while we chat, remind us both what we've got in store. Hmm?'

'Sure,' she says brightly. I'm not convinced she's anywhere near as desperate for this as I am, which means I'll take great pleasure in watching her shed those layers of nerves and brittleness and whatever else is going on as she yields to the way I know I can make her feel.

I refill my drink and we take a seat next to each other in front of the excellent-looking mezze. I adjust my position so I'm facing more towards her and glance down at her bare legs. So smooth. So tantalising. The hem of her already short dress has ridden up, and it wouldn't take much at all to burrow under there and find nirvana.

'Dig in.' I hand her a side plate and take one for myself, populating it with some great-looking falafel and a decent dollop of hummus. 'Want some?'

She nods, and I put a spoonful on her plate.

'Do you have any preference on how we do this?' I ask her.

'Not really. This is my first Seraph audition,' she confesses, which I obviously already knew. Still, it gives me a kick that I'm her first client.

'Have you done this before? Were you doing any sex work on the side while you were toiling away at the RA?'

She gives a little laugh. 'Absolutely not. Um, Camille suggested we use this time to talk about logistics and, um, expectations. Yours and mine.'

'That sounds very sensible,' I say evenly. 'Do you have any expectations, Marlowe?'

'I—no. I—suppose I'd rather hear what yours are.'

I nod my understanding as I bite into a falafel. They're fresh as fuck: perfectly crispy on the outside and soft and fluffy on the inside. I swallow it down quickly and lay a palm on her thigh, just above her knee. Her skin is so smooth and soft it could make a man weep. 'This okay?'

She nods twice, like she's trying to convince herself as much as me. But more telling is the fact that her quad has tensed up under my hand.

'Excellent. Well, I have a lot of expectations.' I brush my thumb back and forth over her thigh, keeping my hand where it is. 'Expectations that I'm going to work you hard, that you're going to blow my mind—which I know you are—and that I'm hopefully going to blow yours. Expectations that I'm going to use you to act out every filthy, depraved workplace fantasy I've ever, ever had, and that you're single-handedly going to save me from the mind-numbing boredom of a desk job. How does that sound?'

She's full-blown, deer-in-the-headlights stiff, her brown eyes wide with what looks like absolute terror, and I realise I may have shown my hand too quickly. Or, more accurately, that I've thrown the entire fucking deck of cards at the poor girl. *Stupid move, Bren.*

'But we can work up to all that,' I say hastily. 'As far as I can see, the most important things are that we've both filled out our questionnaires, and that you give me your safeword, and that we use this evening to test the waters. Basically, tonight's about you taking me for a test drive so you can see if you can bear to work for me.'

She takes a large slug of her wine before staring at me over the rim of the wineglass. 'This is supposed to be my audition, not yours.'

I give her an easy laugh. 'I think we both know that's not true. I'd hire you on the spot without getting any further than this.' I keep my thumb brushing over the skin of her thigh. 'Nope, tonight is for you.'

The line has the desired effect—her shoulders drop a fraction, the death grip on her wineglass loosening slightly. It's a move I've perfected over the years—the art of appearing generous, self-deprecating, while getting *exactly* what I want.

Classic Sullivan negotiation tactic.

But there's something about Marlowe that has me second-guessing my usual playbook. That first meeting at the RA, when my brain completely short-circuited... I can't afford a repeat performance of that epic fail. If she walks away tonight, I'm back to Plain Elaine and my right hand for company.

She holds far more power here than she realises, so I'd better make my "pitch" count.

I jerk my head in the direction of the tinted glass overlooking the main bar. 'Why don't we head on over there so I can kick my audition off in style?'

# CHAPTER 10

# Marlowe

I can already tell Brendan is not a man who's used to asking twice, just as I can tell that wasn't really a suggestion.

It was a charming, casually delivered order.

And, to be honest, I'm so nervous, so out of my depth after years and years of deliberately *not* flirting, that following orders is about all I'm good for.

I give him what I hope is a vaguely coquettish smile and stand, holding onto my wineglass for dear life. This excellent Chablis is my liferaft this evening. He grins back, a sign that I've just passed my first test, and stands up to join me, shrugging off his blazer as he does and giving me the opportunity to check him out properly.

He really is disgustingly attractive, and it feels beyond surreal to be here in this opulent, glass-fronted prison with him. The space is generous, but he's so big, so sure of himself, that he dominates it. I couldn't be more hyper-aware than I am that it's just us in here.

His white shirt is crisp, the unbuttoned collar showing a vee of tanned skin and a smattering of dark hair. It skims broad shoulders and a taut-looking chest and a flat stomach. When he twists to chuck his jacket on the sofa, I get a shot of a firm, nicely rounded arse. He's such a gratifying specimen of the male form that I simultaneously want to giggle and vomit.

Still, he gave me an order.

So follow it I do.

I move towards the front of the room in a manner I hope could be termed sashaying. These heels definitely cause my hips to sway more than usual. As I go, I'm conscious of the sight I must make. Of the skimpiness of my dress, the expanse of bare leg.

I really need him to like what he sees, though his *I can't wait to touch you* comment was encouraging.

On the other side of the tinted glass unfolds a scene that I know is totally normal for a Thursday night in places like this yet seems as alien as if I'd landed on Mars. It's not just the money or the decadence, but the sheer hedonism of it. The concept of folks working all day only to want to go out and socialise even more, to drink and dance and network like they don't have a care or an expense in the world, is categorically beyond my frame of reference. For God's sake, do none of these people have a Netflix show to get home to?

Brendan is undoubtedly one of these people.

This is his world.

I can tell.

His footsteps sound on the polished black floor, then stop. I turn to look at him. He has one hand around his drink and the other fiddling with something in his pocket. Otherwise, he's still, taking me in. I hesitate, unsure what to do. Should I go to him?

'As you were. Please.'

I turn back towards the glass, holding my breath until he announces his presence behind me as a solid wall of heat. He's not touching me, yet I can feel the warmth emanating from his body. Then his hand comes to rest on my hip and he dips his mouth to my ear.

'I should have told you as soon as you walked in. You are stunning this evening.'

His voice is a gruff whisper, his breath hot against my jaw. The foreignness of it, the heady uncertainty, makes me shiver. I can't yet tell if tonight will be one giant out-of-body experience or a giant in-my-body experience. Maybe it'll be a bit of both.

'Thank you.'

His hand slides upwards, cupping my waist. It feels both reassuring and ominous.

'So you want to do this.'

'I do,' I say with a certainty I don't feel.

'What's your safeword?'

'I—uh—is it okay if I just say *stop* if I need you to?'

'Of course it is. I'm not a monster. A woman says stop, I stop.' He turns his lips and whispers into my ear. 'She screams *don't stop*, I keep going. Okay?'

I nod fervently, even if the mere concept of screaming at a man not to stop is downright surreal. I am not that woman.

Never have been.

'Good.' He slides his cold, condensation-laced highball down my upper arm, and I shiver. 'Now, what do you like?'

I suppose this is part of his *tonight is for you* pitch. But honestly, it's the least helpful question he could have asked me. I could give him a comprehensive list of my favourite tropes, microtropes, and bookish kinks, but he's asking *what I like* in my real, honest-to-God sex life, and that's a problem.

I can get myself from nought to sixty like nobody's business, but I've never come with another person in the room. My first boyfriend, who I met when working in a restaurant after I finished Sixth Form, had no clue what he was doing, bless him. And with Joe, it was—I don't know. It felt good—I had certain sensations as well as a whole lot of emotions—but it was usually just blow jobs or straight sex, and I just can't come like that. What I *liked* with him was the intimacy. The attention. The praise. The experience of being worshipped, and the look on his face as he fell apart. I particularly enjoyed it when he got stern and professorial with me—after all, that was what had attracted me to him in the first place—but it didn't culminate in any actual orgasms for me.

I can't exactly tell a man who's already forked out twenty-five grand for the privilege of fucking me tonight that I like intimacy, can I?

So I tell him the truth.

'I don't know, really.'

He laughs softly and drags his beard across my jaw. It's a soft rasp, and it feels good. 'Going to make me work for it, I see. I can respect that. Well, I'll tell you what I like. *I* like good girls who do what I say and stand nice and still while they let me play with them. Can you do that?'

*God*, why is that so menacingly, astoundingly attractive?

'Yes,' I stammer. 'Of course.'

'Excellent. I think we're going to get along just fine, Marlowe.'

He straightens up, inhaling my hair in a way that's not remotely tender but rather proprietary. Assessing. Then he's taking my drink and setting both glasses down somewhere while I stay good-girl still, watching the beautiful people laughing and flirting beneath us, and feeling the bass of the music downstairs thump through my body, and wondering what Brendan's next move will be.

He slides both hands around my waist, then down, skimming my hips, smoothing over my bottom, my dress a flimsy barrier between us.

'You know,' he says from behind me, his hands moving over me, 'when I was working my way up the ranks at the company, my dad made me do six months in each division. Sales was where I smashed it. I'm an excellent salesman, love, and I'm particularly good at closing deals. But *you* might be the most fun I've had closing a deal in a very long time.'

That makes me laugh. He's a charming fucker; I'll give him that. 'Knock yourself out.'

'The plan is to knock *you* out and have a ball doing it. Put your hands on the glass.'

Oh God.

I do, and he drags his palms up my sides and over my rib cage. Then he slides them over my breasts, cupping hard, and I gasp at the fierce physicality of his big hands on my body like this. I may be horrifyingly rusty, but I'm pretty sure that's not a mobile phone pressing against the base of my spine. He's crowding me, and it's not awful.

I've come here tonight with one objective: to put on a good enough performance that I land this job. Contrary to what Brendan said, I am most certainly the one auditioning here. My goal is survival, not pleasure. But if I can relax into this sufficiently, it'll be far less of a challenge to pull off my performance. So I force myself to lay my demons, my insecurities, my nerves aside and focus on the reality of the present moment.

And that reality is this: a very hot man is pressing his dick against me and fondling my boobs.

'Given you won't tell me what you like, I'll have to pay close attention, won't I?' he murmurs. 'That sounded like a good gasp. How about this?'

*This* is deft fingers pinching and plucking at my nipples.

There's a double layer of ruched fabric at the top of this dress, but no padding, and the feel of it is an instant shot of electricity to my core. I've been blessed with extremely sensitive nipples, and they react to Brendan's touch like two little whores as the pleasure of his pinches shoots through me.

I don't even realise I've made a sound until he chuckles, low and pleased.

'Bingo. You like that.'

'Yeah.' I feel shy even admitting it.

'Yes, you do. That's my girl. Fuck, they're hard.'

He ramps up his attentions, squeezing and plucking. I let my eyes drift closed to more fully absorb the hits of sensation, my head dropping back against his shoulder. With his head bent, his breath is warm on my jaw. He releases one nipple and drags his palm down my front so he can snag the hem of my dress and burrow beneath it before cupping my pussy hard, his fingertips pressing right against my entrance.

If I thought having him touch my nipples was shocking, this is so much more: confronting and dirty and *hot*, especially because he's still rolling my left nipple around as best he can through the fabric.

'Legs wider,' he grunts against my jaw, and I widen my stance, keeping my palms clamped to the glass for balance as his fingers flex against the scrap of lace that constitutes my underwear this evening.

'So much to play with.' His voice is more of a purr now. 'I just bought a catamaran, but I can already tell you're going to be a lot more fun, love. I want to see it all.'

The ominous threat has my heart rate ratcheting up, because fuck, this is really happening. He releases my pussy, and I think he's going to go for the concealed zip at the side of my dress, but he takes a step back and slides the slinky fabric up over my bottom until it's completely bared to him.

I squeeze my eyes shut and press my lips together, because

it's so *blatant,* so shameful and excruciating and unseemly, being exposed like this to a man who's paying terrifying amounts of money for the privilege. But the deeply buried part of me that liked the way he grabbed me just now is also forging bravely to life, a tiny, tough seedling bursting into existence with little wisdom and even less heed for the dangers ahead, dangers that seem more imminent when he lets out an anguished, carnal groan.

'Jesus fuck, love.' He gives the slippery fabric an impatient push upwards, and then both his big hands are stroking and grabbing at my cheeks. I can't even imagine how I must look to him like this, skin and lace and heels on display for him, my hands braced against the glass.

He hooks one finger under the string of my thong and runs a calloused knuckle lightly down the cleft of my bottom, abandoning it before he gets too far south and letting the lace snap back into place. His breath is audibly ragged.

'I've wanted to do this since I saw you at the RA looking all cultured and classy and innocent in your floaty dress, and fucking look at you now. The lovely Marlowe is all mine to play with. You should know I'm *this close* to whipping out my dick and shooting my load all over your arse, but I won't. Because this is you auditioning me, so tonight, love, you come first, okay?'

'Okay,' I agree breathlessly, grateful that he's not hiring me for my dirty-talking skills. Because I've got nothing. What I *do* have in my High-Class Hooker arsenal is a couple of recent rewatches of *When Harry Met Sally,* just so I could nail the fake orgasm thing. Except, the way this guy is manhandling me is making me think it won't be very hard at all to sound convincing. He's most definitely pressing the right buttons, even if tonight's pressure and stakes and nerves mean there is literally zero chance of my coming for real.

He lets my hem fall some of the way back down. Then, in

a couple of slick movements that tell me he's had a lot of practice at this, he gathers up my hair and dumps it over one shoulder, slides both my straps down as far as he can with my hands like this, and finds the zip, yanking it all the way down so that my brace position is the only thing holding my little dress up.

Until, that is, he barks out his next order.

'Turn around.'

# CHAPTER 11

# Marlowe

s I turn, instinct has me pressing a hand to my chest to hold the dress up.

Brendan takes a step towards me, shaking his head. 'Back against the glass. Let it fall. I want to see what I've bought.'

Every minute in here with this guy brings a fresh fear, a fresh confrontation, a fresh precipice off which to leap, but this is the highest precipice so far.

His gaze is so intense. So all-consuming. It's like nothing exists for him in this moment except for what lies beneath my dress. He told me during the interview that he had ADHD.

I suppose this is what hyper-focus looks like.

'Go on.' He nods. 'Eyes on me as you do.'

There's a lump in my throat the size of a golf ball. I give myself a mental kick and remove my hand. Surely I'm the first woman he's been with who's ever hesitated to undress for him. Most of them probably chuck their thongs at him the second they get him alone—or even before.

The slinky fabric drops instantly, the tiny, ineffectual

straps slack around my forearms, the dress caught around my hips and my top half completely exposed to him.

Standing here topless in front of a man I don't know while he openly appraises me feels wrong on every level… except for the level where his eyes drop from my face to my naked breasts, and I finally understand what all the romance books mean when they say a man's eyes *burn*, because his are blazing. His mouth opens and shuts again, this moment of silence between us stretching into eternity.

Until he grins.

It's a dirty grin, carnal and dominating and thrilled.

'Unfuckingbelievable. Take it off.'

I choose to take *it* to mean just the dress, so I leave my thong intact and push the dress over my hips, stepping carefully out of the fabric pooled around my heels. I'm barely done casting it aside when he's on me, gathering me up in his arms and smushing my breasts to his chest, my pelvis to what is now an obscene-looking erection, so fully fledged that it's a walking red flag all on its own.

But I'm ignoring that, because the sensation of being almost naked in the arms of a huge beast who smells divine and seems intent on ravaging me is so overwhelmingly unfamiliar and shocking and *excellent* that my cognitive brain withers in defeat.

I'm not prepared for his mouth to find mine, but it does, as soon as he has me in his claws, and he kisses me, hard and hungry and filthy, his lips soft and his tongue insistent as it forces my mouth open while his hands fist my hair and grope my bottom, *hard*, and roam as though they're trying to map every available inch of skin.

It's either self-preservation or good old-fashioned desire that has me hooking my arms around his shoulders as he performs this sensory onslaught. He's not kissing me so much as fucking my mouth with deep, demanding strokes that feel like a menacing foreshadowing of what he'll do to me shortly with other body parts. He's consuming me, milking me, and an actual thought escapes from my cognitive cesspit:

This isn't him giving me a sales pitch. This is him *unleashed*.

As if he can read my mind, he releases me from his mouth and his grasp with an anguished pant and walks me backwards until I hit the glass. 'Stay still,' he orders, his mouth all swollen and wet and lovely. He shoots my breasts a filthy look before bracketing my hips in a tight grip. By tugging them forward and leaving my shoulders slumped against the glass, he has me reclining slightly, and that's when he bends and takes one nipple in his mouth, holding it oh-so lightly between his teeth as he rolls his tongue over it.

I moan in spite of myself, and my palms make a small squeak as they slap the glass for purchase.

'Mmm,' he groans around my nipple. 'Delicious.' His fingers dig more firmly into my hips as his licks become deep pulls on my nipple, and holy, holy shit, this feeling is ridiculously, crazily good. My hips start to jolt, rutting forwards and finding nothing but his grip. That erection of his is too far away from me at this point.

'Stay *still*,' he barks before turning his attention to my other breast. Jesus, this is so, so good. If only the man had two mouths. I want him to never come up for air. I stop rutting, keeping my body still and instead lifting my hands so I can run them through his short dark hair. Its softness is touching, for some reason. With a firm grip, I hold his head to my breast, and he chuckles, jerking his neck backwards and looking up at me, all wet lips and burning eyes.

'Put your hands back where they are, madam, if you want the full sales pitch.'

We smirk at each other, then I sigh and release his head. I

have no idea where this *pitch* is going, but I don't intend to derail it.

'That's my good girl. Now,'—he gets to his knees surprisingly nimbly for a guy his size—'let me show you the killer part of my pitch.'

I press my lips together as he gets level with my crotch. With a thumb hooked in each side of my thong's lace waistband, he slides it down my legs and watches as I step out of it.

I'm now naked, and he's planning on doing *something* down there, and I look down at him as I mentally step up to the highest precipice yet. And as I stare over the edge into the void, Athena's voice rings in my ears.

*Assuming he's not a lazy bastard in bed, he should be* very *good at this shit. So for fuck's sake, sit back and enjoy it.*

She has a point, although *enjoying* something very intimate and very unfamiliar with a total stranger is easier said than done.

'Put your leg over my shoulder, gorgeous,' he says, hooking his hand around the back of my knee and shooting me a very sexy grin.

He looks like he does this every bloody day. Like having naked women drape their legs over his hulking great shoulders is second nature to him.

It probably is.

I balance with difficulty on one stiletto heel, fingers scrabbling against the glass, and allow Brendan to position my leg over his shoulder. His eyes are fixed squarely on where my legs are parted, his expression more that of a kid with a new toy than that of a grown man with a woman he's paying through the nose for.

'That's more like it.' He glances up through eyelashes that are far too thick and pretty for a bloke. 'You are exceedingly beautiful when you're nervous, you know. All quivery and...

mmm.' He leans in and uses his finger and thumb to spread me open for him, and oh my—Jesus, that's—

I stare down, my breath coming more quickly now, transfixed by how quickly his expression has gone from cheeky to rapt and astounded by how different having a man's fingers on my *flesh* feels from having them on my *skin*.

He tuts. 'Oh, Marlowe, Marlowe. All this pretending to be such a good, nervy, innocent little thing, when you're fucking *soaked* already.'

I'm not. I can't be. Except that I can feel how slick it is when he slides his fingers through me, burrowing deeper back until he finds my entrance, and then, God, the ease with which he pushes two fingers in is almost embarrassing. There's a stretch, a burn, of course, but there is definite, undeniable lubrication going on, and I don't know if it's that my brain is in denial about how fun it is having a Very Bad Man do Very Bad Things to me or my body is a traitorous little slut.

It's probably both.

'Oh God,' I say, as mortified that he's called me out as I am happy about this latest development, because that sensation of fullness is really something else, and I have a horrible feeling that if he—

*Jesus.* His thumb finds my clit, stroking over it far too lightly, and I let out a low, shuddering sound that's downright pitiful.

Brendan tears his gaze from his handiwork and stares up at me. 'Looks like we're unravelling the mysteries of what you like pretty fucking quickly. I feel like Miss Marple.'

I snort at that, but it turns into a groan, because he's sliding his fingers out and then back in in a fashion that's as entitled as it is leisurely, his thumb swirling over my clit with not nearly enough pressure.

'Just found my new favourite fidget toy,' he tells me. 'Zoom meetings will never be the same again.' With that proclamation, he tilts his head to one side, licks his lips so sala-ciously it's positively illegal, and leans in to taste me, pulling his fingers out enough to hold me open for him. I mouth a silent *holy fuck* and screw my eyes shut, because the feeling of him using his mouth on me is sinful and shameful and depraved and so perfectly, disgustingly good that I will actually die if I have to watch it.

I've never done this—never had this done to me. I didn't let Pete, my first boyfriend, go there, and Joe never offered. Honestly, I didn't have a problem with that. If it was frus-trating enough failing to come when he played with me, it would have been mortifying beyond belief to let him go to work with his mouth and not produce an orgasm.

But from the low grunts Brendan makes in the back of his throat as his tongue circles in on my clit with the precision of The Jackal wielding a sniper rifle, he doesn't seem to be finding it hard work.

Except—*oof*—closing my eyes and giving in to the fire igniting between my legs while balancing on one four-inch heel is *not* advisable because I promptly wobble and almost fall over.

'Fuck,' he says, emerging from eating me to grab me around the waist. 'Change of plan.' He unhooks my leg and, rising, throws me over his shoulder. I squeal in surprise as he gets to his feet and carries me, fireman's-lift style, across the room before laying me on my back on the sofa quickly enough that dizziness reels through me.

When my head has righted itself, I find him standing beside me—although *towering over me* would be more accu-rate—and looking awfully pleased with himself as he unbut-tons his shirt. I'm sprawled on the cool pleather of the sofa, self-consciousness and apprehension warring with arousal and curiosity, and I can say with confidence that the sight of Brendan Sullivan undressing himself for me has the see-saw swinging in favour of the latter far more rapidly than is decent.

He undresses like I suspect he does a lot of things—hurriedly. He's not putting on a show here, but his smug grin tells me he's not finding my facial expression as ambivalent as I'd hoped.

It's been a long, long time since I saw a man naked, and I've never seen a man like *this* naked. Of my two previous partners, Pete was a still-skinny eighteen-year-old, and Joe had the untoned, if lean, build of an academic.

Brendan does *not* look like an academic.

He looks, as he makes quick work of the buttons down the front of his shirt and battles impatiently with his cufflinks, like a man with far too much energy to burn in the gym. With his crisp white shirt hanging open, the playboy tan is in evidence. He rips the shirt off his shoulders and tosses it impatiently to the floor, giving me my first proper view of a masterpiece of male physicality.

His PT should feel very proud of this masterpiece.

There's a smattering of soft-looking dark hair on his chest that continues down over his flat stomach. His forearms are exactly the kind I tend to ogle on Instagram: not scarily corded but taut and tanned and hairy. His shoulders, as I already knew, are fucking huge, his pecs defined. He's perfectly in proportion, built without being too beefy, and I suspect I'm staring like he's an exotic creature in a zoo.

'Why on earth does a guy like you have to pay for sex?' I wonder aloud, raising myself up onto my elbows for a better look. His ensuing laugh is tinged with self-consciousness.

'Convenience. Dependability.' He wrestles his belt from its buckle and yanks his trousers open. *Holy fuck.* 'Kink, I suppose. It's hot to think of you being my little office fuck toy, baby. But mainly convenience. I don't want to have to go out on the pull or take women out for dinner or have to deal with them falling in love with me and fucking stalking me.'

He kicks his shoes off, pushing his trousers down and stepping out of them. As he tugs off his socks, he looks up at me and finds me shamelessly perving over the sight of tanned, muscular thighs and what looks like a four-seater car parked in his stretchy black boxer briefs. The waistband says Chanel.

Of course it does.

'You're not going to fall in love with me and stalk me, are you?'

I manage, by the skin of my teeth, to avoid an eye roll. The last thing I need in my life as a single mother to a child with a chronic health condition is to fall for a vapid, charming playboy like this guy. Seriously. 'I am not. You're perfectly safe.'

'Glad to hear it.' He shoves his boxer briefs down and Jesus fucking Christ, I have bitten off more than I can chew, because that's not a dick.

It's a monster.

Even Athena would struggle to accommodate that thing. It's insane. Physiologically indecent. Red and angry and leaking precum. He palms it lasciviously and inhales sharply through his teeth.

'How's my sales pitch working?' he asks me with a grin that tells me he caught me ogling. His dick may be intimidating as hell, but he's so ridiculous that I'm relaxing despite myself.

'It's... effective,' I tell him. 'Well-practised, clearly.'

His smile turns self-deprecating. 'It's nowhere near over yet. Now, where were we?'

He crawls onto the sofa, which is wide enough that the designers must have intended it to accommodate lots of shagging, and I lower myself fully onto my back so he can range over me. He's a big, dark, hairy bear, and despite his grin, a thrill of *something* courses through me.

This guy could eat me for dinner. And he probably will.

I don't answer what seems like a rhetorical question, but I do open my legs wider as he slides down my body, kissing my nipples and my stomach as he goes.

He was right earlier. It's far easier to think of this as a random hookup, a "slutty first date", than a transactional precursor to an even more transactional working relationship. Right now, I need to remember that I'm not a mother driven by terrified determination but a woman in her twenties, sprawled out naked in a fancy nightclub and in the—very competent—hands of one of London's most gorgeous and eligible bachelors.

*Lean into that,* I urge myself. *Look at him! He's heaven! And he wants to eat you! Just let him!*

At this point, Brendan crouches between my legs and finds my most sensitive parts with his lips and tongue and fingers, and my inner Mel Robbins shuts the hell up, because the fires of sensation are licking at my flesh and everything else is impossible.

His moves are filthy and decadent and carnal, and they have my nervous system ricocheting between running for the hills and setting off the fireworks.

'I've wanted to do this since the second I met you,' he mutters against my clit, sliding two fingers back inside me and twisting them in a way that's as gratifying as it is painful. 'Been imagining it so much. So fucking delicious. *God.*' He illustrates his point with a lavish lick.

I raise my head so I can stare down at this incarnation of the vision that's been terrifying and titillating me since Athena suggested I interview with Brendan: his broad shoulders between my open legs, dark hair dipped so I can only see the crown of his head, face hidden as he feasts on the most private parts of me, and his huge hand splayed bossily across my stomach, holding me down.

His confession is the most real, raw thing he's said to me, and it sends a tide of heat racing over my skin. I couldn't be more vulnerable right now, and I know this guy probably goes down on a different woman every day of the week, but he makes it sound like *he's* vulnerable too, somehow. That he has skin in the game, even if I'm not much more than a conquest. A trophy sought and won.

Having this gorgeous, sexy man's tongue on my clit is one thing, but having him admit that he's enjoying it, that he's been *fantasising* about it, is the flick of the switch my body needs to go from enduring this to lapping it up. For whatever reason, it seems to get him off, and the idea of him using my body how he wants, burrowing his nose into my flesh and sucking on my clit and fucking me deeper and deeper with his fingers, is every bit as shameful as I imagined it would be and a million times hotter than I ever, ever dreamed.

There's so much oral in my romance books. My favourite mafia men eat their women for breakfast, lunch, and dinner, it seems. And I admit, I've tried to simulate it by myself a few times without knowing what I'm aiming for.

*This is what I was aiming for.* This—the wetness, the silky softness, the—oh my God, the roughness when he laps at me with the flat of his tongue, the precision when he uses the tip. It's like Mother Nature created an all-natural orgasm provider and gave it the ten best settings it needed for totally ruining a woman.

I cannot *believe* fucking Joe never did this to me!

And I can believe even less that I'm having this strong a reaction to a man I barely know, let alone a man I don't have any feelings for. I have never understood how women can jump into bed with random men and survive it, let alone get off on it. I'm not ashamed to admit I've judged them for it.

But it seems the joke may be on me.

The strangest, best sensations are happening to my body. Heat is pricking me all over. Everywhere south of my belly button aches with a visceral, pulsing need. My nipples are so taut with arousal they feel like they're going to snap off. The noises I'm making are zero per cent gleaned from Meg Ryan and a hundred per cent involuntary and possibly a good seventy per cent farmyard.

I am not a woman who has ever asked for what she wants in bed. I have no language, I have no confidence, I have no tricks to seduce a guy or manipulate an outcome.

But I do recall one thing Brendan promised me earlier.

That if I scream *don't stop*, he'll keep on going.

So I channel all this blind, crazy need, and I cast aside the tattered remnants of my inhibitions, and I claw at his hair with one hand, and I throw my head back as he hits the spot over and over and over like the fucking genius that he is.

And I shudder out my plea.

'Please. *Don't stop.* Please.'

# CHAPTER 12

# Brendan

I'm in a fancy club, my nose and mouth and fingers buried in the delicious—and soaking wet—cunt of a hot blonde who's laid out naked on the sofa of a private room for my pleasure.

So far, so on brand for a Thursday night.

But that's where this being any kind of normal Thursday night ends.

Because this isn't a hookup.

It's an audition. A two-way audition.

And Marlowe is not your average hot blonde bombshell who stakes out and seduces men like me so efficiently that she may as well be a professional.

Nope.

The hilarious irony is that this woman, who I'm test-driving ahead of hiring *as a professional*, is reacting to me in a way that's more raw and more gratifying than any other hot blonde I've fucked in a very long time.

Don't feel too sorry for me. I look like this and I'm very, very good in bed. The orgasms I coax out of the others are one hundred per cent real. But those women play the same game as me. They zero in on me for my looks or my money or my reputed prowess in the sack—usually all three. They're practised and cynical, and the whole endless fucking cycle of them is tired, tired, tired.

Whereas I'd bet a lot of money that no one is more surprised than Goldilocks here at the reaction her body is having to mine.

She's barely laid on any moves since she got here. No trite phrases, no trotting out of pretty, fake little moans or coquettish cries. Nope, she's seemed unconvinced at best and shit-scared at worst.

I've never been an academic, but I can read people, and it's clear as day to me that Marlowe is not here because she loves dick. For whatever reason, she wants or needs that paycheque, and who am I to judge? She's been polite and sweet and twitchy, and she's unwittingly provided exactly what I'm looking for so far this evening.

But there is nothing, and I mean *nothing*, more gratifying than having a front-row seat to a beautiful woman unravelling at your hands. Watching Marlowe go from cautious to semi-engaged to unwittingly grinding her honeyed cunt against my face is a bigger and better win than anything I can recall in recent memory—and that includes thrashing my smug mate Ethan at golf last weekend.

I'm so into this it's not funny. The scent of her, the taste of her, are driving me wild, so much so that I've flattened myself onto my stomach so I can hump the sofa. But when she begs me, in that panicked, breathy little voice, not to stop, I mentally punch the air so hard that I mentally dislocate my shoulder.

Fucking *yesssss*.

I knew it.

Marlowe, Marlowe, Marlowe. You were already perfect—*and then you went and begged.*

'I won't stop, baby. I said I wouldn't,' I rasp, looking up so I can enjoy the titillating sight of her red-flushed face and chest, her greedy little tits heaving, her stomach tensing under my hand.

I am going to bring this home, and she's going to fucking explode, and I'm going to enjoy every single second. I use my shoulders to winch her legs even further apart. God, I love having her on her back for me. Mine to pleasure and play with. Once she's working for me, I'll take great pleasure in tying her up and edging her for so long that it will bring new meaning to the phrase *extended lunch hour*, but now is about the pitch. Now is about demonstrating with aplomb the white-hot pleasure she'll know when she becomes my fuck toy.

And so I go for maximum sensation. I'd stick a finger up that snug little arsehole so quickly if she hadn't specified no anal, but we'll get there when I've spent longer earning her trust. Instead, I lick her as roughly as I can while I fuck her deeply, rhythmically, with my fingers. I'd add a third, but she is seriously fucking tight. I'm not sure how I'll survive burying my dick inside this lovely little cunt. I can't resist a low groan at the thought of it.

Her noises increase in volume. She sounds like she's totally out of control and hanging on for dear life, and so help me God, I love it. *This* is what I've hoped for: that the sweet, elegant, polite woman I was so struck by would and could transform for me into this writhing, thrashing creature as she submits to the delights of the Sullivan Pitch.

She's shaking. Shuddering. 'Oh God, oh God, oh God,' she chants over and over.

*I'm going to answer every fucking prayer you've ever had, sweetheart.*

I give her my all, laving at her impossibly swollen clit, and then she's splintering in front of me, sobbing out her orgasm in a broken voice as her climax rips through her beautiful body.

I lick her and lick her, humming my approval, until she comes down and gives a little twitch that tells me it's probably getting too sensitive down there. So I withdraw and instead practically launch myself at her, plastering myself to her front with my cock shamelessly jerking against her stomach and leaking its moisture over us as I kiss her through the aftermath.

I don't just want to *see* her orgasm; I want to *feel* it. I want to savour the chasm that lies between having kissed her earlier, before I'd warmed her up properly, and kissing her now, when she's all wanton and sated and soft, letting her taste herself on my lips and tongue and revelling in the feel of her silky legs as they squeeze the sides of my thighs.

When I release her mouth so I can look at her, her beautiful brown eyes are almost all pupil, and her face is still flushed, and she looks nothing short of shell-shocked. I'm not sure if it's the ferocity of her orgasm that's taken her by surprise or the fact that she experienced it here with me, but I'll take either option.

'You okay?' I ask with all the smugness of a man who knows it's absolutely a rhetorical question.

'Yeah.' Her breathing is still ragged, her eyes darting over my face. 'Yeah—I'm—that was—'

Inability to string a sentence together is an excellent barometer for orgasm quality in my book.

'Part two coming right up,' I say, leaning over to grab my trousers off the floor.

I need to locate a condom and wedge my way inside this snug little cunt *immediately*.

It would be so easy to flip her over, slide an arm under her stomach and drag her up to her knees, but honestly, I'm not sure she'll handle it the first time. She's seriously fucking tight.

From my perspective, there's no such thing as too tight, but I also don't want to cause the poor girl any injuries.

For once, I'll restrain myself and fuck her on her back. Warming her up once she starts working for me will be an absolute joy.

And yeah, I'm feeling pretty good about her saying yes to this job right now. Part one of my pitch was *killer*.

'When you work for me, you'll put these on me,' I tell her as I kneel up between her legs. Her chest is still heaving, her gaze squarely on my dick. I rip the foil with my teeth and proceed to roll the latex over my very fucking sensitive shaft. I didn't bring lube, which in hindsight was an error, but she's pretty soaked, so I hope she can take it.

I suck in a breath through my teeth as I put on the condom. Marlowe is eyeing my dick with what looks like extreme trepidation. 'It's okay,' I tell her. 'I'll go slow.'

*If I'm capable of holding back.*

I don't know why the fantasy of fucking an inexperienced woman does it for me so consistently. It's not like I cross paths with many of them, to be honest. And it makes me feel like a bit of a dick. I know how patriarchal, how revoltingly passé, it is to judge women on different standards from those we men use on ourselves, but I'm not judging.

I'm just expressing a preference.

And that preference is having a lithe little stunner like Marlowe laid out below me, staring at me like I'm a conquering Viking and she's the spoils of my raid. Like she already knows she'll never be the same again after I've filled her up with my monster dick.

She has no fucking clue what a turn-on it is for me—but she's about to find out.

Arranging myself on top of her brings even more clearly home the contrast between my brutish build and her fragility. Going with missionary feels sexist and reductionist and lazily entitled, and all of that has my heart racing. I brace myself on one elbow and take a visual sweep down her body before locating my cock with my hand and positioning it at her entrance.

Beneath me, her beautiful brown eyes widen and she stiffens, her sated laxness ebbing away before me.

'Can you come like this?'

Her expression brightens for a moment into something approaching that put-on peppiness I hate in the women who try to ensnare me, before lapsing into uncertainty. 'Not usually,' she says, screwing up her face like she knows it's not the done thing to admit it. 'But that was a truly excellent orgasm just now.'

It's as if she's forcing her own embarrassment to take a back seat so she can pat me on the back, placate me like I'm a tyrant of a toddler who may throw a tantrum if he doesn't get his way. But that's okay.

I smirk as I reach behind her for a scatter cushion and wedge it under her arse to improve her position. 'People have underestimated me my entire life, love. Luckily for you, my absolute favourite thing is proving them wrong.'

'Oh God, no, it's not you,' she babbles. 'It's me, I just— clearly you're very good at what you—'

She breaks off with a strangled sound as I notch my crown into her plush little pussy.

'I'm *very* good at what I do,' I pant out. My dick is on fire and my head is reeling. 'Just try to relax, love, so I can get in there and show you.'

I'm not a huge fan of kissing while fucking. I enjoy both acts immensely, but together they feel... unwise. I need her to loosen up, though, so I dip my mouth to hers and give her a leisurely, dirty fucking with my tongue. I wish I'd tied her up, but it's still indecently hot to have her splayed out below me as I kiss her and roll my hips over and over, edging into a glove so tight it will be a miracle if I don't disgrace myself after all my big talk.

Inch by inch, I work my way in, her internal muscles squeezing me all the way. I'm sweating like a pig with the effort of holding off on throwing her wellbeing to the wind and ramming the fuck home.

But then I'm in, and I practically weep at the relief of it. My slutty kiss swallows up Marlowe's surprised little noise as I bottom out in her.

We are fucking *on*.

My dilemma is this. I want to talk dirty to her—I have a feeling it'll speed up whatever orgasm she is intent on *not* having. But I'm fully aware it'll speed mine up too if I let rip the stream of filth I want to pour into her ear.

Unfortunately for me, withstanding impulses is not my strong point, especially not at this time of day and *especially* not when I'm buried balls deep inside the vice-like cunt of a delightfully skittish woman hell-bent on refusing to entertain the likelihood of me and my big dick coaxing another orgasm out of her.

Never mind *coaxing*. I'm going to *ram* it out of her, and I'll enjoy every moment of those huge eyes going from dubious to glazed to molten.

'Next time we do this, I'll be bending you over my desk,' I rasp in her ear. Fuck, that's a white-hot visual. I drag my dick out of her body and push back in slowly, both to torment us and because I'm not sure she's fully acclimatised to my size yet. When I bottom out, I roll my hips, loving the feeling of being so tightly held.

'You'll be in the middle of something, and I'll call you into my office when I'm on a really boring call and make you hike up your skirt. I'll play with you for a bit to get you wet, but you'll have to stay perfectly still like a very good girl.'

She makes a noise in the back of her throat, and I turn my head to see her. 'Do you like the sound of that?' I ask.

'Yes.' It's little more than a whisper.

I increase my pace, and she curses under her breath. 'What do you like about it, baby?'

She closes her eyes and turns her head away from me.

'Marlowe. This is what I want, remember? I want to know what gets you off. You told me you don't know but I think you do.'

She's silent for a moment. Unfortunately for her, I have no compunction about weaponising my dick, so I pull out and slam in, harder than I have so far. Jeeeeeesus, that's good.

The impact has her eyes flying open. 'Well? What do you like about that scenario?' For good measure, I dip my head to pull a pretty pink nipple into my mouth and suck hard. It has the advantage of removing what she might deem excessive eye contact, too.

'Oh, God,' she stutters.

'I'm waiting,' I say with my mouth full.

'Um. I want you to give me orders like that.'

I hum my approval, because this little nipple is too good to neglect. It's so hard as I roll it around with my tongue. 'Go on,' I mumble.

'I like the idea of being at your beck and call.' Her entire body arches under me, into me, as she says it, and I know she's being honest.

She's beautiful, she begs, *and* she's naturally submissive. Fuck me, I think I'm getting even harder. I pull off her nipple and rear up so I can brace myself on both elbows and really give it to her.

'Damn right you'll be at my beck and call.' *Fuck.* 'You'll be mine every single fucking way I can have you. You have no clue how hard I'll work you. On your knees, on your back, any fucking way I want, when I want.' I piston my hips into her over and over. Attempting to withhold my own finish is a special kind of hell, but as I grit out the words, as I fuck her over and over, I'm rewarded with a special kind of heaven, too: the sight of Marlowe unravelling in real time beneath me.

Her face is growing more anguished as she chases the climax she swore she couldn't have, her thrashes more violent and useless and desperate. I doubt she's aware of it, but she's clinging to my shoulder with one hand as she digs the fingernails of the other into my arse. She's a cowgirl employing her own brand of spurs, and I'm her lucky, lucky ride.

It's not her fault. She may not usually come this way, but she's never been fucked by Brendan Sullivan before, and she probably hasn't been subject to my brand of dirty talk—or dirty promises, rather.

It's a devastating combination if I say so myself, and she's not the only one getting carried away here. The fantasies I have of railing my newest toy against every flat surface in my office are a shot of Viagra to my performance, turbocharging my dick to the point that I have no fucking clue how I'm this hard and how the hell I haven't shot my load yet.

We're both slick with sweat now, or maybe we're both slick with *my* sweat. Our breaths are ragged, heat is coursing through my body, and her cries match my grunts with every fevered thrust. I'm an animal in this moment, rutting and rutting with no finesse and no endgame except for chasing my release and Marlowe's.

Her face registers total surprise before she lets out a series of anguished cries as she goes hurtling over the edge. Her entire body is wracked with convulsions as I fuck her through her orgasm, and it's a fucking spectacular sight.

Thank God.

I did it.

Now I can let go with my fragile male ego intact.

'Fucking yes,' I tell her as I stiffen impossibly more inside her, and then I thrust and thrust and thrust, burying my face in her neck and roaring into her hair as my orgasm winds me up and spins me out like a spinning top. I'm powerless and weightless, hurtling through the air in ecstasy as I ride it out deep inside her body before collapsing my weight on top of her.

My brain is wiped clean.

No noise.

No friction.

Just blessed stillness.

I'm vaguely aware of her releasing my hair from her death grip and sliding her hand down my back.

Mmm. Feels nice.

It's not until she flinches beneath me that I realise I'm practically spatchcocking the poor woman with my body weight. With enormous difficulty, I find the strength to rear up onto my elbows, but the sight I get is worth it.

Now that's what I call a woman who's just discovered the life-changing power of a really great fuck.

I smile down at her, amused and smug and blissed-out, and tuck a strand of pale gold hair behind her ear. 'We'll probably need to work on our noise levels in the office.'

ATHENA

WELL??????

How was it? How are you?

Totally shellshocked

Good shellshocked or bad? I can't tell

Hello?

Answer me

Double orgasm shellshocked

I came harder and louder than I've ever come in my life. TWICE. I'm so embarrassed. Who even am I?

Fucking YESSSSSSSSSS

You are exactly who you should be

I knew your inner goddess was hiding somewhere

Well played, Mr Sullivan. Well played.

# CHAPTER 14

# Marlowe

Dr Marcus Elliott may just be my new favourite person. He is patient, unflappable and reassuring, but his attraction lies mainly in the air of competence that streams out of him in waves, even from across the Atlantic and through my computer screen.

Yes, I can confirm that Dr Elliott is an insanely experienced paediatric cardiothoracic surgeon based at Duke Children's Hospital in North Carolina, and he will be leading the team that takes on Tabby's operation.

It's happening.

OH MY GOD, IT'S HAPPENING!!!!!!!!!!!!!!!!!!!!

Sorry.

It's just that the relief of knowing, after so many months and years of worrying about this operation, of having it hanging over me, that my daughter's chance at a normal life will come at the hands of such an intensely skilled, experienced team is a rush the likes of which I've never, ever had.

The knowledge that this valve replacement is necessary has overshadowed every single day of my life for the past couple of years. In recent months, that dark shadow has morphed into a ticking time bomb that colours every moment I have with my daughter and robs me of my sleep and my sanity.

Sometimes, when Tabby's sleeping, I'll sit on the edge of her bed with my hand on her chest, feeling and listening to her little heart beating. It does the best it can, but without a right-sized pulmonary valve, it's not enough, and it's falling more short every single day.

Dr Elliott and his team have a plan to end her suffering: to laparoscopically replace the valve with minimal invasion and the least risk to Tabby. My vocabulary around heart stuff is pretty good these days, but he speaks to me in plain English, laying out our journey and his plan. This initial meeting is heavy on information exchange and the lining up of our ducks in a nice, neat row. We discuss my daughter's medical history, her recent blue spells, or *tet spells* as the professionals call them, and her medication. He already has the full details of her previous operations from Great Ormond Street.

'I know this must all seem very overwhelming,' Dr Elliott tells me. His silver hair is neatly side-parted, and his smile is patient. He's a good kind of older—experienced rather than doddery. I'd put him at late fifties. 'But my team pioneered this kind of procedure in children. We see kids from all over the world with Tetralogy of Fallot. Without wanting to downplay the extreme importance of what we do, it's our bread and butter. Tabby will be in excellent hands.'

I nod. It's exactly what I needed to hear, but it's still scary as fuck.

A transatlantic trip.

A new, strange hospital and medical team.

A major operation on the most important organ in her body.

'I know,' I say weakly. 'In terms of timing, I'm hoping we can do it during the school holidays, but my job is in the UK. How long do you think she'll need to be in hospital?'

He purses his lips in thought. 'I would say the absolute minimum would be eight days. I'd be more comfortable with two weeks. I realise this is an extremely costly procedure in its own right, but if you could secure flat beds for the flight home, that would help with her discomfort.'

I scoff internally, because what the hell is another few grand when I'm already forking out six figures for this? The costs keep getting higher and higher.

Dr Elliott continues, oblivious to my spiralling. 'A timeline that tight would require us to complete as much of the preparation as possible remotely at GOSH. All final pre-op tests would be carried out on the day you arrive, with surgery scheduled for the next day. You're looking at three to five days of observation, either in or outside of the ICU, depending on how Tabby's body responds to her new valve, and then another few days of short-stay monitoring. How does that sound?'

I'm nodding, I realise, and it's an attempt to persuade myself as much as this kind man that this is doable. That Tabs and I can handle it. 'Yep. Mmm-hmm.'

'I know it sounds like a tight timeline,' he says. 'She's welcome to stay longer, depending on your budget and your demands back in London. Just remember this, Miss Winters. Tabby isn't systemically ill. She's missing one crucial piece of equipment. And when we've switched that out, the effect on her entire system will be nothing short of miraculous. Yes, there's a recovery period, but, barring any complications, we'd expect to see an immediate improvement in your daughter's cardiopulmonary function. That means higher sats and much improved exercise tolerance, for starters.'

He smiles at me, and I can feel the reassurance of it through my screen. 'What that means in practice is that she'll be doing cartwheels and dancing her little socks off before you know it.'

*T*abby *isn't systemically ill.*

Dr Elliott's words stay with me for a long time after our call. He's right, of course. It's just that the *crucial piece of equipment* she's missing is so fucking critical to her survival that it's always been hard to think beyond that.

But now I begin to allow myself to do just that. After our call finishes, I collapse on the sofa, and I dream about a version of my little girl with rosy cheeks and boundless energy.

I see her turn cartwheel after cartwheel across the grassy area in our local park.

I imagine myself picking up a flushed, sweaty, overexcited little thing from ballet or street dance or whatever dance classes she decides she wants to do. She loves to dance so much —I bet she'll want to do them all.

I shut my eyes and visualise her heart beating and her beautiful new valve pumping all that glorious blood into her lungs for oxygenation.

And I know, somewhere somatic and visceral, deep inside or even beyond my body, that my brave, beautiful daughter will get her life force energy back. That she'll have everything she needs to live a full and magnificent life.

*P*utting into place these tentative, terrifying, exhilarating plans for our US trip is one of my top priorities during this week off before I start my unique role at Sullivan Construction next Monday. The twenty-five grand Brendan paid for my audition facilitated this call with Dr Elliott. The operation itself will require a horrifyingly large deposit, but I get a hundred grand sign-on bonus next week, so that will cover it.

I'm still reeling from how easy things become when you have money to throw at them. A consultation with one of the top surgeons in the world when it comes to my daughter's condition. *No problem.* Scheduling an operation for the surgery that will change her life with the minimum of invasion. *Done.*

Is this how it is? Is this how Brendan feels every single day? That doors open and everyone says yes and the road rises up to meet you on every fucking thing? God knows, it's heady and it's addictive and it feels so, so wrong.

I have fought for months and months for a grant that would fund this exact trip. I have spent so many evenings after work doing research and writing out applications and lobbying every relevant individual, from MPs to doctors to governors of Great Ormond Street, and peanuts. *Peanuts.*

But I spread my legs for a filthy-rich guy and immediately it's open sesame. The money rolls in. The hospitals roll over. And I get what I've wanted for Tabby all along.

A few short weeks ago, taking a job with Seraph felt like the hardest thing I could do, the highest hilltop on which to sacrifice myself for my daughter.

Now it feels like the easiest.

It wasn't even awful! That's what I can't get my head around. I'm supposed to be making the ultimate sacrifice for the ultimate cause, and instead the orgasms are flowing as abundantly as the money, and I can't get my head around it. I'm under no illusion that Brendan will go easy on me, but I had a fantastic night with a hot, generous and disgracefully skilled lover, and for some reason, I feel more guilty than relieved.

And don't get me started on the money.

My very pleasant chat just now concluded with Dr

Elliott's assurance that one of the hospital concierges will be in touch to help me with everything from getting travel clearance from GOSH and liaising with Duke's international patient services department to organising medical visas and supplemental oxygen on our flight should Tabby need it.

Like I said. Open sesame.

I sold my body and instantly jumped all sorts of queues, and I'd do it a million times over, because it got me exactly what I needed. But I can't let myself get used to it.

This money—and this job—goes away as soon as I've paid for this trip and stashed away some savings so Tabby's ongoing medical care isn't purely dependent on the over-stretched folks at Great Ormond Street. The empowerment it's giving me is temporary, as is my ability to book business-class flights, and the decadent workwear shopping trip Brendan has insisted on for my first day, and any orgasms he sees fit to throw my way.

None of it's real. None of it's permanent. The life that people like Brendan live is not for me, and it will serve me to keep that in mind as he dazzles me with this tantalising glimpse of a parallel universe.

What's real is Tabby securing a new "piece of equipment" in the safest possible way so that she can live a normal, active life.

And who knows, the orgasms may not even be a thing. He made it very clear that he was pitching me.

He pitched me.

He closed me.

Just like he said he would.

It's entirely likely that, from here on in, he'll just use me and reward me very handsomely for the privilege.

Maybe it's a good thing. I've always thought (or hoped, rather) that I was the kind of person who didn't believe in the end justifying the means. It turns out I am *so* that person it's not even funny. But at the very least, it seems indecent that I should enjoy the means any more than I have to.

Brendan Sullivan is a means to an end for me, and I am for him the latest in what sounds like a long list of endless acquisitions: the newest and shiniest toy to which he's treated himself. He told me he has ADHD, just like he told me he'd bought himself a fucking *catamaran*. How long until I lose my lustre?

I'm sure I'll be a fun novelty for him the first few times, a new gimmick to stave off the boredom of his dreaded Zoom calls. But I know from Athena and from the gossip columns that this guy has a different woman in his bed every night. He probably enjoys the hunt as much as its spoils. I'm not convinced he's thought through how quickly it'll get monotonous for him to have the same willing dead cert lined up for him every single day at the office.

If I didn't already have a firm expiration date for this job, I suspect he'd produce one fairly bloody quickly.

After we came around from our orgasm stupor the other night, he was surprisingly businesslike. Not unfriendly at all, but brisk and efficient. He helped me get my hooker dress back on and handed me a glass of water as he told me with a grin and a wink that the job was mine if I wanted it. There were no lingering looks, but neither was he at all awkward, and I realised that what had just gone down was nothing more or less than a straightforward transaction completed to mutual satisfaction.

I suppose from his perspective the sex was just a slightly more structured version of what was an everyday occurrence for him, but I'll readily admit that, after he'd put me in a black cab with a perfunctory kiss on the cheek and handed over a wad of notes to the driver, I sat and stewed the entire way home.

I'd achieved my goal. Secured Tabby's future.

But I'd enjoyed the process far too thoroughly, and I wasn't sure what to make of that at all.

The next morning, when Athena called me for a debrief so lengthy and detailed it had her declaring she might never be able to look Brendan in the eye again, she warned me not to catch feelings.

I mean, I get where she's coming from. I'm massively out of practice, and I don't have casual sex, especially not with guys that loaded and attractive and eligible.

I won't lie. A shameful, secret part of me is turned on every time I think about how hot it was when his head was between my legs or how deeply he fucked me. And that same part is partially terrified and partially titillated by how it will be next Monday when I rock up for my first day on the job.

Like, will it be awkward seeing him for the first time after we've fucked?

No. No, I can't imagine a guy like Brendan being awkward about sex at all.

Should I wear underwear? Will he touch me immediately? Will he push me straight to my knees? Should I pre-empt him and just get straight on my knees anyway? After all, Athena said she went down on Gabe within minutes of arriving at his office. She totally blindsided the poor guy with some kinky priest fantasy.

I am not Athena, and I have no clue what to expect, except that anything and everything is fair game. But honestly, her concern made me laugh. I don't have feelings for Brendan Sullivan. What I do have is many, many feelings *about* him, and what he represents.

Possibility.

Power.

Pleasure, it seems, judging from my slutty performance the other night.

And definitely danger. Danger that he'll get bored, that

he'll chew me up and spit me out before I've assembled the funds I need, and, more than anything, that he and his heady, hedonistic existence will suck me into a whirlwind of excess and luxury and debauchery. He's taking the morning off on Monday so he can take me to Selfridges and get me kitted out, for goodness' sake.

Like I said, I'd do well to remember that none of it is real.

Keep your head down, Marls, and your eye on the prize.

There's only one prize. And, no matter what every other person out there with a vagina seems to think, it is *not* Brendan Sullivan.

# CHAPTER 15

# *Marlowe*

'I have some amazing news,' I tell my parents, Tabs, and Daniel the Spaniel at dinner. 'Well, *two* amazing pieces of news, actually.'

They—my folks and Daniel—usually pick her up from school and keep her until I've finished work, but I've been on school run duty since I got sacked, so they haven't seen her as much. I know they miss their afternoons with their grand-daughter, but God, have I loved seeing her huge smile every afternoon at the gates as she hurls her slight frame against me. I'm treasuring these brief times together, because my job at Sullivan Construction will be a whole other level of commit-ment and intensity.

Tabby squirms in her seat, her wide smile showing off the two huge adult front teeth making their slow descent into her mouth. I try to keep things positive around her, but we're not exactly drowning in good news these days, so it's no surprise she picks up on the excitement in my tone. 'What kind of news?' She's not so interested that she can't forage in the depths of her stir-fry for a piece of chicken and feed it to Daniel, who is sitting by her chair with all the wide-eyed, vibrating intensity of a hunting dog in the presence of a high-value treat.

I shake my head at her firmly, because he's a fucking nightmare if you encourage him, before grinning at my parents'. I can feel my eyes filling with tears even as I prepare to lie to the three people I love more than anything else in the world. The lies are necessary, but I'm intent on keeping them to the bare minimum, for practical purposes as much as ethical.

The tears aren't because I'm lying.

The tears are because this news will change their lives.

We're sitting in my parents' small flat, which is a five-minute walk from my flat in New Cross. When I got the job at the RA, they gave up a pleasant suburban home and down-graded to an underwhelming ex-council flat so that they could support me in raising Tabs. Even worse, they gave up their beloved garden in favour of hanging baskets on their dingy balcony and a share in an allotment a mile or so away.

They've never uttered a word of complaint.

I've never stopped feeling guilty.

'Okay, first,' I say with a watery smile at them all, 'I got a really good job.'

Their faces light up right on cue, and Tabby pushes back her chair so she can round the kitchen table for a hug.

'That's amazing, honey!' my dad says. He's a quiet Englishman, far more mellow than his fierce Dutch wife and, since the appearance of his granddaughter, anyway, a total softie.

Mum nods at me. 'Huge relief. Well done. Doing what? Daniel, come *here*.' She's still formidable, a former model and singer with posture that puts mine to shame. At fifty-six, her pale blonde hair is growing silvered. She has it up in its usual dignified French twist, and her don't-mess-with-me vibes are as strong as ever. They don't go unnoticed by Daniel, who reluctantly abandons his sentry position next to Tabs and ambles stiffly to Mum's side. At eleven years old, her beloved golden show cocker spaniel is starting to show his age.

Here goes. 'So Athena introduced me to her boyfriend Gabe's brother Brendan. He runs the family construction company—he's the CEO. Anyway, he needed a new executive assistant and, thanks to Athena putting in a good word, he agreed to interview me. And, well, I got the job!'

Mum and Dad exchange a delighted look. I know they've been worried sick since Dean the Dick fired me.

'That's amazing,' Mum says. 'And it's a good job?'

'It's a great job,' I say softly, hugging Tabby to my side and enjoying the sensation of her arms around me. 'The pay's a lot better than the RA, too.'

Dad reaches across the table and squeezes my hand as it rests next to my bowl of stir-fry. 'That's bloody marvellous, honey. We're so proud of you. Isn't your mummy clever, Tabs?'

I allow myself a second of genuine pride and happiness before the guilt kicks in. Yes, it's great news. Yes, it'll change Tabby's life. And yes, I've taken this role for all the right reasons. But my parents are looking at me like I'm their golden girl, and it's the way they've always looked at me, and I don't deserve it.

I fell for my professor and for all the silken lies he poured into my ear, and I got myself knocked up, and I had to take a year out, and since then, my parents have made sacrifice after sacrifice for me and Tabs. And now I'm selling my body and agreeing to be the fuck toy of some rich, entitled guy, and it makes me feel so dirty and grimy and sullied and ugh. Just *ugh*. So yeah, it's shitty to sit here and feel the light of their pride shining on me when it would one hundred per cent *kill* them to know what I really have planned for my summer.

It would finish them off, truly.

A swift gulp of water has me pushing on. 'The other news

is even better, guys.' *Here goes. The lie won't hurt them, because the news is so wonderful.* I twist my body so I'm facing Tabby and wrap an arm tightly around her. In this position, we're exactly at eye level. 'We've been awarded a grant, my love, and it means we can go to America, you and I, and get your heart fixed very safely by doctors who are the best in the world at what they do.'

Mum's whimper is matched by Dad's shocked inhale, but my gaze is fixed firmly on my daughter's face, which seems to light up before my eyes.

'America?'

'Yep,' I tell her with a smile that feels far too wobbly. 'You and I are off to the States in a month or two.'

She gasps theatrically. 'Can we go to Disneyland?'

That makes me laugh. 'Not Disneyland this time, I'm afraid. We're going to a very fancy hospital that has very good doctors and very clever machinery, and they'll be able to replace your valve without even opening you up. They'll make a tiny hole the size of a keyhole, and they'll do it that way.'

'No open-heart surgery?' Dad asks, his voice cracking, and I tear my eyes away from Tabs.

'Nope. No open-heart surgery. They can do it laparoscopically. They're experts in this kind of procedure for kids.'

My parents are staring at me like I've pulled off nothing short of a miracle. If you remove the ethics from the situation, I suppose I have.

'But how?' Mum says. 'How did you get it?'

'The grant? One of the applications finally came through.' I clear my throat and blink away the tears from my eyes as I stroke up and down Tabby's back. 'Here's the thing, though. It covers a lot, but it doesn't cover everything, so this is where the new job is really important. I'll be able to afford it all,' I add hurriedly, because I absolutely don't want my parents worrying about the money side when I'm about to have the fruits of my prostitution raining down on me.

'But the downside is that, for the next month or two, I really have to put my nose to the grindstone.' I turn back to Tabs. 'That means I have to work really, really hard. So Nana and Grandpa will start picking you up from school again, if that's okay with them—'

'Of course it is!' Dad interjects forcefully.

'Okay then. Thank you. But the other thing is'—I scrunch up my face—'I have to prove to my boss that I'm really committed. So if you have to go to hospital during school hours, it might have to be Nana and Grandpa who go along with you and not me.'

I can't believe I'm saying this. I can't believe I'm telling my daughter that I'll have to prioritise my new job over being there for her during one of her terrifying trips to A&E.

'But it's just for the first few weeks,' I hasten to add. 'Because once we're back from the US, you should be right as rain and you won't need any more hospital trips. Not emergency ones, anyway.'

'Really?' she asks, her brown eyes wide.

Yeah, she got my eyes. Fuck you, Professor Joseph Penn, and your recessive genes.

It hits me that she hasn't fully processed the implications of her operation, and why should she? She's eight years old, for crying out loud.

'Really, sweetie. The doctor I spoke to earlier put it really well, actually. He reminded me that you're not sick, you've just got one little piece of equipment that doesn't work so well. It's a bit like a bike that has a punctured tyre. If you change the tyre, it's all good. So once they swap out your valve for a bigger one that can carry enough blood to your lungs, you should be dandy. No more blue spells. No more feeling faint. No more trips to A&E. That's the plan, anyway. He said you'll be turning cartwheels in no time.'

I give her my brightest, most optimistic smile, and she returns it.

'Can I start rollerskating?'

'Rollerskating. Dance lessons. Parkour. Whatever you like.' I make a mental note to save a few extra grand for my daughter's fully fledged extracurricular fun.

'Will your new boss be okay with you taking time off to go to the US so soon after you've started?' Mum wants to know. A worried frown creases her forehead.

Time for the next porky.

'He's been really understanding,' I lie smoothly. 'He says I can take it as holiday or work remotely. He gets how important this is.'

# CHAPTER 16

# *Brendan*

The bad news is that Mum and Dad have come into London for the evening and issued a three-line whip for a family dinner. The good news is that they're off to the theatre with my sister Mairead and her husband Peter, so dinner is early and I'll be off the hook by seven.

Apparently, there's a new hot shot stepping up tonight to play Jean Valjean in their all-time favourite show, *Les Mis*. Cue endless reminiscing (a euphemism for *ribbing*) about the time when they took us along as kids and I asked at the interval after an endless first half, 'Which one is Les?'

They've never let me live it down.

Because Gabe and Athena are Madly in Love and playing house, they've offered to host everyone for a pre-theatre supper, and because my brother knew it would be a hard sell for me, he has a Nobu chef coming to serve everyone up some excellent Japanese. Not that Gabe's not a decent cook. He is, but after a decade in the priesthood, his style can tend towards the meat-and-two-veg-sad-singleton-meal-for-one, which is not my idea of a fun Saturday night.

Even better, he's promised me that the meal will be served up grazing style in the kitchen. He pitched it as a chance for everyone to be able to catch up and mingle, but really he knows there's no way I'll acquiesce to a sit-down dinner after a week at my desk.

Anyway, I rock up dutifully at five for early cocktails so we can get some adequate family time in before my parents and sister are spirited away to the West End and I can embark upon the next stage of my Saturday night, AKA the Getting Laid stage. From the way my brother is touching Athena by the wine fridge, it looks like they're headed for the Getting Laid stage later too.

How my formerly celibate brother managed to land himself the hottest woman in London is a mystery that'll haunt me to my grave. Though I suppose I'm about to level the playing field with Marlowe. Just thinking about the two orgasms I gave her—left-field for her and one hundred per cent predicted on my part—makes me smirk.

That was a lot of fucking fun.

Gabe has a really nice pad, even if it couldn't be more different from my glass-heavy penthouse in a mixed-use, Sullivan-constructed building overlooking the Thames in Battersea. He took over one of Mum and Dad's properties—a big Georgian redbrick house in Manchester Square in the middle of town—but his interior designer has done a great job on it. With its warm neutral palette and no-expense-spared finishings, it hits exactly the right notes between the serenity this former priest still values and the opulence he's probably still adjusting to.

'They'll be a few minutes late,' he tells me, handing me a bottle of Peroni.

'Not a problem.' Our parents and Mairead live out near Newmarket, where we were brought up, right in the middle of the horse racing folks. It's like a really boring version of a Jilly

Cooper novel out there. As far as I can tell, all the action happens at my sister's stud farm.

'Before they get here, I want a word about Marlowe,' Athena says, moving closer. Oh, boy. Here we go. She looks like she means business. She's in a long, green silky dress that has a lot of buttons and does a stellar job of showcasing the curves that corrupted my very willing brother. I find myself thinking that she's curvier than Marlowe, whose body is more athletic.

'Does Marlowe like sports?' I blurt out, and she stops in her tracks.

'Yes. Why?'

'I dunno.' I scratch at the corner of my Peroni label with my fingernail. 'She looks sporty.'

'She likes running, for some unearthly reason. And she's bloody brilliant at tennis.'

That perks me up. 'Really? Huh. Interesting.' I'm a member of a very high-end racquets club near our office. Maybe I can lure her there for the odd game of tennis or padel.

'Anyway. I wanted to thank you for giving her the job.' Her tone is clipped, and there is no doubt in my mind that her thanks is an opener to her main agenda.

'You're welcome. She earned it.'

I try to keep my voice neutral, I really do. I want Athena to know that I didn't do her a favour, that Marlowe got the position on her own—very compelling—merits, but the words sound sleazy as soon as they're out of my mouth, and she frowns.

'I don't want to know.' She leans in and lowers her voice. 'Just remember. She's your employee, not your toy. She's a human being. Treat her with respect.'

'Jesus. I'm not a total prick. I know all that. She's lovely, and I'm not about to fuck her up. That said, I'm paying her a fuck-load of money for this job, and we're both adults. Maybe give us both the chance to work our relationship out for ourselves?'

She surveys me for a moment with her lips pressed together. She really is terrifying. Kudos to my brother for being able to handle her.

'Good,' she says finally. 'And you're right, it's between the two of you. It's just—' She hesitates, looking uncharacteristically lost for words. 'Don't judge people by their roles, Brendan, okay? Yes, you're paying her for sex, but she's not just some whore. She seems really strong, and she is, but she's also more vulnerable than she looks. Just—do me a favour and look after her, okay? She's worth it.'

There's something about the intensity in her voice and her face that's sobering. It's almost like she's trying to warn me. But Athena's super protective of Marlowe; I know that much. So maybe she's just looking out for her friend.

'I will,' I say quietly. 'I know she is.'

My mother and sister can mainline chardonnay like nobody's business, so I'm making myself useful opening another bottle of Meursault when the folks show up. Mum enters in a cloud of that pungent eighties Dolce and Gabbana perfume she always wears. I swear you can practically see the leopard print and big hair wafting off that stuff.

'Look at my gorgeous, strapping son,' she says proudly, as she always does. It's as if my gym-honed body is the modern-day equivalent of being a well-built farmer's lad. I dunno. I won't attempt to guess what goes on inside that brain of hers, opting instead to pour her a generous glass of her favourite wine.

She's all excited because they've taken a box for the night. I honestly don't get the appeal of boxes. They're all the way on the side of the theatre and they face the wrong fucking way. Seriously, they're like the theatrical equivalent of the Emperor's new clothes. Who wants to sit through three hours of *Les* fucking *Mis* only to emerge with a crick in their neck?

Not me.

Mum releases me to go fawn over Athena. I won't lie; things got pretty hairy there a few weeks ago when a former board member of mine—total wanker—outed her as a hooker in front of the entire family at a fancy charity gala. Never has the fear of having to perform CPR on my parents felt so real. Honestly, I thought they'd pass out from the shame of it. It made Gabe leaving the priesthood seem as innocuous as missing Mass on a Sunday.

But in a move far more legendary than I'll ever admit, my mild-mannered brother finally located his balls and gave Mum and Dad a giant bollocking. They've subsequently agreed to accept Athena as the CEO of our family foundation—the newly named Audacity Foundation—and Mum seems to have forgiven her for being a *shameless little hussy* (Mum's words) remarkably quickly. I suspect it's that the likelihood of Athena popping out mini Angel Gabriels ramps up with every passing day.

I have to say, though, even if we've put that particular episode of the Sullivan Family Soap Opera to bed, it's a timely reminder that Mum can never, *ever* find out the full scope of Marlowe's new role.

Dad comes over and gives me a hug that involves backslaps hearty enough to displace my lungs. He's wearing a navy suit with pinstripes so wide they call for a cigar. Unlike Gabe, Mairead and me, who have only ever known extreme privilege, Dad grew up on the Dublin docks before emigrating to the UK with his father to make fortunes beyond their wildest dreams. As a consequence, Ronan Sullivan is a bon viveur, a man whose wealth and status are still novel enough for him to simultaneously struggle with them and enjoy the fuck out of them.

Or so it seems from my vantage point, anyway.

Finally, he releases me, gripping me by the shoulder tightly enough to remind me that he's still the boss, even if he's passed the reins of his businesses onto the next generation now. 'How's my boy? Behaving yourself, Bren?'

It's a loaded question that probably has two desired responses: a reassuring *absolutely* regarding our behemoth of a construction firm and a cheeky *fuck, no* for the women in my life.

'Only in the ways you'd want me to,' I tell him with a wink, and he laughs right on cue.

'Good man, good man. Glad to hear it. I can't persuade you to come along tonight? There's a seat going spare in the box, and it would mean the world to your mam. Sure, we could look for Les.' He nudges me forcefully with his elbow.

And there it is. The ribbing and the guilt trip, all rolled into one tidy package.

'I can't, Dad. I'm catching up with some friends later. And you know I don't take my meds on the weekends. I'd be a liability.'

If reminding my father of the time when surviving a trip to the theatre with me was his worst nightmare is the easiest way to get out of thespian jail guilt-free, then I'll happily throw myself under the bus.

A therapist once explained to me that a family system is like a play. Everyone has their role to perform, and if you choose to reject your role and reinvent it, it does not go down well, because it throws everyone else's role into disarray. If I wasn't the disruptive troublemaker, Gabe wouldn't have been the academic saint, and Mairead wouldn't have been the dutiful little mother. Never mind that I run a company with an equity market capitalisation of eleven billion pounds.

Dad reacts exactly as predicted, rearing back with a laugh as if he's dodged a bullet. 'Damn, you're right, son. You go and blow off some steam or you won't be of any use to anyone on Monday.'

He still has a way of making me feel like my position at Sullivan Construction is a tenuous one, contingent solely on the blind luck of my circumstances and not the hard graft I've put in ever since I graduated from uni. Sometimes, it seems as though he sees me as the pesky but charming mailroom guy who would do well to tamp down his personality so as not to ruffle any feathers, rather than a CEO who has repeatedly proven his mettle.

But there's no point in saying anything. Not to Dad. So I nod without a comment and wave him off as he heads over to join Mum and Athena.

My sister zeroes in on me, and I hastily pour a glass of wine for her.

'If it isn't my favourite stallion wrangler,' I say, kissing Mairead's cheek. 'How are the horny beasts doing?'

'The four-legged ones are fine,' she shoots back, looking me up and down. 'But you didn't put that porno black shirt on for us. So I suspect the two-legged ones will be going on the prowl later.'

'Ha fucking ha. Sour grapes aren't a good look on you, sis.' I jerk my head in the direction of her long-suffering husband. 'When's the last time you let Peter near you without a riding crop?'

She smirks, sipping her Meursault with irritating *sang-froid*. 'Quality over quantity, dickhead. I'd rather have one thoroughbred than a stable of ponies. Speaking of which, heard you've got a new filly starting Monday.'

I look over my shoulder at Mum. It's not a secret, but the

last thing I need is my eagle-eyed sister dropping any unwarranted speculation. 'News travels fast.'

'Athena mentioned it. Said she's gorgeous, smart, and way too good for you.'

I narrow my eyes at her. Women. Why do they always have to have an angle? I don't know for certain *what* her angle is, just that there is one and it probably involves tripping her brother up with her devious conversational skills just as effectively as she used to with her skipping rope.

'She seems smart and highly qualified,' I say, hoping my tone sounds as sniffy as I feel. 'And the job pays well, so I don't see why she'd be too good for it.'

I ignore her point about Marlowe being gorgeous. I'm not touching that with a bargepole, no matter how true it is, because her looks shouldn't be relevant to her role as far as anyone else is concerned.

I'm aware my sister's trying to get a rise out of me, but Athena's comment has pissed me off. I did her a favour, for fuck's sake, gave her friend a job. I'm a big deal. Just take a look at *Tatler* or *GQ* or *The Financial Times*. I'm not some bum who's punching above his weight. On the contrary, I'm one of London's most eligible bachelors, and my extended family would do well to cut me some fucking slack every now and again.

None of that is to detract from the truth that Marlowe is gorgeous, and that, even on a Saturday night when my mind should be squarely on what mischief I can make later, I'm growing increasingly impatient for Monday morning.

I've had Plain Elaine, who is vocally happy about the prospect of having the EA portion of her admittedly onerous job taken off her plate, block out the morning in my diary for Marlowe's *onboarding*. Fuck, that sounds dirty when I consider that it will most likely involve bending her over my desk.

But first, I've told her we have an appointment with the personal shopping team at Selfridges. I'll meet her in town first thing so we can get her kitted out in precisely the way I want. Camille at Seraph has assured me it's not necessary—that with the salary these women command, their work wardrobe is their problem.

It's not about what's *necessary* for me, though. It's about having the maximum amount of fun with my new favourite toy. It'll make the pleasure of showing up for work even more intense, knowing that this woman will be waiting for me in the sexiest looks, her exquisite body showcased in the finest lingerie money can buy.

We'll grab more items along the lines of the pink dress she wore for her interview while veering into Sexy Miss Moneypenny territory as firmly as I can get away with.

That's my new favourite fantasy.

Marlowe, swathed in an ivory silk blouse and tight pencil skirt, all that long, golden hair pinned primly up, with knockout lace right below the surface. It'll make plundering her or showing her off or ordering her to her knees all the sweeter.

Shopping for this stuff will be a damn sight more engaging than picking out linen swatches for my fucking catamaran, that's for sure.

In fact, it'll feel like extended foreplay.

*Jesus Christ.* Maybe I shouldn't go out later. Maybe I should just head home and spend my evening erupting all over my shower tiles as I imagine all the ways I'm going to *onboard* my delectable new plaything.

Looks like Monday morning is the new Saturday night.

# CHAPTER 17

# *Marlowe*

I can confirm that those first-day-of-school nerves have nothing on the nerves you get on your first day in a new job where you know you'll be shagging your boss from the outset. I'm in absolute pieces, and it doesn't help when I emerge from Bond Street station to find a text coming through from Brendan.

> Running 15 mins late. Stuck in traffic. See you in there. Third floor.

> Tell them I'm your boyfriend. Otherwise it'll seem too weird if I'm picking out your lingerie

Um, that's because it *is* weird to most normal people that my boss is picking out my lingerie.

Jesus.

I'm slightly early. I stand and wait by one of the main sets of doors with a handful of other people until a doorman unlocks and opens them on the dot of ten o'clock. The shop floor is still empty of customers. The fanciful displays in the

Dior and Hermès and Chanel handbag concessions are immaculate, as are the sales assistants in their chic all-black outfits.

I make my way up to the still-deserted second floor, winding through rail after rail of clothes that look more like hanging works of art than things you would wear when going about your daily life. The personal shopping department announces itself with a huge arch above which hang the letters in the store's distinctive font: LADIES' PERSONAL SHOPPING.

Here goes. I peer through the arch, my heart dropping when I see the young woman at the reception desk. I've made an effort for my first day, obviously, but I haven't bought anything new. I was working under the assumption that Brendan would want me to wear one of the dresses he'd picked out, so I'm in a grey pre-loved shift dress. It's from Vinted and originally came from one of the higher-end brands on the high street. It's smart and work-appropriate, but it doesn't scream *money*, and a single raised eyebrow from this woman tells me she's got my number.

'Good morning,' she says coolly, not rising from the desk. 'Can I help you.' It's as if she can't even be bothered to make it a question. Her impeccable but dramatic makeup suggests she moonlights as someone who gives contouring and lip-lining tutorials on TikTok, and the long dark ponytail draped over one shoulder gives new meaning to the term *sleek*. She looks me up and down like the judgiest and most world-weary X-ray machine.

'Morning.' I'm instantly intimidated, flustered. I had a fantasy of walking in here with serious moral support in the form of Brendan, but that's clearly been shot to hell. I'm not used to places like this. I never even go *into* places like this. Zara is a stretch for me. 'Um—I think we have an appointment under my boss's name—Brendan Sullivan?' There's no way I can say *my boyfriend*. Brendan may be able to bullshit like that, but I know that if I said it, my entire face would go red. I'd be as obvious as Pinocchio.

Her entire demeanour changes. She shoots up out of her chair and cranes her neck, her gaze going behind me. 'Of course. Is Mr Sullivan not joining?' The last sentence is said with a distinct squeak of panic.

'He's, um, running a few minutes late. He said we should start without him.'

She visibly relaxes. 'Okay. Great. Let's take you through. Coffee?' She's already marching ahead of me down a wide corridor that's all rosy lighting and flawless cream carpets. The red soles of her spiky-heeled dominatrix boots flash as she walks. She's in some super edgy, asymmetrical, zip-heavy black dress that looks a million dollars on her. If she's the one styling me, I really hope she goes with a more classic look.

Scratch that. If I have to undress in front of this woman, I've got bigger problems on my hands.

'Can I get a tea with oat milk, please?' I squeak out.

'Sure.' She stops in front of a door and holds out her hand to usher me through.

Holy crap. In front of me is a stunning and surprisingly large room. It's cream, just like the reception area, with accents of brass and a wonderful scent of flowers. One corner has a big brass rail tracking around it, the heavy cream velvet curtain pushed all the way to the side, while beside it stand two rails on wheels. One is absolutely *stacked* with clothes, the other with underwear, while pairs of beautiful, scary shoes sit below each item.

To my left, there's an ivory-coloured sofa and, in front of it, a coffee table bearing an array of white flowers profession-ally arranged across a selection of vases and bud holders.

It's all glorious, and it's all intimidating as *hell*.

'I'm Terri,' the fearsome brunette says without offering

her hand. 'Fiona will be assisting us today. You can put your bag there.' She gestures to a little upholstered footstool next to the sofa, which is probably meant for bearing Birkins rather than my Coach-from-TK-Maxx handbag. 'I'll fetch your tea. Take off your dress and put on that robe if you like, while we talk you through the clothes.' She points to a silky robe hanging in the changing corner.

With a swish of her ponytail, she strides off, shutting the door behind her and leaving me alone.

I sink onto the sofa and blow out a slow breath.

Holy fuck, what am I getting myself into?

'Mr Sullivan suggested a palette of blush and neutral tones,' Terri colleague Fiona tells me as I sip my tea from a china teacup and hold my robe closed over my boobs.

Fiona is equally polished and terrifying, only with a platinum bob so perfectly styled that not a hair is out of place. 'The descriptors he gave us were professional, feminine with both softer and sleeker elements, and sexy.' She gives me some side-eye, which seems not unwarranted, because a boss requesting *sexy* for his assistant's office wardrobe is definitely dodgy as hell.

'Mmm-hmm,' I murmur, eyeing the rail and refusing to rise. I edge closer to the beautiful pieces. From what I can see, they're a gorgeous concoction of silk and cashmere, of frothy blouses and elegant dresses and—oh my God, is that a pale pink leather skirt? It looks so soft.

Athena would die for this stuff. It's far more her kind of taste than mine. I love big prints and florals and bright colours. This is so refined, so sophisticated.

But then the Marlowe who will be wearing these clothes only to let Brendan Sullivan undress her is not me. She's a facet of me that I've invented solely for the purpose of paying Tabby's medical bills, and it's actually a good thing that her vibe is completely different from that of the real Marlowe.

'What is it you do for Mr Sullivan, exactly?' Terri asks, not even bothering to hide her curiosity.

'I'm his executive assistant. Today's my first day.'

They exchange a look that strikes me as loaded with subtext.

'I see. He also requested a significant amount of underwear...'

She trails off, and I assume she's hoping for clarification.

'Great!' I say brightly. 'So, should I start trying this stuff on?'

'Of course,' Fiona says coolly. She pulls out an off-white sleeveless shift dress with a chunky exposed zip running the whole way down the back. The phrase *easy access* immediately pops into my brain, and I stifle a smile. These ladies are onto my dirty boss, it seems.

'What's it made of?' I ask her. It's hanging on a crazily wide hanger, and even I can tell that the tailoring in this thing would inspire those in the know to whisper awed prayers of gratitude for its perfection.

'It's wool crepe. It's one of Dior's signature fabrics.'

Oh, shit. It's Dior, and it's the kind of colour that would get dirty if I stepped foot inside a tube station. This is not good. I set my teacup down and hold out my hand for it. 'May I?'

'Of course.'

She hands it over, and I rummage inside the neck for the price tag.

Three thousand pounds. Oh my... Immediately, I hold the dirt magnet at arm's length. 'Did Bren—Mr Sullivan give you a budget?' I ask weakly, because this is insane. There's having some fun kitting out your new toy in a few nice dresses, and then there's this. Excess so ludicrous that it's actually unethical. This dress costs at least twice as much as that consultation I had with Dr Elliott. It costs the same as flying Tabs home in business class from Raleigh-Durham Airport!

It's out of the question, that's what it is.

But Terri is shaking her head like my question is distasteful. 'He made it clear there is no budget.' She looks behind her, probably wondering where the hell Brendan has got to. Aren't we all, sister? 'Let's try it on,' she insists. She picks up the pair of shoes sitting right below it. They're stunning stilettos with narrow heels, and they're exactly the right shade of ivory—in suede. Those shoes wouldn't last two minutes in London without getting trashed.

I sigh and make my way over to the changing room corner. There's no point in being modest, no matter how judgy and hostile these two women seem. I'm under no illusion that they're here for me. They're here for the big fat commission they'll earn when they ring all this stuff up.

With the robe off, I step into the dress that Terri holds out for me. I've left my regular underwear on. It's a new set I bought for the job, and it's way nicer than anything else I've got at home, but it's just from the high street. I'm not touching the lingerie issue until Brendan turns up.

Terri zips me up, and I step into the shoes. Everything fits perfectly. How the hell do they do that? I turn towards the trio of full-length mirrors angled for a comprehensive view, smoothing the dress over my hips self-consciously. These two definitely aren't the most comforting audience.

Wow. The woman staring back at me looks glossy and expensive. And, even if she's a very different kind of glossy and expensive from the version of my reflection that gave me such a sense of dissonance when I dressed up as High Class Hooker Barbie, that same surreal feeling hits me again.

I wonder if this was why Brendan insisted on this appointment. I wonder if he wants his new fuck toy to be a sleek, designer-clad arm candy and not the boho woman he met at the Royal Academy all those weeks ago.

I wonder if he knew that he'd need to step in and polish me all the way up to the standard needed to be a Brendan Sullivan trophy. The thought that he did smarts a little, but I shrug it off. He's paying a fortune to have me at his beck and call. He's entitled to shape me into whatever the hell he wants.

Behind me, there's a stony silence. Terri surveys me and our eyes meet in the mirror.

'I think it could work,' she says, nodding at my chest, 'if you fill it out a bit more. It's a shame to ruin the line of the dress.'

What the fuck? A single glance at her tells me that the twin tennis balls protruding aggressively from her edgy dress are unlikely to be a part of her God-given, very slight figure.

'Agreed. I've got just the thing,' Fiona adds. 'Here. Try these.'

She stoops to a pile of packaged underwear stacked beneath the hanging bras and panties. I watch in my peripheral vision as she approaches with a box. My boobs aren't letting the dress down—I don't think so, at least. I may only be a B cup, but they're in good shape. And Brendan seemed to enjoy them the other night, which is all that counts in this situation.

But Terri already unzipping the top half of my dress as Fiona briskly unpacks two silicone chicken fillets. She hands one to me, and I weigh it in my hands. Ugh, it gives me the creeps. And surely Brendan doesn't want to undress me and find *these* in my bra?

'Go on.' Terri nods bossily. 'Try them. They'll give you a far less boyish line.' She slides the dress off my shoulders.

I sigh and pointedly turn my body away from them as I stuff the fillet into my cheap bra, wincing at the cold, slimy feel of it against my skin. I do the same with the other one. They feel too heavy, too bulky, for the thin, lacy cups of my bra. 'I don't know,' I tell the assistants.

'Let's zip you back up again before you decide,' Fiona says before I can take them out. I'm not sure what happened to the customer knowing best, but I obediently stick my hands back through the armholes and let her zip me up.

I look more... buxom. Curvy, definitely, but it's not me. The dress is undeniably beautiful, but it's hard to feel at ease here in this luxurious room with two not-remotely-friendly sales assistants for company.

Before I can put my foot down, the door flies open, and Brendan strides into the room.

Oh my *God*.

# CHAPTER 18

# *Marlowe*

I haven't seen Brendan since that night in the club. Some parts of the evening are seared onto my brain, obviously, but I've been trying to conjure Brendan up in my mind on repeat since then, and it turns out my imagination was sub-par. Because, as I turn around in my all-white outfit to greet him, the sheer *physicality* of him hits me anew like a brick in the face.

Holy crap, he's big.

And hot.

And... everything.

How can a man have so much swagger just walking through a doorframe?

He grins at me, and it's slow and dirty and seemingly dripping with every memory of everything we did together a couple of weeks ago. He's wearing just a pristine white shirt and navy trousers and he looks a million dollars. No tie, no jacket. Men seem to find it so easy to leave the house with absolutely no personal belongings, although I guess if you have a driver, which I'm sure he does, it makes it easier.

'Mr Sullivan, *hiii*,' Terri says breathily, injecting far more enthusiasm into her greeting than she's shown to me in the past twenty minutes.

Brendan ignores her. He ignores both of them, in fact, making a beeline for me. 'Fucking hell. Look at you.' He gives a low whistle.

'Hi,' I say. I sound so blooming shy I could slap myself, but come on. He's looking at me like that, and I haven't seen him since we got naked, and there are two scary women judging my every move. I'm hardly in the right frame of mind to channel my (non-existent) cool inner goddess.

I'm preparing for, I don't know, a cheek kiss or something, but he slides an arm around my hip and pulls me to him. His hand finds my very fancy Dior-covered bottom and gropes it as he dips his dark head and kisses me hello.

It is *not* a cheek kiss.

It's a familiar, *you left my bed a few short hours ago* kiss on the lips, and it's leisurely and entitled and contains the slightest glimpse of tongue, and I'm so taken aback by the shocking hotness of it that I freeze.

He releases my mouth and slaps me on the bottom. 'This is a great colour on you. How's it going? Sorry I'm late, love.'

I'm not the only woman who froze at the Brendan Sullivan Effect. Fiona and Terri have been stuck to the spot, silently gaping since he barged in here and kissed me.

Perhaps all the blood in their brains has flooded south.

I know mine has.

Fiona finally speaks up. 'You're not...' She clears her throat. 'I'm sorry. I thought she was your employee.'

'It's Ms Winters to you, and she's my girlfriend *and* my newest employee.' He narrows his eyes at me. 'You didn't tell them, love?'

'I—um—it didn't come up,' I stammer.

'No harm done. So, how are you getting on?'

'This is the first dress, Mr Sullivan,' Terri pipes up. 'And we think she—ahh—Ms Winters looks fantastic in it.'

*Fantastic.* Not an opinion either of them have volunteered before now.

'Great.' Brendan nods brusquely. 'We'll take it.' He may want to dress his little fuck-doll up, but I can't imagine the actual process of shopping is any fun for him at all. Nor is it a good use of his time, I imagine.

He holds me by the forearms and pushes me towards the changing area before pulling the curtain shut around us. 'I'll help her get changed. Give us the next one, please.'

'It's three grand,' I hiss as he turns me around so he can unzip the dress.

'Don't care. Worth every penny. Just don't come near me when I'm drinking coffee or eating chocolate. I'm a clumsy bastard, and you'—he pulls the zip open with great relish and far too little concern for the dress itself—'are ravishing.'

He pushes the dress off my shoulders, exposing me down to my waist, and our eyes meet in the mirror. He licks his lips. 'Nice to see you again,' he whispers. He brushes his fingertips lightly down my upper arms, and I shiver. 'Welcome to Sullivan Construction, Ms Winters.'

Brendan threads his hands between my body and my arms, those same fingertips gliding over my ribs, his blue eyes holding my gaze in the mirror. Fiona and Terri are right on the other side of the curtain, and this is really inappropriate, and I can't look away from him. Can't look away from the sheer size of him behind me, from the way he's checking me out so proprietarily. He brings his hands up to cup my bra and stops.

'What the fuck are these?'

Oh shit. The fillets. 'I, um—they said I needed them to fill out the dress. Something about the line?' I whisper, my eyes darting nervously between the reflection of my boobs and that of the outrage on his face.

'Like fuck you do.' He sticks a hand down the front of my bra, his warm skin grazing my nipple, and yanks the silicone thingy out. He does the same with the other, then rips the curtain aside enough to step out.

'Don't you fucking tell her she needs these to look good in a dress,' he shouts at the sales assistants. I hear one wet slap as a fillet presumably lands on the glass coffee table, then another. 'Her figure is fucking perfect, and you know it. If you can't stick to your job, which is picking out clothes and handing them to us, then you can get out and leave us to it. Do I make myself clear?'

Bloody hell, he's got a temper. I press my lips together to hold in my shocked laughter as they stammer out their apologies.

'Give me that,' he spits. A moment later, he reappears in the changing area holding a dove-grey silk dress that looks even more high-maintenance than the white one and a matching grey lace lingerie set so exquisite I'd rather frame it than wear it. He gives me a cheeky wink, and I allow myself a silent giggle.

'Let me help you with this, madam,' he murmurs, hanging the lingerie and dress on the hook before unzipping me the rest of the way. The silk lining of the dress slithers sensually over my hips before falling to the floor and pooling around my heels, leaving me in just my underwear.

I may have been naked with the guy a couple of weeks ago, but it's mid-morning on a Monday, and standing here like this for him while he openly checks me out feels as confronting as it does salacious.

'Part one of your *onboarding* process,' he whispers, his emphasis making the term sound filthy. He finds the hooks of my cheap bra and slides it down my arms. My nipples have hardened—they're no more immune to Brendan's charms than the rest of me—and believe me, he's noticed.

His gaze rakes over my bare breasts in the mirror, dark and filthy, before he takes the beautiful grey lace bra off its hanger and holds it by its straps in front of me. I slide my arms through it and he pulls it up, fastening it behind my back.

'That's more like it,' he murmurs. He reaches around and cups my breasts through the lace, his thumbs strumming over my nipples. My eyes stay locked on the sight of his big hands caressing me as I stand here in this exquisite lingerie he's insisting on buying me. It's such a decadent, taboo concept— that he's paying for my body and I'm selling it to him—that it has my heart thumping behind my rib cage.

Abruptly, he pulls away. 'I'm very invested in getting this shopping trip over with quickly,' he says. He bends his head to nip me on the shoulder before reaching for the grey dress. 'Come on, let's give this one a whirl.'

One hour, a dozen speedy outfit changes and tens of thousands of pounds later, we leave the palatial changing room and its toxic sales assistants and emerge through a side entrance of Selfridges to where Brendan's driver is waiting. At my new boss's insistence, I'm wearing the off-white dress and heels while, behind us, three smartly dressed porters carry an array of distinctive yellow carrier bags and garment bags to complete my *Pretty Woman* moment.

Really, though, it's the man striding along beside me who commands most of the attention. I can't miss the glances from my fellow shoppers, which range from curious to downright feral. I can't blame them. Even if they have no idea who he is, even if he's only wearing half a custom-made suit, Brendan Sullivan cuts a dashing figure. I'm as bad as them, shamelessly ogling his very nice arse as I scurry along in my heels, trying to keep up with him. He's bored now, and he wants out.

Yan, his driver, directs the porters as they load the fruits of our shopping spree into the boot of Brendan's shiny black car while an excited Mark, paws up on the back of the seat, yaps at us through the open boot hatch.

I have an instant stab of guilt. 'Has he been in there the whole time?'

'Nah,' Brendan says easily. 'Gabe lives just behind here. Yan took him for a runaround in his garden.'

Oh, thank God for that.

Brendan opens the back door for us. 'Let me get in first and secure this mutt. Hiya, mate. Who's my best boy? Did you have a nice walkies? Did you dig up Uncle Gabe's garden like a good boy?'

I eye the back of the car warily—it seems I am now a woman who must inspect every surface before plonking her Dior on it—but the cream leather seats look immaculate. Either Mark is a very clean doggy, or Yan tidied him up after his romp.

'Hi, sweetie,' I coo at Mark as I slide in behind Brendan. The dog is now sitting nicely in the footwell, his enormous head resting on the empty middle seat between us. I pet his smooth head and allow him to sniff and then lick my hand. If I'm honest, my first day is off to an intense start. I'm already exhausted between dealing with those two snobby women, the three million outfit changes, and the confusing charge I've been feeling since Brendan showed up.

It's a lot, and Mark is a grounding force.

I glance over at Brendan. He was so sweet in there. I love

how he looked after me and dealt with their crap. Honestly, it was pretty attractive. This whole situation I find myself in may be as fake as anything, but I can't deny he made me feel special in that changing suite.

He's frowning down at his phone. 'Gotta make some calls.'

'Of course,' I say brightly.

He gives me a nod and sticks in an earbud. 'Elaine. Yep. Heading back now. You'll need to give Marlowe a tour at some point this morning. Did the plumber come back with a quote?'

I quietly check my phone with one hand, leaving the other on Mark's sleek head. Camille has sent a message wishing me luck for today, which is sweet, and Athena has added me to the Seraphim group chat. I don't know any of them yet except for Athena's good friend Sophia, but they've all chimed in with tips and messages of support that range from sweet and supportive to filthy and hilarious.

I smile to myself, grateful for the reminder that, no matter how weird this new lifestyle might be, I'm not the only one out there living it. I'm in no doubt as to my reasons for doing this, but it hurts to imagine little Tabs going about her innocent day at school when I've had a dangerously hot man dressing and undressing me in designer rags all morning.

If I'm making a sacrifice, surely it should feel harder?

When I've locked my phone, I close my eyes and zone back into Brendan's conversation. He's still on the phone with Elaine.

'No. Tell him he's got to liaise with the boiler guy. I've had enough of his muppetry. Oh, and send flowers to that woman from Saturday night, will you? Ava? Eva? I'll text you her address... I dunno, something pretty and expensive.'

My hand freezes against Mark's comforting warmth. Because, just like that, Brendan has hit me with a very timely, very helpful reminder that I'm not the only woman he's lavishing with *pretty and expensive* goods.

I'm an employee. A new novelty. But I'd do well to remember that this gorgeous, charming guy is most likely spinning a hell of a lot of plates.

I just hope I don't shatter into pieces when he drops me.

# CHAPTER 19

# *Brendan*

I'm antsy as fuck by the time we approach our offices, which are based in the heart of the Docklands, in Butler's Wharf. Crawling through Monday traffic from the centre of town is not a good use of time by anyone's standards, and spending a good chunk of my morning in Selfridges isn't a good use of time by *my* standards.

The parts where I got to watch Marlowe trying on sexy AF lingerie were fan-fucking-tastic, don't get me wrong, but the rest of it was excruciating. I spend most of the journey firing off admin requests to Plain Elaine and dealing with emails. My email strategy centres around deleting everything possible and shooting back replies to everything else. It's an endless game of tennis, and as we approach Butler's Wharf, every single ball I had is now littering someone else's court.

Marlowe is quiet in the car, either staring out of the window or at her phone. While I'm working, I shoot her surreptitious glances between smirking to myself. She looks spectacular in that white dress—every kinky Seraph fantasy I've entertained since I learnt about the agency come to life. She's every bit as ravishing as she was that night when we met, when her beauty turned me into a total muppet, but the dynamic is very, very different now.

I'm the one in control, and she's a sure thing.

She's no longer some elusive, artsy angel to be admired from afar in her creative milieu but very specifically a seraph. Now we're in my milieu, and I'm paying a shocking sum of money to admire her up close.

Fuck, the thought has me hardening in my seat.

Can't get in there soon enough.

I'm springing out of the car as soon as Yan's pulled into my designated bay in the basement of our building. Mark, who's found the journey just as boring as I have, bounds out after me, no doubt happy to be back in his second home with hundreds of adoring fans.

We take the lift up to the main reception, and I stride across the polished palatial space. I fucking love this building. Our footprint in this part of London tends to straddle both ultra-modern new builds and sensitive but ground-breaking restoration of old industrial buildings, and this former Victorian tea warehouse is a stellar showcase for our capabilities, if I say so myself.

Our architectural team designed the double-height ground floor around the original, unapologetically industrial features, keeping the weathered brick walls and the enormous cast iron girders. The timber columns and beams have been lovingly restored and lit to perfection, while a sleek poured concrete reception desk reaching across the far wall provides the necessary modern contrast. Behind it, huge illuminated black and white photographs celebrate the building's illustrious history at the centre of Britain's tea-trading heritage.

It looks like we're arriving just as the first outflux of staff leaves to grab lunch. In an industry known traditionally for being pale, male and stale, I'm proud of the energy, the diversity, we've cultivated among our workforce, which is young and hungry. Our initial public offering a few years back has proven a fantastic way to lure in the smartest, brightest minds with stock options, and I can't deny the changing of the guard (Dad to me, basically) has attracted new talent, too.

I'm used to causing a stir wherever I go in the company, and today is no exception. As Marlowe, Mark and I proceed across the vast lobby, the women of Sullivan Construction react in ways as predictable as they are varied: the more brazen among them tossing me knowing smiles while eye-fucking me with indecent indiscretion, and the more timid clearing a path with those deer-in-the-headlights eyes that my presence always seems to trigger.

As we approach the bank of lifts, Serena, our front-of-house manager with legs longer than some motorways, finds an urgent need to rise from her chair and lean over the reception desk, conveniently displaying both her cleavage and her ability to make eye contact through her lashes. The gaggle of women checking their phones by the lifts suddenly fall silent, their whispers replaced by not-so-subtle glances. Even that pain in the arse from Legal, who spent last year's Christmas party telling me how much of a liability I am, suddenly develops an intense interest in smoothing her skirt while stealing glances my way.

It's the usual parade. I'd like it stated for the record that I have never, ever dipped my nib in the office ink—I'm not that fucking stupid—and normally I'd find these reactions tedious or amusing depending on my mood.

But today there's an added edge to their behaviour. These women aren't just eyeing me; they're assessing Marlowe too, this stunning blonde in pristine Dior walking beside me. The calculation behind their eyes is transparent: sizing up the competition, measuring how long she'll last, wondering what makes her different from the others. Little do they know she's both my EA and my plaything, and I've got plans for her that would make HR spontaneously combust.

Plans that are making my fingers twitch with impatience as we cross this endless fucking lobby.

Still, it's a solid reminder that whoever I'm seen with regularly will assume a certain level of profile by association, and I'd do well to make my interactions with Marlowe as discreet as possible. The last thing she needs is every woman in the building staring daggers at her because they think she's caught my eye. And the last thing *I* need is the guys standing by the lift checking her out, even if a part of me can't blame them.

I catch one guy behind her openly ogling her arse until he clocks me next to her. The smirk on his face vanishes as he visibly pales and clears his throat.

'Mr Sullivan.'

I don't grace him with anything more than a *don't even think about it* frown—I have no fucking clue who he is. Usually, I make an effort to engage with my employees, even when I don't feel like it. Even when I don't know their names or their faces. It's important. Our success depends on everyone here feeling invested in this firm, and if a kind word or smile from me can help with that, then I'm all for it.

I'm all for it unless they're mentally undressing my EA, that is.

We enter the lift, everyone else yielding to me, Marlowe and Mark, who trots obediently by my side. I nod my thanks to the person holding the doors for us and settle at the back of the metal box, allowing myself a quick glance at Marlowe. She was here fleetingly for her interview, of course, but it's always different turning up somewhere for your first day of work.

She's taking everything in with her quick, darting gaze. I

suspect she has no clue she's the object of both male and female scrutiny, but there's no question that she stands out. It's not like I can parade her around—the entire basis of success for this relationship will rest on our discretion—but it doesn't matter, because the kick I get from knowing that this woman is bound for the executive floor with me, to be my secret little reward whenever I choose, is hot beyond belief.

And I want to remind her of that.

There's no one behind us. I put a hand on the small of her back and let it slide down until it's cupping the curve of her arse.

Fucking glorious.

She stiffens and shoots me a quick, alarmed glance that I return with a neutral, professional smile. Nothing to see here, folks, just a horny CEO groping his sexy-as-fuck EA with benefits... because he can.

As soon as we get to the executive floor, Mark scampers off in search of love, validation and treats. He'll get all three here. I practically drag Marlowe past the bank of desks that house the various administrative roles supporting the management team.

'This is Marlowe, everyone. I need to go through some urgent paperwork with her—I'll introduce you properly later.'

Marlowe smiles and gives them an apologetic *hi* as she trails after me into my office. The wall facing the main area of the executive floor is glass, but it turns translucent or opaque at the flick of a switch and, thank fuck, is currently fully opaque.

I pull her into the room.

Take her bag from her and put it on the floor.

Slam the door shut.

Hit the lock.

Lean back against the door and slide my hands into my pockets.

My newest, shiniest toy is standing in the centre of the

room. At the sound of the lock turning, she spins back to face me.

I cock my head as I assess her.

Long, blonde hair loose and perfectly styled.

Stunning white dress.

Willowy figure.

Legs to die for.

And the expression on her face somewhere between wariness and abject panic.

Hmm.

*Where to start?*

# CHAPTER 20

# Marlowe

The soft metallic shunt of the lock slotting into place has me spinning around where I stand. And when I do, I'm in no doubt as to its significance. Brendan settles his huge frame against the doorframe and slides his hands into his pockets as he assesses me. Sunlight dances across his face, across that broad, white-shirted chest, as he lounges with the easy assurance of a predator who has his prey cornered and knows dinner is moments away.

Because the indulgent shopping trip was just a prelude, and I should make no mistake about it.

*This is why I'm here.*

He extricates a hand from his pocket and crooks his finger at me. 'Come here.' His voice is much lower than usual, and it sends an ominous thrill through me.

'Turn around,' he says when I reach him, and I do. He smooths his hands down my hair, twisting it into a rope and placing it over one shoulder. 'So pretty,' he coos as he eases the chunky zip all the way down my back. 'Remember when I said we'd have to be quieter in here?'

'Yes.' He said that jokingly in the club when he was still

inside me, but it *feels* important now, because it's broad daylight, and there are dozens of people getting on with their jobs mere metres from us, and thick glass walls don't strike me as the most robust privacy measure.

'Keep that in mind,' he says against my ear before he bends to undo the zip all the way down to my hem so he can straighten up and slide the dress off my shoulders like a coat that's on backwards.

He's seen me naked in the club, in that opulent dressing room, but here I am in nothing but heels and lingerie in the sunlit office of a kinky CEO, and it all hits me at once—the vulnerability of my position. The shame of it. The unavoidable truth of my being paid to be here, to do this. To let him strip me and use me. It sluices over me like a bucket of water, and I'm glad he can't see my face. I feel stricken; there's no other word for it. Stricken and alone and uneasy.

Brendan caresses my waist, my hips, like he did in the changing room earlier. He sighs, and it's warm against my shoulder. 'Turn around.'

I steel myself, and I do, and God, his eyes are *so* blue in this light as I look up at him. It's astonishing, really. His gaze drops to my chest in its new lacy Agent Provocateur bra and then moves lower, and he groans a little as he slides his hands back to my hips. Honestly, that feels astonishing too, because I'm pretty sure I just witnessed spontaneous ovulation from dozens of women down in reception.

Walking through the building with him, looking at him through their eyes, was eye-opening to say the least. Yes, he's the CEO, so he's bound to garner some level of attention, admiration.

But there was *nothing* professional about the way those women were mentally undressing him.

And now I'm here with him, in his palatial corner office, and he's mentally undressing me in exactly the same way. The only difference? He intends to do a hell of a lot more than that. Despite my nerves, despite the surreal, intense charge of this situation, that gives me a kick, because there's no denying the man is beautiful.

*You lucky bitch,* I admonish myself. *This guy is the prize everyone in this building wants, and he wants to play with* you.

His gaze comes back up to my face, and we stare at each other as I wait for him to make his move.

He smiles slowly, confidently, and I know it's game on.

'Get on your knees, love.'

And there it is.

I really, really hope I was right about blowjobs. I hope it's like riding a bike, because I am seriously out of practice.

Brendan takes my hands and holds them tightly so I can sink to my knees in four-inch heels without going sideways. I hit the plush white carpet and look up at him. Holy crap, he's tall from this angle.

'Take me out like a good girl.'

His voice is strained, and there's already a serious bulge going on behind those very nice wool trousers. I'm under no illusions as to the size of this guy, but his God-given blessings practically hit me in the face as I pull down his flies and rummage in the small space to find the slit in his boxers. Can I even get him out like this, or do I need to undo his belt buckle and buttons too?

Jesus, I'm rusty.

He doesn't seem to notice my lack of elegance, though. He groans again, low in his throat, as I abandon any hope of getting his dick out this way. It brings new meaning to the analogy of trying to fit a camel through the eye of a needle. Anyway, he'll want me to play with his balls, I assume. I may as well give myself full access.

I shift on the carpet and mentally grit my teeth. I can do this. I have a degree and an MBA. I'm a professional overachiever. I can work out how to get a guy off, even if the dizzying amount of money he's paying me to do it makes the stakes terrifyingly high. I make quick work of his belt buckle, conscious that the only sounds in here are those of leather against metal and his ragged breaths. For the most part, I'm holding mine. Belt undone, I undo the little metal hook thingy and the button and slide his trousers down. His boxer briefs are black again, his monster dick making a valiant break for freedom.

I wrench down his boxers and it springs out, hard and hot and as intimidating as a fully loaded assault rifle. Jesus *Christ*. I glance up at him, for reassurance maybe. The expression on his handsome face gives me pause. He's flattened his palms against the door as if seeking strength and balance, but the look on his face is feral, *desperate*, and I feel a weird surge of power.

He's using me.

He's paying me.

But look how much he wants me. Or, at the very least, wants what I have to offer.

There are dozens, if not hundreds, of women in this firm who'd be happy to suck the CEO's dick for whatever reason, but only one of them has her mouth inches from its engorged, angry crown.

I wrap my hand around his shaft—so satin-smooth, so *hard*—and I run my tongue over his slit.

The man practically shoots through the ceiling. He slides his hands through my hair, cupping my jaw, his fingers taut, vibrating with tension.

'That's very good, love. Do that again.'

This low, commanding Bedroom Voice he's using is so ominously hot that a spot of moisture hits my thong.

So I do it again, and he groans.

Okay, so I was right, and Athena was right. Men are pretty

basic. This isn't rocket science. When a guy is this turned on, it's hard to get it wrong.

He tastes—good, I think. Clean. Earthy. Male. God, it's been so long since I did this, so long since I smelt this scent and tasted this part of a man's body.

'Take me in your mouth,' he orders me. I have a feeling he's going to talk me through this whole thing, and why shouldn't he? He's paying for the privilege, after all, and honestly? I kind of like it. Let's not forget what this is.

I look up at him through my eyelashes before focusing on wrapping my lips around his crown. I use my tongue to find that little notch on its underside—Joe used to go crazy when I licked that—and he moans his satisfaction. Seems to me he may want to heed his own advice around noise levels.

His hands drag along my jaw so his fingers can flex in my hair. 'Look at you. So fucking angelic this morning with your blonde hair and white lace, and look at you now, sucking my cock like the perfect little whore. So fucking good. I've wanted you on your knees for me since the first time I saw you.'

I moan my agreement. It's intentional, part of my performance for him, but his filthy brand of appreciation is doing it for me. Blow jobs aren't supposed to be hot for the woman—they're the ultimate act of service, of submission—but this whole fucked-up power dynamic is getting me hot and bothered, and I have no idea why.

He tightens his grip on my hair so he can use it as a kind of rein. It seems his entire body is vibrating before me, and I marvel that my mouth has the capability of undoing a man as powerful and fierce as Brendan Sullivan, but it does. His breath is harsh and noisy, his thighs are trembling.

The next time I move to take him all in, his hand forces me further down around his dick, and I have to inhale sharply through my nostrils to override my gag reflex. Sweat pricks me everywhere. Fuck. I claw at his thigh with my free hand as I focus on my single objective—to survive this. To take him as deep as he wants and needs without retching.

We find a rhythm. It's messy and punishing, and I'm gasping and flailing, my eyes watering, but he seems to like that, because his thrusts and his grunts and his fingers in my hair all grow more desperate, it seems.

Until he pulls out of me with a strangled gasp, and I stare up at him through my watery eyes.

'Jesus fuck. Fucking look at you.' He blows out a breath. 'Okay. Here's what I want. Turn around and crawl away from me, nice and slow, until you get into the middle of the room. I want you to wait there on all fours so I can come and fuck you like that. Got it?'

# CHAPTER 21

# *Marlowe*

C*rawl.*

Oh, sweet Lord.

Right. Okay. I can do this. For what he's paying me, I can humiliate myself. My opinions aren't relevant. The only route to success here is doing exactly what he wants.

The happier he is with me, the more secure my job is.

It doesn't hurt that he's staring at me as if I will deliver him to the Promised Land if I abide by his wishes, all hooded eyes and harsh breaths and strong fingers closing over his hard dick.

I twist my body, dropping my palms to the carpet so I'm on all fours, and I start to crawl—cautiously, because crawling is not second nature to me, funnily enough, and it's even tougher when the pointy toes of your new shoes are catching in the thick pile of the carpet every time you move. The logistical challenges are a relief, partially absolving me from fixating on how my rear view must look in this flimsy thong as I channel my inner Baby from *Dirty Dancing* and attempt to slink away from Brendan in a seductive, feline manner.

'God, yeah, that's it,' he rasps behind me. His validation is an instant shot of dopamine to my insides. 'Oh, fuck. Look at the way your arse moves when you crawl. Keep going. *Just* like that.' I sense him approaching and stop when I reach the centre of the room, forcing myself to arch my back a little so my bottom sticks out.

He must squat behind me, because he slides his knuckles down the now-damp strip of my thong, and my nerve endings dance to attention as, deeper inside, my core clenches in antici-pation. This couldn't feel filthier—parading around on my hands and knees in gifted lingerie for a guy who's bought my services.

There's a rip of foil, followed by some heavy breathing as he wrestles the condom on. Then Brendan pushes my thong to one side, exposing me properly, and teases me with his fingertips.

'Would you look at that?' he mutters as his fingers move noisily through my wetness. 'Absolutely fucking drenched, already. So you like sucking me off in my office then, hmm?'

'Y-yes,' I manage.

'That is very good news. I'm such a lucky bastard. Now, you'd better stay nice and quiet like we discussed.' He steps between my legs on his knees, and I widen for him, bracing on my hands for balance. I hope he'll fit. I may be wet, but it'll be seriously deep like this.

Seriously deep, and seriously dirty.

No wonder he said it was his favourite position.

Then he's pushing in, and—God—it's so big and invasive, stretching me as he goes, but it's a relief, too, to know how fully he'll fill me up. All those fancy new presents and lingering touches and charming, cheeky whispers earlier, and it's all led to this: my new boss getting ready to rail the living daylights out of me on his office floor.

'Fuck, you're tight,' he says with a disbelieving laugh. 'I'd almost forgotten how—bloody *hell*, love.'

I'm sweating as he edges his way in. My wrists ache already. I can tell he's trying his hardest to hold off for my sake. But, finally, he's all the way in, and it seems we both pause in sync to marvel at this physiological wonder. He smooths a hand down my neck and back, glossing over my hair and tracing the column of my spine before both his hands come to my hips and grip tightly. When he pulls out of me, he sucks a sharp breath in through his teeth.

'I wish you could see what I see. Best sight ever. You're so fucking gorgeous.'

I love that. I'm so exposed for him like this, so I love that he's getting off on the view. All I can see is the carpet, the city skyline through the bank of windows in front of me and, if I hang my head, Brendan's knees between mine, his trousers pooling around them. The slivers of thigh are thick and hairy, and it feels so brutish for him to be taking me like this.

I suspect that's what he is: a big, sexy brute in a beautiful suit.

And now I rhyme, apparently.

He gets into a rhythm—thrusts punishing, balls slapping against my thong and my skin, fingers digging in so hard I suspect they'll leave bruises—and the fit is so tight, the drag of his dick along my inner walls so fucking amazing, like *life-affirmingly amazing*. I brace myself as well as I can, but I find myself shunting back to meet him when he bottoms out in me and then rolling my hips before he withdraws.

None of it's performative. It seems my body knows what to do better than I do, because neither of my previous partners ever took me like this. My moves are instinctive, purely to maximise my pleasure and, I hope, Brendan's, but on some level I'm aware that I am an active participant in this; I'm bucking and arching and taking every drop of sensation he's giving me just as he seems to be wringing me for every drop he can take from *me*.

I chase it and chase it, more shamelessly than I thought I was capable of doing, and the pressure inside me builds as he fucks me and fucks me, because *Jesus,* this man has stamina. It's sweaty and messy, and we may not be crying out or screaming, but we're definitely both grunting and panting in a way that makes me hope no one out there has their ear pressed to the door.

'You're going to come, aren't you?' Brendan huffs out. 'You're so close.'

'Yeah,' I gasp. 'Yeah, I just need—'

'I know, baby. I've got you. Here, take this.'

Bloody hell, he ramps up his pace and intensity, ploughing into me with such blunt force that my vagina should really develop a survival instinct that comes with several alarm bells, but it just carries on drinking up everything this guy has to give it.

Which is a *lot.*

I'm powerless against such a spectacular show of dominance, such a marathon of masculinity. Every single thing in my life reduces to this one point of contact where he's doing battle with his majestic dick. The heat builds and then releases inside my body like the most beautiful crescendo, and I'm molten and boneless and gooey as my orgasm wrings me out over and over, vaguely aware that the gorgeous man behind me is letting rip with a string of filthy curses at how gratifying he finds my reaction to him.

'The way you fucking *milk* me,' he rasps. 'Jesus fuck, it should be fucking illegal. I can feel every fucking tremor.'

He's not far behind me, going impossibly swollen and rigid before coming with a strangled roar and a volley of pumps that feel so staggeringly good against my sensitive flesh that they have me wondering what it would feel like if he were bare and emptying himself inside me rather than a condom.

*No, Marlowe. Bad thought. Bad. Not only is this guy prob-*

*ably fucking half of London on his nights off, but he probably has super sperm. No more unplanned pregnancies, thank you very much.*

When he's done, he collapses on top of me, bracing himself on one hand so he can wrap the other one around my waist. Against my back, his chest radiates heat through the still-crisp cotton of his shirt. He lets out the most enormous sigh into my hair—the sated sigh of a victorious predator after a cardio-heavy hunt—before stroking the skin of my stomach with his hand. Deep inside me, his dick twitches. He releases me, straightening up, and I feel the loss of his body heat keenly.

I wince as he pulls out of me, and he slaps me on my bare bottom.

'Well, that was very fucking good. I must get HR to add it to the onboarding manual.'

# CHAPTER 22

# Marlowe

'The smoothies here are amazing, I have to say,' Elaine tells me, gesturing around the palatial staff cafeteria. It's a couple of floors down from the executive floor, a mainly white, light-filled space that looks like it's been designed by a Zen master. Sure enough, there is an actual juice and smoothie bar that Tabby would love.

Apparently, the food is all fantastic and also *free*, which I thought was something that only happened at tech giants like Google. As I gaze around the food court at the grill, the salad bar and the omelette station, I can't help but calculate not only how much money I'll save, but how much time and headspace. No more assembling the next day's lunch after Tabs has gone to bed. Now I just need them to do my laundry for me, too.

A woman can dream, right?

'Great!' I say brightly. Elaine is a lovely woman whose age I'd put in the mid-forties range. Her light brown hair is styled in a long bob, and she has the most genuine smile. I'm grateful to her for taking me under her wing, because to say I'm feeling discombobulated after Brendan's particular brand of *onboarding* is putting it mildly.

I'm actually compiling a mental list of things I need to stock up on. Lube, for sure, because that fit was *tight*. Wrist supports, possibly—a high plank has nothing on doggy-style on the floor for putting undue pressure on the wrists—and definitely an ice pack. I anticipate feeling very sore by tomorrow.

One thing I *don't* need, it seems, is moisturiser. Athena told me that Camille makes a big deal about aftercare with its clients. Seraph has all kinds of tutorials about it, apparently. Brendan's brand of aftercare appeared to be mainly a cheeky slap on the bottom for a job well done, so it surprised me when I emerged from putting myself back together in the swanky marble bathroom attached to his office to find him patting the sofa next to him.

Annoyingly, he didn't look like he'd just had a shagathon. He was back to being perfectly put together, dark hair raked effortlessly back and his attire immaculate. He winked at me, dropping to his knees on the carpet once I was sitting and picking up a tub of what looked like fancy body butter. He then proceeded to rub said body butter into my carpet-burnt knees with a charming grin as I stared down at him, completely dumbfounded.

Now *that* was discombobulating.

After our tour, I make myself comfortable at my new desk. I'm sitting in a spacious, low-walled cubicle next to Elaine and across from some of the other assistants who look after the rest of the management team on this floor. My sleek computer makes the one I had at the Royal Academy seem like an ancient relic. I just hope I don't embarrass myself working out how to use it.

Elaine is a godsend. Brendan mentioned to me that he was

in dire need of an executive assistant to assume the bulk of his professional workload from her, but he certainly hasn't shown any interest in the more administrative side of my, um, onboarding process. When she and I settle ourselves on some sleek sofas over by the coffee machine for a debrief, three things become clear. One, she's had way too much on her plate juggling both jobs, two, she's pretty hilarious, and three, she's a gold mine of information on my new boss.

'There are a few things you need to know from the outset,' she tells me, and I lean forward, eager to get the inside track on Brendan Sullivan, billionaire CEO and sex god.

'If you have pens you like, hide them. He fidgets with everything, especially in meetings. During the last quarterly management meeting, I made the mistake of leaving my favourite fountain pen on the table. By the end, he'd completely disassembled it—springs, ink cartridge, the lot—while explaining our expansion plans to the management team. Never found the bloody cap. Now I keep a drawer of cheap clicky pens just for him. He *really* likes clicking things. He has a fidget toy in his pocket, but basically nothing is sacred.'

I laugh out loud. That was *not* what I was expecting her to lead with. 'Okay, got it. Cheap pens.'

'Cheap *clicky* pens, remember. Right, next thing. He operates on what I call "Sullivan Standard Time". He's either fifteen minutes early or forty minutes late—there's no in-between. For important meetings, I tell him they start half an hour before they actually do. He thinks he's chronically late, but he's actually been surprisingly punctual for the past year. He has no idea.'

'Understood,' I say, making a mental note to keep Brendan's calendar on this adjusted time going forward.

'Oh, but he absolutely hates it if anyone else is late, especially if he's turned up early. He throws a total toddler tantrum. There's nothing worse to him than people wasting his time, and it's your job to chivvy everyone along so they don't rock up late and derail everything. I usually call the key attendees up fifteen minutes before a meeting starts.'

I can see that. I can easily imagine Brendan pacing, throwing his toys. And it's not much of a leap to understand why a guy who hates wasting time might incorporate his sexual needs into his office hours.

'That makes sense,' I say. 'Uh—does he throw many toddler tantrums?'

'A few. He doesn't exactly have a filter, and it can come off badly. But don't get me wrong—the guy has a heart of gold. Last summer, we had this intern on our floor for a few months. Harry. Brendan took a real shine to him. The poor kid was in floods of tears one day—he was only about twenty —and Brendan took him out for a walk. Turns out his mum had suspected skin cancer, but the waitlist on the NHS for her to get biopsied was months and months.

'Brendan forked out for her to see a private dermatologist and then for all her treatments after that. Turned out she did have skin cancer, and it cost thousands and thousands to get it sorted privately. But he didn't bat an eye. He thinks nothing of stuff like that. He's one of the most generous people I've ever met.'

I smile dreamily. So he's a big softie when it counts. 'I'm so happy to hear that.'

'He definitely has his moments,' she agrees, picking up her coffee. 'But then he can also be a gigantic twat. My little boy was off sick loads last term, so I had to work from home. My job's a lot more flexible than my husband's. Anyway, Brendan made me feel really shitty for it. I was totally capable of getting the job done, but he behaved like such a baby because he had to go out and get his own lunch for a few days. He can be so self-absorbed sometimes. And don't get me started on the way he treats women.'

I stiffen. Brendan's multiple personalities are giving me whiplash. The lifesaver who forks out on medical treatment for a woman he doesn't know, and the guy who has zero tolerance for accommodating working mothers. It's a good wake up call, and a vindication of my decision to keep Tabby's entire existence a secret, as well as abdicating her emergencies to my parents, no matter how wrong that feels on every single level.

And now another alarm bell is ringing.

'How do you mean?' I ask faintly.

'Well, I probably shouldn't say, given it's not in your job scope to bother with this stuff, but his personal schedule needs... creative management. Last month, he somehow double-booked himself with two different women on the same night at the same restaurant.

'I had to call one pretending to be from the restaurant, saying they had a gas leak. Then I sent flowers from him with a handwritten note I forged apologising for the cancellation and offering to reschedule at an even fancier place. She actually thanked him for being so thoughtful. I have no idea how he gets himself into these pickles, except that the sheer volume of women he goes through makes it hard for him to keep up with the details, I suppose.'

'I heard him asking you to send flowers to someone today,' I venture.

'Yes. That's very standard. He likes to follow up, keep them on the back burner. But he gets bored so easily, bless him. Variety is the spice of life where that man is concerned.'

Jesus. How long will I last? How long before he runs out of ways to fuck me in his office, before being with the same woman day in, day out has him running for the hills? I sigh. I may need to hit Athena and the other seraphim up for some tips on how to keep things novel, at least for as long as it takes me to pull together the vast funds for Tabby's US trip and beyond.

The familiar spiral takes hold, the blind panic that her fate lies in my hands. That it's down to me to pull this off when I'm more out of my depth than I've ever been. I feel like Anne Boleyn and every other wife Henry VIII ever had, desperate to keep her mercurial king happy and focused on her and her interests for as long as possible.

The anxiety is so forceful it almost drowns out Elaine's next piece of advice.

'And for God's sake, don't let him anywhere near that coffee machine.'

One of the rules Seraph is very big on is keeping strictly enforced business hours. Obviously, these EA positions are critical roles with a tonne of responsibility and, as with any other important role, work-life balance can be tricky to manage. It's assumed that there will be evenings where we're on our laptops late at night or can't unplug from our email or have to juggle key deadlines. But here's the crux of it:

*We can't do it from the office.*

Camille drummed this into me on the phone call where she formally passed on Brendan's post-coital job offer.

'Being a seraph is intense,' she told me in her calm, modulated tones. 'Intellectually, physically, and emotionally. And the men who hire seraphim are usually powerful and often entitled. They're used to getting whatever they want and they're not used to hearing *no*. If you don't leave that office by six each night, before you know it, you'll be their arm candy at every function. You'll be their fully fledged escort. If they want you at your best every day, they have to understand that you need to protect your downtime fiercely.'

As a working single mother, this was music to my ears. The time when Tabby was at school was fair game for me to work on earning a living, but even at the RA, I always hated when three-thirty rolled around and I knew she'd be walking out of those school gates to her grandparents and not to me. Every minute I wasn't with her felt like a lost opportunity. Less rationally, it felt like I was letting her down. Ridiculous, obviously, and probably more than a little co-dependent. But when you have a chronically unwell child, you learn to value every moment with them.

So it's with relief that I go to get changed in Brendan's bathroom on the dot of six. Apparently, Yan will drop by with my scores of Selfridges bags later this evening to deposit my new wardrobe. I'll need to Marie Kondo the heck out of my current one to get my new designer threads into my closet, but that's what I call a high-quality problem. I mentioned to Brendan that I'd probably cycle to and from home from work each day, and he instantly offered me the use of his swanky ensuite. This evening I'll rent a bike, but from tomorrow I'll be on my ancient, barely roadworthy one.

Into my big rucksack go my new dress and shoes as well as the outfit I arrived in. I've created space by leaving my so-called "hooker kit" in the spacious bottom drawer of my desk: all the stuff Athena told me I'd need to do my job without looking just-fucked all the time. You know, toothpaste and intimate wipes and a *lot* of spare underwear.

Brendan is still at his desk when I emerge in a tank top and cycling shorts, my hair tied up in a big bun, because it's warm out there. It seems rude to be leaving before the boss, but I remind myself that upholding healthy boundaries is critical in this job, and I need to implement that from day one. But more urgently, I'm not sure what constitutes an appropriate farewell.

*Thanks for the orgasms?*

*Can't wait to see what you have in store for me tomorrow?*

*Not sure how I'll ride home with my pussy this bashed up?*

In the end, I settle for none of those.

'Bye. See you tomorrow.'

He looks up from his laptop and stills. 'Fucking hell. Feel free to just wear that tomorrow.'

I give him a shy little smile. It's so surreal to think this big, beautiful man railed me right here where I'm standing earlier. 'Not sure it's dress-code compliant.'

'You're probably right. More's the pity.' He pauses, assessing me, and then pushes his chair back. Before I know it, he's strolling towards me. 'You doing okay? Today was a lot.'

I nod quickly. 'Yeah. I'm good. It was... good. Thanks again for all the clothes.' *And, you know, the ridiculous orgasm.*

'My pleasure.' He hesitates before sliding a warm hand around the back of my neck. 'This is all new for me too, you know. This kind of arrangement. So when you're not happy, I need to know you'll speak up.'

I make myself come out with it. 'I'm a bit sore. I might need to... be careful tomorrow.' Ugh, I hate saying it. He's bought a new toy, and he's played with it precisely once, and it's already defective. 'Let's just see,' I add hurriedly. 'I might be fine. I'm out of practice, but I'm sure I'll get used to it.'

He's shaking his head. 'No, no way. If you're sore, you're sore. You're not a blow-up doll, love. I don't expect you to just put up and shut up, okay? Like I said, we're both new to this. And for it to work, we both have to be happy.' A dirty smile spreads across his face. 'For the record, you did great today. I went hard on you.'

'Okay,' I whisper. 'Thank you.'

'I'm the one who should be thanking you.'

Our eyes are locked. He really is indecently attractive, but I'm still trying to figure him out. He clearly has a heart of gold, but, from the sounds of it, my early instincts about this being a nannying job may also be right.

I wonder what a Monday evening for Mr Brendan Sullivan looks like.

'Do you have any plans for this evening?' I blurt out.

He looks for a moment like a deer in the headlights. His fingers flex on my neck. 'I've got a... dinner. In Chelsea.'

I nod brightly. *A dinner.* It's none of my business. Our sordid little arrangement ends at six each night, and that goes for Brendan as well as for me.

'Have a lovely time,' I say cheerily.

I'm pretty sure his eyes stay on my bum as I walk out of his office.

That bike ride definitely didn't help my swollen undercarriage. When I walk gingerly into my building, it's weird on so many levels. I feel like a weary traveller who's seen another world and can't unsee it.

Tabs and I live in New Cross, just south of the Docklands in South East London. It's an area that can optimistically be described as "up and coming", but there are still far too many grotty parts. Its only positive, really, is that it's close to my new place of work—around a fifteen-minute bike ride if I pedal quickly.

Our flat is in a sprawling estate which is a mix of government-owned council flats and those which have been sold to private owners or landlords. Ours is one of the latter—we rent it from a rental company—but it looks and feels every bit as depressing as a council flat, and don't get me started on the communal areas.

I punch in the code for the outside door and creep past a gang of youths in the concrete hallway. Even in the summer, it feels damp in here. They're all in black hoodies, faces barely visible, the stench of weed thick in the air. They're swearing loudly, and they're intimidating as fuck. They're blocking the mailboxes, and I quickly decide I won't be checking my post today. I hate that my parents and Tabs have to make the journey through this area to get upstairs to my flat, and it's a miracle that Athena ever braves this place at all.

Not that any gang would dare mess with Athena.

As I climb the stairs and leave the fog of weed behind me, the smell turns to piss. Yes, my neighbours piss in the stairwell from time to time. Can they be any more revolting? It's such a world away from the huge flower arrangements and gorgeous windows and soaring architectural details of Brendan's offices. This place is a roof over our heads and not much more.

I'm sweating and out of breath as I reach the fourth floor. There are lifts, but they're often out of order and I use them as little as I can. I don't like the idea of Tabby and I being trapped in a smelly metal box if some of our less salubrious neighbours decide to join us. It's always a relief when I can lock the door of our little home behind us, because it means we've reached our sanctuary safely.

But here's where my return gets more surreal. When I shut the door and drop my rucksack behind me, I'm met with a vignette of domestic bliss in this basic little shoebox, and it hits me like a blow to my stomach.

Tabs and my parents are sitting at the small kitchen table, dirty plates stacked neatly to one side and an array of playing cards between them. The evening sunlight streams through the kitchen windows, bathing the room and its occupants in a golden glow while also drawing attention to the urgent need for an updated paint job in this living area.

But while the white paint is greying and peeling, especially in the corner that was damp all winter, the vibe of our home is cosy and safe. It smells deliciously of Dad's cooking—his carbonara, if I'm correct—and it's spotlessly clean. My parents are as protective of me as they are of Tabby, and it looks like some serious housework has gone down while I've been out.

I'm scrupulously tidy myself—if we're going to live in a little box in a dodgy building in a dodgy neighbourhood, then I'm damn well going to make sure it's immaculate—but I know it'll only be a matter of time before the housework starts to pile up, given the intensity of this job.

My parents may not know exactly what my new gig entails, but they know it's a step up from my last role, and they also know it's a necessary part of the funding for Tabby's op. They can sense I'll need extra support, even if I don't ask for it.

And, on day one, they're already stepping up.

All of it should make me happy: the clean kitchen; the card game; the delicious food that awaits me; the contented faces. I should be ecstatic as Tabby launches herself out of her chair and flings her little body against me. Mum's religious about her changing out of her uniform after school, so she's in white daisy print shorts and a lemon-yellow T-shirt with a huge daisy appliqué on the front.

And I am ecstatic; I am. I hug her back and pepper the top of her blonde head with effusive kisses. I'm delighted to see her, delighted to be home.

But it's as if I'm viewing my daughter and my parents through a veil of sorts. Because while they've been carrying on with their wholesome, innocent days of learning and child-care, of housework and family time, I've been permitting a man I barely know to buy me tens and tens of thousands of pounds' worth of clothes. I've allowed him to get me on my knees, to order me about, to put his dick in my mouth and in my pussy in the aggressive splendour of his office, and in return I've taken his money. *Gladly.*

So forgive me if knowing that the three people I love most in the world are ignorant of the depths I've plumbed in the name of money is horrifying rather than reassuring.

Don't get me wrong. They can never know.

I just wish I didn't have to sell my soul quite so comprehensively to ensure my daughter's future.

# CHAPTER 23

# *Brendan*

I've always loved my job. I thrive on it, in fact. I love this company that three generations of Sullivans have created. I love the challenges, the creativity, the wins. And I adore this beautiful space we've built to house our people, to nurture their talents and coax the very best out of them.

But I have never enjoyed coming into work quite so much as I'm doing this week.

Marlowe's new position got off to a cracking start on Monday with that shopping spree. For the first time, I understood why little kids love dressing up their dolls. Marlowe is a highly intelligent, well-educated and talented woman. She seems organised as fuck and I have no doubt she'll whip me and all my admin firmly into shape while taking a huge load off Plain Elaine.

All that is undeniable. *And yet.* She is also my brand-new fuck toy, and she's glorious. Just glorious. Stunningly, head-turningly beautiful, for starters, all long-limbed and molten-eyed and golden-haired. She's an absolute knockout, and she wears her new clothes so perfectly that a guy is incapable of doing anything but taking them right off her.

She also has a temperament I can really get on board with. She's articulate, assertive, but not aggressive. She's not afraid of hard work, and she's no snowflake. While I was sold on her looks, I can't afford to have an EA who's purely decorative, and Marlowe is earning her salary across the board. She's warm. Friendly. Upbeat. Resilient. Funny.

I suppose what I'm trying to say is that I like her. As a person. I'm not a woo-woo guy, but her vibe is positive. She has a good energy about her, an energy that draws you in and has nothing to do with those astounding looks.

I went easy on her yesterday—a quick blow job because she was sore from Monday. But today is a hoot. I get Alo to send over a sexy little white tennis dress and I drag her along to my racquets club at lunchtime where I proceed to beat her at padel by the skin of my teeth. Considering it's her first time playing the sport, she's fucking amazing. She's seriously sporty: great eye for the ball; great stamina (a fact I duly note); and my absolute favourite trait—a total refusal to yield a point until she's done absolutely everything in her power to win it.

She puts up such an amazing performance, in fact, and looks so hot doing it with her long legs and lithe figure and hair in a wholesome plait, that I feel compelled to drag her into the disabled changing room afterwards. Not only is it private, but the open-plan shower gives it more of a wet room dynamic.

'Brendan!' she gasps. 'We shouldn't be in here! What if someone needs it?'

'*I* need it.'

'You know what I mean.'

She presses her lips together, unimpressed, and I sigh. My little rule follower. My good girl in her tiny white dress and schoolgirl plait, her smooth, golden skin slick with sweat. 'There are three disabled changing rooms. Three. And are any of them in use? *Nope.* So stop worrying and come the fuck here.'

For good measure, I peel off my t-shirt and chuck it in a damp pile in the corner. That gets her attention. She takes in my bare chest and drifts over, biting her lip.

'Come here,' I repeat. 'I thrashed you fair and square, now I want my spoils of war.'

'You didn't thrash me—you beat me by a small margin—and has anyone ever told you it's not polite to gloat?' Her brown eyes flash as I push down my tennis shorts, leaving myself naked. But not before I openly remove a couple of condoms from the pocket and place them on the shelf, arching my eyebrows in a challenge.

I suspect my delicious little EA has a fiercely competitive streak. Bring it on. Racquet sports as foreplay is something I can definitely do.

'I'm going to gloat over you very, *very* hard. So why don't you take off that dress, and your bra, and your panties and bend over like a good little loser? Because I want to take my prize for a ride.'

Her breath catches. *She likes that.* Hmm. I lick my lips and watch avidly as she pulls her dress up over her head, leaving her in just a white sports bra and plain white cotton panties which might actually be the death of me. They may as well have *DEFILE ME* printed all over them, for fuck's sake.

She toes off her shoes. Bends to pull off her socks, then strips out of the bra and panties and stands before me, skin still flushed from our exertions on the court.

Yep. She'll do very nicely indeed.

I crank the shower on without breaking her gaze. 'Are you wet yet?'

She takes a step forward. 'You tell me.'

Fuck, she's a fast learner. I like that a lot. I shoot her a filthy smile and crook my finger at her. It seems she likes what she sees, because her eyes drop to my already-hard dick and stay there.

I wind her plait around one hand to bring her gaze back up to my face as I slide my fingers between her legs.

Slick as fuck.

'Soaked,' I pronounce, and she blushes more. I gesture at the shower. 'Get in there and bend over for me.'

The sight of Marlowe under the torrent of water, hands flat on the tiles and long golden plait hanging over one shoulder and perfect little cunt presented perfectly for me, is so intensely gratifying that I suck in a harsh breath. I don't waste any time, getting straight to my knees and parting her arse cheeks so I can stick my nose and mouth straight into warm, wet nirvana as the water sluices over us, lubricating everything.

She is fucking delicious. I burrow in further. My movements are ravenous and unrefined, but she doesn't seem to care. Quite the opposite. She squirms and moans as I feast on her. I keep going until she's coming violently, pushing her cunt into my face like she feels no shame at all, only blind need.

I know how she feels.

I was planning on fucking her like this, but given I took her from behind the other day, I'd like to see her face this time. I'd like to see how she looks post-orgasm, how she reacts to my cock driving into her over and over. So I straighten her up and turn her. She's every bit as pliant and floppy as I expected: face flushed, eyes glazed to the point of looking drugged.

'Stay there,' I say, settling her against the wall so I can make quick work of rolling on a condom. As soon as it's on, I close the gap between us, finding her under the water and lifting her easily into my arms. 'Hold on tight, love.'

She wraps her long limbs around me, her arms around my

shoulders and her legs around my hips. Our faces are so close now, and it strikes me that I haven't actually kissed her this week, an oversight I need to rectify straight away. I push my body up against hers, my rock-hard cock jerking against her pussy, and I indulge in a filthy, heated kiss, our lips sliding wetly against each other's, my tongue fucking her mouth, my body enjoying the welcome weight of her weary, post-orgasm limbs draped over me.

I may have beaten her on the court just now, but she's proven herself a surprisingly worthy adversary, a well-matched partner.

Now it's time to remind her how good it feels when I'm putting her to work off the court, too.

Without releasing her from the kiss, I reach between us and direct my dick straight at the soaking softness of her cunt. 'Tell me if you're still sore,' I mutter into her mouth, and she shakes her head.

'I'm not. I want it.'

'That's my very good girl,' I sigh. 'Sink down on it. *Fuuuck*, just like that.'

She's doing exactly as I've asked, bearing down on me inch by inch, wriggling a little in my arms to aid herself. I use both hands to support her arse and lean my forehead against hers as she pants her way through this part.

I'm in, and it's a fucking miracle. We stay like this for a moment, me sheathed in her, her breaths soft against my face, her beautiful little tits brushing against my chest, her arms and legs so tight around me.

This is a very, very good position.

I pull back a little so I can watch her face as I fuck her, deep and slow. Her fingers claw at my hair, grip it hard. Her face is so expressive, the impact of every thrust shimmering across it in what looks like awe and need. She's not the only one in awe. I push her up harder against the tiles, hoping the smooth limestone won't hurt her too much, and I let her have it, because my new goal in life is to have her face play out every single sensation she feels as my dick impales her.

There's nowhere for her to hide like this, and I don't want her to hide. I want her stripped back and exposed for me; I want her to give me every last vestige of strength she has left in her. I want to fuck her so thoroughly that I turn her inside out... and I want a front-row seat to the entire blessed show.

I grit my teeth and ignore the screams from my already worn-out thighs, and I focus on fucking Marlowe with a rhythm so even, so deep, that it'll unravel her like a ball of yarn. And my efforts are rewarded with breathy little whimpers, with her hand twisting in my hair and her legs tightening around my waist and her huge brown eyes going even wider as she attempts to ride this one out.

'Come for me, my filthy girl,' I growl. 'You looked so fucking innocent on the court, but you need my dick so badly, don't you? Hmm?'

'Yes,' she manages, letting her head fall back against the tiles, her eyes drifting closed as she grips me tighter.

'Yes what?'

'Yes, I need your dick.' She squeezes her eyes even more tightly closed, as if embarrassed, and I experience the most shameful wave of utter delight that she's still bashful about this shit. God knows, fucking the embarrassment out of her will be no hardship at all.

'Yes you do. Feel how deep I am, baby. Feel what it's doing to you.'

'Oh, God,' she moans. She sounds utterly defeated, and I know why, because her inner walls are fluttering around my cock, just as her eyelashes are fluttering against her wet cheeks, and my only mission is to take her over the edge into a place where nothing else exists for her but this shower and my dick.

I fuck her harder, and my legs shake harder, and my own orgasm builds and builds.

She shatters around me, fucking *shatters,* her head falling forward so she can bite down on my shoulder and scream out her climax, and she's a sight, she's such a fucking sight to behold that I let rip, freeing myself up to follow her over the edge, to yield to that incredible heat ripping through my balls and up my dick until I'm rutting and rutting and rutting deep within her body.

And, as I come, it's with her teeth on my skin and her screams in my ear and the extraordinary feeling of intensity, of *intimacy,* this watery cocoon simulates.

# CHAPTER 24

# *Marlowe*

I won't see Tabby before she goes to bed tonight, because this evening I have drinks with the infamous seraphim. There's something so depressing about knowing that when I sneak into her room later to inhale her skin and kiss her cheek, she'll be totally oblivious. But Athena says these drinks are important, that in the unique isolation of a role like this, you need your tribe around you. You need women who know exactly what you're going through.

And tonight is my chance to build those relationships. Aside from Athena and her friend Sophia, whose brainwave this was in the first place, I don't know anyone.

Besides, I've survived my first week of being Brendan's seraph, so I'm pretty sure I deserve a very large drink.

I've purposely worn one of my most gorgeous new dresses today: a sleek pale grey Miu Miu shift with an embellished neckline. Elaine commented on how beautiful it was earlier. She said it genuinely, but I could hear the unasked question in her voice—*exactly how much is he paying you?*—and I couldn't really blame her. Anyway, I hope it's worthy of the seraphim. I imagine them all to be total glamazons who actually live this crazy, opulent lifestyle rather than just pretending to live it during office hours.

Before I leave, I lock myself in a toilet cubicle so I can call Tabs and catch up on her day. It sounded largely uneventful, which in my book is a good thing. I tell her how much I love her and promise her that we can go for breakfast tomorrow at a cute little place not far from us. After all, what is a hundred grand a month of blood money if I don't get to treat my daughter occasionally?

Back at my desk, I check Brendan's emails one last time. I've added a few new rules this week, and it's helped to streamline the ridiculous, relentless tide of crap that streams into his inbox. It's in pretty good shape now—good enough for me to close it up and head out, in any case.

I suddenly remember that, in all of my handover discussions with my parents this week, I've neglected to nag them about Tabby's supplements. Vitamin C isn't going to magically enlarge her pulmonary valve, but keeping up her overall health is of vital importance going into a gruelling operation. I pick up my phone and message my mum, hitting the dictation button as I absently close out of Brendan's email.

'Hey, can you get Tabs to take her supplements before you give her dinner, please? They're on the counter by the sink. Thanks. Love you.'

'Who's Tabs?' a deep voice booms behind me, and I swear I almost fall off my chair in fright. It's fucking Brendan. Mark is next to him. How the hell did I not hear him *and* his dog sneak up behind me?

'Uh, what?' I ask, my brain spiralling in blind panic. I bend to stroke Mark and massage his jowls, playing for time.

'Tabs? You said something about Tabs and dinner.'

My initial reaction is to lash out. Tell him it's none of his business. But that's not the way to speak to your boss, and it would also sound seriously shady. 'Tabs. Oh, yeah, Tabs. She's, uh—she's my dog.'

Thank you, God—and Mark—for that timely moment of divine inspiration. I exhale shakily and keep my head down. The main problem with this entire plan I've hatched is that it involves a great deal of deception and I'm a totally useless liar. Like, a red-faced, shaky-voiced, deer-in-the-headlights kind of liar.

'Your dog?' he asks, and the sheer delight in his voice has me glancing up at him. He's positively beaming.

'Yeah.'

'You have a dog called Tabs?'

'Well, Tabby, but yes.'

'Tabby's a cat's name, not a dog's name.'

Seriously? He's really going there?

'Most people would argue that Mark is a human name, but here we are.'

He grins. He looks so unreasonably handsome when he grins, but I really wish he would drop this. Unfortunately, and appropriately enough, he's like a dog with a bone. He pushes his hand through his hair. 'What kind of dog is she? Can I see some pics?'

'Absolutely!' I say with a perkiness I do not feel. 'You know what—let me just send one final email and then I'll come through with my phone in a sec. Okay?'

'Okay.' He gives me an easy smile and turns. 'Come on, Mark. Let's give the lady some space.'

They trot off together, and I'd enjoy the rear view if I wasn't so busy spiralling. Fuck fuck *fuck*. I put my computer to sleep and pick up my phone. Once in my camera roll, I scroll through to the People & Pets section. I still think it's creepy that my phone is this clever. Sure enough, there are loads of photos of Daniel the Spaniel from over the years. I quickly rename his collection to Tabby and do a quick scroll through to make sure there aren't any photos where he's lying on his back and showing off his crown jewels. Now *that* would be tricky to explain.

'Hey,' I say breezily as I walk into his office. He's lounging on the sofa, long legs stretched out, one hand on his flat stomach and one on Mark's head. The fact that he loves his dog so much makes him a million times more attractive, in my view. Not that he needs any help in that department.

'Hey.' He pats the sofa next to him and sits up straighter. I sit down next to him and hold out my phone.

'So Tabs is a golden show cocker spaniel,' I force myself to say. So weird. God knows, I am not built for duplicity. 'My parents bought her for me when I was sixteen, so she's getting on a bit.'

'Ahh, she's gorgeous,' Brendan says, leaning in to see the phone screen. 'Look at her! What a beautiful coat. Sorry Mark.' He caresses his dog's smooth head. 'Yours is beautiful, too.'

'She is gorgeous,' I agree. 'And so are you, Mark. The coat is high maintenance, though. It gets so messy, because she loves mud, and she loves puddles. She's basically Peppa Pig.'

He frowns, confused.

'Who's Peppa Pig?'

*Okay then.* Just another reminder that our lifestyles are galaxies apart. 'Just a cartoon character who likes muddy puddles.'

But he's moved on, taking my phone off me and scrolling through the "Tabby" camera roll. 'Why don't you bring her into work with you? Mark would love some company.'

Um, because one look at his little doggy penis and the jig will be up. Plus the small fact that Daniel's not actually my dog.

'She's, uh, pretty anxious. She doesn't like lots of people. I don't think she'd feel comfortable here,' I say hastily.

'Oh no! Poor little thing. And who's this?'

Brendan points my phone at me, and my worlds collide. On the screen is a photo of my beautiful Tabby, golden and gorgeous last summer, her arms thrown around Daniel's neck, and a huge gap where her adult front teeth are now half-grown.

I stare at the image, feeling sick to my stomach. It's not a rational thought in the slightest, but, aside from the clear practical need to keep her a secret from Brendan, I don't want this existence and my real life to overlap at all. I don't want any of what I'm doing here with him to sully the innocence of my daughter's childhood.

My brain shudders to a halt. 'That's my—um…'

'You alright, love?' he asks. He sounds concerned, which should be a red flag.

'That's my niece,' I supply triumphantly.

'She's cute. So, do you have a sister?'

His dirty grin snaps me out of my panic. I deliver both the side-eye and the barefaced lie that kind of question deserves. 'A brother. Listen, I have to go. We've got Seraph drinks.'

'Jesus Christ, that's a visual I don't need,' he groans, handing me the phone. I snatch it back with relief. 'Every man in the bar must hit on you guys. Where are you going, and what do you guys get up to when you go out on the tiles?'

I stand. 'One, I have no idea because I've never been out with them before, two, it's none of your business where we're going, and three, if I had to guess, I'd say we'll spend most of the time sharing salacious details about our bosses.' I wink at him. 'Have a good weekend. Try to leave some fuel in the tank for me on Monday morning.'

And with that, I sashay out of his office like the brazen ho I now apparently am.

# CHAPTER 25

# Marlowe

Apparently, it's Seraph tradition that a new hire puts her card behind the bar for the first team soirée she attends. Athena has made it clear to me that this is categorically not happening on her watch. She told me that the seraphim all know about my situation and that everyone has agreed to split the tab tonight.

I'm equal parts mortified and relieved. Much as I hate being a charity case, I know the guilt would kill me if I watched these women drink thousands of pounds' worth of champagne and spirits. And it really would be thousands. Athena said the champagne they drink at this place is like seven hundred pounds a bottle for table service.

A bottle!

So yeah. When two bottles of champagne could fund a consultation with a cardiothoracic surgeon, then I'm more than willing to swallow my pride and save my cash. Besides, I'm not going to drink much tonight. I'm exhausted after the week I've had, and there's no way I'm going to risk feeling crappy tomorrow when I get to spend quality time with my little girl.

I get myself across the river and meet Athena in Mayfair before we show up at the bar together. As usual, she looks immaculate in a strappy black dress, her auburn hair styled in glossy waves. She greets me with a tight hug and an aggressively worded warning that she wants and expects a full debrief of absolutely everything that's gone down (pun intended, I'm sure) with Brendan this week. Clearly, she thinks she's above NDAs, and clearly I won't hold back from dishing the dirt to her.

After all, she's even more of a vault than her priest boyfriend.

This place is like an alternate universe. It's on the top floor of a swanky hotel, with huge windows showcasing a three-hundred-and-sixty-degree view of the London cityscape. It's *incredible.* The weather is perfect this evening, and as the sun lowers in the sky, it bathes the beautiful people in a golden glow.

And the people really are beautiful. It's a wealthy, shiny crowd for whom this is a standard Friday night. Confidence rolls off everyone in waves. These are not people who have a problem taking up space. It's no surprise when Athena steers me to the glossiest, noisiest corner of the room, where the seraphim stand by a huge window facing due west. This must be the most sought-after corner of the entire bar. If I survive long enough, the sunset will be spectacular.

Despite the armour of my fabulous Miu Miu, the imposter syndrome kicks in immediately, because these women all look like supermodels who've probably moonlit at the UN and the White House, too. You know the type? Fiercely intelligent. So much panache. So accomplished. The kind of gilded darlings who float through life like it's a lazy river.

I went to school with lots of girls like that, but a glance tells me that these women are in a different league. More worldly. More sophisticated. More competent. I take a moment to drink them in. They're a bunch of gorgeous, glittering birds of paradise, and their sparkling laughter and glamorous looks are definitely drawing attention, but they seem oblivious.

Almost at once, I spot Sophia. She comes towards us, arms outstretched in glee, her smile wide. This woman is ridiculous. She's indecently tanned and absolutely glowing, her long dark hair a shiny mane. She wears her fringe long and feathered so that her brown eyes peek seductively out from underneath it. Her dress is skintight, electric blue, and has her incredible boobs out on a platter.

It's a wonder her boss gets any work done at all. She told me he's in his *sixties*—some old, horny Greek shipping magnate. I can't even imagine. I'm suddenly even more grateful that my dodgy moneymaking scheme comes with an outrageously hot man who serves up outrageously hot orgasms.

'Ladies!' she shouts. 'The guest of honour is here! Let the festivities commence!' I can't tell if she's already drunk or that's just how she is. She's one of those people who are so vivacious that their sobriety level is not always obvious. She lunges forward and throws her arms around both of us, air kissing me on both cheeks before hugging Athena. 'I mean Marlowe, by the way. You shouldn't even be here, you horrible little turncoat.'

'Once a seraph, always a seraph,' Athena replies blithely. 'Even if I'm giving away the goods for free these days.'

Sophia gives a chic European shrug. Her accent is pure Oxbridge, but she's apparently also from a big Greek shipping family. 'Gabe's a lucky fucker, but I'm far more interested in how Brendan Big Dick Sullivan is treating our little ingenue here. Marlowe, prepare to get drunk and spill the beans.'

I laugh. I can't imagine sitting around with these women and casually swapping sexual exploits, or sexploits, as the seraphim apparently term them. Camille has explained that our NDAs purposely exclude our fellow Seraph members so that we have a safe pool of people with whom to be frank—critical in this job—but that doesn't make me any less horrified at the prospect of openly sharing with anyone beyond Athena what Brendan and I have got up to. It's disrespectful to him, for one, and it's far too... complex, I suppose, for me to make light of it. It's still fresh, still raw. Fabulously so, don't get me wrong, but yeah. Nope. No beans will be spilt tonight. Not by me, anyway.

'I'll definitely take a drink,' I tell Sophia now, because she strikes me as the kind of person to relent a little if you throw her a strategic bone.

'Of course you will. Fuck knows, you've earned it this week. Come here, come here. Ladies—I give you our newest seraph, Marlowe.'

I allow her to clamp an arm around me and pull me into the circle, Athena bringing up the rear. There's a chorus of effusive greetings and a generous smattering of smiles so full-wattage I'd swear there were paps around.

'I feel exactly like the new girl at school,' I whisper to Sophia with a shaky smile, but it's true. I remember showing up at Cheltenham Ladies' College on a full scholarship, one of the only girls whose father wasn't rich and either famous or titled. In this moment, I'm right back there.

She doesn't smile back but instead cocks her head and studies me with compassion. 'That may be a younger part being triggered, but that's understandable. We're going to show her that this is your tribe. You're wanted here, and you belong here. Got it?'

Okay then. I have no idea what she's talking about, but I

nod. Even if I couldn't feel less like I belong, I appreciate the sentiment, and I know Sophia and Athena have my back. 'Got it.'

'Marlowe,' Camille says, coming forward with a warm smile. 'You survived! How are you feeling?'

I lean in as she greets me with a kiss on each cheek. 'I'm good. I'm—yeah. It's all good. He's really sweet, he's taken good care of me. The office is lovely. So yeah.' I nod. 'All good, really.' *So articulate, Marlowe.*

She smiles kindly. 'Oh dear. You're a bit dazed still. It's absolutely to be expected. The first few weeks are a *lot.* Aren't they, Bree?'

This is directed at a tall, slender Black woman who's drifted up next to us. She looks like a supermodel. She's in a coral pink halter-neck dress that showcases skin so glossy it doesn't seem real. It's actually shimmering. She's so beautiful it's ridiculous.

'Hi, sweetie,' she says, holding out her hand. 'I'm Bree. We need to get you a drink. And yes, the first week or two can range from the surreal to the downright bonkers. These guys get so overexcited when they get their new toys. It's ridiculous, if you ask me. So if you're still standing and you can still walk, you should take that as a win.'

I laugh at that, because she's nailed the situation perfectly. 'I couldn't really sit down on day two,' I confess, which is probably all the dirt I'm going to dish on Brendan. Bree throws back her head and laughs, and I admire the huge diamonds flashing in her ears, the delicate column of her neck.

'I have a feeling I'm going to regret knowing so many sordid details about my future brother-in-law,' Athena says with a groan, shoving a goldfish-bowl-sized glass of rosé into my hands. 'Relax, darling, I put some Pellegrino in it.'

'Thanks,' I tell her. Bree gives her a hug that's clearly genuine and supremely elegant at the same time.

'Did you get engaged?' Bree asks, and Athena gives her trademark dismissive face.

'Nah. But we both know it's going to happen.'

'Ahhh,' everyone choruses.

'Come over to the window,' Sophia urges me. 'This view is spectacular.'

'When did you get in?' I ask her as we approach the edge of the seating area. From what she's told me, she's based in Athens with her boss, but he also spends a lot of time treating the Med as his personal playground. She definitely didn't get that tan in London, that's for sure.

'A couple of hours ago. Thad lent me his jet. The flight was fine, the traffic from Luton was a disaster.' She shudders, and I marvel at the insouciance that comes with a lifestyle where hopping around Europe by jet is as normal as jumping on the Tube.

'He loves you,' Athena coos, and Sophia laughs.

'He loves my body. It really is a fab gig.' She stretches. She's like a cat, so comfortable in her own skin and so sensual. They all are, actually. 'Think it might be coming to a close, though. Oh, hey Tal.'

She breaks off as another gorgeous woman joins us. Like Sophia, she has Mediterranean looks, with dark brown hair and olive skin, but it's her eyes that are striking. They're a pale green-grey, and they're startlingly beautiful against her skin.

'Sorry to interrupt. I had to come say hi. Aren't you gorgeous?! Look at that dress. I'm Talia, by the way.'

'Marlowe,' I say. I startle as she pulls me into a giant hug. Wow, she smells incredible. Athena swipes my wineglass from me just in time. She's staring at Sophia.

'What do you mean, Soph?'

Sophia sighs, and Athena hands me back my glass. 'He's retiring, and his wife wants him to stop jetting around and settle on the estate. Their eldest son is expecting his first kid—it's a big deal.'

'Wow,' Athena says. 'How do you feel about that?'

Sophia shrugs. 'I mean, it always had an expiration date. Either he was going to keel over and die from Viagra overload, or his wife was going to put her foot down. It's not a huge surprise.'

I stifle a giggle. Apparently, Sophia's boss treats her more like a full-on mistress than an assistant, and she seems fine with it. To be fair, her lifestyle is insane, from what I know.

'You can have my boss,' Talia says through gritted teeth. 'I'm washing my hands of him.'

Another giggle threatens to break free. I could listen to these women all evening. The men they're discussing are presumably some of the wealthiest, most powerful men in Europe, but they're talking about them as if they're annoying kids.

'What's he done now?' Athena asks. To me, she says, 'Talia's boss, Ethan, is very hot and a total wanker. He has a face like a slapped arse most of the time.'

'Oh no,' I say. I may still be trying to figure Brendan out, but for the most part, he seems to be a good guy. A little immature, maybe, but he's very good-natured. It must be rough to have to manage the moods of someone with a difficult personality, especially when you have to be intimate with him.

'It's just death by a thousand cuts, you know?' Talia takes a big slug of the neat amber liquid in her tumbler, and I realise she's already pretty drunk. 'To be honest, I gave him my notice this afternoon. That's why I'm getting hammered tonight.' She brandishes her drink.

'Oh, darling,' Athena says. 'I'm sorry. That's seriously shit. What the fuck is his problem?'

'Ugh, he has so much baggage, I don't even know where to

start. But I'm sick of him taking it out on me. He yells at me all the time, and it's just not worth it. I'm sick of crying in the loos every day. The cleaning lady had to comfort me the other day. He's an aggressive dickhead and he needs to find a way to work through those anger issues instead of bullying his assistant.'

'Damn fucking right he does,' Sophia seethes. 'Was he aggressive in bed?'

Talia pouts into her glass. 'That's the worst bit. Yes he was, and it was fucking excellent. I'll miss all the angry sex. Fighting was definitely our foreplay, and it was the only part of the whole bloody job I actually enjoyed.'

I frown. I'm glad she enjoyed it, but that's not really my style. Thrashing it out with Brendan on the padel court this week was about as belligerent as I like my foreplay to be.

'Hmm, interesting.' Sophia appears to be turning over this new information. 'I could stand up to him. I'd fucking kill him with my cheeriness. But if that failed, I'd take every inch of fat, angry dick he could throw at me.'

I can't help it. I burst out laughing. These guys are absolutely hilarious, though I can already see how important it is to be able to laugh about this job.

'You'd wipe the floor with him,' Bree tells Sophia. She's been watching the interaction with silent focus. 'You should talk to Camille and get her to hook you up, babes. And you, Tal, should go find a nice, good-natured man who worships the ground you walk on. God knows, you deserve it after putting up with that shit.'

As the sun sets, Sophia, Athena and I drift toward a quieter corner of the bar, leaving the rest of the seraphim debating the merits of various investment opportunities with the ferocity—and, it seems, expertise—of Wall Street traders. Sophia secures us a small booth partially hidden behind a cascading crystal installation that catches the fading light and transforms it into prismatic fragments across our faces.

'Honestly. How are you finding it?' Soph—she's told me to call her that—asks. 'Fun? Hot? Creepy? Confronting? Terrifying? All of the above?'

I take a sip of wine as I consider my answer. 'Definitely all of the above.'

Sophia leans in, her dark eyes sparkling with the promise of salacious gossip as she swirls her martini. She's been knocking them back since I got here, but I still can't tell if she's hammered or just being herself. 'First week with the infamous Brendan Sullivan. Give us the uncensored version. I bet he put a lot of noses out of joint by making a beeline for you.'

I hesitate, glancing at Athena, who responds with a knowing smile. 'It's just us, Marls. Safe space.'

'I don't even know where to start,' I admit, taking a fortifying sip of my drink. 'It's been... intense.'

'Details, darling. We need details,' Sophia purrs. 'Is he as demanding as Athena said he'd be? I don't know the man from Adam, so your secrets are safe with me.'

I feel my cheeks heat. I'm sure that, for most women in their twenties, dissecting their sex lives over cocktails is totally standard, but I missed that stage entirely. I couldn't even tell my friends at uni about Joe—not till he knocked me up and the cat was out of the bag, anyway. So this feels downright bizarre, even if these women are professionals when it comes to shagging. 'He's... thorough.'

Athena laughs. 'Look at you blushing! You weren't this coy when you called me after your interview.'

'That was different,' I protest. 'That was just us.'

'And this is just us, plus Soph, who has literally done things that would make a porn star blush,' Athena counters.

Soph shrugs. 'Facts. But seriously, how are you holding up? I feel responsible for your wellbeing given I was the one who put the idea in your head in the first place.'

I stare into my glass, finding the right words. 'Physically? I'm sore in places I forgot existed. Emotionally? I swing between feeling like I've hit the jackpot and feeling completely out of my depth. I mean, it's not Brendan. He's gorgeous. It's no hardship to let him do whatever he wants, you know? It's just the whole... thing. It's completely surreal.'

'Welcome to the club,' Sophia says, her voice softening. 'That pendulum swing never fully goes away, but it does slow down. Sometimes the transactional aspect makes you question everything about yourself, and sometimes you eat it the fuck up. Am I right?'

'So true,' Athena observes.

'What I wasn't prepared for,' I confess, 'was how much I'd... enjoy it.' I've been wrestling with this since my interview, but the admission feels even more shameful to say aloud.

Athena reaches for my hand. 'You think we don't all feel that? That weird guilt when you realise you're getting off on something that should be a transaction? But the straight-up exchange of sex for money gets confusing when you get money *and* orgasms into the bargain.'

'Exactly!' I'm relieved these seasoned professionals understand. 'And then his assistant Elaine was telling me stories about him—how he paid for some intern's mother's cancer treatment, and then in the next breath, how he's terrible to working mothers.'

I don't add the part about how terrified that makes me

feel. Soph planted this genius seed in my head. Athena lobbied all the relevant parties to bend the rules and make it happen. The ball's in my court now. It's up to me to overachieve on all fronts so that Brendan doesn't get tired of me or irritated with me.

I can't give the guy any rope to hang me with.

Soph leans back, crossing her legs elegantly. 'Men like Brendan are walking contradictions. That's what makes them interesting. Thad once flew a specialist from Johns Hopkins to Montenegro because his chef's daughter had a rare condition. Then the next day, he fired his PA for taking too many bathroom breaks. They're honestly all like mercurial toddlers.'

'How do you reconcile that?' I ask.

'You don't,' Athena says simply. 'You use it. The contradictions mean there's a gap between who they are and who they want to be. That gap is your leverage.'

I blink at her. 'Holy shit, that's... extremely philosophical.'

'What did you think we were, just pretty faces who give great head?' Soph laughs, the sound rich and genuine. 'This job is psychological warfare disguised as world-class blow jobs.'

'I would never for a single second underestimate anyone here,' I tell her. 'You women are terrifyingly smart. And I'm used to Athena blowing my mind. Believe me, after a decade and a half of friendship, you get used to it.'

'Speaking of psychological warfare,' Athena interjects, 'how are you handling the office dynamic? That has to be trickier than the bedroom stuff.'

I think about the women in reception, the man who Brendan told me ogled me, and how he reacted. 'Everyone watches him, so we have to be careful. All the guys look up to him and the women just want to jump him. It's ridiculous. And I want to make friends, which means I can't be seen as having any special favour with him, but I also feel quite isolated, especially because I'm always watching what I'm saying, how I'm interacting with Brendan publicly... It's exhausting trying to figure out the politics while also... you know.'

'While also timing your boss's orgasms around his meeting schedule?' Soph supplies helpfully. 'Been there. Get a planner specifically for that. It's not the sexiest thing, but he'll be counting on you to carve out sexy time for him. You'll need some good code names to get that into the shared calendar.'

'Oh my God, oh my God, *so* much potential.' Athena claps her hands briskly. 'Right. Let's see. Hands-on Training? Deep Dive Analysis?'

She says *Deep Dive* in a low, pervy voice. I snort, and Soph cackles loudly.

'Fucking amazing. How about Mindfulness Monday? Tension Release Tuesday? Feel-Good Friday? Oooh. This is so much fun.'

'Elaine will think Brendan's gone full yogi,' I say between giggles.

'I bet he could make downward dogs very fucking dirty,' Soph muses. 'Mmm, delicious.'

'You've been fucking an old man for too long,' Athena tells her. 'Maybe you should take Tal up on her offer. Angry sex is better than old-man sex.'

'Facts.' Soph holds her once-again-empty martini glass up in a salute.

We all burst into laughter, and for the first time all week, I feel the tension in my shoulders release.

'Seriously though,' Sophia continues when our laughter subsides, 'the trick is to remember that you're the asset here. Not just your body—your entire skillset. These men could fuck anyone. They're paying for the whole package—and that's *you*. Also, remember he's been mooning over you for weeks and weeks.'

'Exactly,' Athena agrees. 'You didn't get selected because

you're just a pretty face, M. You got selected because you're brilliant, capable, and yes, gorgeous. Own all of it.'

I take another sip, contemplating. 'I guess I've been thinking of this as something happening to me, not something I'm actively choosing.'

'And that,' Soph says, tapping a perfect red nail against my glass, 'is the difference between being a victim and being a seraph. These men may think they own us. God bless them, they don't know how wrong they are.'

Athena's eyes meet mine. I know this expression. It's her stern, bossy, I-love-you expression. 'You're doing this for Tabby, we know that. But don't let that be an excuse to disconnect from your power. You chose this path because you're brave enough to do whatever it takes for her. That's strength, not shame.'

I feel something shift inside me—a subtle realignment. 'I never thought of it that way.'

'Well, start,' Sophia says firmly. 'Because the minute you own this, Brendan will sense it. And trust me, nothing gets a man like him hotter than a woman who knows her worth. He may like it when you submit, but that's because he knows how meaningful that submission is. How *valuable*.'

Athena raises her glass. 'To knowing our worth.'

As we clink our drinks together, I catch a glimpse of our reflection in the mirrored wall across from us—three glamorous women with knowing smiles and fierce eyes. For the first time since signing up as a Seraph, I don't think of myself as an imposter among them.

I may even allow myself to believe I belong.

'Have you had any more ideas about how you're going to get leave to take Tabs to the US?' Athena asks.

'I've pretty much thought about nothing else. It just goes around and around in my head.'

'Have you booked the operation yet?' Soph asks. Her tone

is far gentler than any she's used so far this evening, and I can sense her compassion from here. But she doesn't need to go gently on me, because this is a good thing. Having to nail both the logistics and the duplicity around sneaking off to save my daughter's life is what I'd call a high-quality problem.

I nod. 'It's booked in for the first week of August. That's the absolute earliest I can do it after this month's pay cheque drops.'

Soph grimaces. 'Three weeks from now? Okay, so you need to get your ducks in a row with Brendan quick-smart.'

'I know. I need to do it this week. My current plan is to tell him a family member needs a procedure and to ask him for the time off.'

'I have a far better plan,' Athena says crisply. 'It came to me the other day. Tell him you've been called up for jury duty. It's by far the most bulletproof option. He could be a real pain in the arse if you ask for time off for a family member, but if you say you've been called up to do your civic duty, he'll legally have to agree to it.'

I stare at her. Trust Athena to come up with the most effective lie. 'That feels so dishonest, though. And can't you get out of jury duty?'

She nearly spits out her drink. 'Darling, you've lied through your teeth since you applied for this job. What's one more lie? The key is that it preserves your credibility and your job for afterwards. Just tell him you've already escalated it and they won't waive it. This way, you save face *and* you get the time off without him being able to do anything about it.'

She's right, of course. But my mind is still whirring, turning over potential obstacles. 'Wouldn't he ask to see a copy of the summons?'

She shrugs. 'Honestly, I can't imagine he'd bother. He trusts you, so why would he question what you tell him?'

Ouch. She's right—he does trust me. Which is why the

idea of abusing that trust even further is so painful. That said, I've known this entire time that I'll need to come up with a plausible reason to secure two weeks off from a brand-new, very highly paid job.

I'm already going to hell. One more lie won't make any difference. And if it gets me on that plane with Tabs, it'll be worth it.

# Brendan

Marlowe has proven to be a most excellent hire these past couple of weeks. Not only does her beauty strike me just as much each day as it did at that first meeting when I crashed and burned, but she's quickly proving herself to be smart, proactive and competent as an assistant and genuinely excellent company as a human being.

I've very much enjoyed putting her through her paces. We've even managed to sneak out to a nearby hotel for a couple of lunchtime quickies where we can really let loose. Marlowe has put those sessions in my calendar as *Contract Fulfilment Assessments,* which made me chuckle. I've tried to coax her out for post-work drinks a couple of times, but she's really dug her heels in around any after-hours socialising. It pisses me off, but I have no choice but to respect her decisions.

What I haven't done yet, though, is anything too kinky. I haven't needed to, if I'm honest. I'm as horny as a schoolboy just being around her. As someone who likes my sex the dirtier the better, I've been remarkably slow to add in bells and whistles. The simple knowledge that she's sitting outside my office and can be summoned *into* my office to suck my dick at any point is kryptonite enough.

Today, I plan to ramp things up a notch. I made it clear in my questionnaire and in that first audition with Marlowe that I intend to show her off and work her hard. I intend to get full use out of my stunning little fuck toy, and I plan to kick things off this afternoon.

I told her yesterday to make sure she came in today wearing the black dress with a flared skirt and the very special underwear I'd bought her: namely some black lace, crotchless panties and the matching lace bra whose cups are held in place by a tiny fastener. When the fasteners are undone, the centre panels of the lace cups hang down, exposing her breasts.

I really enjoyed helping her try that lingerie set on last week.

After lunch, I had her come and perch on my desk while I indulged in a little leisurely fingering to ensure that she was indeed wearing the panties.

She certainly fucking was.

Aside from that, I haven't touched her.

I can tell she's in a state of suspense.

I can tell she's wondering when I'll make my move.

She'll find out soon enough.

Yan drives us across the river, into the City. I told Marlowe that we were meeting with the head of The Kingsley Group, a global luxury hotel chain that contracts Sullivan Construction for all their London hotels. I haven't, however, suggested that this is anything other than a regular business meeting.

Until now.

I'm on a call with my strategy team about the upcoming International Green Building Summit. It's a mouthful, but it's also a massive deal: a gathering of the world's top developers, government officials, and sustainability leaders to address the environmental responsibilities of this industry. This year London is hosting it and Sullivan is being recognised for the carbon-neutral construction techniques it's pioneered.

The keynote speaker, you may ask?

Yours truly.

It takes a lot to get me excited about a conference, but this one checks all the boxes. It's fucking gold when it comes to cementing (see what I did there?) Sullivan Construction as a leader in sustainable luxury construction. It's a huge validation for me and a *major fuck you* to everyone who's ever written me off as the playboy Sullivan brother. And, of course, the financial opportunities are sky high. If I get this speech right, we could hit the jackpot on multiple ten- and eleven-figure contracts from governments and developers worldwide.

Yep, this is the big leagues, baby.

That said, I can't write schmoozy speeches for shit, so my strategy and PR teams are working endlessly on my behalf to craft the perfect keynote. Words like "rhetoric" and other wanky terms are being bandied about far too much for my liking. I'm chiming in occasionally with my opinions, my camera turned off so I can zone out without being busted, and growing sufficiently bored out of my brain that I seek out some light in-car entertainment.

We're about ten minutes away from the Kingsley Group's headquarters near the Bank of England. Plenty of time to have some fun. I slide the privacy screen up, separating us from Yan, and flick the intercom off.

'Open your legs,' I mouth at Marlowe. Her jaw drops in surprise, and I nod curtly to show her I'm serious. She does as I ask, widening her legs beneath the roomy skirt of her dress. I push the fabric upwards and run my fingertips along her thigh until I find the lovely, exposed spot I've been searching for. It's so warm and soft and wet. So inviting, I could get on my knees right here and eat her.

But I won't.

I'll make us both wait.

I mute myself for a second.

'You'll have to be a very good girl when we get into this meeting,' I whisper, pushing two fingers inside her. Her mouth makes an O shape as she takes me. It makes me want to grin, but I don't. I want her to get the Stern Brendan experience. Because she really is *such* a good girl. 'And you'll have to be very quiet now,' I continue, holding my phone up so she can see me unmute myself.

For the next few minutes, I toy with a squirming Marlowe as I pretend to give a shit about what my project managers are saying. Really, my focus is on getting to Kingsley.

That's when the real fun will start.

This is all a test.

That's what I tell myself.

It's a test to see if my very expensive new EA with benefits can handle the more extreme parts of her job. A test to see if she's willing to earn the salary that makes her the most well-compensated person at my company, myself and our Finance Director aside.

It's a test to see if she *enjoys* it. To see how much she can handle. Just how filthy she's capable of being.

It's not a case of me being a horny, entitled dickhead.

Not entirely, anyway.

# MARLOWE

These offices are as opulent, as stylish, as you'd expect for the headquarters of a seriously high-end hotel group. I've never been in a Kingsley hotel, not even to have a drink, but I follow them on Instagram and I can confirm that their feed makes me drool.

As my diabolical boss leads me into the sleek lift, I'm still worked up from the way he edged me on the way here. I swear, this man is frustrating. He orders me to wear the most porno set of underwear he bought me, he ignores me all morning, and only on the way to meet one of his most important clients does he start to play. Ugh! I could cheerfully strangle him.

'What's the agenda for the meeting?' I ask him, attempting to pull myself together. He's cool as a cucumber except for the hand in his pocket fiddling with what I now know is a fidget toy.

'Just a general catch-up.' He seems evasive, but then he winks at me. 'Nothing too serious.'

'Got it.'

The lift doors open and Brendan ushers me down a wide corridor whose walls are lined with a taupe-coloured linen. At the end of the corridor, a man stands perfectly still, his hands in his pockets. It looks like he's waiting for us. As we approach, I can see that his hair is somewhere in the dark blond slash light brown region, swept back from his face. He's tall and lean—less bulky than Brendan—and he doesn't crack a smile as we stop before him, even though I'm smiling at him in a way that's more jittery than anything else.

His lack of smile is unnerving.

*He's* unnerving.

'Hiya, mate,' Brendan says easily.

'Bren. Good to see you.' He sounds friendlier than he looks, although his face seems to soften a little as he shakes

Brendan's hand. Up close, his eyes are an astonishing colour—cold and light grey and strangely beautiful—but it's his impassivity that stands out the most.

'This is my new EA, Marlowe,' Brendan tells him. 'Marlowe, meet my good friend Ethan Kingsley.'

'Marlowe.' He turns those eyes on me as he takes my hand. 'It's a pleasure.' I don't miss the lightning speed with which his gaze darts down my body and back up. I hope he can't tell that I was halfway to orgasm about three minutes ago.

'How do you do?' I ask, but he doesn't grace it with a response. Instead, he drops my hand and gestures to us to go through to the room beside him.

The space is clearly a meeting room, but it has all the Insta-worthy opulence of the suites on Kingsley's feed. The walls in here are also linen-lined, but in a dark steel grey that makes it feel atmospheric, despite the brightness of the day outside. There's a big conference table on one side, a glossy brass bar cart that looks remarkably well stocked, and two white sofas facing each other over a glass coffee table. Several small console tables line the walls, each bearing a vase of beautiful pink-and-white orchids. It isn't necessarily any fancier than Brendan's meeting rooms, but it feels far less corporate.

We take a seat, Brendan and I on one sofa and Ethan sitting opposite us. He opens a big bottle of sparkling water and pours us all a glass.

'So,' Brendan says, sitting back and crossing one ankle over his opposite knee, 'how are you holding up since Talia walked out?'

I stiffen. I suddenly realise I know exactly who this guy is, and I have no idea how I should react. He's the guy Talia was talking about at the Seraph drinks last weekend. The one she said she'd quit on because he was so mean to her. The one Soph is considering as her next boss.

Holy crap.

I mean, he's hot. Seriously hot. And he doesn't look like he has a temper. To be honest, he looks cold as steel. But I can imagine that if he pulled that stick out of his arse and let all the emotions he doesn't show out, it could get pretty intense. He's intense enough right now.

But I'm not supposed to know any of this. And surely these guys have NDAs? They can't discuss their Seraph employee.

Can they?

In the split second that it takes for me to panic, Ethan produces an expression somewhere between impassive and unimpressed. 'Not ideal. I've got someone from the admin pool filling in, but she's not...' He trails off.

'Yeah,' Brendan says. 'That's rough.' He turns to me. 'Ethan had a Seraph EA working for him. Talia. Do you know her?'

My eyes dart in a panic to Ethan, then to Brendan. 'Yes.' I clear my throat. 'I, um, met her at drinks last week.'

Brendan touches my shoulder. 'It's okay, love. He knows exactly who you are and what you do for me. Turns out I was the last fucker in London to cotton onto the Seraph thing.'

Oh my *God*. This is excruciating. So far, I've been in my own little bubble with Brendan. I knew there would come a time when someone else would stumble on the truth, but I didn't expect to be blindsided like this in a business meeting. It's beyond horrifying to realise that this stranger knows Brendan is fucking me, even if he's been doing the same with Talia.

I force myself to look at Ethan. He's settled back on his sofa, nursing his sparkling water as he openly assesses me.

'You're very beautiful.' There's no inflection in his voice when he says it. None at all. Somehow, his statement of fact feels more intense, more ominous, than if he gushed.

'I—thank you?'

Brendan slides his arm around my back so his hand hangs over my shoulder in a way that feels proprietary. 'Poor Ethan. He's got no one to fuck because he's such a grumpy bastard. Meanwhile, I really like watching and I have a sexy-as-fuck assistant who explicitly agreed to being shared in her questionnaire. If that doesn't scream *serendipity*, I don't know what does.'

My mouth goes instantly dry. My palms break out in pinpricks of sweat, and I press them to my fabric-covered thighs. I jerk my head around to see if he's being serious, and whatever is on my face makes him laugh.

*Shared.*

Oh my holy fucking Christ alive.

'So sweet,' he croons. 'You know the innocent routine really does it for me, don't you, love? You're really not helping yourself when you look at me like that.'

I swallow, beseeching him with my eyes to read my mind and get us the fuck out of here. Besides the fact that I don't know Ethan from Adam, outnumbered is outnumbered. And it's three o'clock in the afternoon, for crying out loud!

'If you have something to say, say it now,' Brendan tells me with a little nod, and I know he's giving me an out.

*Stop.*

I could say it right now and all this would go away. We could walk out of here and I'd never have to see this Ethan guy again. I could excuse myself from any future meetings with him.

But it's not fair. Because Brendan is correct. I did tick the "group activities" box on that questionnaire. I knew Brendan was into kinky shit, into watching, and I still ticked it with all the desperation of a mother who'll do anything to get in the door. Land the job. Collect the sign-on bonus.

And now it's time for me to come up with the goods. If there's anything that would make me feel even worse about selling myself, body and soul, to Brendan, it would be fucking him over. I wouldn't be able to live with myself if I didn't at least give him what he's paying for.

Besides—and it's a very big *besides*—he might let me off the hook and take me back to the office if I safed out, but it would be a red flag to him. The first time he tries to push the envelope, I bail. I need this job for at least another month, and I told myself I'd do anything necessary to ensure Brendan held onto me.

Falling at the first hurdle is not an option, not when I'm so close to funding Tabby's operation. Nor is bailing as soon as the going gets tough.

I look at Brendan's blue eyes, and I realise I know something else to be true. No matter how much he's planning on pushing me outside of my comfort zone, I trust him.

I really do.

So I give him my answer.

'I'm good.'

# CHAPTER 27

# Marlowe

'Have you ever had two men use you before?' Ethan asks in an arrogantly casual monotone.

He's basically asking me if I've ever had a threesome, so I'm unclear as to why his turn of phrase is so charged.

I drag my gaze to him. 'No. Never.'

He closes his eyes briefly as if he can't handle this information.

'God,' Brendan whispers beside me. 'This is going to be so fucking good. You'll fucking adore it, love. I know you will.'

I admire his confidence. I wish I shared it. But I turn back to him and give him what I hope is an encouraging smile. 'I'm sure I will,' I lie.

'We'll tell you everything you need to do,' he tells me. Those big blue eyes are softening with desire, and I'm struck all over again by how ridiculously, disgustingly attractive he is. 'Just give yourself over to us. The more you surrender to it, the hotter it'll be for everyone. Understand?'

I nod.

'Say it.'

'I understand.'

'Good girl. Now stand up.'

I stand. I can't help but notice that Ethan's eyes are fixed on me. They haven't left me at all. Knowing that I've been ambushed, that the guys have set this whole thing up, gives his intensity a whole new meaning, and a tiny part of me—my inner whore, I suppose—feels a thrill to be the sole focus of these two obscenely powerful, attractive alpha males.

I stand, and Brendan rises with me. My hair is tied back today, its style a world away from Old Marlowe. Gone are the messy, easy buns and in their place is a glossy ponytail. I secured the ponytail before carefully curling my hair in sections and back-combing it a little so it's all bouncy and elegant.

He starts to undo the zip that runs down the back of the dress. I'm facing Ethan, who can't see anything interesting just yet. Still, he's spread his legs wide and is leaning forward, elbows resting on his knees and fingers interlaced and facial expression, if not quite avid, then laser-focused. His pale blue shirt is as crisp and crease-free as if he's just put it on, the folds in his navy suit trousers razor-sharp, and his effortless polish throws into sharper focus the fact that these two plan to destroy me.

'I got her to wear her best lingerie for you, mate,' Brendan says conversationally. '*And* I warmed her up in the car, so you can thank me later.'

The zip is fully open, and he slides the feminine black dress I'm wearing off my shoulders so the slinky fabric falls down my arms, the front of the dress dropping to my waist.

Oh my God. My boss is undressing me, and my boobs are now on display for this random guy in lingerie that screams *high-class hooker.* I'm well aware that my nipples are still taut from Brendan's ministrations to my pussy in the car, and that Ethan can likely see them through the lace.

'Believe me, I will,' he mutters. 'Now, take it off. Take it all off.'

Brendan pushes my dress down over my hips and the expensive fabric falls heavily to the ground with a swoosh. I stand, frozen, for a second in only my heels and my lingerie, the dress pooled around my ankles and the air conditioning cool on my skin.

'Very good,' Ethan says, his eyes glued to the spot where the black lace of my panties gives way to a scalloped edge and then the bare flesh of my pussy.

Brendan kneads my bottom with his hands. 'Get rid of the dress, love,' he reminds me gently.

I start. 'Oh—of course.' I step out of it and push it to one side with my stiletto.

'We're going to tell you exactly what to do, and you're going to do it,' Brendan says. 'So you just clear your mind and let us take charge. Okay?'

'Okay.' That does actually sound like a plan. I can let them use me, but if they wanted me to choreograph something, they'd be sorely disappointed. I may be a trained performer, but I have *never* performed like this.

'Good girl.' He sits down heavily behind me, which surprises me. 'Open your legs.'

I widen my stance. I have no idea what to do with my hands, so I let my arms hang to the sides, but I'm pretty sure neither of these guys are focused on my hand movements right now.

He brackets my waist with hands, his grip strong. 'Now come and sit on my lap.'

I lower myself into a seated position. The wool of his trousers feels somehow forbidden against my bare skin. Ethan collapses back on the sofa and spreads his arms out along its back. There's something arrogantly expectant about the pose —it suggests he sees a lap dance or a blow job in his near future—but the deep sigh he lets out tells me he's more agitated than he's letting on.

Brendan, on the other hand, seems in his element. I know from his questionnaire that he's a voyeur, and all my experience of him tells me he likes to show off, too.

'Right,' he says, 'I want those legs even wider. Hook them around the outside of my knees.'

I take a deep breath and do as he says, stepping each foot wider. He widens his legs too so that I'm straddling him. Which, of course, means that Ethan now has the money shot.

'Can you see?' Brendan asks him.

'Indeed I can.' Ethan's voice is low. Gruff. His eyes flicker back up to my face before returning to my pussy, which is on a platter for him. My skin heats with mortification and shame and something else, something darker and far less predictable.

'Does she look nice and wet?'

'She does, yeah. She really fucking does.'

'Let's see, shall we?' Brendan takes one hand off my waist and slides it around to my front so he can finger me in front of his friend, and oh my God, the shame of it. The shame of being played with like a little toy, of wearing this kinky lingerie that gives him full access to his fuck doll, of my boss fingering me *in front of his friend who I've only just met.*

But that's not the worst part. The worst part is that I'm wet. Seriously wet. Wet enough that it's actually audible when Brendan's skilful fingers slide over my still-swollen clit and push inside me. I'm so slick. I know it, and so do they.

Ethan is holding himself still, breathing slowly and steadily like it's the only thing tethering him to reality. His eyes haven't left the spot where Brendan is breaching my body.

Brendan pulls his fingers out, and I let out a completely involuntary whimper of distress.

'Such a greedy, needy little thing,' he tells me. 'You're going to come in front of both of us, aren't you? So fucking filthy. Shame you're not into anal, but we can still plug your other two holes with our big dicks. How does that sound?'

Fuck, it's going to happen, and the hideous, awful, unthinkable part is that it doesn't sound hideous or awful or unthinkable. It sounds hot. It sounds like I'm a lucky bitch who's going to get well and truly seen to by two gorgeous, dirty men. And it also sounds like I'm a total whore, because it's taken me approximately thirty seconds of clit action from my boss to go from *I'm terrified* to *give it to me now.*

I make myself respond to Brendan, because vocalising this stuff is still one of the hardest parts for me, even after three weeks on the job with Mr Dirty Talk. 'Um, yes please.'

He groans and grinds against me. He's fully hard now, his dick straining against the fabric of his trousers and pressing into my lower back.

'That's my girl. Ethan, you want to come and do the honours?' To demonstrate his meaning, he slides both hands up my sides and cups my breasts. My nipples tingle and strain.

'Why not?' Ethan pushes himself off the sofa and comes to stand in front of me or, more accurately, to tower over me. I raise my face to his. Fuck he's tall.

'They open,' Brendan tells him. 'See the buttons?' He slides his hands back down to my waist.

'Yes, I certainly do,' Ethan says. He looks down at me. He's so different from Brendan, who's like a very, very dirty golden retriever. This guy is freezing cold. Intensity absolutely radiates from him. He and Sophia would be fire and ice together if she deigned to work for him.

More pressingly, his dick is at face height and practically punching a hole in those nice trousers. He cups my breasts hard, thumbs dragging over my nipples. Fucking hell. 'Here's what's going to happen. Let's get you a little more warmed up, then you can suck my dick and Brendan here can watch, and then he's going to fuck you while you finish me off.'

Oh my God oh my God oh my God. I don't know what I feel, or what I should feel, but every word is like a shot of a million emotions.

'Okay,' I say in a shaky voice.

'It wasn't a question,' he snaps, and his dismissively arrogant tone sends another wave of desire and self-disgust rolling over me.

*It wasn't a question.*

*Oh Jesus.*

He makes brisk work of the tiny fasteners at the top of each bra cup and lays the lace down with something approaching reverence, exposing my breasts.

'Perfect,' he says with an approving exhale, and it's as if the sun has come out after a hailstorm.

'Isn't she?' Brendan's fingers flex on my waist before smoothing over my hips.

'Yeah.' Ethan sinks to his knees in front of me, but it couldn't be less deferential. I know he just wants a closer look. I hold my breath as he takes one nipple and plucks at it before he reaches down and slides a couple of fingers over my clit and through my soaking flesh.

Oh God, that feels so good.

'Jesus,' he remarks, like my wetness has shocked him. He slides his fingers inside me and glances downwards. 'Fuck, I've missed this,' he groans.

Behind me, Brendan sniggers. 'It's been a week, mate.'

'And your point is?' He twists his fingers inside me and watches my expression. Our faces are so close, his eyes a silver ring around endless pupil. I'm not expecting him to kiss me, not at all, but he leans in and tugs my bottom lip briefly, sharply, between his teeth. Then he's bending his head to my breast and sucking, hard.

The soft, hungry pull of his mouth against my nipple is a shock that sends its waves right to my core. I gasp and arch into the sensation as his fingers twist and crook inside me.

'Brendan, take her other tit,' he gasps against my skin before diving back in.

'Fuck, yes,' Brendan sighs. 'Let's make her come like this first.'

He finds my free breast and begins to tug at my nipple. The stimulation of these three points, not to mention the fact of being trapped between these two men, played with for their own edification, is so fucking hot I can't breathe.

Ethan starts to finger-fuck me harder. His mouth is still glued to my nipple, and his hair smells of very nice, very expensive, very manly product. Or maybe it's just him. He smells amazing. Behind me, Brendan's bulk is reassuringly solid, his body heat radiating off him and warming me in this too-cold room.

'If you want to please us, love, you won't hold back,' he urges me. 'Just fucking let yourself fall apart.'

'Okay,' I manage. I'm honestly holding on for dear life here. I don't know which way is up. But then Ethan applies his thumb to my slippery clit and I practically shoot off Brendan's lap. His strokes are strong, rough, even, and the heat builds further within me.

There's something so unashamedly primal about this, about hearing nothing but the ragged, desperate sounds of our breaths as they work my body. Pinned as I am between the two of them, with Brendan's thick thighs acting as stirrups, my only outlet for the building tension is my voice, and I allow myself to make the noises I'm so dying to make.

'That's it,' Brendan croons. 'You love it, don't you? Such a beautiful, golden little princess when we're in the office, and yet you'll let two men touch you like this. It's fucking filthy.

How are his fingers, hmm? Do they feel tight? Are they stretching you nicely for my cock?'

It's his words, and the thought of what's to come, that does it. I drink up every last drop of this feeling, of their fingers and Ethan's mouth on me. I douse myself liberally in the shame of it all and I let Brendan's dirty talk set me alight.

# CHAPTER 28

# *Brendan*

I'm so fucking jealous of Kingsley's view right now.

Seriously, I don't know why I thought it would be a good idea to put Marls on my lap while he got to do all the good stuff to her.

Except I do know.

I wanted to show off. To come over here and taunt him, show him how stunning my new fuck toy is, rub his nose in it and then waltz off with her afterwards. I don't know why I'm like this, but I've been like this since I was a kid. When you're used to being the disappointment, to being outdone by your siblings, you become overly fixated on finding gimmicks, external trophies, that will allow you to shine. To dazzle.

I'm a modern-day Bishop George Berkeley, except the Brendan Sullivan school of philosophy goes like this:

If I bag myself the hottest EA of all time and I get to fuck her, does it count unless at least one of my disgustingly competitive friends gets to see exactly what's so great about her?

Other examples of this great philosophical question include everything from my cars and boats to my golf swing and my mogul skiing. It's an endless, shameless quest for vali-dation. Praise. Envy. It's one-upmanship, and I'm not proud of it, but I still fucking love it, and it's that knowledge that stops me from going nuclear because *my* beautiful assistant is writhing on my lap, coming all over Ethan fucking Kingsley's fingers.

Even if I feel like a little boy who agreed to share his toy and regrets it instantly.

I want to stomp my feet.

*He's playing with* my *toy and I want it back.*

*Her* back, I mean.

But, in about an hour, I'll get to walk out of here with her, and he'll be left to speculate what it is about his undesirable personality that has his being deserted by wives and EAs and PAs, left, right and centre.

So yeah. I'm showing off. I'm using Marlowe as a flex while also spinning out that it's not my fingers inside her *and* also loving the fact that I'm privy to this moment between two other people, that it's my dick she's grinding against and my legs she's straddling and my nose in her hair as I fondle her nipple for dear life.

It's my own private 3D porno, and all this FOMO, this jealousy, this frustration, will be worth it in a second when she's sucking Kingsley off and I'm pushing deep inside her.

This orgasm is a strong one; I know her well enough now to be able to tell. I can't imagine Kingsley is *that* fucking good with his hands, so it must have been this scenario that's done it for her. All of which bodes well for our future working rela-tionship, because I have so many plans for this woman.

I kiss her hair, her neck, as she comes down, firstly because Kingsley wouldn't recognise aftercare if it punched him in the face, and secondly because I am very proud and very turned on right now.

'That was amazing,' I tell her, smoothing my hands down

her arms. 'Such a good girl. You're going to be so ready for my cock.'

Kingsley gets to his feet and sucks his fingers into his mouth. 'Sullivan was right. You're a delicious little thing. Let's see you return the favour.'

He saunters back to the sofa across from us and eases himself down gingerly. His boner looks as painful as mine. He resumes his previous position with arms laid out across the back of the sofa, and I put my hands around Marlowe's waist and lift her off my lap.

'He's right. You're very lucky that we gave you such a nice orgasm. It's time for you to suck his cock like a very grateful girl, and if you do a good job, I'll reward you with *my* cock.'

She turns to me, her blonde ponytail cascading over her shoulders. Her face is uncertain, but she has that gorgeous post-orgasmic flush on her cheeks and neck. She's so fucking gorgeous like this in her black lace with her tits and cunt on full display, and the sick beast in me revels in how unsure she seems. How off-kilter.

'Remember I said that we'd call the shots so you didn't have to? All you have to do is free your mind and do as we tell you.' I pause. 'Unless you want to say your safe word.'

That snaps her out of her trance.

'No. I'm good.'

'Okay then.' I rise and turn her around to face Ethan. 'Show me how nicely you can take him out, and then you can show *him* what a lucky fucker I am to have this mouth whenever I want it.' The key with Marlowe is to keep her on that knife edge of praise and something darker. What she responds to, I've found, is that very particular combination of praise and filth and dominance.

I lean in to whisper in her ear.

'Don't you want him to know why I pay you and no one

else to get on your knees and use that sweet little mouth? Men would do a lot of very bad things for that mouth of yours, love. So get down there and let him slide his cock past your lips and see for himself. He's ready to blow, I know it. He needs to use you for a few minutes like the lovely little fuck doll you are.'

I'm getting more and more turned on with each word. They seem to do the trick for Marlowe too, because she gets slowly to her knees between Ethan's legs and, with a shy glance up at me to check she's doing it right, reaches for his fly. He lets out a grunt of what sounds like agonised pleasure and shifts his arse forward so he's reclining further, giving her more access.

I'd like to say for the record that I have no interest in dick whatsoever. None of this is an effort to see Kingsley get his cock out. Christ, no. But, like I said, I *do* get off on watching something as taboo as people fucking up close, and I particularly enjoy being able to watch a man take Marlowe for a ride.

He's felt her cunt; he's felt how tight she is and is presumably all too aware of how snugly she'll fit around a dick; he's seen how sexy she is when she abandons her self-consciousness enough to come; and now he gets to feel her mouth on him and know, even while he's drowning in the sensation, that it's a one-off.

And when I bury myself balls-deep in her, he'll feel every single thrust as the back of her throat hits his dick.

He owes me a *very* nice bottle of whisky for this.

Marlowe makes quick work of his belt buckle and zip before pulling down his boxer briefs. I'm intensely annoyed that he doesn't have the pencil pecker I was hoping for and instead looks not much smaller than me.

'Don't come in her mouth,' I order him.

'I plan on coming on her tits,' he tells me with a churlish

glance up at me. He interlaces his hands behind his head. 'Go on. Suck it. Show me what all the fuss is about.'

And, like the champ she is, Marlowe lowers her beautiful mouth to his dick.

# CHAPTER 29

# Marlowe

I have never in the past three weeks felt so much like a sex worker as I do right now, on my knees to service a stranger at my boss's behest as that same boss looks on. I feel like a toy, an object with no real agency and no relevance except for my holes, and I have no bloody clue why that sends waves of heat flooding my body. I'm the nameless whore, and yet, I'm the centre of two powerful men's attention.

I tell myself to remember that last part. To hold it close, to harness it.

Ethan is sprawled out in front of me, long legs outstretched and hands cradling his head, like he's at the receiving end of this kind of treatment every day. I suppose he was, until Talia quit. She told me she was his third Seraph EA. I'm not surprised, really. The way he spoke to me just now is so fucking nasty, so contemptuous, that if a man spoke to me like that in my place of work I'd probably crack a plate or two over his head.

Unfortunately, him speaking to me like that in *this* context is, for some reason, hot as hell.

I'll show him what all the fuss is about.

Arrogant twat.

His dick is, in my limited experience, very nice indeed—long and thick and clean and very, very hard, a fact I confirm when I wrap my hand around its root. I bend and look up at him through my eyelashes. His steeliness is still there, but it's banking, building into something far more ominous. He's a black thundercloud rolling in after an oppressive day: all pent-up danger.

And he's planning on unleashing it all on *me*.

I dive in, acutely conscious of Brendan's eyes on us. I want to wipe the smug entitlement off Ethan's face, I want to unravel him just like he unravelled me right now, and I also want to prove myself to Brendan. I want his envy and his praise; I want him to think I'm the best hire he's ever made.

Basically, I'm performing for both of them, and it galvanises me.

I lick him like an ice cream. I take him in my mouth and suck, marvelling at the weird thought that, even if you blind-folded me, I'd know that this wasn't Brendan. I embrace the strangeness of blowing a random guy in his office in the middle of the afternoon and I let rip. I take him as deep as I can. My eyes fill with tears as he hits the spongy flesh at the back of my throat, but it's worth it, because the sound he makes is so low and guttural and so full of unwilling apprecia-tion that it almost makes me smile around his dick.

'Fuck,' he hisses through his teeth. 'So good.'

'Good enough to earn a fucking?' Brendan enquires through gritted teeth.

'Yeah. Fill her up.'

Brendan comes around to kneel behind me. I'm bracing with one hand on the sofa, back arched and bottom in the air. I'm basically doing the cow part of cat-cows but in porno crotchless panties. My exposed pussy is still pulsing from its orgasm, still sensitive to the cold air circulating. As Brendan kneels between my legs and I feel his heat, I experience the oddest sense of rightness.

This Ethan guy is very sexy. Terrifying, but sexy. It may be fun and unusual and arousing to be messing around with him, but the sensation of Brendan ripping foil and sheathing himself and dragging the beautiful, blunt head of his crown back and forth over my entrance to lube himself up with my arousal is a homecoming, a key turning in a lock. And when he pushes inside me and I attempt to accommodate him with shimmies of my hips, the dick in my mouth goes from being my sole focus to a hot gimmick.

Because when Mr Brendan Sullivan is intent on burying himself balls-deep inside you, it's hard to focus on anything else.

Even when your face is buried in another man's crotch.

Taking both of them like this is beyond dirty. I'm on my knees for them, my breasts jiggling freely as Brendan clamps his hands to my hips and begins to move. His first full thrust has me shunting forward onto Ethan's cock. I gag. He groans. The wrist bracing on the sofa screams. And my traitorous, still-swollen pussy rejoices.

'Fuck, this view,' Brendan huffs out behind me. 'It's sensational. How does she feel, Kingsley? Too bad you won't get to fuck her. Her cunt is so. Fucking. *Tight.*'

'She feels amazing.' Ethan leans forward a little, just enough that he can wrap my ponytail around his fist like a rein. 'I'm gonna come so hard all over her.'

'She's a lucky, lucky girl,' Brendan muses. He must be white-knuckling my hips. He eases out of me and pauses, and I brace myself as hard as I can for impact before he drives forward. The way he fills me up is so sublime. He's so, so deep in this position, and he's practically performing this blow job for me, because his thrust pushes me forward again onto Ethan. My eyes are watering, I'm struggling for breath, but Ethan holds me here for a beat with my ponytail as he lets out a ragged exhale.

'Let me tell you, love, the sight of you taking my dick from this angle while you suck Kingsley off is so fucking hot,' Brendan says. 'Maybe I'll make you do this to all my mates, hmm? God, I love the thought of that.'

Even in the heat of the action, I bank this thought: Brendan is getting his pound of flesh from me right now. I'll remember, when I'm sitting on that plane with Tabs having lied through my teeth to him and taken his money, how blithely he passes me around his friends and treats me like a plaything, a free-for-all.

Brendan Sullivan is not a victim here.

It seems my and Brendan's machinations on Ethan's dick are working their magic, for he's growing more agitated beneath me. The fingers of his free hand flex on my jaw, he grips my ponytail more tightly, and my glances up at him through my lashes show that impassive face of his contorting as his arousal builds. And for all that I'm stuck between the two of them, impaled at both ends by their dicks, I get that heady rush of power, because all this grunting and grimacing and gasping around me? *I'm doing that.*

'Fuck, I'm close,' Ethan rasps in a borderline panicked voice that's a world away from his previous entitled drawl.

'Let go of her, then,' Brendan orders. As soon as Ethan has released my hair, Brendan is bending over me and wrapping his arms around my chest and hauling me up onto my knees. He moulds me to him, my bare back against the firm bulk of his cotton-covered pecs, one hand stroking over one of my exposed breasts and the other sliding down between my legs to find the gap in my panties. 'Put your arms around my neck, love,' he tells me, and I do. I lean back and I grip the back of his head as best I can as he dips his face to my shoulder.

It's only then that my gaze meets Ethan's. The expression on his face tells me exactly what kind of sight I must make, stretched out like this for Brendan in my useless scraps of black lace, his fingers working my clit, my knees bracketing his. Ethan looks unleashed. There's no other word for it.

Gone is the bored arrogance, the insouciance, with which he greeted us. His jaw is clenched so tightly that the muscles are jumping on both sides of it; his eyes are wild; and he's managed during the course of his blow job to mess up all that dirty blonde hair pretty impressively. He gets to his feet, gripping his cock like it's an unexploded grenade, his shirt undone and trousers hanging by a thread around his hips.

'Show her who's boss, why don't you?' Brendan goads him.

'I fucking will,' Ethan says in a low, rough voice that would be terrifying if it wasn't so hot.

Brendan moves the hand that was on my breast and wraps it around my neck.

He has me by the neck and by the clit.

I am, to all intents and purposes, naked between two riled up, still-dressed billionaires.

They're using me as a pawn in their weird, fucked-up game of rutting horns.

Brendan is huge and hot and hard inside me, his dick pulsing angrily inside my front wall as he holds off on thrusting again until Ethan's done his part.

My lips feel puffy, and I can still taste Ethan's precum.

I don't think I've ever been so turned on in my life.

Brendan circles my soaking clit with infuriatingly light, slow circles, and I attempt to bear down against his finger, but I can't. I'm held in place by his dick and his chokehold.

'Stop it. Stay nice and still like a good girl and let Kingsley use you how he wants, and then I'll make it all feel better. Got it?'

'Got it,' I whisper, fixing my eyes on Ethan, who's towering over me. I watch, transfixed, as he runs his hand over his shaft once, twice, three times. Each time he does it, he closes his eyes as if he's in agony.

And then he's coming, shooting great white ropes of cum that hit me on the jaw, the chest, with warm, wet lacerations, his exhales laced with low, anguished cries.

One man has marked me as another man pulses inside me, and I feel the oddest mixture of debased and triumphant.

Brendan releases me from his grip and uses both hands to smear Ethan's cum over my skin, rubbing it into my nipples and my stomach. 'Look what you made him do,' he croons. 'Little fucking seductress. You're too fucking lovely for us not to want to mess you up.' Then, 'Out of the way,' he grunts at Ethan, who's standing, head thrown back and hand still wrapped around his cock, looking utterly spent and not a little dazed.

'Hands and knees,' he tells me, and I brace once again. Brendan wraps one arm tightly around my cum-smeared stomach and proceeds to absolutely let rip, his thrusts hard and fast and aggressive, as if he's trying to get as many in as humanly possible before he, too, capitulates.

It's so much sensation and exactly what I need, and I'm powerless to withstand it in my current, hyper-aroused state. So I brace, my marked skin growing cool, my pussy utterly molten, and I fix my gaze on Ethan's shiny black shoes as Brendan pummels into me.

It's too good it's too good it's too good—

I shatter. *Shatter.* I soar through the air, oblivious to the excruciating vulnerability of this situation, oblivious to everything that's not the white-hot pleasure Brendan's dick is wringing from somewhere deep inside my body.

'Look at that,' Ethan says in a still-strained voice. His shoes move to my left, presumably for a better view of the action, as Brendan hardens and stills in that glorious, miraculous way, before he too shatters inside me with noisy grunts that make me feel like I'm being fucked by the Beast himself.

Two guys.

Two holes.

Orgasms all round.

It's a new low.

Or a new high.

In this moment, I genuinely can't work out which.

It strikes me on the way back to the office that this is the perfect chance to notify Brendan of my intention to take leave. I'm not sure if it's an opportunity to regain some semblance of control or if I have a vague belief that he owes me one, that it would be unseemly of him to complain about my taking leave when I've just accommodated one of his most taboo fantasies.

I may have had a couple of orgasms, but I'm in no doubt as to who was servicing who this afternoon.

Besides, he's doom-scrolling on his phone and largely ignoring me, which, given what just went down, is an excellent reminder that what we have is purely transactional in nature. At no point since we left Ethan's office has he checked in to ask me how I'm doing. Sure, I'm about to lie to him, but this job is a means to an end, and when the *means* get as extreme as that, it's even more important for me to secure my end.

The final payday I require to front Tabby's medical bills

isn't until next week, but even if Brendan threw his toys fully out of the pram and sacked me over taking leave, he'd still have to give me a month's notice. It's unlikely, though. I'm counting on the fact that I've earned some serious brownie points this afternoon and shown him that I've got what it takes to be a valued Seraph EA.

'Have you got a sec?' I ask him.

'Sure,' he says without looking up from Strava. I roll my eyes at the side of his stupidly handsome face. So hot, but so rude. It's a standard correlation in men. Just as today's little threesome is probably standard for guys like Brendan— though usually he's probably juggling multiple women.

'I've been selected for jury duty, I'm afraid. It starts in two weeks and they expect to need me for another two.'

He looks over at me, frowns, then returns to his phone.

'That's fine. We can get you out of it. Elaine can help you.'

'I'm afraid I've already tried. I got the call-up a week ago and I've been fighting it, but they're resolute.'

That gets his attention. He throws his phone onto the expanse of leather between us. 'Fuck's sake. Escalate it. I can't spare you.'

'I have escalated it,' I say, trying to keep my voice steady. 'They won't budge. I've declined it twice before, which hasn't helped my case.'

He glares at me. 'What the fuck am I supposed to do while you're away?'

'I checked the protocol with Camille. She said they can send in a replacement.' Though the thought of sending in another woman to bend over for my gorgeous, entitled boss while I'm away is strangely horrifying. Maybe it's just because our entire setup is so strange, or maybe it's because having someone else take over both sides of my role would underscore precisely how disposable, how replaceable, I really am. 'Or I can ask Elaine to cover,' I add. 'And I can get online every evening and play catch-up, too.'

In reality, I'll be logging in from the hospital, but he doesn't need to know that.

He's still scowling. That good-looking face of his gives excellent petulance. He's actually sticking that plump, suckable lower lip out. He's so sulky it makes me want to burst out laughing, but it also hardens my resolve.

'It's ridiculous,' he spits out. 'Let me know who to call and I'll do it. People like us don't need to bother with shit like that. There are enough lazy tossers sitting around on their arses and collecting the dole while we hold down actual jobs. Why can't they find someone else to do it?'

This is the problem with people like Brendan—people who've accumulated so much wealth and power that they believe it absolves them from any civic responsibility, or any responsibility that causes them the remotest inconvenience, for that matter. He thinks that because he and his company pay billions in taxes, that lets him off the hook, and it bloody well doesn't. His attitude is the epitome of entitlement, and elitism, and double standards, and just—*grrrrr.*

I may not be doing jury duty this time—I may be taking the time to save my daughter's life—but what Mr Sullivan doesn't know is that I've done it before. I've never turned it down. I did a week's worth of it two years ago, and it was, as a working single mother, a gigantic pain in the arse to juggle it. But I did it, because I believe that every person in the UK has the right to be tried before a jury of their peers. My sense of being inconvenienced, and Brendan's, should come a distant second to that.

'That's a terrible attitude. Having everyone pull their weight is part of our democratic process. Besides, I like to think I'd add something to the process. We need our juries to be a good mix of professions and intellects and emotional intelligence.' I clear my throat. 'So I'm not interested in trying to wriggle out of my duty. I'm genuinely sorry to have to take leave so early on in this role. But I'll speak to Elaine later, and I mean it when I say I'll pick up as much of the slack as I can out of hours.'

'Shit!' he says suddenly. 'You'll miss the summit. I was counting on having you there.'

I grimace. I know what a big deal this summit is for Brendan and the management team as a whole, and I hate that I'll be AWOL. At the very least, I suspect he could do with a cheeky blow job to take the edge off before he goes on stage to deliver his address.

'I know, and I'm so, so sorry. I really am. But I'm going to include Elaine on all the handover stuff from here on in. It seems like the strategy team is planning on doing the whole presentation, and Elaine seems to be a font of knowledge about the event.' It's true. Apparently she's managed the firm's appearances at all the previous summits, which I believe have been dotted around Europe.

He gives me a death stare and picks up his phone again. 'Fucking idealistic bullshit. This had better not affect me or mess up the summit in any way. Just because you're a fantastic lay doesn't mean you're indispensable, you know.'

*What* a gigantic wanker. The hurt slices through me like a jagged knife. It's not that I expect the guy to fall in love with me, but to put me in a position like the one back there and then to dismiss me out of hand is disgustingly obnoxious. By focusing solely on his own needs, he's made me feel cheap. Disposable. *Dispensable.*

When people show you who they really are, you should take heed.

*One more payday. One more payday.* I chant my mantra as I silently plot his castration all the way back to the office.

# CHAPTER 30

# Marlowe

Soph, I met Ethan Kingsley today

SOPHIA:

Oooh

Thoughts?

ATHENA:

Hang on

By "met" you mean…

😳😳😳😭😭😭

ATHENA:

OMG! Baby's first threesome I assume?
Unless Brendan lent him to you???

Nope. He SHARED me with him

(Can't believe I wrote that)

SOPHIA:

Fucking hell

HOTTTTTTTTTTTT

You ok babes?

ATHENA:

That should have been my line. How are you feeling?

A bit wrung out. In a good way. But my boss is an entitled dickhead

This bloody job

What a head fuck

SOPHIA:

FACTS

ATHENA:

What did they do to you?

I really don't want to spell it out on text. I feel weird

ATHENA:

They didn't DP you did they? I'm assuming not unless your No Back Passage rule went out the window the second two hot men got their claws into you

NOOOOOOOO! Jesus

ATHENA:

You just had a threesome. Not sure you can take the moral high ground with me young lady

True 😢

SOPHIA:

So what did they do?

I sat on Brendan's lap and Ethan finger fucked me 😳

Then I went down on Ethan while Brendan took me from behind

SOPHIA:

NICE

(Dirty bitch 😂😂😂)

ATHENA:

So they spit roasted you. Excellent work 👣 👣👣

SOPHIA:

Thanks for being my canary down the coal mine w Kingsley

What's your verdict??

Might take him for a spin once Thad gives me the boot

On Ethan? He's really hot. But he's as cold as ice. Seriously, the guy was scary. I can't imagine you two together. But definitely hot

SOPHIA:

Remember babes, when fire meets ice, fire wins out every time

He'll be nothing but a puddle on the floor when I've finished with him

ATHENA:

Got to love your confidence

Marls - next up: gang bang

He'd better fucking not. He seriously pushed his luck today

Also I told him about "jury duty" and he hit the roof. I think he thinks it's something only poor people should have to do.

ATHENA:

What a shocker. He's such a man-child.

Only a few more weeks, babe. Hang in there. It'll all be worth it in the end, I promise you xx

# CHAPTER 31

# Marlowe

My and Tabby's plans for our US trip are seriously building momentum. I was up late last night and early this morning completing the endless rounds of paperwork that Duke requires before we travel. Next Friday, Tabs and my parents will head to Great Ormond Street for a final round of check-ups to ensure she's flight-fit and to gauge her current cardio-pulmonary levels for the team over at Duke. I hate more than anything that I'm not going, but my job here is to earn the money that will get us onto that flight and into that operating theatre.

Speaking of which, next Friday is my July payday, and then we'll be out of here.

It's really, really happening.

Today, Brendan is working from home and I'm going to base myself from there, too. Things between us may have reverted to normal after his little hissy fit over jury duty, but that insight into his personality definitely firmed up my resolve not to trust him with anything that's going on in my life. As Athena said, he's a man-child. A gorgeous, successful, filthy-rich man-child who's spoilt rotten. He hasn't earned the privilege of gaining the confidence of the grown-ups.

I've got to say, I'm a little nervous about being all alone with him, in a residential setting and without the buffer of our colleagues a few metres away. Still, I'm curious to see his pad. Elaine told me it was indecently palatial but a little on the Kardashian side, which made me laugh.

I cycle the six miles from my flat to Brendan's penthouse in the fancy complex surrounding the restored Battersea Power Station. The final part of the ride, along the south bank of the Thames, is stunning. I take my time, not wanting to arrive a sweaty mess, although Brendan has—quite pervily, I think—demanded that I stay in my cycling gear all day.

He *really* likes my cycling gear. So much so that he ordered me a new blush-pink outfit from Alo the other day. I'm wearing it now, and I'm convinced it makes me look naked from a distance.

Maybe that was his point.

I cycle up to the covered drop-off area outside his building, where a burly doorman stands, dressed in a black top hat and tails.

'Can I help you, ma'am?'

'Hi,' I say a little breathlessly. 'I'm here to see Brendan Sullivan? I'm his assistant,' I add hastily.

'Ms Winters? Welcome. We'll park your bicycle securely.' He clicks his fingers and one of his minions appears, right on cue.

'Oh. Thank you!' I dismount, and off the minion trundles, wheeling my crusty old bike. I cringe inwardly as the clicky wheel does its thing every time it revolves past a certain point. It's the chain; I know it's the chain. I just need to find the time and money to get it sorted.

As if he's a mind reader, the doorman frowns in the bike's direction and clicks his fingers again. 'Paul.'

The minion halts and looks back at us.

'Would you like us to have that clicking attended to while you're with us today, Ms Winters?'

'Oh, no, I—' I begin, but he cuts me off.

'It's no bother. We have a bicycle expert on hand. He can replace the chain or whatever needs doing. It's all part of the service we offer to residents and their guests, ma'am,' he adds. He can probably see my *how much will this cost Brendan* frown.

I brighten. 'In that case, yes please. That would be amazing!'

'Very good, ma'am. This way, please.'

I follow this new fairy godfather of crapped-out bikes through the glass doors and into a cavernous lobby: ultra-modern; gleaming white marble; ostentatious displays of flowers everywhere in vases that stand taller than Tabby. You get the picture. I mentally compare it to the concrete urine-scented box that is the lobby of my building, complete with its resident gangs, and shudder. Brendan wouldn't last five minutes in my building if this is what he's used to.

Then again, if you have the money, why not? Athena told me that Brendan is deeply unsure about his family's pledge of most of its billions to the Audacity Foundation. My personal take is that losing his billionaire status would mean a serious identity crisis for him—even if they'll still be revoltingly rich by most people's standards. So he's spending money like it's going out of fashion.

Exhibit one—the catamaran he's ordered, the admin around which Elaine is having to deal with.

The doorman deposits me in a vast glass lift and swipes his security card before pressing the button marked PH. *Penthouse*, I assume.

'Enjoy your morning, ma'am.'

'Thank you.' I swivel as the lift starts to rise. This building can only be ten or so storeys tall, but the glass walls still offer me a stunning view of the Thames, blue and hazy on this stunning morning. Before I know it, the lift is sliding smoothly to a halt and the doors part for me.

Oh holy crap.

This place is outrageous.

The space before me is so big it must surely take up this entire floor. It's *vast*. There are huge floor-to-ceiling windows on both sides. In front of me: a massive terrace facing the Thames. To my left: the majesty of the restored power station, now a major shopping destination. It must look so cool when the entire thing is lit up at night.

It's simply incredible.

And sure, I could imagine Kim or Khloe hanging out here —something about all the neutral tones and that cream and coffee chequered Hermès blanket laid across the arm of the massive sofa—but honestly, it's like something out of a dream.

The apartment is open plan, with most of what I can see given over to a very fancy, cohesively decorated living area. The ceilings are double-height, a shallow cantilevered staircase to one side leading up to a mezzanine from which I assume you access the bedrooms. Beyond it, the kitchen area is an expanse of glossy white marble with chunky taupe veins: masculine and opulent in equal measure. It's a kitchen to be seen, admired—to show off in.

If Brendan actually cooks for himself, which is a big *if*, it makes total sense that he'd want a spectacular backdrop against which to perform.

I bet it's full of the toys he loves so much.

I'm just clocking the heavenly sight that is a glossy black grand piano over by the terrace when I hear my name and the man himself appears at the top of the staircase.

Well that grabs my attention.

He's wearing nothing but a pair of bright blue running

shorts and a heart rate monitor strapped around his chest, upper body bare and tanned and so shiny with sweat that it has the effect of his having covered himself in baby oil. Thick white sports socks accentuate the hairy muscularity of his legs. He has a towel in his hand, and the damp mess of his dark hair suggests he's been towelling it. Mark shoots down the stairs ahead of him and bounds over to me.

'Morning,' I say, feeling suddenly shy, which is ridiculous. Still, working for the guy in his offices is one thing. Showing up here to his penthouse pad to find its master half naked is quite another. I bend to greet Mark, who's rubbing his wide head over my calves as if he can't believe I'm here, in his home.

I suppose that's fair. It's not like I've ever been here before. As far as he knows, I'm firmly an office fixture.

Brendan trots lightly down the steps and comes to stand in front of me. He's still out of breath from whatever he's been doing. I look up from Mark and take in the chunky globes of his biceps, the expanse of slick, flat stomach, the dark, dampened hair covering his pecs, and make a mental note to coax him out of the office more often so I can get him fully naked. Suddenly, the at-work trysts where he stays mostly clothed feel like a bum deal for me.

Because this man is spectacular.

'I was on the Peloton, doing my FTP test,' he explains. 'I'm sweaty as fuck.'

'FTP?'

'Functional Threshold Power.' He grins at me, his eyes roving over my cycling gear. Clearly I'm not the only one enjoying our working-from-home dress code.

'How fun,' I deadpan. I have no clue what that means, but it sounds horrifying.

He laughs. 'Give me five minutes to have a shower, yeah? Make yourself comfortable. There's coffee on the counter.'

Sure enough, there's a glass French press standing on the

huge marble island. I shamelessly watch his arse as he skips lightly back upstairs. As soon as he's gone, I move over to the grand piano as if bewitched. Coffee has nothing on the allure of this baby.

Holy shit, it's a Steinway, and it's their Model D—their concert grand piano—in the glossiest black. If it's not tuned I think I might cry, and I'll definitely never be able to speak to Brendan again.

Gingerly, I take a seat and lift the lid, letting my fingers brush over the keys before I attempt a couple of chords.

It's tuned. Holy hell, is it tuned. I've died and gone to heaven, it seems. I hope Brendan doesn't have much work for me today, because he'll have to physically tear me away from this thing.

I let my eyes flutter closed, and I play Bach's beautiful prelude from *The Well-Tempered Clavier*, the one to which Charles Gounod set his *Ave Maria*. It's one of my all-time favourite pieces of music.

I may not have had my hands on a piano for a few years, but this is less muscle memory than a melody scored deep into my DNA. It's *who I am*. My aura is probably made up of musical notes instead of colours. My love of music is at the very essence of me, yet it's been subjugated so much these past few years since graduating. It's been squashed down in favour of other, more important passions like keeping my daughter alive. But it's never far from the surface, and there's nothing like a Steinway and an empty room the size of a concert hall to coax it out, to allow it to stream from me.

Eyes still closed, I begin to sing.

# CHAPTER 32

# *Brendan*

My shower is quick and perfunctory. I crank off the torrent of water and towel myself down impatiently before moving through to the dressing room that sits between my bathroom and bedroom. I find any sort of self-processing, from showering to brushing my teeth, boring as hell and a total waste of time.

I'm pulling a t-shirt on over my still-damp torso when I hear it.

To call it merely *singing* would be like calling Mark just a *dog*. It's soaring and operatic and spectacular, and it's accompanied by my piano. Unless Katherine Jenkins has surreptitiously entered my home while I was in the shower and set up camp, this sensory heaven must be my assistant singing.

I pull on some clean running shorts and pad out of my room in as much of a trance as a kid bewitched by the Pied Piper. If I'm honest, it feels like the music is pulling me along. I'm a sailor, sucked in by a siren's call. I stand at the top of the stairs and I take in the sight, the sound, in amazement.

Marlowe is sitting at my Steinway, her back to me. She's pulled all of that long blonde hair out of its perky ponytail and it cascades down her back in untamed waves. Her back is straight, but she's swaying. Her fingers are featherlight as they move over the piano keys. She's singing some version of *Ave Maria*—not the Schubert one, but I can't recall which. It's the one my sister had performed at her wedding, I think. Mark, wise man that he is, is lying on the floor beside her, head resting on his paws, gazing up at her in awe.

Her voice is extraordinary. *Extraordinary*. Her speaking voice is lovely, sure—feminine and melodic—but her singing voice is rich and pure, with a gravitas I can't articulate. It packs a serious punch, filling the vast room. As the hymn progresses and the tension builds, I find myself gripping the balustrade. Marlowe sings the *Sancta Maria* part, her voice soaring, making every note sound as effortless as breathing.

Every Catholic knows the Hail Mary by heart. It's a hymn we've all recited thousands upon thousands of times, most of us without ever thinking about what the words mean. But, even in Latin, Marlowe sounds like she's praying. Her voice is nothing short of beseeching, the lofty vocals of her *nunc et in hora* desperate, and I find my eyes pricking with tears. It's the weirdest feeling, but it's like I've trespassed upon her as she prays hard for something she wants very, very badly.

I stand here and let the music wash over me as I watch the performer below turn my home into a concert hall.

Marlowe is an impressive woman. Of that, there is no doubt, even if I can, in my more introspective moments, admit that I'm guilty of taking her for granted and, worse, objectifying her. Her looks, her presence, have affected me from the first moment I laid eyes on her. Since stepping foot in my office, she's overachieved. She's an extremely capable assistant and a great lay.

But this is something else entirely. I may not be a classical music aficionado. I may approach evenings at the opera with the same horror as the prospect of root canal. But I have no doubt that what I'm bearing witness to is art and alchemy and God-given talent, the splendour of which has my skin breaking out in goose bumps and my breath stalling in my lungs and my heart swelling. There are gifts—and there's greatness.

I let that final *Amen* in her flawless soprano wash over me. I never, ever want this private performance to end. But when her voice fades off, my need for more has me heading for the staircase.

'Please sing it again,' I say, practically running down the stairs. 'Please. That was incredible.'

She turns to me, and I can tell I've taken her by surprise. Her eyes are wide, like she's forgotten where she is, and, as I approach, the tears tracking down her cheeks glimmer in the morning light.

'Please,' I beg her, stopping just short of the piano. 'Sing it again. Just pretend I'm not here and don't hold back.'

She considers, then nods and lets her eyes drift closed, and the haunting melody starts up again.

I may have told her to pretend I wasn't here, but I don't take my eyes off her for a second. The woman not only looks like an angel; she sings like an angel. She's also a performer. She's captivated me in two minutes flat. I have no doubt she would captivate anyone who watched and listened to her sing.

It strikes me that she sings the first few lines of the hymn a little more self-consciously. She doesn't falter, but her voice is fainter than it was. Then she finds her stride and goes for it. She's probably already forgotten I'm here.

Marlowe is beautiful every single day, but when she sings, she lights up. Like this, in her casually sexy cycling gear, sitting at my piano with the sunlight casting a halo around her hair, she commands every ounce of my attention.

As she concludes the hymn once again with that breathtaking, transcendent *Amen*, I fight the urge to tell her *again* like a little boy who's just watched something so cool he never wants it to stop. She's not a performing monkey. She's a very, very special person, a person whom, I suspect, I've repeatedly underestimated so that I can treat her as an object and a convenience.

When she opens her eyes and smiles self-consciously at me, she finds me staring at her.

'I don't know what to say. That was... beautiful. So moving.'

'Thank you,' she murmurs.

'May I?' I ask, gesturing at the wide piano stool.

'Of course!' She shifts to the side so I can sit beside her. 'Please tell me you play.'

She says the words in a rush, as if she's trying to brush off whatever awkwardness she perceives from having just performed for a man who had no clue she could sing. A man who should have paid far more attention to her CV, because I knew she was a choral scholar at school, for Christ's sake.

I give her a self-deprecating smile. 'I do, but I'm not good at classical stuff.'

She grins at me. 'Thank God. If you owned a Steinway and couldn't play it, I might have to strangle you.'

'I'm not that much of a wanker.' That said, I may enjoy playing my piano, but it's guaranteed that I don't appreciate it enough. Not the way Marlowe so clearly just appreciated the hell out of it. 'You can come over and play anytime,' I tell her. 'It's no hardship for me to have the odd private concert.'

'Thank you.' She tilts her head to one side and plays a couple of wistful one-handed chords. 'What kind of stuff do you play?'

'You really want to know?'

'Absolutely.'

'Alright then. Don't say I didn't warn you. Move up.' I nudge her over further on the stool and let my fingers attack the keys, going straight into *Great Balls of Fire*. She lets out a gasp of surprise as I launch into the lyrics, channelling my inner Jerry Lee Lewis, and deliver a sweet glissando. When I hit the chorus, she joins in.

It's clear she doesn't know the lyrics of the verses, so I keep going with my little one-man show, giving it all my swagger. I hunch my shoulders; I pull back dramatically; I make my voice growl; I hit the keys so hard you'd think I was trying to punch through the keyboard. It couldn't be more different from her beautiful, pared back version of *Ave Maria,* but she asked for a Brendan Sullivan Special and I'm damned if I'm not going to deliver.

By the time I finish, she's laughing and clapping her hands beside me. She twists around to face me.

'Oh my God! That was *so* good!'

'It was a party piece,' I tell her. 'A good one, but just a bit of fun. It's nothing like your talent.'

She shakes her head. 'It was amazing. When did you learn to play like that?'

'*Top Gun,*' I confess. 'My parents were on me to learn the piano when I was little, but I found it really boring. Trying to get a kid with undiagnosed and untreated ADHD to practise his chords? Not happening. But when I saw Goose play this on *Top Gun*, I was like, that's pretty fucking cool. I remember I marched out to the stables and told my dad that I'd learn the piano as long as I could only learn rock and roll songs. He agreed, and here we are.'

'You must be great at parties,' she says.

'I'm *great* at parties, love.' I brush the stray locks of blonde hair off her shoulder and stare at her bare skin. 'But what you have is a very, very special talent. So what the fuck you're doing being my assistant and taking fucking meeting notes, I have no idea. Why the hell didn't you pursue a career in this?'

I glance up at her face, but she turns her head, gazing out the window.

'It's not an easy career. You're very kind, but I had no guarantee I'd make it. And the lifestyle is hard—long hours, travelling, really unpredictable. Life got in the way, and my priorities changed, you know? So now it's just a hobby.' She looks down at the piano and smooths her fingers over the keys. 'And it's a very nice hobby when I get to play one of these.'

'But you love it.' It's not a question.

Finally, she raises her eyes to meet mine. 'I love it,' she whispers.

'Do you ever sing for other people?'

'Just my d—' She stops abruptly and blinks, her face going instantly red. What the fuck?

'Your what?'

She stares at me as if she's choking or something. It's weird. 'Just my dog,' she says finally on a big exhale.

'Tabby.'

'Yeah. Exactly.'

'Lucky dog.'

We're silent for a moment, taking each other in. I'm no angel, but I've never found any woman as arresting as Marlowe. She's the real deal: gorgeous and smart and wonderful, with more talent in her little finger than most people could dream of possessing.

What's growing rapidly clear is that she has depths I haven't begun to plumb.

I let my gaze drop to her mouth. I had plans for us to work through my diary for the rest of the month, but those will have to wait. 'Can I kiss you?' I ask her. My voice sounds gruff to my ears.

'Of course,' she says. She looks a little surprised that I've asked. Or maybe she's surprised that I'm considering a kiss rather than just bending her over my desk. I suppose at work

I'm a bit more presumptuous, but it would feel weird to jump on her here in my home without warning, right after we've been discussing her musical talent. The rules feel different here.

She isn't buttoned up and glamorous today. She's soft and supple and undone with that cascade of long, silky hair and this thin athletic gear and all that gorgeous skin on display. Her arms are bare. Her midriff. Her chest. It's all good, because I feel undone like this, too. I'm in shorts and a t-shirt, barefoot in what is honestly more of a trophy pad than a real home. Right now I'm not the big boss man prowling through his corner office in extortionate tailoring.

I'm just Brendan.

# CHAPTER 33

# *Brendan*

**S**he sighs softly as I gather her up in my arms. So often, I act on impulse. I'm all about the destination and, in Marlowe's case, the orgasm. See her. Fuck her. Make her come. Let myself come. Boom.

And repeat.

She's a means to an end. A beautiful vessel that pours forth an endless stream of sexual gratification.

This morning, I'm going to bloody well enjoy her.

And I do.

I smooth her hair off her face with one hand and take a moment to absorb her before I dive back in. Her eyes are molten chocolate, her eyelashes fluttering, lips so soft and pink and lush. I can't not kiss her. I tilt my head and I close my mouth over hers again, testing the seam of her lips lightly with my tongue. They part for me, and I'm flooded with *her*: her scent, her taste, sensory delights I've already grown to crave.

There's always an element of time pressure in the office. Much as I like living on the edge, I don't actually *want* anyone to barge in on us. Here, though, there's a stillness, even as the sounds her voice made hang in the air like beautiful ghosts. I have a sense of presence that even my meds can't always deliver.

We're properly making out now, and it's seriously fucking cool. I twist my body as much as humanly possible as I cup her jaw and stroke her skin and thread my fingers through her hair and entangle my tongue with hers. The more I give myself over to this kiss, the more it gives me. The more *she* gives me.

She pushes the short sleeve of my t-shirt up further and wraps her hand around my bicep. Her lips move against mine, her tits press against my pecs, our athletic gear far less of a barrier than our workwear usually is. Her other hand finds my hair and tugs at it. And a thought comes to me unbidden.

Does she really like this? Or is she acting? After all, Marlowe is pretty implacable as far as women go. She's also the consummate professional. I have no doubt that all the orgasms I've doled out have been real—no one is *that* good a performer —but it doesn't mean she's into me.

I may not want anything serious here—after all, this pay-for-play relationship suits me down to the ground—but I really, really want to believe that she's kissing me on a Friday morning on the stool of my grand piano because she's digging it, not because I'm paying her to.

Only one way to find out. I need us both bare and on a bed. Usually, the client-hooker dynamic really gets me going, but today I just want to take this beautiful blonde upstairs and show her how good it can be when she's with me.

'Can I take you to bed?' I mutter against her lips.

She gives a little hum of approval. 'Mmm. Yes please.'

I stand up and hold out my hand. When she looks up at me and takes it, it feels as though the girl I like has agreed to go on a date with me.

'Brendan Sullivan's bedroom,' she murmurs as I lead her upstairs by the hand. 'I'm almost scared. Do women come here on pilgrimages and scatter flowers at your bedroom door?'

Cheeky little minx.

'Mostly they just bring empty bottles so they can collect holy water from my bathroom taps,' I bat back.

'Kind of like Lourdes?'

'Exactly like Lourdes. The healing power of a few hours with me and my dick is miraculous.'

She doesn't miss a beat. 'Explains a lot. I wondered how that weird rash of mine had vanished so quickly.'

'Oh ye of little faith. You'll see, baby.' I wink at her.

'As long as you change the sheets between all your "miracles".'

'Joke's on you.' I usher her through the open double doors of my master suite. My housekeeper, Val, made my bed first thing this morning before I gave her the rest of the day off. I don't need anyone cramping my and Marlowe's style. 'You're the first woman who's ever been in here.'

She stops stock-still on the threshold. 'You're kidding me.'

'Nope. As you well know, I don't require a bed to have a good time.' I let go of her hand and stick my hands in my pockets. 'Plus, getting rid of them is way harder than getting them in here. So I just don't do it.'

'Aren't you a charmer?' she asks, but she sounds distracted. She looks around my room, taking in the dark grey linen-covered walls, the vast white bed and the views out to the private terrace and the river beyond. My room is a knockout. Serene. Luxurious. Simple. It has to be. My exhausting, exhausted brain needs a safe space to crash each evening, and this place is my sanctuary.

'This is absolutely amazing,' she says.

'Thanks. And I don't care if it sounds rude. It's the truth. I have enough headaches without dealing with needy women who refuse to leave. You don't count,' I say hastily.

She laughs. 'I'm not sure if that's a compliment or an insult.'

'It's a compliment. We have a very productive, well-defined working relationship. And you always shoot out the door at six like a scalded cat. I don't flatter myself that my bed is good enough to keep you hanging around like a bad smell.'

'Such a charmer.' Her smile is coquettish, and I think once again how bloody gorgeous she is. 'It's increasingly obvious why you have to pay for sex.'

I frown in a faux-menacing manner. 'I'll wipe that smile off your face with my dick. Now take those fucking clothes off and get on that bed.'

Why having Marlowe naked and spread out on my bed for me is quite so different from having her stripped and on all fours in my office, I'm unclear. But I'm staring at her like I've never seen her clearly before.

Every inch of her is stunning, sure. But this morning there are parts of her that warrant special attention, parts I've been guilty of neglecting thus far.

The impossibly thin, silky skin along her collarbone.

The freckle below her left breast.

The dip between her hip bone and her navel when she's lying on her back.

I lie next to her, propped up on one elbow and as naked as she is, and I play. I explore. I trace the contours of her body with my fingers just as I marvel at the softness of her skin. I flip my hand and brush my knuckles over one breast, grazing her nipple softly, and she shudders.

'Do you like me touching you?' I ask quietly, and she turns her head to stare at me.

'Of course I do. Can't you tell?'

I hesitate. 'Mostly I can. But, at the end of the day, I'm paying you to say that, aren't I?'

'Yeah, but—Jesus, Brendan. I'm not *that* good an actress. I mean, surely you can see the kind of effect you have on me? I *love* you touching me.'

'Let's see, shall we?' I ask, and I dip my mouth to her nipple, sucking on it lightly. The skin puckers into a sweet little rosebud between my lips, and she arches against me.

'Come here.' I release her nipple and slide an arm under her head, wrapping it around her shoulders and pulling her against my body. 'That's better.'

It is. She's flush against me, her head cradled in the crook of my arm, her face so close to mine. Don't get me wrong; I love flipping her over and fucking her from behind. I go crazy when she obeys my commands to crawl away from me only for me to dive on her.

But this is cool, too, even if it's uncharted territory for me to cuddle a woman while I bring her to orgasm.

She tilts her face up towards mine, a silent plea for my mouth. I bend my head to meet her, parting her lips with my tongue as I hold her close against me, my hard-on flexing against her hip. 'Open your legs for me, love,' I whisper against her mouth before diving back into the kiss and using my free hand to stroke her breasts. At this angle they're almost flat, the taut nubs of her nipples the best kind of fidget toys.

I play with them for a few moments as our tongues entangle and she makes soft noises of appreciation into my mouth. Then I let my hand trail down between her breasts, over the velvety-soft skin of her stomach, to the neat little triangle of fair hair that marks nirvana for me. Her knees are drawn up, her legs parted, one of them resting on my thigh, and I marvel at the intensity of this position: of feeling so close to her. Of being able to see every flutter of her eyelids.

When I slide my fingers between her legs, she's wet and silky, her promised land exposed just for me. I stroke her flesh so, so softly, in awe that this lush, fertile habitat can unearth itself for me, that the female body is such a subtle and intelligent and complex thing. I brush my fingers over the glossy button of her clit and explore the delicate petals that enfold it before circling her entrance.

And all the time, I kiss her.

It's always been clear to me that the female sex organs are far more complex than the blunt instruments with which we blokes are gifted, but my hyper-focus has never quite zoned in on the intricacies of a woman like it's doing now. I'm usually thinking mainly about chasing my own pleasure. The woman's pleasure is more marginal: it's an ego boost to me and a channel for getting her wetter and the sex hotter.

But in this moment, all I can focus on is exploring Marlowe. Being *allowed* to explore her. Having free rein over her stunning, incredible body.

'How does this feel?' I murmur against her mouth as I return to her clit with featherlight touches.

'Like you're teasing me and teasing me,' she says with a little gasp.

'You want it harder?'

'Yeah, but I kind of like the teasing, you know? It's making me lose my mind.'

'That's very good, baby. That's exactly what I want you to do. I want you to lose that incredible mind. Just lie back and pay attention to every little touch.'

I hold her more tightly and lift my head so I can watch her face. Her eyelids have fluttered closed again. Her dark-blonde eyelashes lie fanned out against her cheeks. She's wearing no makeup today, and she looks wholesome as fuck. I continue to touch her lightly, and with every touch I wonder how it feels to her. How much each stroke teases her. Torments her.

Ignites her.

She writhes beneath me, pushing into my fingertips. Her body is warm and lithe against mine.

'I'm close. I'm—'

'Look at me,' I order her. 'Look at me and I'll give you everything you need.'

She opens her eyes. They're magnificent. I could lose myself in them. Their huge pupils, their frantic movements, tell me everything I've wanted to know. She's not faking this. She needs it. Right now, she needs *me*.

'You're so fucking beautiful,' I tell her as I slide two fingers inside her cunt and use my thumb to rub her harder. She's silken inside. *Silken.* Our faces are inches apart. I blame the rasp in my voice on the fact that my cock is rock fucking hard. 'I've never been so blown away by a woman's beauty as much as I was that time I first saw you. Never.' *And every time I've seen you since.*

She arches harder, lifting her hand to grip the bicep of the arm I'm using to get her off as if she's scared I'll pull away.

'I want to tell you something.' She swallows and looks away. 'It's kind of embarrassing.' I'm not the only one whose voice is strained. Hers is breathy with desire

'Hey,' I say, and she looks back at me. 'You can tell me anything.' God knows, Marlowe plays her cards close to her chest. If she wants to open up to me, I'm damn well going to make sure she feels safe to do so.

'No other guy has ever made me come before,' she gets out. 'You're the only one.'

She may be growing close to orgasm, but she also looks like she wants to sink through the floor with mortification. I can tell it's the truth and I can tell what it's cost her to share this with me.

I swear, I feel a hundred feet tall. In light of my little moment of insecurity just now, this is the greatest gift she could have given me.

'You're serious?'

She nods, her huge brown eyes fixed on me.

'Well, I'm embarrassed for them. Not for you. Fuck's sake.'

That gets me a glimmer of a smile, and I seize the opportunity to preen a little.

'You come for me like a little champ, don't you, love?' I withdraw my fingers slowly and push them inside her, hard. 'You come on my fingers.' *Pump.* 'And my tongue.' *Pump.* 'And my dick. You love coming on my dick, don't you?' *Pump.*

She flushes but nods. She's such a good fucking girl. Comes off all innocent, but she's so fucking responsive. To me, anyway. Fuck knows what all the other losers were doing.

'Yeah, you do.'

'It's not just your body parts. It's you.'

I swear I grow harder.

'Yeah?'

'Yeah. You're so, so gorgeous, Bren. I thought so from the second I met you.' She gasps as I reward that endearment with another firm pump and a swirl of my thumb over her clit. *Bren.* 'And you're so dirty. It's such a turn-on.'

'You like me corrupting you?' I lean in closer and let her have it with my fingers, thrusting and rubbing in a way I hope will give her maximum stimulation.

'I love it.'

Her admission is a red rag to a bull. We may be enjoying what I strongly suspect is that nebulous concept of intimacy, but that doesn't mean I can't milk the sheer heat of this moment for all it's worth. 'Good girl. That's so good. How does it feel to know I'm paying you a fortune to spread your legs for me in broad daylight and let me fuck you with my fingers so I can warm you up with my cock, hmm?'

'Oh God,' she moans, writhing in my arms. 'It's so good, I can't bear it.'

'That's right.' I dip my head, dropping my forehead to hers. 'I can feel this greedy cunt sucking me in. So fucking needy. I want you to come as hard as you can for me.'

I keep our foreheads pressed together, my arm banded around her body as I work her harder and harder. She spreads her legs as far as she physically can, her breath growing more ragged, her whimpers more desperate. I inhale them as if they belong to me, which they do. She's consuming me like this. I want to consume her, to swallow her whole. I can't get enough of her. If we leave this bed today, it'll be a miracle.

She begins to babble. 'Bren, I can't—I'm—oh god. Oh my god.'

'You can.' I hold her even more tightly. Our foreheads are both slick with sweat. 'Take it. Just fucking take it, you little beauty. Show me what you've got. Give me what you've never given any other guy. Show me that you only come for *me*.'

My words sent her hurtling over the edge. She comes around my fingers with a violent shudder that seems to go on forever, her beautiful body wracked with spasms as she rides out her perfect orgasm. I swallow her cries with my kisses, fucking her slowly, thoroughly with my tongue as I marvel at this front row seat I have to unravelling the most beautiful woman I've ever laid eyes on.

As her shudders subside, so do my kisses. I lift my head and enjoy the sight of her lying in my arms, breathless and boneless from pleasure. Even the throbbing of my desperate dick doesn't distract me from this sudden thought:

Here is a woman made to be worshipped.

# CHAPTER 34

# Marlowe

The only way to survive Brendan Sullivan is to ration him. Ring-fence him with very careful boundaries.

And that's precisely what I've been doing until now. I serve at his pleasure, both professionally and sexually, during working hours, and I leave the office religiously at six every day. When I'm at home, I focus on my amazing little daughter and I studiously avoid all thoughts of my sexy boss.

As a coping strategy for an extremely irregular professional dynamic, it works well.

None of my careful boundaries accommodate lying naked in his arms, in his *bed*, half-dead from orgasms while staring into his gaping, blue-ringed pupils as he gazes back at me with an expression of which a playboy like him shouldn't even be capable.

Nope.

I don't know if it's being in his home or the musical bonding we enjoyed, but this doesn't feel like a boss-slash-EA-with-benefits scenario. These last few minutes felt like something far more akin to a relationship, which is really not good.

Unfortunately, I'm too awash with endorphins to muster

up the energy to worry about it, because Brendan is kissing me again, and all I'm capable of is taking what this big, beautiful, hairy, blue-eyed man sees fit to give me. I reach between us and wrap my fingers around his gorgeous dick, and he breaks away from me with a groan. I fully expect him to flip me over and pull me up until I'm in his favourite position, but he doesn't.

He twists his body away and locates a condom from his bedside table, handing it to me. 'Ride me, love. I want to watch you ride me.'

Let me tell you, when Brendan Sullivan gazes into your eyes and tells you to ride him, there's only one option. I smile at him, a smile he returns with what looks like a sense of wonder as I climb on top of him. That sense of dissonance returns as I take him in. How is this my job, naked on a Friday morning and straddling the world's hottest guy as he lies, sprawled out on his huge bed for me, a mass of muscle and hair and smooth, tanned skin?

It's ridiculous, that's what it is. But, for once, I experience no conflict. No shame. There's nothing but well-being with a heady shot of arousal as I roll the condom down over his hardness like the pro I now am. It's all part of the foreplay, sheathing Brendan. Revelling in the anguished anticipation on his face as he endures my teasing touches.

He got me so wet just now. I brush his crown between my legs, right where his fingers were moments ago, until he's at my entrance. We stare at each other wordlessly. We gave each other the gift of vulnerability just now, when he said those incredible things about my looks and I admitted that he was the only man to have made me come, and I swear those confessions have supercharged the energy between us.

I lower myself carefully, slowly, down on him, and the expression on his face has a lump forming in my throat. He may be a playboy; he may have tonnes of energy and not enough focus as he goes through his daily life; he may have hundreds of other women that he sees outside of the office—I don't know—but in this moment I have him, and the delight of being the sole object of his attention is a drug so heady that I suspect I should run for the hills right now.

But I don't. I sink lower, until I've accommodated every glorious inch, and I plant a hand by his shoulder, throwing my weight forward so that my hair hangs loose, brushing his pecs. This busy, impatient, distractible man clamps one hand to my thigh and takes a lock of my hair between his fingers.

'Don't move for a sec,' he whispers, and I nod.

'Feel that?'

'Yeah.'

*That* is his dick pulsing inside me like a racehorse desperate to get out of the gates. Yet we both hold our positions. By his standards, this is basically tantric sex. I've never seen such quiet, such stillness, in him, especially when he's in this state of arousal. On instinct, I lower myself further forward so I can kiss him. His beard tickles my chin in the best possible way as he kisses me back hungrily, his fingers flexing against my thigh and his other hand finding the back of my neck, gripping me hard and pulling me further into the kiss. My nipples are brushing against the hair on his chest. Mmm.

He releases me. 'Now you can ride me,' he grits out. I bestow another kiss on his lips and I pull myself upright.

'You look like a goddess. You're how I imagined Boudica to look, all gorgeous skin and glorious hair.'

I grin. 'If I'm Boudica, does that make you my horse?'

His laugh is pained. 'Fuck, yeah, so you'd better fucking show me how you can ride me.'

And so I do. There's no doubt I feel exposed, self-conscious, in this position, but I embrace it and I drink up Brendan's avid gaze as I revel in the performance I'm putting on for him. As I drag myself up and down on his dick, that sense of exposure sharpens into something darker, more intoxicating. I'm simultaneously servicing him and taking my own pleasure from his glorious body, and it's hot as hell.

He grips my hips hard, his powerful body undulating beneath me, his jaw flexing and hips thrusting. This is a private porno with a very lucky audience of one. He's so bloody gorgeous, so supremely *male*, his voracious sexual appetites just an extension of that. I have a fleeting and totally inappropriate memory of Joe, whose intellectual arrogance and professional gravitas were undoubtedly sexier than what actually lay beneath his clothes. While I dismiss it immediately, it provides a wave of gratitude for this fine specimen of a man beneath me. I thought I was a woman who went for that tortured, cerebral, unobtainable type, but time has proven me wrong, it seems.

It strikes me that beneath those sharp suits, Brendan only ever overdelivers.

'Fuck me harder,' he orders me, accompanying his command with a vicious thrust, and I groan and obligingly up the intensity of my movements, grinding down on him until my thighs are burning and my skin is slick with sweat.

Our breaths are ragged. The feral look on his face as his climax builds would be enough to send me over the edge again all on its own. He's so often behind me that I don't get to see it enough. And the drag, drag, drag of each punishing inch of him against my inner walls is like nothing else on earth. The way he stroked my clit was one thing, but this pleasure is deeper, more primal. I feel it in my womb.

Until I met Brendan, I thought penetrative orgasms for women were mythical creatures, but the heat that builds and builds with each powerful upward thrust from him tells another story.

'You're so fucking gorgeous like this,' he rasps. It's more of a snarl, in fact. 'God, I love seeing you lose control, baby. This is the best sight ever.'

'Same here,' I pant.

He releases my hips and holds his hands up. I interlace my fingers with his and continue to move. He grips my hands tightly and it gives me the stability I need to meet his thrusts, to push down harder, to yield to the growing ache inside me. I let my eyelids flutter closed.

'Look at me,' he orders, and I open them. 'If I'm giving this to you, I get to see it break you. Understand?'

'Yeah,' I say. I'm trembling with effort and desire, seconds away from detonating. I fix my gaze on his gorgeous mouth and dilated pupils even as my face contorts with the tsunami of pleasure that's now on the cusp of overtaking me.

'That's it,' he croons as I grind down on him as hard as I can, shamelessly seeking out every drop of friction as I ride this endless, beautiful wave. 'Fucking milk me. Jesus *fuck*.'

I do. I milk him. I ride his dick in a way that will ruin me for every man and every vibrator in my future, because nothing and nobody hits the spot like Brendan Sullivan in all his glory. He pumps up into me as hard as he can while keeping hold of my hands, his abs flexing in a way that should be illegal and every other muscle group in his body conspiring to give me as good a time as they possibly can.

The pleasure is blinding. His face blurs as I come so hard that my peripheral vision goes black. I grip his hands like a cowgirl trying to stay on a bucking bronco and I ride it out as he swells inside me, his astonishing body going rigid before he pumps and pumps and pumps through his own orgasm in a desperate volley. His grunts and my cries intermingle, and the whole experience is so raw and dirty and intense that I feel as though I've been vaulted through the air, weightless and insubstantial and free.

When he's finished fucking me through his climax, he pulls me down and I collapse on his chest, panting and laughing into his neck at the intensity of it all. He twitches inside me, and I clench around him.

He groans into my hair, wrapping his arms around me. 'Fuck. Does your cunt go to a special cunt gym? Because it's fucking ripped. Does it lift weights? Do squats?'

'No, but it has an excellent personal trainer,' I quip.

He stills beneath me. 'I know I don't have the right to ask you this, but... just the one trainer?'

'Just the one,' I whisper, and he squeezes me tighter.

'Good.' There's a pause, then he clears his throat. 'My dick only has one PT too, and she's bloody gorgeous.'

CHAPTER 35

# Marlowe

I'm determined that this trip will be cause for celebration for Tabs, something for her to embrace rather than fear. She's known for years that a valve replacement operation is in her future, and we talk about it as one of those great, delineating events in life, as if a new pulmonary valve is as momentous as the coming of Christ. Which, of course, it will be for her and for those of us whose happiness depends solely on the health of this little girl.

*After the operation, you'll be able to run as far and as fast as you can!*

*After the operation, you can learn how to ice-skate!*

*And do parkour!*

*And trampoline!* (God, how badly she wants to go trampolining. I'll spend every hour of my weekends in those hellish, neon-lit trampoline parks that I've heard other parents from school complain about if I have to.)

So, yes, this procedure will mark a seismic shift in my daughter's life. It will, quite literally, give her a new lease of life, as if, by moving heaven and earth and paying hundreds of thousands of pounds, we've purchased a lease agreement that promises athleticism and freedom and boundless energy, for the next few years at least.

That's worth celebrating. So I take her into the centre of town to get some bits and pieces for the hospital: new PJs, some reading books and sticker books. She skips along beside me as I hold her hand and navigate the crowds of weekend shoppers.

'Take it easy, sweetie,' I say as gently as I can. Every time I have to remind my eight-year-old daughter to tamp down her natural little-girl energy and *take it easy*, a piece of me dies.

'Sorry, Mummy,' she says reflexively, and I squeeze her hand and smile down at her.

'You don't need to be sorry. I'm sorry I have to say these things to you. But in a few weeks you'll be running and skipping all you like, won't you?'

Her smile is huge. 'Yeah. And dancing.'

'And dancing. A *lot* of dancing. I can't wait to see you dance everywhere we go.'

'Will I be able to run through the airport?'

'On the way home, maybe. It depends on how you're feeling, honey. You may still be really tired from the operation. But you won't be out of breath. Isn't that amazing?'

'Will the airplane be like the one in *Home Alone?*'

'Um...' I cast my mind back to the movie. I'm pretty sure the McCallister adults travelled at the front of the plane. 'It won't be as fancy as that on the way out, but on the way back it'll be far fancier. We'll have seats that turn into actual beds. How cool is that?'

She beams at me and instantly starts to skip again. 'So cool! Will we get a pillow?'

I squeeze her hand gently to remind her to *take it easy*. I do not need an ambulance trip to the nearest A&E to become part of our day out. 'I think so. I've never flown in the fancy part before.' I've never flown long haul at all, in fact. 'Now, where to first?'

'Waterstones?' she suggests.

'Waterstones it is.'

Like me, Tabs loves reading. It's lucky, given that the range of physical activities available to her is pretty tiny. She's smart for her age and devours books quickly. Thank heaven for our local library. We don't buy many books, except on birthdays and Christmas—my wallet can't keep up with her reading pace. So the smoke comes off our library card. But I'm determined that she'll have some beautiful new books to enjoy on the flight and at the hospital.

Waterstones has always smelt like home to me: that scent of printed paper that's as dependable, as comforting, as a swaddle. I was a child of varied interests—I sang, and I played a lot of tennis, and I read as many books as I could get my hands on. Tabs doesn't seem as interested in singing, unless it's Taylor Swift or Gracie Abrams, and tennis has been out until now, but books are her jam a million times over.

'Oh wow,' she says reverently, glossing her little hand over the intricate gold foiling on some special editions of Penguin Classics. 'So pretty.'

'We can get one or two,' I tell her. They really are gorgeous. 'You might like *The Secret Garden*. There's a little boy in it who everyone thinks is ill, but he gets super strong by being out in nature, and he's running around in the secret garden by the end of the book.'

She throws me a *you poor, deluded woman* look. 'I don't think nature will fix me,' she says solemnly, and I don't know whether to laugh or cry. I do neither, in fact.

'No, but you'll be able to enjoy it a lot more when the *doctors* fix you up.'

She turns the book over and looks at the price.

'It's 'spensive, Mummy.'

I inhale sharply through my nose and get to my knees so I'm at eye level with her. It kills me that my eight-year-old girl worries about money, that she doesn't run into a bookshop and demand things like other kids her age might but instead frets about how we'll afford those things.

She's seen me scrimp all these years.

She knows that the material kind of treats don't come along much outside of Christmas and birthdays.

She's accustomed to there being precious little money to go around in the Winters household.

I recall something Athena said when she insisted on funding Tabby's opulent bedroom tent as her Father Christmas present last year and I tried to put my foot down. She told me, in her inimitably forceful and candid way, that *this is about ramming home a very important message to a sick little girl—that sometimes, in a world full of shitty disappointments, sometimes, just sometimes, life not only delivers but blows your fucking mind. It's always worth believing.*

I'll be damned if I'm going to let Tabs worry her way to this momentous and gruelling operation. If ever there was a time to channel her godmother and ram home the importance of an abundance mindset, it's now.

'It's more expensive than the others, yes, because it's a beautiful special edition,' I tell her now, putting the book into her hands. 'More love and care has gone into making this book, so it has a higher value. It's special, just like you're special, and this trip we're going on is very, very special. So how about we treat ourselves, because a special trip deserves a special book. Hmm? What do you think?'

She nods slowly, her face still solemn. 'Do you have enough money?'

'Oh, sweetheart, of course I do. I have this great new job, remember? And it means that we can afford to get some nice treats for our trip. *Special* treats. And you can put this pretty book by your bed in the hospital, and hopefully it'll help to comfort you. We'll bring Bartholomew, too.'

Bartholomew is Tabby's new Jellycat bear. Athena bought him for her as soon as we got our date for the operation. He's soft and solemn and sports a very smart pair of red-and-white pyjamas. He'll be our wingman for the trip.

'Mummy,' she says, and then pauses in that way that tells me she has something on her mind.

'What is it, my love?' I tuck a strand of hair behind her ear, still on my knees.

She looks at the carpet. 'Will you be with me the whole time in the hospital? I don't want to be alone, even with Bartholomew. I want you.'

So this is what's bothering her.

'I will be with you the whole time, except when they're doing the actual operation,' I promise her. 'I'll be stroking your hair when they make you go to sleep, and when you wake up afterwards, I'll be there. I'm not allowed in the oper-ating theatre in case of germs. They have to keep it really clean.'

Her chin wobbles. 'But I don't want to be without you. It's scary.'

I blink my eyes rapidly to stem the tears threatening to well up. 'I know it's scary, sweetie. I *know*. But you won't be awake during the operation. So you'll have me with you all the times you're awake. And do you know what? It'll just feel like a few minutes that you're asleep, but when you wake up you'll have a whole new valve. Isn't that amazing?'

'What if I can't go to sleep?' she mutters, reaching for a strand of my hair and rubbing it between her fingers. She's done this since she was a tiny girl.

'You don't need to worry about that, because they have this magic sleepy gas. It's so funny! You breathe it in, and then the doctor will ask you to count backwards from ten or some other number, but you'll start snoring before you finish. What do you think of that?'

Her smile is slow and wondrous. 'No I won't. I can count backwards.'

'Yes you will. I promise you. It'll feel lovely, like you're floating through the clouds.'

What I don't tell her, of course, is that watching your child go under is one of the most distressing things a parent can witness. Stroking your little girl's hair as she drifts off under anaesthetic on a cold, clinical gurney is so strikingly similar to how I imagine it would be if she passed away that I can't bear it. I really can't.

I'm not sure how I'll survive those hours after they wheel my unconscious child into theatre, sitting in the waiting room all alone as strangers operate on the most important organ in her body, rocking and waiting and praying for good news until my tears run dry and my knuckles turn white.

I honestly don't.

# Marlowe

'Mum? What's up? Is Tabs okay?'

I hurry into the ladies' loos at work, praying they're empty. They are. As soon as my mother's name flashed up on my phone, I bolted from my desk like a greyhound after a mechanical rabbit.

'We're at A&E,' she says in a shaky voice.

'Oh God. Oh God.' I squeeze my eyes closed and press my lips together, clapping a hand over my mouth. I'm not sure if I'm trying to stay quiet or squeeze away the pain through sheer force of will.

'We took her for a little walk in the park. It was such a nice day, but we kept it very slow. We just wanted her to get some fresh air.'

'I know. It's okay.' My parents treat Tabby with kid gloves, even more than I do. They're so devoted and so conscientious, and I won't have them beating themselves up over something that could have happened on my watch. 'What happened?'

'Her fingers and mouth turned blue, and her eyes went glassy. It was so terrifying. We didn't know what to do, so your dad carried her out to the street and flagged down a cab. We're at Denmark Hill.'

'What have they said? What are her other symptoms? Have they triaged her? They need to take her sats. Have you shown them the form?'

The questions are pouring out of me now in a deluge of panic. I trust my parents implicitly. I know they'd run into traffic for my daughter, just as I know Mum has an oximeter in her handbag and a copy of Tabby's medical information form on her phone. But nobody knows her condition as well as I do. No one has more experience than me of managing her A&E trips, producing all the information and educating every single medic who has contact with her.

In short, no one can advocate for Tabby like me when it's crunch time.

'We gave them the list,' Mum tells me, her voice still quavery. 'Um, a nurse said she'd be triaged within the next few minutes.' She's a level-headed woman, but the pair of them are getting on in years, and an emergency like this is discombobulating for anyone. They've been with me and Tabs to A&E a couple of times, but they've never taken her by themselves.

'Have you taken her sats?' I ask in a rush. 'Do you have her knees to her chest? You need to. It prioritises the blood flow to her lungs.' My tears are falling freely now. I can't help it. We're so close. We're so fucking close to this operation, to getting Tabby a solution that will last her until she's in her early teens, at least.

When your child is oxygen deficient, time is everything. Any dithering around or failure to take Tabby's condition seriously could lead to all sorts of horrific outcomes. I can't even think about it. I feel so fucking helpless as I listen to my parents fannying about. 'Robert, she needs to tuck her knees up higher. That's it, Tabs. Good girl.'

'Sats, Mum,' I prompt her. God, I feel so fucking helpless,

standing here in this marble bathroom as my daughter fights for every breath in a crowded A&E.

'We have the oximeter on,' Mum says. 'Hang on, darling. Let's see. Eighty-one.'

I blow out a breath. This is hopeless. 'Mum. Listen to me. You need to do whatever it takes to get her seen, okay? She needs oxygen *now*. I don't care how busy it is or how big of a bitch you need to be. You need to track down whoever you can and shout as loudly as you can until she gets treated. She needs you to be her voice. Don't let her down.' My mum is usually a strident woman, but I can tell this is knocking her for six. I feel bad as soon as I say that last part, but now is not the time to be meek and polite. Not for me. Not for my parents. If I can't get there, then I damn well need them to forget about their natural inclination to bow to medical authorities and behave nicely. I need them to shout and scream their way to getting Tabs the help she requires.

'Okay, darling,' Mum says, and I wish, I really wish that I could hear less fear and more steeliness in her voice right now. I glance at my watch. Just after five.

'I'll be there as soon as I can, alright? I'll try to sneak out of work early. Keep me posted. Can you put me on with Tabs?'

'She's struggling to breathe,' Mum says. 'She won't be able to talk.'

'I don't care. Just put me on, please. And go flag down a doctor over there.'

There's some feedback and the mutter of voices as Mum gives Dad the phone and instructs him to hold it to Tabby's ear.

'Tabs? You there, sweetie?'

I hear some ragged breathing and a choked whimper, and I swear it makes me want to rip my heart out of my lungs and give her my own bloody pulmonary valve. I sniff hard and make my voice sound as calm as possible.

'Listen to me, darling. I'm so sorry I'm not there, but Granny and Grandpa are going to keep you safe while you wait for a doctor, okay?'

The door to the loos flies open and Elaine comes in, concern written all over her kind face. She stops dead at the sight of me in such a state but doesn't leave. Fuck. Right now, having Elaine rumble me is the least of my worries. I force myself to keep talking to Tabs as if I'm alone.

'We've done this before. Remember what an old hand you are at this. It's horrible and scary, but you'll get some oxygen soon, and until then I know your tricks will help you. Are you hugging your knees?'

She whimpers, and I take it as an affirmation.

'Good girl. Breathe nice and slowly. As slowly as you can. Nice deep breaths. It'll all be over soon. Once you have this operation, these scary trips will be a thing of the past, okay? Remember that, my love. Remember what a strong, brave girl you are. I love you so, so much, and I'm going to be there as soon as I can, okay?'

'Okay,' she manages, sounding as wheezy as a mini Darth Vader.

'I love you. Bye.' My voice fails me on that last word. As I go to end the call, I can barely see the red button through my tears.

When I dare to look up, Elaine is still staring at me. I put my phone on the vanity and wipe both hands under my eyes.

'I'd ask you if everything's okay, but it's clearly not,' she says, and then she's closing in and wrapping me up in a huge hug. Even as she squeezes me, I hold back. If I let myself collapse on her, I'm not sure I'll be able to pull myself back together enough to get myself to Denmark Hill Hospital.

'Your daughter?' she asks, pulling away enough to scrutinise me.

'Yeah. Brendan doesn't know about her,' I add hastily, and she nods sagely.

'There are a lot of things in this job that Brendan doesn't need to know about, bless him. Is she in hospital?'

'She's in A&E with my parents. She has a congenital heart defect and she ends up there quite often,' I tell Elaine as I grab a couple of tissues from a box beside the washbasin. I blow my nose noisily.

'Oh my dear. I'm so sorry. That's just tragic. How old is she?'

'She's eight.'

'Well, you should go be with her then.'

My face crumples again. I can feel the panic welling up. 'I want to, but I told her that when I took this job I might not always be able to make it to the hospital.' I take a look at Elaine's face, contorted with sympathy. She's a mother and a lovely person, as straight as they come. There's no need for politics or game-playing with her. I know I can trust her.

'It's only for a few more days,' I tell her. 'We're going to the US to get her operated on privately. She needs a new pulmonary valve.' I hesitate. 'That's why I told Brendan I had jury duty next week.'

Her lips press together in an attempt to prevent a smile. I suspect Elaine's been working on a need-to-know basis with Brendan for a long time. 'Well, he's thrown his toys enough about that, hasn't he? Let's not add any sick kids into the mix. I told you what a total twat he was when my son was ill.' Her face grows more serious. 'Listen to me, love. You do what you need to do. Brendan's a big boy, and I'll hold the fort when you're away. But for now, you get yourself over to that hospital and go be with that little girl of yours, where you belong. I'll tell Brendan you weren't feeling well.'

'Okay,' I say with a watery smile. She's such a lovely lady. 'Thank you so much.'

'It's not a bother. I hope you don't mind my asking, but I assume this job is funding the US trip?'

She raises a meaningful eyebrow, and I nod, feeling a flush of mortification sweep over my cheeks. Oh my God, *Elaine knows*. This is horrifying.

She pats my hand. 'I'm well aware of the sacrifices you're making for your daughter. She's a very lucky girl to have a mother like you. Now, get over there and raise hell until those doctors give her everything she needs, you hear me?'

# Marlowe

The sound of my alarm is exactly as violating as a power drill to the head. I don't actually possess the energy to sit up, so I turn my exhausted body over with great difficulty and slide out of my bed on my stomach before crawling over to where the alarm is ringing shrilly across the room. I plugged my phone in over here on purpose last night—I knew that if it was within reach from the bed I'd most likely turn it off in my sleep.

The only motivation I have to shut the damn thing up is the acute desire not to wake Tabs, who is hopefully sleeping the sleep of the exhausted next door. She was too broken to sleep in her warrior princess tent last night—or at one o'clock this morning, rather—when we got home from the hospital, instead opting to curl up in her bed. They put us through the wringer last night, with a million tests and the inevitable hours of waiting before and after each one.

I stroked her hair until she fell asleep, but I sat on the edge of her bed for hours afterwards, gazing at her in the dim light of her nightlight and willing her heart to give us just another week.

Just one more week until we can get on that plane. Until my little girl's heart will finally be in the hands of the people who can make her suffering go away.

I turn the alarm off and reach deep within me to find the strength to get to my feet and into the shower. I am, ironically, on my hands and knees.

It's probably not the last time I'll find myself in this position today.

I cannot think of anything my poor, broken heart and exhausted body is less capable of this morning than having to be someone's sex toy. No matter that Brendan is objectively drool-worthy, or that the dynamic between us has been super-charged and, dare I say, intimate since we "worked" from his home. Yesterday, I gave everything I had to ensure my child survived the night, which means that today I am broken, broken, broken.

The good news is that, after depositing Mark at the office and grabbing some files, Brendan heads out on a site visit for most of the morning, buying me some breathing space. Elaine, bless her, is very solicitous, bringing me a delicious double espresso and a pain au chocolat from the fancy, overpriced café across the square. She enquires after Tabs and is endlessly patient while I spew out all my worries. After all, I can't vent to my parents. I sent them home when I got to the hospital yesterday evening. If nothing else, I needed them well-rested to look after Tabs today.

'Just take it as easy as you can this morning,' she tells me. 'There are some beds in the basement by the doctor's surgery. You could take a nap there?'

'I'm good, thanks,' I tell her, hoping that my layers of

concealer will do their job and conceal the purple bruises under my eyes, even if they can't do much about the reddened puffiness. 'I want to get through as much as possible before we fly.'

She nods, mouth pursed. 'Okay, but just look after yourself. You'll be no good to that little girl of yours if you're an exhausted shell.'

The bad news is that Brendan texts me from the building site he's visiting.

> Got us a suite at the Kingsley Canary Wharf

> I'll be there at 1

> I want you naked and waiting for me in
> that bed

Fucking excellent.

Holy crap, this suite is *gorgeous*. Not to mention vast. I can't even imagine how much it costs. Thousands and thousands, probably. What a waste of money to use it for an hour. Usually, I'd be drawn to the incredible west-facing terrace that looks out over the iconic chrome-and-glass skyline of Canary Wharf to the Shard and beyond, but today there's only one siren's call in this room, and it's the bed.

The huge, white bed with its fluffy-looking duvet and its mountains of plump pillows.

Oh my dear Lord. I may not be religious, but someone up there is answering my prayers.

I undress as swiftly as my poor, dulled motor skills will

allow, draping my clothes over the back of a nearby *chaise longue* and chucking several pillows off the bed so I can get access. As my exhausted body slides between the cool sheets I let out an actual moan of appreciation. What is this sorcery? Did angels pluck feathers from magical geese to stuff this mattress topper? I have never in my life been in a bed quite as comfortable, as cosseting, as this. After the tribulations of last night, it's like going back to the womb.

A very soft, very expensive womb.

I snuggle further down into the bed, one perfect pillow cradling my cheek, and I close my eyes.

## BRENDAN

I feel like the king of the fucking world. This building, a mixed-use skyscraper encompassing retail, residential and some office space, is set to be the fucking bomb. It's green, it's glamorous, and has Sullivan written all over it. (Literally. Our hoardings are heavily branded.) I'm obsessed with momentum. Each project we undertake needs to build on the ones before. To push the envelope in terms of aesthetics and construction expertise. To show the world—and our shareholders—that Sullivan Construction will never rest on its laurels.

I grab a key card from the very attractive, very interested brunette at The Kingsley's check-in desk and take myself up to the tenth floor where my suite is. I feel like a rockstar, and I want to fuck like one. I've been thinking all morning about how I'm going to take Marlowe. Maybe pressed up against the shower tiles first—a scorching hot quickie to take the edge off —before tying her up and edging the fuck out of her.

Yeah.

That's what I'll do.

If this morning's site visit was foreplay for my ego, having the most beautiful woman I've ever laid eyes on restrained and writhing and begging for my cock will have my self-confidence going stratospheric. I know she loves it when I'm in alpha mode. I know submitting to me gets her off like nothing else.

Except that when I swagger into our suite, the very same beautiful woman is not lying back for me, legs spread and smile teasing, like I'd demanded. Instead, she appears to be out cold.

You've got to be fucking kidding me.

'Hey, love,' I say quietly. I don't want to scare the bejesus out of her, as my parents would say.

Nothing.

I tiptoe closer. She's snoring very softly and very prettily. One arm is folded over the covers, its hand under her cheek, its shoulder temptingly golden. The rest of her is concealed. Her gorgeous hair is splayed over the pillow.

'Marls?' I whisper.

Still nothing.

*Fuck.*

I debate heading into the bathroom and getting myself off in the shower, but I'd like to think I'm not that weak-willed. I cast my mind back to first thing this morning, when I saw her briefly, and begrudgingly admit that she didn't look great. Stunning, obviously, but not too well. She looked bloody exhausted, come to think of it, and I recall too late that she went home early yesterday because she was feeling sick. I sigh.

Fuck's sake. Looks like I'm sleeping with my executive assistant today without actually *sleeping* with her. I strip off my clothes and lay them next to Marlowe's, noting with interest that her lacy bra and thong are on top of her pile. So she's naked under there, is she?

This should be fun.

Carefully, I turn back the covers and lose a pillow or two before sliding in next to Marlowe. The sheets are cool, but my skin picks up the warmth of hers even without touching it. She has her back to me, but as I pull the duvet over myself, she stirs with a whimper and rolls over.

I freeze for a second. She's still fast asleep, and, honestly? It's a captivating sight. I never, *ever* spend the night with women, so I never get to see women sleeping up close. Her face is so peaceful, it tugs at my heartstrings. The little crease she so often has between her eyebrows is gone, smoothed out by sleep. Her long lashes, black with mascara today, fan across her cheeks.

She looks like an angel. An actual seraph, in the most literal sense of the word. And, as I watch her sleep, something akin to awe floods my body like warm treacle. If she'd ever stop bolting for the doors at 6 pm every day and agree to go out with me one evening, I'd gladly let her sleep over, if just for this.

I know this: my dick may be hardening appreciatively at her scent, at the proximity of all her soft, golden skin. But the rest of me has no intention of waking her. If she needs a nap this badly, I won't be the one to deprive her of it.

Besides—and this is pretty creepy, to be honest—I can do without sex this once if I get to watch her sleep instead. I thought both our walls were coming down after that amazing sex at my place, but she's still so bloody boundaried in many ways. I still don't feel like I know her properly—like I've earned the right to know her properly. In this moment, she's giving me something without knowing it. A piece of the side of her she keeps so carefully hidden away.

And I'll damn well take it. I'm paying her for plenty of exclusives. I can still feel that flash of pleasure I got when she confessed that I was the only guy she was fucking, let alone the only guy who could make her come. But for some reason the knowledge that I'm the only one who gets to see her like *this*, sleeping and vulnerable and trusting, feels even more precious.

I ease in closer to her, sliding an arm around her waist and tugging her in more flush against me. She shifts a little, snuggling even closer, and my chest tightens in a way that usually only happens when Mark and I are cuddling. I settle her with a whispered *shh* and stroke my fingertips lightly down her spine until she stills again, her head tucked in beneath my chin.

As her breathing returns to that slow, steady state I assume is normal for someone sleeping, I lie there, tense and alert. Tense because I don't want to wake her and I also don't know what the fuck I'm doing here. Alert because my consciousness has shrunk to this little world under the covers, where my entire focus is on her shallow, even breaths, and the rise and fall of her ribcage, and the sensation of her satin-smooth skin beneath my fingertips, and the way her hair smells when I inhale it and feels when I brush my lips over it.

This is not the way it was supposed to be.

I was supposed to hire a Seraph PA to run my office and ride my dick on demand, both equally competently. Marlowe has upheld her end of the bargain. After all, she nails both sides of the role admirably. *I'm* the problem here, the creepy boss snorting his EA's hair like an addict and holding her while she sleeps instead of fucking me like I'm paying her to.

Let's revisit that last part.

*Holding her while she sleeps.*

I don't do girlfriends, commitment, even regular dating. Marlowe is the person I've racked up by far the highest number of orgasms with. I suppose, if I think about it logically, regular fucking would engender some level of... familiarity, for want of a better word.

But it honestly never occurred to me that fucking the same woman day after day would make me want *more*. If anything,

I was worried I'd get bored and want to trade her in after a month or two. I never, ever thought to worry that I'd get attached, that I'd want evenings with her. It never struck me that I'd lie here one day and feel grateful to be having an experience with her that feels more intimate than a quick fuck at lunchtime. And I certainly never expected to find myself daydreaming about this very thing happening on a lazy Saturday morning in my bed.

Jesus fuck, no, Brendan!

Intimacy is not a dynamic I've ever, ever craved. It's just not. Why would I want that? My sister may be happy, my brother may have fallen hard for Athena, but I've always wanted more. More wealth. More success. More validation. More *adulation*, if I'm honest. Recognition. And all the trappings that come with that. Models on my arm at events. Sports cars. Penthouses. Catamarans. I don't want to tie myself down, for fuck's sake.

More accurately, I don't want to *want to* tie myself down. I have no desire to put limits on my success or my rewards. Because if I limit myself to one woman, no matter how incredible, it's just a fucking waste. My FOMO will go through the roof. I want to live a big life, a fast life, a life where the pace keeps me on my toes and the prizes get more and more glittering and the steady stream of women hotter and hotter. I want to be untethered. Unencumbered.

I *don't* want to be feeling sick to my stomach because my EA is taking off for two weeks on some fucking civic duty that she's insisting on seeing through because she thinks society's needs are more important than my needs.

I don't want to be so thoroughly disinterested when I look at any other woman. When I even *think* about the parade of willing, gorgeous women I'll take out on the town when she's off martyring herself to our judicial system.

I want my mojo back.

I want my self-respect back, for fuck's sake.

And I'll get them.

I'm Brendan fucking Sullivan.

Having Marlowe is supposed to make my crazy schedule run more efficiently. I know that. But for now, I'll just let myself lie here and inhale the honeyed scent of her hair for a few more minutes, and I'll allow each warm exhale she makes against my chest to bleed into my heart and warm it up, and I'll try my absolute damnedest to bottle up the way this makes me feel.

God knows, when she's gone, I'll need to pull myself the fuck together and get back on that damn horse.

# CHAPTER 38

# Marlowe

Our bags stand packed and ready in the living room of our flat. I've dotted every *i* and crossed every *t* of the endless paperwork I've had to complete for this journey Tabs and I are about to undertake. Apparently, what we're doing is known as "medical tourism". I'm pretty sure that term is better suited to jetting off to Turkey for some cheap boobs than travelling across the Atlantic to give my daughter her best chance of survival, but whatever.

And today is my last day of work before my so-called jury duty. We fly tomorrow, and Elaine, who is now fully briefed on my darkest secrets, has vowed to hold the fort for Brendan.

If I'm honest, I'm looking forward to putting some distance between me and him. The vibe's been weird this week, to say the least. I was so, so mortified when I woke up in his arms the other day. He had to wake me—we'd been lying there for an hour, apparently. He forked out all that money on a suite and it was wasted because I was too busy being unconscious to do my job properly. The job he pays me very well to do.

I will say it was the best (and most badly needed) nap of

my life, and waking up in the warm, hairy, muscular cradle of Brendan's body was fairly spectacular, too. As soon as I had my wits about me, I started apologising profusely and kind of grabbed his dick, but he just laughed very sweetly and said he considered napping an even better use of time and money than sex.

He was definitely only saying it to be nice, but he did prise my fingers off his dick before he pulled me back into his arms and cuddled me some more. I'm pretty sure he sniffed my hair, too.

If napping with my boss-with-benefits is a red flag on every level, then his behaviour since then has been even more of a red flag. Once we left that suite behind us, the caring, cuddly Brendan I'd woken up with disappeared. In his place, I've had to deal with childish, cocky, mercurial, alpha-hole Brendan, who's more interested in throwing his weight around and getting quick fucks than anything approaching the intimacy we've enjoyed in recent weeks.

Yesterday morning he called me into his office, told me to lock the door, pushed his chair away from his desk and pulled out his dick. As soon as I'd made him come with my mouth, he uttered the immortal words, *Go on. Clear off now.* The day before that, he fucked me wordlessly over his desk while he was muted on a conference call, something that was indescribably hot and yet left me feeling grimy. Especially because he pulled out, wandered off to deal with the condom, and then threw himself on the sofa to continue the call, leaving me bent over and exposed.

While this kind of treatment is nothing worse than I expected when I took this job, it's a far cry from the treatment he gave me in his bed and in that hotel suite, and that makes it a million times worse.

Maybe he's pissed off that I'm leaving him in the lurch and he's taking it out on me. Maybe he's freaking out that his solidly transactional no-strings-attached office sex is turning into piano duets and daytime naps. I don't know, and to be honest it doesn't matter.

Because you know what? He's right. He may not be communicating his emotions in the most evolved way, and his entitled, dismissive behaviour may be hurting me more than I care to let on, but the guy is right to pull back, to redraw his boundaries. God knows, one of us has to.

So yes. I'm determined to view this trip as a forced reset, a chance for us both to regroup. When I return, my daughter will be in possession of a shiny new, fully functioning pulmonary valve and I'll be in a position of greater strength. Once I have a better idea of the cost of her ongoing medical needs over the next few years, I can set myself an end date for this job and stick to it.

And I vow to myself that I'll exercise more agency next time. I'll choose a position that doesn't involve me selling my soul. I won't even tolerate dickheads like my previous boss, Dean. I'm done with being at the mercy of power-hungry guys at every level of management.

There's only today to get through. I dress carefully. I'm sure Brendan will want his fill of me before I go off on leave, and why shouldn't he? I wear a flirty little pale blue fit-and-flare dress and some of his favourite white lace underwear, and I go to work prepared to service my boss in whatever way he requires today. In my mind, his treating me like a whore this week is my penance for lying to him. For using him to secure my daughter's future.

It's just one day. I can handle whatever he gives me.

'I'll miss this while you're gone,' Brendan comments, but his tone is idle, borderline disinterested. Which would be fine if we weren't in the position that we're in right now. As it is, I'm lying in my underwear on the carpet in his office as he straddles me, his huge body braced above me, his thick thighs in their fine wool trousers bracketing my head. With one hand he pins my wrists above my head, while he uses the other to feed me his dick.

I don't answer him because I can't. My mouth is too full of his dick, my focus entirely on not suffocating and not choking. From here, he looks evil and powerful and foolhardy: a dangerous combination.

'You're very good at it, you know,' he continues, his tone callous. 'If you do a truly excellent job of making me come then I promise I'll fantasise about it when I've got another woman in this exact position next week.'

It's the most backhanded of compliments, and it stings, humiliates, just as much as he intends it to do. I hope he considers himself lucky that my mouth is too full to answer him.

He pulls out slowly and groans before jamming his dick so far down my throat that I audibly gag. Even through my blind, teary panic, I register how gorgeous he is. He's right, of course. He can have as many women as he wants lying here for him next week, sucking his dick when I'm not here to entertain him. But with the jealousy comes disgust that he would be as tasteless as to ram that point home right as he's ramming his dick home inside my body.

He's lashing out, going on the attack like a hurt little boy, and it makes me despise him. God knows, it's occasions like this that underscore just how fully we seraphs earn every penny of our money.

'Don't think I'm going to make you come,' he's saying now, seemingly fascinated with the sight of his dick disappearing past my lips. 'I have a plan for you later. If you want that orgasm, you can have it. Just remember, love, beggars can't be choosers.'

*Ain't that the truth, mister.*

Ahead of the International Green Building Summit, Brendan has organised a Friday afternoon working lunch at the office for some of his bros (his word) at competing firms. The theory is that, every now and then, they get together to shoot the breeze, bitch about some of the biggest contractors, and share trade secrets which I imagine include which government officials have palms they can grease and other equally shady topics.

I just hope his bro-lunch improves his personality. While his aggressive blow job earlier seems to have taken the edge off his foul mood, it could use more help. I really don't like this churlish, sulky side of him.

He meant what he said about bros. When his business associates file into the large meeting room down the corridor from his offices, there is not a single female-identifying professional among them. Sullivan Construction may talk the talk on diversity and equality, but it seems that at the upper echelons of this industry, the old boys' network still runs like clockwork.

I leave them to their silver buckets full of champagne and endless platters of Nobu sushi—no coffee and dried-out sandwiches for these big hitters—and settle at my desk. I'm intent on ensuring that I've done everything possible to make this handover as smooth as possible for Elaine.

The strategy team is still putting the finishing touches to the high-tech slideshow that will accompany Brendan's speech, but I've been working with them on compiling a briefing document for Brendan with answers to the most likely questions he'll field.

I've also spent a large chunk of my time liaising with our in-house PR team to fill his schedule of press interviews and with our Commercial Director and her team on prepping him for meetings with various European governments who may be keen to commission Sullivan for overseas projects.

It's a lot, and it doesn't assuage my guilt about leaving Brendan in the lurch for the biggest event of his year, even if I tell myself that the majority of the work—and skill—lies in the pre-event organisation. By the time he rocks up at the conference, he should be fully prepped and ready to smash it.

After a couple of hours, I take a call from the console in the meeting room. It's Brendan. 'Come through for a sec, will you, love?'

'Sure.' He shouldn't really be calling me *love* in front of his mates, but it's not an uncommon term of endearment, so hopefully it'll slide. I stand and grab my notepad and pen, heading down the corridor to the meeting room. I hear them before I see them—a rowdy, unintelligible jumble of male voices. And when I open the door, the odour of booze hits me. It smells like a brewery in here. The table is littered with empty champagne bottles and remnants of food, and most of the men have ditched their jackets and rolled their shirt sleeves up.

'Here she is!' Brendan shouts. 'The woman of the hour.' He leans back in his chair at the head of the table and grins at me. He looks gorgeous, if pretty dishevelled, and I smile back at him.

'Come here, come here!' He beckons me over in an exaggerated manner and I go to him. 'Guys. *Guys.* This is Marlowe, my *very* beautiful assistant, who's also incredibly competent at *everything* she does. Isn't that right, baby?' He clamps a hand to my bottom, and I freeze. What the hell is he doing?

There are disorderly catcalls at Brendan's crude words. I feel like a stripper who's been booked for a stag party. I stare down at him, willing him with my eyes to rein it in or let me go, but his grin has turned dark, and there's a callous expression on his handsome face now.

'Did you need something?' I ask, hoping the stiffness of my tone tells him how low my tolerance level for this shit is.

He pretends to consider. 'I don't know. Do we need something? I know *I* need something. I always need something from you, but you don't care, do you? You're buggering off for two weeks.' He squeezes my bottom before sliding his hand down the back of my thigh. When he finds the hem of my dress, he burrows underneath it and moves his hand upwards. My entire body goes still, and there's a flash of heat across my face and neck.

'Brendan,' I hiss.

'What? Like I said, you're fucking off for a fortnight. I think you owe me. Who here thinks this pretty little lady owes me?'

There's another rowdy chorus that apparently sounds to Brendan's drunken ears like assent, because his hand moves even higher. I clench my thighs together, trapping it. I want to reach down and slap his hand away. I want to run for that door, but I'm frozen to the spot. All I can focus on is the smoothness of the fancy Sullivan pen in my hand and on the ruddy cheeks of the guy sitting closest to Brendan.

I wonder if he knows champagne makes him go red?

Or maybe it's having his host try to finger his assistant in plain sight that has his colour heightened.

These men are all strangers. All people who have actual business dealings with Brendan. People with whose assistants I've probably had email contact. Phone contact. Outside of my specific arrangement with Brendan, I've conducted myself with perfect professionalism these past few weeks. I'm representing both him and his firm at the highest level, after all.

And here he is treating me like a two-bit whore in front of his drunken cronies.

'Open up, baby,' he stage-whispers now. His voice sounds so nasty.

'No.' Every muscle in my body is tensed so hard that I'll probably pull them all. I glare down at him, because I cannot look at anyone.

'Aww, come on, darling,' someone jeers from the other end of the table.

Brendan edges his fingers further up, working against my locked thighs. 'Look, there's no reason to be shy. They all signed NDAs before they got here—they know the score. I've told them all about you. We've had lunch, but I've promised them a little show for dessert. They want to see your tits, and they want to taste your sweet, sweet cunt, and Anthony over there was hoping you'd blow him because it's his birthday this weekend. So why don't you do us both a favour and remind yourself exactly what I'm paying you for?'

Every single disgusting word crawls over my skin like a cockroach. I have never in my life felt simultaneously so invisible and so splayed open. I usually love him touching me, but every second that his hands are on my skin feels like a violation of the highest order. His touch has nothing on his words, though.

It's obvious he's drunk, but *NDAs*? He cooked up this entire plan, and I'd bet every fucking pound he's paid me that it's because he's pissed off with me for taking leave. He's admitted as much. So he's expecting me to strip off and put out and behave like some party piece, to tolerate a mauling from him and his revolting, drunken, chauvinistic friends? He expects me to get on my knees and put on a show?

I've done a lot to save my daughter's life. I've sold myself body and soul, to this man, I've jumped so far into the deep end I don't know if I'll ever find land again, and I've momentarily feared that I was gaining feelings. I've sunk to lows I could never have imagined, but these are depths I cannot plumb.

He's paying me to fuck him. He's paying me to relieve his stress and his boredom, to fulfil his fantasies. And I know he said he liked to watch, so maybe I should have seen it coming. But nothing is worth this level of shame and humiliation and invasion.

*Nothing.*

I think about my tiny, sick daughter. About our bags packed and ready. About the operation she's going to endure. I think about the money, Brendan's money, sitting in our bank account. We're good to go for now. I don't need to endure this. He may, in this moment, be trying to make me feel like I have no agency, but I do. I fucking do. I've done enough to save Tabs, but I bloody well won't do this.

I summon every ounce of that fierce mama bear energy that I can draw on so readily when it's Tabs I need to advocate for. I throw my notepad and pen on the table and reach behind myself, digging my nails into his wrist and pulling his hand out from between my legs.

'Stop,' I spit at him. *My safeword.* The word I haven't even had in reserve for the past few weeks, except for one brief moment with Ethan Kingsley. I look down at his brattish, entitled face and feel only contempt. Disgust. 'Stop, stop, stop. You can blow the birthday boy yourself for all I care, you sick fuck. I'm out.'

# CHAPTER 39

# Marlowe

Tabby's hospital gown is pale blue and dotted with Peppa Pig and George Pig's heads. She outgrew Peppa years ago, but I suspect these little piggies represent a safe space for her. She's tired and a little faint after a long morning of the obligatory fasting, but she's in good spirits.

For the millionth time, I am in awe of her resilience and her courage. I've hoped and prayed for this procedure for so many years. More than that, I've fought and sacrificed and gambled my own wellbeing on taking back our power from the NHS and pulling this operation off on our terms. I've fixated on pretty much nothing else for the past three years.

And now the moment is upon us, and our medical team is a veritable who's who of paediatric medical qualifications, and I am utterly terrified. I've been shaken up since I gathered my stuff up at the speed of light on Friday and stalked out of the office, reassuring a very concerned Elaine that I'd handled the situation and was okay. And when we got on that plane, much as I was glad to put space between myself and Brendan, I couldn't help feeling that I was leading Tabby to her certain death like a lamb to the slaughter.

I know I'm being irrational. I know too well that emotions like that are intrusive thoughts, nothing more. I know she's in great hands and that this operation is a lifeline and not a death sentence. Still, I can't quash the relentless anxiety. It doesn't help that I'm jet lagged and exhausted—spending last night on a plastic pull-out couch in Tabby's hospital room wasn't conducive to a restorative night's sleep.

And it definitely doesn't help that I'm all alone over here, the sole adult in charge of a terrifyingly fragile little girl. In hindsight, it was stupid not to cobble together the thousands of pounds needed to bring Mum and Dad over with us and put them up somewhere cheap nearby. I'm kicking myself, because I hadn't realised how desperately I'd want another adult here to hold *me* and parent *me* and tell *me* everything was going to be okay.

The only thing keeping me together, to be honest, is the unwavering determination I have to be a brave, reassuring face for my daughter. She's the vulnerable one here. She's the one who's about to endure a serious operation in a strange place, thousands of miles from home, and she deserves the support of a mother who isn't falling apart herself.

I stroke her hair as she lies on the gurney. A woman with a wide, friendly smile and the most beautiful dark eyes approaches. The anaesthetist, I guess, judging from the big badge on her scrubs that features a sleeping cloud emitting a stream of Zs.

'Hi, Tabby!' she says in a perky voice. I have to hand it to the Americans; they're way more effusive and cheery than us Brits, and right now Tabs and I will take all the peppiness we can get. She keeps talking. 'I'm Dr Martinez, and I'll be your sleep doctor today. Do you know what that is?'

'You make me go to sleep?' Tabby whispers, so shyly it's almost inaudible. I stroke her hair again.

'Exactly! My job is to help you fall into a special sleep during your heart operation and make sure you don't feel anything. When you wake up afterward, your heart will be working better! Have you ever fallen asleep for a doctor before?'

Tabs cranes her neck to look up at me. 'Have I, Mummy?'

'You have,' I tell her. 'A few times. But you were too little to remember.' *Which makes one of us, because I'm still traumatised.*

'It's a lot of fun,' Dr Martinez tells Tabs. 'Because guess what? We put a special mask on you and it smells good! Tell me, do you like the smell of cherry, or strawberries, or bubblegum, maybe?'

Tabby's eyes meet mine again, and I smile. I know just what she'll choose.

'Bubblegum,' she says, a little more loudly this time. 'But I'm not allowed to eat it at home.'

Dr Martinez laughs. 'Right? It's not great for your tummy if you swallow it. But this way, you get to enjoy the yummy smell without all that chewing. When you put the mask on and you start to smell the bubblegum, it might feel like you're floating or spinning. That means the sleepy medicine is starting to work. You'll drift off, just like the cloud on my pin right here, and you won't feel a thing. When you wake up, you'll be with your mom and your operation will be all done.'

'Can I have some food when I wake up?' Tabs asks.

'For sure. You hungry?'

Tabby nods, and the vehemence of it makes me and Dr Martinez laugh.

'Yeah. It's rough having to starve yourself. You can eat as soon as you feel ready for it, so you just let us know, okay? Now, are you ready for some special stickers?'

A nurse approaches us and begins to prep Tabby. I move to her side so I can hold her hand.

'Tabby, I'm going to place these pretty heart stickers on your chest so we can see your heartbeat on our special TV screen, okay?' He brandishes an adhesive patch at her. It's bright yellow and covered in tiny red hearts. 'And this clip goes on your finger like a little hat—it helps us see how much oxygen is in your body.'

'You mean my sats,' Tabs says, and both medics laugh.

'Uh oh, we're in the presence of an expert, I see,' Dr Martinez says. 'No pressure, Nurse Jayden, but I hope you know what you're doing.'

'Well, I did until now,' Nurse Jayden says. 'Tabby, do you know what this is called?'

'An oximeter,' Tabs says, and they laugh again.

'Tabby, if you want a job, come back and find us in about ten years, alright?' Dr Martinez tells her.

Her beam of delight has my heart constricting, even if this light-hearted banter makes me feel the tiniest bit better. This is routine for them. It's all in a day's work. They wouldn't be so relaxed and animated if Tabby's life was on the line, surely?

As Nurse Jayden affixes the electrodes to my daughter's little torso, her surgeon, Dr Elliott, wanders into the room. Tabby and I have seen him a couple of times since we checked in yesterday morning, and I'm delighted to report that his air of quiet competence is just as notable in the flesh as it is over Zoom.

'Afternoon, Tabby,' he says. 'How are you doing? Mom, you holding up?'

I nod and give him a bright smile for Tabby's benefit.

'Glad to hear it.' He focuses his attention on me. 'We expect that the surgery will last three to four hours,' he tells me quietly. 'We'll have someone come and let you know when we're done.'

I nod. 'I appreciate it.' He ran the timings past us yester-day, so I know that the actual valve replacement will take two to three hours. I'll be notified when the closing-up begins and then again when Tabs is out of theatre.

Eventually, Dr Martinez produces the mask, and I steel myself. There will be other operations in Tabby's future, but I will never, ever get used to this part, to watching my child lose consciousness and being forced to walk away, leaving her there for strangers to cut open.

I bend over far enough that my face is all Tabby can see and I give her my best, brightest smile. 'This is it, my love! I'm so proud of you, and I love you so much.'

'I love you too, Mummy,' she says, reaching up her skinny little arms and pulling me down for a hug. I drink in her scent for a moment before forcing myself to pull away.

'I'll be right beside you when you wake up. I promise.'

She nods, her face so trusting, so brave. I pick up her hand and hold it between mine.

'Now I'm going to hold this mask near your face,' Dr Martinez tells Tabs. 'It might feel a little cold at first. Can you practise taking some deep breaths like you're blowing out birthday candles? Perfect! Now I'll place it on your face, and you'll start to smell that bubblegum flavour. Keep taking big breaths... you're doing so well!'

The mask is child-sized, but it dominates Tabby's face. She keeps her eyes on me until they start to flutter closed, and then she's gone, drifting away on a cloud of bubblegum-scented anaesthesia, and I have that awful, terrifying moment where I can't shake the feeling that I've just said goodbye to my baby for the last time. I release her hand. Dr Martinez gives me a reassuring smile as the medical team wheel Tabs through to the operating theatre, and I stumble blindly away, wiping the tears off my cheeks.

I know that each second of the next four hours will feel like an eternity.

# *Brendan*

There's nothing like your shiniest, most expensive new trophy, the trophy you boasted about to all your mates, letting you down in front of every last one of them. The way Marlowe reacted in my office yesterday was the humiliation equivalent of my catamaran sinking like a stone during its own launch party, and it was a massive fucking middle finger to everything we'd signed off on in our introductory questionnaires.

I may have been tipsy, and I may have blindsided her, but that's the nature of the job, I'm afraid, love. It's not like anyone is being exploited here. I pay her north of a hundred grand a *month* to do whatever the fuck I want, and I damn well expect her to put out when the situation demands it.

I'm still seething at the way she looked at me in front of all my business associates, like I was some scumbag hell-bent on assaulting her and not the man bankrolling her lifestyle.

The problem is that when a woman is as beautiful and talented and unique as Marlowe, there's always the risk that she'll get under your skin. That you'll blur the lines and bend your own rules and forget that she is, at the end of the day, a whore.

I'm paying her for sex.

It's as simple as that.

I'll admit that we've both bent the rules in recent weeks, but that weird little midday slumber party I let us indulge in last week was a much-needed red flag. When you veer off course, in business as in relationships, you course-correct. You redraw the lines.

Yesterday was an attempt to do not only that but to scratch that familiar itch of mine. The itch that yearns to show everyone how well I've done. How far I've come. How fucking big I've made it. Most of those dickheads yesterday are highly successful men. Not as successful as me, mind you, but they've done alright for themselves.

We all enjoy the same trappings, just as we judge each other on them. Strippers. Lambos. Yachts. Strippers *on* yachts. Snorting coke off strippers on yachts. Spraying four-figure bottles of champagne over topless women at Nikki Beach in St Tropez.

It gets tired pretty quickly. The toys lose their shine. So when you have the best toy of all, you want to wheel it out, take it for a ride in front of all your friends until they're half sick with jealousy.

But what you don't want is your toy safe-ing out after you've promised the bros a show and then suggesting you blow your own friend.

Not cool, Marlowe. Not cool at all.

I was half minded to call up that Camille woman and complain, to just pull Marlowe's contract and find me another seraph to replace her. After all, they're all interchangeable, aren't they? But something stopped me, and I'm choosing to believe that it wasn't the thought of replacing Marlowe. I was just sober enough to know that Camille wouldn't take kindly to a drunken rant, and plenty sober enough to remember Athena's threat to skin my balls with a rusty butter knife—or was it castration she threatened?

Either way, I don't want to poke the bear, and her silence over the past twenty-four hours suggests Marlowe hasn't gone crying to her. Not yet, anyway.

So I'll sit tight. I'll bide my time, and I'll give Marlowe the chance to return in two weeks with her tail between her legs. Meanwhile, I'll employ some old tricks to ensure that I don't spend the next fortnight moping around like Mark does when I've taken away his favourite bone.

Fernanda Luz da Costa is, objectively speaking, as big a trophy as they come. And, unlike certain other people, she doesn't mind me showing her off. She's a Brazilian supermodel working and living in London and, critically for my internal trophy value calculator, she was on the cover of British Vogue last month.

Put that in your pipe and smoke it, Marls.

Full disclosure: we've hooked up before, and, even if she's physically flawless, she was one of the least interesting fucks I've ever had. Lay on her back like a limp fish. Nobody else needs to know that, though. I shoot her a text and she agrees, with indecent haste, to be my escort to a lavish fundraiser for Great Ormond Street Hospital, of which Sullivan Construction is a patron.

Thank fuck there are people in the world who actually devote their time to caring for sick kids. I may not be one of them, but I'm always happy to open my chequebook for a good cause, and I'm equally happy to show up when the paps are out.

Fernanda's conversational skills may not be a huge selling point (just like her libido), but as far as arm candy goes, she's top-notch. And I have to admit, we look fucking hot together on the wide, pink-lit steps of the Natural History Museum, me in my Zegna tuxedo and her in a barely-there sequinned number that shows off her miles of satiny limbs. The paps eat us up, and it's a few minutes before we're moved on to allow the next celebrities to take our places.

'Your arms are so big,' Fernanda purrs in her sexy accent, her slim fingers tucked into the crook of my arm as we make our way across the iconic space to the bar. 'So hot.'

'You know it, baby.' I shoot her a smile—she's so tall I barely need to dip my head—and, all at once, a memory hits me in a flash.

Marlowe, cradled in my arms on my bed.

Gazing up at me with those huge brown eyes.

*No other guy has ever made me come before. You're the only one.*

The shyness in her voice.

The intimacy of that moment.

Fuuuuuuck. Fuck. Fuck. Fuck.

'Let's get that drink,' I tell Fernanda through gritted teeth.

When your assistant-with-benefits is both AWOL and pissed off with you, and your supermodel date's appeal begins and ends with taking her out in public to make every other guy on the face of the earth jealous, and your new Alchemy membership card is burning a hole in your pocket, there's only one way to end your night.

I got Yan to take Fernanda home. She pouted as I kissed her on both cheeks and put her in the car, but her bedtime game isn't exactly compelling. It's enough of a win for me to know that I could fuck her if I wanted to, and God knows she can't compete with what I've heard about Alchemy. And first impressions tell me this place will live up to *all* my expectations, because holy shit.

The club is based in a white stuccoed villa in Mayfair, and, from the moment I walk in, the vibe is exclusive. Opulent. The lobby is gorgeous, as is the woman manning the reception desk. I'm still in black tie, and she eyes me appreciatively as she greets me. If this is the welcome I get at reception, then things are looking up for the rest of my evening.

Through a set of double doors, there's a pink-hued bar. If we were anywhere else I'd be happy to linger here, nursing a scotch and sizing up my options. But this is a sex club. I don't need to hang out at the bar to pull. I neck a shot and, with a nod of thanks to the two brutes on security, head through the next set of double doors.

The Playroom.

The space I've been itching to experience ever since my bloody brother got a membership. And on this Saturday night, it doesn't disappoint. My first impression is of high ceilings, white pillars, white drapes, pink lighting and naked bodies. I feel like I'm at an orgy in Ancient Greece, and I'm fucking here for it.

The heavy beat of the dance music thrums in my veins. This is more like it. I'm restless and feverish, burning up with the need to make mischief. To cause carnage. I reckon I've spent more evenings at home since Marlowe started working for me than I have in my entire thirties. I've been in some little fuck bubble with her, and that ends now. I'm a sought-after guy with real needs, and just because my otherwise perfect assistant has gone all frigid and left me in the lurch, that doesn't sentence me to a life of celibacy. My brother may have gone without sex for a decade, but there was only ever going to be one priest in this family, and it was never, *ever* going to be yours truly.

I strip off my jacket and fling it over my shoulder, holding onto it with a crooked finger and surveying the debauchery in front of me. Where to start? The woman at reception told me that the female hosts wear little white dresses and the male hosts all-black. I can see one brunette mounted on one of the St Andrew's crosses, a little white scrap of fabric banded around her middle. Her tits are out and her cunt is on full display and she's being ravished by several gentleman. She looks like she's having the time of her life.

I look to my left and catch the eye of a gorgeous young Black woman who has to be a model. Her scarlet dress is sinfully sexy and matches her lips to perfection. She gives me a coquettish smile, but something about her immaculate appearance puts me off approaching her. I've already put one flawless woman in a car tonight. I'm not convinced these model types know how to let loose and have a good time.

Tonight I want something messy. Something real. I wouldn't mind some anal, come to think of it. That's another area in which limiting myself to Marlowe has curbed my ability to meet my needs. There are times when only something utterly transgressive will quieten the incessant static in my head, and I'm pretty sure wedging my cock into the forbidden chokehold of a beautiful woman's arsehole will be just the medicine I require.

Right. Now that I know what I need, I can search out someone whose entire demeanour screams *I take it up the arse and I love every filthy inch.*

Bingo.

Little white host's dress.

Messy strawberry blonde hair and big blue eyes that make her a dead ringer for Kelly Reilly.

And such an incredible-looking rack that it makes me

think tonight's the night I could finally fulfil my *Yellowstone* spank bank favourite of Beth Dutton giving me a tit wank.

I just hope she's less prone to random acts of violence than Ms Dutton.

Most importantly, she screams sex. She's the polar opposite of my blonde, classy and wholesome assistant about whom I absolutely will not think. I need this, and I bloody deserve it.

Beth's doppelgänger is loitering by the bar, looking bored. When I saunter over, she visibly perks up, pulling herself upright as she openly looks me over.

'You look like James Bond.'

'You look like you take it up the arse.'

She doesn't miss a beat. 'Charming. But not wrong. I should probably reward your powers of observation.'

She moves towards me, and I hold my hands up. 'I should warn you, I'm just looking for a quick fuck. Nothing more.'

The eye roll she gives me is quite something. 'No shit, Sherlock. This is a sex club.'

'I know, I'm just—this is my first time here. I want to be clear.'

'Aww. That's sweet. So I get to pop your Alchemy cherry? Anyway, you don't need to worry. There seems to be a fascinating misconception by the punters here that we're all trying to snag an engagement ring. Do you know how many guys I've tried to ensnare here? Zero. Do you know how many proposals I've had? Three of actual marriage and fuck knows how many to be a fully paid-up mistress. So don't you worry your little cotton socks about me.' She drops her voice to a stage whisper. *'Because I just want your dick.'*

I laugh. I like this girl. She's funny and refreshing, and those tits really are a gravitational marvel. I just wish my attraction to her felt less theoretical and more... red-blooded. More immediately carnal.

'Consider me reassured. What's your name?'

'Ivy.'

'I'm Brendan. Can I fuck you?'

She shrugs. 'As long as your fucking is better than your banter, Brendan, then sure. Knock yourself out.'

I laugh again. She's a hoot—assuming she's not serious about my chat, which I'd say is pretty strong. 'My fucking is excellent. Can I fuck your arse?'

She turns away from me and puts her hands up on a pillar. 'Yep. Just do me a favour and lube up, okay?'

Holy crap. She wants to do it right here, in the middle of the room? Okay then. I suppose I shouldn't be surprised. We are in a sex club after all, as she pointed out so sweetly.

Ivy moves her feet further back from the pillar and hinges forward so she's bent over for me. I step in behind her and push her short dress up so that her arse is bared to me. She's not wearing panties. She has long legs and a fantastic, toned bottom and a bare pink cunt. Everything about her is objectively a knockout. But the strangest thing happens—my instant reaction is that she's WRONG WRONG WRONG. Just like that. It's like my body is screaming at me: *No! This isn't what you want! You only like Marlowe's body, remember? Wrong woman!*

Well, fuck that for a game of shits and giggles. Just because I've allowed myself to get comfortable with one partner recently, doesn't mean I can't enjoy mixing it up a bit. I stare at Ivy's lovely white arse as I give myself a stroke through my trousers. Weirdly, I'm still completely limp. Maybe it's because I'm in public? Maybe my dick hasn't got the memo that it's okay to fill up in this context?

'Mmm, you're very sexy,' I tell Ivy. She is, after all, and it feels like the polite thing to say. Her little arsehole is right there, all tight and puckered and forbidden and *mine for the taking* after weeks of Marlowe keeping hers firmly out of bounds.

I want this. I do.

I need it, basically.

I exhale harshly through my nostrils as I rub my hand harder over the area covering my poor, sad, flaccid dick, as if it's a bottle and I'm hoping this will awaken the genie. Still NO fucking THING. Nada. Maybe it has stage fright? Maybe it's scared of this strange new land and is reminiscing about more familiar terrain.

Another memory lances through me. Marlowe on her hands and knees for me on the floor of my office, her incredible body braced to take me. Whenever she's in that position she exudes the strangest mix of vulnerability and courage and carnality. I can't explain it, but I wish I could bottle it.

Fucking hell. I need to give myself a serious talking to here.

*This is not Marlowe.*

*Marlowe has fucked off for a few weeks.*

*Marlowe won't let you anywhere near her arsehole. She won't even let you lick it.*

*This woman is gorgeous, and she's* literally *bent over double so you can take her up the arse, so what the fuck are you waiting for, you wanker?*

Ivy cranes her neck to see me. She, presumably, has the same question for me. 'You okay?'

'Yeah,' I lie. 'Just… warming him up.'

She frowns, then straightens up and looks down at the notable lack of bulge in my trousers.

'Oh, mate. That's not good.'

'It's fine.' I rub it so hard that my boxer briefs chafe against my poor dick. 'I just need a minute.'

She bites her lip. 'You want to get it out for me? I can have a go.'

I flinch. I actually flinch, and my feet take a step backwards of their own accord. 'No!' I say. I think I may snap it, which is neither cool nor intentional.

She raises her eyebrows. 'Okay, okay. Look, you're obviously not feeling it. No bother. I'll just go and find someone who can rail me nice and hard.'

'I'm so sorry,' I tell her lamely, watching her cut through the crowd. I have never had to apologise for any lack of sexual prowess before, and here I am, falling at the first hurdle. It seems my dick did not get the memo that we are here to have a good time tonight. It seems my entire body is repulsed by the fact that this beautiful, willing woman is Not Marlowe.

And nothing about that is okay with me.

I look around in a panic to see if anyone is watching, if anyone is laughing at the guy who's all talk and no trousers. But they're not.

No one is paying me any attention whatsoever. I duck my head and make a beeline for the doors.

I can never show my face in here again.

That's for sure.

# CHAPTER 41

# *Brendan*

he Bach accompaniment to Gounod's version of Ave Maria is pretty straightforward, actually. I've steered away from classical music as long as I've played the piano, but I downloaded the sheet music for this after hearing Marlowe sing it here a couple of weeks ago, and I've been practising it ever since. The melody is flowing and arpeggiated and creates a serene foundation for the soaring vocals.

When I was first learning it, it made me feel happy. Connected to Marlowe.

Now it just makes me feel sad. And, honestly, it's not as enjoyable without her here to sing along.

Eventually, I abandon the piano and pace around the room. The summit is tomorrow, and I really need to practise my speech. The problem is that my speech is boring as fuck, which means practising it is also boring as fuck. At this time of day, my study buddies have worn off, meaning I'm in total ADHD paralysis. My therapist has explained that this happens when my sympathetic and dorsal nervous system states collide and oppose each other at full force. Whatever. All I know is that I'm full of pent-up energy and frustration and unable to channel it into something meaningful and productive.

Like practising my fucking speech.

I should probably record myself delivering it on my iPad. At least if I play it back it'll put me straight the fuck to sleep.

With a frustrated sigh, I pick up my phone and see a message from Plain Elaine. She's sent me a link to a research report one of the big investment banks has put out today ahead of the summit. Her message says that their estimates for our industry's projected carbon emission reductions over the next decade are way more pessimistic than mine and suggests that I arm myself with more hard data to back up my numbers in case anyone challenges it during the Q&A.

Well, that's very fucking helpful, thanks Elaine. Marlowe put those stats together for me. She worked with the strategy team to pare them down to the ones that would paint the clearest picture.

Jesus Christ. I have no interest in dealing with this, or any last-minute curveballs for that matter. I'm tired and cranky and nervous and sexually frustrated. My Beth Dutton tit wank fantasy didn't cut it in the shower this morning, and I was forced—*forced*—to succumb to the memory of spreading Marlowe out on my desk and eating her sometime last week in order to get myself over the edge.

It was humiliating, and it wasn't enough.

I glance at my watch. 7pm. Marlowe should be done with jury duty for the day, shouldn't she? Courtrooms usually finish up pretty early. I'll just call her quickly. I'll keep it polite and professional and brief. I'll explain the situation and ask her to send over more of the context for the stats she gave me. Then we can bid each other farewell like adults.

Yeah. I'll do that. No big deal. I'm a billionaire wheeler-dealer in a bespoke suit. I pull off eight- and nine-figure deals without breaking a sweat. I can sure as hell speak to my assistant without pissing my pants.

I bring up her number and hit the speaker button. There's a pause before it starts ringing. Weird. That doesn't sound like a UK dialling tone. I'm frowning at my screen in confusion when the call connects.

Here goes.

I brace myself, unsure why my heart rate has picked up, but it's not Marlowe who answers. Instead, a perky woman with an American accent says, 'Ms Winters' phone! How may I help you?'

Who the actual fuck is this? 'Um. I need to speak to Marlowe.'

'I'm afraid she's not available right now, sir. She's in the ICU. May I take a message?'

ICU? I rack my brains. Is that—'You don't mean intensive care?' I ask. My heart is now hammering. No no no. Why the fuck would she be in intensive care? Has she had an accident?

'I do, sir. But I can take a message.'

'Why the—what's wrong with her?! Is she okay?' Oh my God oh my God oh my God.

'I'm afraid I can't share any client information, sir. But I'll have Ms Winters call you back just as soon as she can, unless you'd like me to take a message?'

I look up from my phone. This room feels alien, as if I don't even recognise it. 'Hang on. I don't—who is this? And where the hell are you?'

If she thinks I'm insane, she doesn't say so. 'My name is Norma, sir. I'm one of the duty nurses in the Paediatric Cardiac Intensive Care Unit here at Duke Children's Hospital, North Carolina.'

Paediatric.

Duke Children's Hospital.

My head is spinning. I can't—does that mean Marlowe's not in the ICU herself? Why the fuck would she be in a children's hospital in *North Carolina?*

There's only one reason that I can think of. Only one reason she would have lied to me to get this time off.

Marlowe has a child, and that child is ill, and my assistant is not on jury duty as I thought but instead holding some kind of bedside vigil in intensive fucking care in North fucking Carolina, and I can barely breathe, I can barely function as my overwrought brain attempts to absorb and compile and process this information. I do the first thing I can think of and pull up Athena's number.

She answers after a couple of rings. 'Brendan.'

'Does Marlowe have a kid?' I blurt out.

She lets out a long, defeated sigh. 'Yeah. My goddaughter, Tabby.'

'Tabby.' I whisper the name to myself, wondering why it sounds familiar. 'And she's ill?' Pressure is building in my sinuses, and I pinch the bridge of my nose.

'She is. She was. But—'

'Why the fuck are they in North Carolina?'

She sighs again, even longer and harder. 'Tabs needed an operation to save her life. Duke is the best place on the planet to do it. Look, have you spoken to Marlowe, or...?'

*Save her life save her life save her life.*

'I just called her, but this woman answered her phone. And I tried to talk to her, but this nurse said she was in the ICU, and she wouldn't fucking tell me anything, and so— then I—but I don't—'

'Brendan. Breathe for me, okay? It's all okay.' There's some rushed, low-level mumbling as she presumably talks to Gabe.

'I need to know,' I say, because she's being obtuse. I thought Athena was smart, but she's too calm. I don't understand why she's—doesn't she realise how bad this is? 'I need to know how—what's the—like, is there a fucking plan here?'

I've started shouting without realising it. I just want to make her understand the urgency here.

'Brendan. Listen. Can you make it over here? Come over and we'll have a proper chat, and I'll tell you what I can, though the story is really Marlowe's to tell.'

My mind is reeling, but the only thing I'm certain of is that I need answers. 'Yeah. I'll take the bike.' I have a bespoke Falcon in the garage downstairs, and it's going to be by far the quickest way of taking me across London and getting me some answers.

'Okay.' She sounds doubtful. 'Don't kill yourself. You'll be no good to anyone if you come off your motorbike.'

'I won't. Athena?'

'Yes?'

I can barely get out the words. 'How old is—how old is her—Tabby?'

'She's eight. Nearly nine.' Athena's voice is soft when she says it in a way I haven't heard before, except when she's mooning over my brother.

My beautiful Marlowe is mother to a gravely ill eight-year-old little girl, and I didn't know a damn thing about it.

I don't take the time to put on my leathers, which is probably really stupid, but I don't care. Besides, it's a warm night and I'd rather stay in my shorts and t-shirt. I get across the river quickly on my Falcon and then make my way to my brother's house in Manchester Square as speedily as I can risk without getting pulled over.

Athena answers the door. She surveys me with a grim countenance. No doubt she thinks I'm having some kind of breakdown. She wouldn't be far wrong. The entire way here, my brain has been downloading question after question. I don't understand what's going on here, and I need some answers before I lose the fucking plot.

I follow her through to the kitchen where my brother is putting the finishing touches to what smells like stir-fry. On the nearby table is a huge stack of Audacity Foundation brochures. They have a stall at the green summit tomorrow. He comes over, slaps me silently and heartily on the back once, and slides an open bottle of beer over to me. I take it with an equally silent salute and raise it gratefully to my lips. Jesus, that's good.

While my mind was busy formulating questions on the bike ride over, it was also busy prioritising them, so I go ahead and blurt out what is by far the most important one. 'Is Tabby going to be okay?'

Athena picks up her glass of white wine. 'It seems so, yes.'

I blow out a breath. 'Good. That's good. What's wrong with her?'

'She has a rare congenital heart defect.'

Congenital... 'She was born with it?'

'Yes. Her pulmonary valve, which takes blood from her heart to her lungs, was too narrow when she was born. She had an operation at birth to replace it, and one aged three, but she's been overdue another one for some time. She had the replacement done yesterday, and from what Marlowe tells me, it all went smoothly, thank God.'

She's been speaking to Marlowe. Marlowe has shared this emergency with her. Of course she has—her little girl is Athena's goddaughter.

'But I thought she was in the ICU.'

'It's standard for a major operation like that,' Athena says, and her voice is so calm and assured that I could kiss her. 'They're just observing her.'

'Okay. Great. That's good. And—sorry, why go to the US?'

'Duke has the world's leading paediatric cardiothoracic surgeons,' she explains patiently, and I realise she's already told me this over the phone. 'Plus, they did it laparoscopically. Over here, it would have meant open-heart surgery. The NHS was dragging its feet and Great Ormond Street couldn't operate before November in any case. Tabby didn't have time to wait.'

Great Ormond Street. The gala that I treated as a chance to flaunt my boring-as-fuck supermodel trophy on the red carpet was actually raising money for families like Marlowe's. A wave of nausea and self-disgust rolls through me.

'How do you know she didn't have time to wait?' I ask. My voice sounds thick. My brain feels thick. Cotton woolly.

Athena and Gabe exchange a glance that looks significant. 'Her blue spells have been getting more frequent,' she says. 'That's what we call it when her lungs are deprived of blood— she starts to turn blue in places. Her A&E visits have been ramping up.' I stare at her in horror. Every single new piece of information is like a blow to the stomach, but she's rattling them off matter-of-factly, as if all these nightmare scenarios are something she's profoundly familiar with. 'They used to only happen when she exerted herself,' she continues, 'but they've been happening more and more. We've all been on tenter-hooks over it.'

*We've all been on tenterhooks. We.* I glare at my brother. 'Do you know her?'

'Tabs? Yeah, I've met her once or twice with Marlowe at Athena's,' he says, and I flinch. Tabs. They've all been playing happy families and sharing this burden with Marlowe and I've been fucking oblivious this entire time.

'Then why the fuck didn't she tell me?' I ask, the frustration in my voice audible even to me, because I'm feeling stupid now.

Athena gives me a *don't be obtuse* look. 'Come on, Brendan.'

'Come on, what? How the hell does my assistant have a sick kid and no one thinks to tell me?'

'It was deliberate,' she says in her measured voice, 'and I'm sorry if that stings, but there was no way you would have hired her if you'd known her circumstances, and she really needed this job. She needed the money.'

I feel like I'm wading through treacle here, but my brain is fuzzy and overstimulated and I can't work out what the fuck connection I'm failing to make. 'What for? The flights? The trip?'

'For the *operation*, Brendan. It's costing her a fortune, but she was out of options. GOSH had a six-month waitlist and Tabby needed that operation urgently. It was looking increasingly likely that an emergency op would happen, which would have been far too risky and far too invasive.' She steps forward, her brow creased, and puts a hand on my arm. 'Marlowe needed to find a way to get hold of hundreds of thousands of pounds as quickly as possible, and she flat-out refused to let me pay for it.'

She clears her throat delicately. Her hand is cool against my bare arm, but it doesn't help to dispel the nausea that's rising inside me like a relentless tide. 'The only option was Seraph, and I suggested you, because I was absolutely bloody terrified for her and I knew you'd look after her. I knew I could trust you. Honestly, it was the only way I could, in all decency, propose her for Seraph. Yes, she was insistent on earning the funds herself, but the way I saw it, someone as inexperienced as Marlowe signing herself up for sex work was like throwing herself into the lion's den. She hasn't had a boyfriend since Tabs was born, for God's sake.'

I stare at her, bile filling my mouth with rancid acid.

*She needed the money.*

*I knew you'd look after her.*

*I knew I could trust you.*

*Throwing herself into the lion's den.*

*She hasn't had a boyfriend since Tabs was born.*

I hired a beautiful, smart, sexy, obliging woman so I could use and abuse her. I knew Marlowe was classy, knew she had integrity, but figured she had experience, at the very least. I figured she wanted a certain lifestyle and was prepared to do what it took to fund that lifestyle.

I fucked her in every position.

I made her suck my friend off while I took her from behind.

I dragged her into my blokey, boozy lunch and tried to finger her. Oh, Jesus.

I intentionally humiliated her.

I treated her like a whore.

I used every trick in the book the other day to make her feel like a piece of fucking meat in front of my mates.

*And she was doing it all to save her daughter's life.*

She isn't a slick professional operator.

She's a desperate, terrified mother who will do anything, endure anything, to save her little girl's life.

And Athena was looking out for her—Athena engineered the whole thing, thinking she could trust me to act properly. To look out for her friend and treat her with respect and decency.

Her face the other day in that meeting room.

*Her face.* Oh dear God, I can't get it out of my mind.

Another wave of bile seeps into my mouth, and my entire body convulses.

I slam down my beer bottle and I turn, running out of the kitchen and across the huge hallway into Gabe's downstairs cloakroom, where I fall to my knees and proceed to noisily, messily, empty the poison of my sickened stomach and my blackened heart into his toilet bowl.

# CHAPTER 42

# *Brendan*

I return to the kitchen on shaky legs, my face still damp from the cold water I threw over it.

'You alright, mate?' my brother asks, holding out a glass of water.

I take it and shake my head. 'Not even close.'

'Sorry if this has been a bit of a shock for you,' Athena says. 'But Tabs will be okay. And know this: by giving Marlowe the job, you saved her daughter's life.'

An image flashes into my head. A little blonde girl cuddling a dog. *Tabby.* The girl, not the dog. Marlowe was so antsy when I spotted that photo. And no wonder.

I shake my head. 'I've treated her like shit, though,' I say mournfully. I may have inadvertently bankrolled Tabby's operation, but fuck did I make her mother jump through hoops to earn it.

Athena's eyes narrow. 'I thought you two were getting on well. What did you do?'

'She didn't tell you?'

'No. Spill it.' She crosses her arms.

'Don't think I will, thanks.' I'm not that fucking stupid. I take a tentative sip of water. 'How does it work, then? They stay out there until Tabby's better and then come back?'

'That's the plan.' Athena's still frowning at me. 'A day or two in ICU and then another week or so in hospital before they clear Tabs to fly.'

'Does she have anyone else out there with her?'

'No. She's close with her parents—they look after Tabs when Marlowe's at work—but she couldn't afford to fly them out there and put them up.'

By my estimates, Marlowe is raking it in, even after hospital bills. 'Why couldn't she afford it?'

She rolls her eyes. 'Because every penny she gets from you is going towards hospital costs. She wants to save a chunk before she quits so Tabs can have private care over the next couple of years, but there isn't any spare cash knocking around.'

*Before she quits.* Something on my face must reflect my shock, because Athena rolls her eyes. 'Come on, Brendan. Knowing what you now know, it can't be a surprise that she doesn't want to be your whore forever. That's not who she is, believe me.'

I'm very glad Athena isn't a doctor, because her bedside manner is shite. I may have been furious with Marlowe; I may even have been idly considering trading her in for a more promiscuous model, but it hasn't occurred to me until this moment that she might end things on her terms, that she could just walk out of my life when her daughter's medical coffers were adequately funded.

I have no intention of confirming that, yes, it is a surprise. Instead, I force myself to focus on the issue at hand, the issue which, in my eyes, is a major fucking problem.

'So, she's all alone over there with a sick little girl, and she's got no one looking out for her?' Just saying the words makes my chest feel tight.

'That's right,' Athena says. 'I wanted to go out there with her but she wouldn't hear of it.'

'How's she holding up?' I whisper.

She grimaces. 'So-so. She's relieved it's over, but she's exhausted and emotionally drained. She finds it very upsetting when Tabby's in surgery, obviously, and there aren't any parents' beds in the ICU so she spent last night in an armchair. So yeah. I think it's pretty shitty for her, even if she's been putting on a brave face for me.'

Of course she has, because that's what she does. She turns up for work every morning looking perfectly professional and breathtakingly beautiful, and she focuses on me and my child-ish, irrelevant fucking needs like I'm the centre of her universe and she doesn't have a terrifyingly sick kid waiting at home for an operation that needs to happen yesterday. She's a grafter, and a trooper, and I wonder when the last time was that she put herself first.

I bet she wouldn't be able to tell me if I asked her.

My heart has been breaking for this little girl I don't know, but now it's breaking for her amazing mother, the woman who got under my skin. The woman I treated like dog shit when I got the fear that I was catching feelings.

There are a lot of things I'm not good at, but I *am* good at throwing my weight around and throwing my toys and throwing money at situations where palms need to be greased —I'm good at throwing things, basically.

I may not be fit for Marlowe to wipe the floor with, but I can definitely make myself useful. I can go over there and be the person to advocate for her. I bet she's fierce when she's advocating for her daughter, but I bet she's meek when they tell her they can't do better than an armchair. We'll soon see about that.

And if she needs a break, then maybe, just maybe, she'll trust me enough to sit with Tabby so her mum can take five for herself. I imagine her pale and drawn, with those same dark circles under her eyes that she had the day we napped together.

Well, that's decided then.

'I'm going to go over,' I tell them. 'She needs someone in her corner. It's fucking ridiculous that she should have to face this alone. I mean, what was she thinking?'

Athena gives me a small smile that I think means approval. 'I'll come with you. Then I can spend some time with my goddaughter so you can get Marls out of the hospital for some air.'

I like that idea. I like it a lot. And I can see that if I were a sick eight-year-old in a strange hospital in a strange country with a hole in my chest, I'd rather be with my godmother than some random guy. 'You're on.'

'But you've both got the summit tomorrow,' my brother points out, and I blink. The fucking summit. It feels like it's happening in an alternate universe. The idea of turning up like some smug fuck and boring everyone senseless with my wanky speech while Marlowe sits, pale-faced and exhausted and alone, in some hospital room, is unthinkable.

'Not happening. I'll call Pl—Elaine and get her to sort the jet out. They'll have to find someone else to take my slot.' I glance at Athena. Her turn.

'You'll have to man the stall, darling,' she tells my brother, wrapping her arms around his neck. He slides his hands around her waist and gazes at her like she's the living embodiment of Our Lady, who was definitely his favourite woman before Athena came along.

It's the way Marlowe deserves to have me look at her. It's the way I should have looked at her this entire time, except that I've been a big, hairy coward.

'Not a problem,' he says like the serene fucker that he is, and kisses her softly on the lips. 'You guys should go and be with Marlowe.'

'Let me call Elaine. We should go tonight.' I'm fully mobilised now, all my impulses coursing through my veins like crack. I've made my decision and I'm ready to take action without delay.

But Athena, ever the pragmatist, shakes her head. 'You won't get clearance to fly this evening. Anyway, Tabs is still in ICU so we couldn't visit even if we wanted to. Apparently they're hoping to move her in the morning. We should go first thing tomorrow.'

I hate that she's right. 'Fine.' I turn away to call Elaine. She doesn't sound thrilled to hear from me, and there's a kid making noise in the background. Usually I wouldn't think twice about interrupting her evening with her family, but Marlowe's bombshell has me rattled.

'Hey. Sorry to bother you, but it's an emergency. I need you to get the jet ready to take me to the US tomorrow so I can go see Marlowe.'

There's a silence that I take for confusion.

'She's over there with her daughter,' I explain. 'Tabby. She had an—'

She interjects. 'Yes, I know.' Jesus fuck, was everyone in on this except for me? 'But I'm not convinced she'll want to see you.'

My face heats. I feel like a naughty little boy who's been found out.

'What do you mean?' I bluster.

'I don't usually speak to you like this, but honestly, you've behaved like a Grade A twat to that poor girl. The way you treated her on Friday was nothing short of disgusting. She was in pieces when she left.'

The idea of her being *in pieces* rather than fucking furious, which is how I perceived her emotional state when she safed out, is yet another gut-punch. I can see it all too well from Elaine's perspective, unfortunately: if she's been privy to

Marlowe's secret struggles, then seeing the fallout from me and my mates trying to have some fun at her expense must seem horrific. Still, I'm not about to let my PA's judgement derail what is an important mission here.

'I don't disagree, but I'm trying to make amends. Look, she's all alone over there with no reprieve and no one to look out for her. I'd like to go and make myself useful, so sort the jet, please. I'll tread carefully, I promise.'

Elaine's right. There's an excellent chance Marlowe shows me the door as soon as I turn up there, but I have to go along anyway.

I have to at least try to take some of this burden from her.

# CHAPTER 43

# Marlowe

If there is a more depressing combination than eating a sweaty, plasticky cheese sandwich while doom-scrolling Instagram photos of a supermodel draped all over your gorgeous boss, then I'd love to know.

Actually, I wouldn't. Things are crappy enough already.

I take that back. I feel guilty even thinking that, because nothing is crappy. Tabs has a new pulmonary valve, and she's out of the ICU and sitting up in bed, and her cheeks are a lovely pink colour, and all of that is amazing. Miraculous. It's the dream!

For as long as I can remember, I've prayed for this outcome. My entire future happiness has hung in the balance as I've desperately fought for a way to get this life-saving operation for my daughter. So it's safe to say the big things in my life are going really, really well. They're fantastic, really. I've secured a few more years of optimal health for Tabs, and nothing else matters.

I say that last part to myself through gritted teeth, because gratitude in these moments is important, and I shouldn't be sweating the small stuff. I'm not, really. It's just that I've spent two nights sleeping in an armchair next to Tabby's bed in the ICU, and exhaustion seems to have robbed me of all perspective. They have a no-parents-overnight policy, which is far from sensible if you ask me. Why am I any more likely to spread infection at night than during the day? I was just lucky that the duty nurses looked the other way as I sat in that chair all night.

Now we're back on the paediatric cardiology ward, which is great. It's just that it's noisy, and I'm so tired. My head is throbbing, and the poor little girl diagonally across from us keeps screaming in pain. There's a family visiting in here, and their twin toddlers are running around and yelling at the top of their voices. I've given Tabs my noise-cancelling headphones so she can nap, and I'm kicking myself for not bringing earplugs, too. I have no idea how she's supposed to heal in here. Busy paediatric wards are the least restorative places on the planet.

I'm not usually one to throw a pity party, but I'm not normally so sleep-deprived either. I wasn't doing too badly, actually, until I scrolled through Instagram in a vain attempt to distract myself from this revolting hospital cafeteria sandwich and my feed served up GOSH's posts of its latest fundraiser.

The very first post on the carousel?

Brendan Sullivan grinning and looking like every woman's wet dream in black tie with the ridiculously gorgeous Brazilian supermodel Fernanda Luz da Costa on his arm. She's so leggy and flawless, and he looks so suave and, let's face it, smug. They're perfect together. They both look like megastars.

Do you know what? It's a good thing. It's a helpful reminder that this guy's lane is a motorway and mine is some country road full of potholes and *I should stay in my lane.* I should be grateful for this additional piece of evidence that the universe has served up to nudge me back on course. He and I have had a very specific kind of relationship, and he made it clear exactly what kind of worth I have in his mind on Friday. I shouldn't require any more data.

I throw my phone onto the bed in disgust and pick up the little pink notebook by Tabby's bed. It's her gratitude journal, a habit I've tried to instil in her even while I've failed to take my own good advice. We write in it together every single night. When she was little, I would do the writing, but now she does it. I open it and leaf through the pages.

*Mummy sang to me when I couldn't breave.*
*I gave Daniel chease and he gave me his paw.*
*Mummy says were going to Amercia and a special doctor will fix me.*

I feel breathless, suffocated by that constant chokehold of love and terror and gratitude and unresolved intrusive thoughts.

Last night's entry, written in the ICU, was this:

*My hart is better and i had strawberry jelly.*

It's the perfect reminder from my greatest and most treasured teacher that we can give thanks for the big stuff and the small stuff alike. But right now I'm so broken that it feels impossible.

I close the notebook and slump forward on my hard plastic chair, creating a cradle with my arms so I can lay my weary head down and attempt to nap alongside my daughter.

## BRENDAN

Our nine-hour flight proves an excellent opportunity to interrogate Athena on every aspect of Marlowe and Tabby. Having been Mr Boundaries for so long, the dam has burst and I'm insatiable in my thirst for details.

But there's one area where she's unyielding.

'Talk to me about Tabby's father,' I demand, and she shakes her head.

'No.'

'Why not?'

'Because that's Marlowe's story to tell. If you want to know more, you'll have to ask her.'

Fair enough. Her intransigence makes me like her more, actually. It's been clear to me since I met Athena that she's ridiculously hot and ridiculously competent, but she strikes me as a bit of a cold fish. It's made me question at times whether she's the right person for my brother, who has the most golden heart you could wish for.

But the more I understand about her relationships with Marlowe and Tabby, the more I understand what a fiercely loyal protector she is, and I'm glad. Glad my brother has found happiness with her, and glad Marlowe has her in her corner.

'Just tell me if he's still around.'

She toys with a piece of mango on her fruit platter, spearing it elegantly, before locking eyes with me.

'He hasn't been around since Marlowe told him she was pregnant.'

'Fuck.'

'Yeah.'

'What a loser. So he's not in the picture at all—he has no relationship with Tabby?'

'He's never met her. And that, mister, is all you're getting from me.'

My contempt for this guy grows even as some kind of sick relief hits me that I'm not competing with anyone else here. How the hell do you walk away from a woman like Marlowe, and how the hell do you make the decision to miss out on fathering her child? It's fucked, that's what it is.

'So she got pregnant at uni?'

'She completed a three-year degree in four years. What do you think?'

So she got knocked up at uni and then not only went ahead with the pregnancy but went back to finish her degree. Plus, she got herself an MBA afterwards. Seriously fucking impressive. But I realise that trying to push Athena for more is a fruitless task. She's a vault. I change the subject.

'So how do you two know each other?'

'We became friends at school—Cheltenham Ladies. She doesn't come from money—she was there on a full choral scholarship. She's an incredible singer, you know.'

'I know,' I tell her. 'I caught her singing Ave Maria at my place. It was unfuckingbelievable.'

Her face softens. 'Yeah. She's really something.'

'Do you think she'd ever want to pursue it professionally?' I venture.

Athena fixes me with a steely look. 'That's not a dream she's ever had the indulgence of entertaining.'

I nod. Life got in the way, and she was stuck raising a sick kid and making enough of a living to support them. I ask the question that's been circling around and around in my head. 'You said her parents were in the picture, but how the hell has she juggled working full time with all the hospital visits? It must be a lot.'

Her face is grim. 'Sheer determination, and commitment, and immense sacrifice. Not to mention organisation. She has these printed fact sheets at Tabby's school with her full medical history. They get doled out every time an ambulance is called. It's the same as for most single parents, with the added kicker that she never knows when she'll get the emergency call.'

'Does it happen often? It hasn't happened since she worked for me, has it?'

I rake over my memories of these past couple of months of Marlowe's employment. She's always been so professional. So put together.

'She had one a couple of weeks ago,' Athena tells me now. 'You have to understand, Marls was adamant when she took this job that she wouldn't let her personal life interfere. She knew what an opportunity you were giving her, and she got fired from her last job for leaving early to go to the hospital.'

Fury washes over me in a scorching wave. 'Wait. She was *fired*?'

'Yes, because her boss was a total dick. And she couldn't afford for that to happen with you. So she'd already made it clear to Tabs that if she got sick during the week, it would be her grandparents taking her to hospital.

'But she had a bad spell the other day and they had to call an ambulance. Marlowe's mum called her at work to let her know, and apparently your PA found her crying in the loos and bundled her off to the hospital.'

I stare at her, horrified, trying to understand how she could have suffered through so much drama under my very nose while I remained totally fucking oblivious.

'She went home sick a week or two ago,' I say slowly. 'At least, Elaine told me she was sick.'

'That was probably it. She had a late one, I think. She told me you found her asleep the next day and were very sweet about it, but she was mortified.'

Jesus. That day in the hotel room. She was sleeping off a night in hospital?

This narrative I've woven for myself which, like everything

else in my life, has me at the epicentre, is, I now realise, completely unreliable. All this time, Marlowe has existed as some kind of side character, there to humour and entertain and service *me*, and this entire time she's been dealing with the kind of shit I've never encountered in my cushy, entitled life.

'She was exhausted,' I whisper. 'I remember. Fucking hell.'

I remember far too much about that hour in that bed with her. I remember the feelings that lying there with her elicited. The feelings that prompted me to freak out and behave like a callous, disrespectful twat.

That ends now.

'It's going to be different now,' I promise Athena. 'Now I know the score, I'll look after her.'

She puts down her fork and lays her elbows on the table between us, glaring at me with her signature ferocity.

'Let me be very clear. If you think what's happening here is that you'll swan in and save the day, then you're wrong. Marlowe's not a victim. She's stronger than any of us. This is about you having the privilege of seeing her clearly for the first time, and fully appreciating what makes her so special, and then supporting her. It's about her and Tabs. She's been rescuing herself and her daughter for the past eight years without much help from anyone, so she doesn't need you swooping in like Superman now. Got it?'

Yeah.

For what feels like the first time since I laid eyes on this beautiful woman at the RA, I finally get it.

Jesus, hospitals give me the heebie-jeebies. Like most unpleasantness in the real world, my family's money has insulated me from this sort of stuff. I'm happy to keep things that way, even if I know deep down that money doesn't guarantee good health. Far from it.

But I could really do without being reminded up close of the existence of a world where people are ill and suffering. Where *kids* are ill and suffering.

As Athena and I walk along the bright corridor, it occurs to me that this is an integral part of Marlowe's life. Hospitals and valves and oxygen levels and God knows what else are all part of her existence, her vernacular. They're second nature to her. Unlike yours truly, she doesn't have the option of burying her head in the sand and pretending these parts of society don't exist.

I'm a bit of a mess, to be honest. I barely slept last night, and I was up well before dawn packing my bags. Athena's revelations on the flight over have hit me hard, and I'm still struggling to process, to recalibrate everything I thought I knew to be true. I'm also nervous as hell—nervous that Marlowe will hate me, that she'll be furious with me for overstepping. And I'm scared of confronting her in this new reality, of having the truth of her suffering laid bare for me.

Luckily, my brother's impressive girlfriend takes the lead, marching me briskly down endless corridors and stopping to ask staff members for directions when we get ourselves lost.

It's when we get to a cheery nurses' station decorated with the words *THE HEART HEROES UNIT* in colourful paper letters that I suspect we've reached our destination. Again, Athena takes charge, giving Tabby's name to the duty nurse. I watch in trepidation as the woman points towards an open-doored ward.

'Tabby is in bay nine,' she tells us with a friendly smile.

'Come on,' Athena says impatiently. 'What are you waiting for?'

I follow the noise, which escalates as we enter the ward. Fucking hell, this is utter carnage. Machines beeping and kids screaming and a hum of chatter—it's like a refugee camp or something. Why the hell didn't they get a private room? I look around in abject horror, attempting to process this hellish overstimulation of colour and noise.

And then I see them.

At least I think it's them.

The third bed has a tiny blonde girl in it. She's asleep, and she looks frail as fuck. The oversized headphones she's wearing dwarf her small face.

Next to the bed sits a woman, her upper half slumped over the bed. She too looks to be asleep with her head in her arms, long blonde hair tied in a messy topknot.

*Marlowe.*

Even from here, she looks utterly defeated.

The two of them are still and quiet at the centre of this total fucking circus, as if even the chaos around them couldn't stave off the demands of their exhaustion.

I take them both in, and I know for certain that I will never be the same again.

CHAPTER 44<br>*Marlowe*

I'm sucked rudely back into consciousness by a gentle hand shaking my shoulder and a familiar voice whispering in my ear.

'Marlowe? Babes, it's me.'

I jerk upwards with a shocked gasp from where I've been face-planted against the bed, adrenaline flooding my system. *Athena?* I look up and to my left, and there she is, a vision of well-groomed serenity in the midst of this zoo.

'Oh my God!' I croak. I can't believe what I'm seeing. 'What are you—how did you—'

She jerks her head towards the door with a knowing smile, and I follow the gesture.

Oh God oh God oh God.

Now I really am dreaming.

Because standing right across the bed from me, looking like a walking thirst trap in a dazzling white t-shirt and jeans, is Brendan.

I blink and reflexively reach up to brush my hair out of my eyes. I must look like shit. I must *smell* like shit. I haven't showered in days. I'm groggy as hell from that nap, and I'd put money on having blanket creases on my face, and this guy looks perfect. Just perfect.

We stare at each other for a moment. The expression on his gorgeous face is so far from the usual easy smugness. It's more akin to total devastation, and I realise in a rush that the very fact that he's here means he knows. *He knows everything.* Instinctively, I reach my hand up to grab Athena's for comfort. She squeezes hard.

'I can't believe you're here,' I say lamely to both of them, but mostly to Brendan.

'We came on Brendan's jet.' Athena bends and kisses me on the cheek. 'He was worried about you. We both were.'

I brave eye contact with Brendan again.

'I hope it's okay that I'm here,' he says. He sounds far more subdued than normal.

Rather than open that can of worms, I shoot him a look I hope communicates my conflicted feelings about seeing him. 'How did you find out? Did you tell him?' I ask Athena.

'No,' he says. 'I called you last night and one of the nurses answered the phone. She wouldn't give me any information except that you were in intensive care, so I called Athena.' He pauses. 'She filled me in.'

'So you found out my secret and decided to just show up?' I can feel the defensiveness rising. 'After what happened at that lunch, you think you can just fly across the Atlantic and every-thing's fine?'

Even as the words leave my mouth, I know I'm being a bitch. Dropping everything to fly over here is a massive deal for him. But I'm so exhausted, and I'm all out of fucks to give. He doesn't get to erase all that nasty shit he pulled last week with one grand gesture.

'No. *No.* Not at all. I know'—he clears his throat—'I fucked up. But I was hoping I could come and lend a hand anyway.'

He turns to Tabby, who's still sleeping. I watch as he takes her in, watch as my two worlds collide in a way I could never have imagined. The man on my Instagram feed, the man who knows me more intimately in some ways than anyone else on the planet and from whom I've kept this side of myself a secret, the man at whose hands I've had my highest highs and lowest lows, has flown across the Atlantic Ocean to be by my side, and I can't compute it at all.

'How is she?' he asks gruffly.

'She's good. It's all gone smoothly. The surgical team has been amazing. We got out of the ICU this morning.'

'Glad to hear it.' He shoves his hands in his pockets and looks around the chaotic ward. For a childless guy with a life-style like his, this must feel like the Twilight Zone. 'Oh,' he says. 'She's—'

I turn towards Tabby. She's blinking sleepily and reaching for her headphones. I smile at her and lean over so I can get them off her. 'Hey, sweetie! Look who's come to see us!' Her look of shock is downright comedic.

Athena squeezes behind me so she can get to Tabs. 'Hey, darling!' she cries, leaning over her for a careful hug, because Tabs is still hooked up to various monitors. 'Oh my goodness, I'm so proud of my brave girl! Surprise!'

My daughter gets the most animated, most demonstrative side of Athena. They have such a special relationship. I watch as she wraps her little arms around her godmother's shoulders to hug her, my heart filling with warmth at what it will mean to Tabs to understand that we are not alone, that we are loved, that we have people in our lives who will cross oceans to be with us.

'How did you get here?' she asks with wonder in her voice.

Athena releases her and straightens up. 'I flew here in Brendan's jet! Imagine that!'

Tabby's mouth drops open. 'Cool!' She swivels her head

to Brendan and takes him in, going instantly quiet. I'm not surprised she's shy around a huge, bearded stranger.

'This is Brendan, my love,' I tell her. 'My boss. Isn't it so kind of him and Athena to come and visit?'

'Is it *your* jet?' she asks quietly, and I stifle a grin. Brendan may have found a rapt audience to show off his toys to.

'Well, it's my company's jet,' he says a little awkwardly, but then he winks at her. 'I kind of stole it.'

Her jaw practically hits the bedcovers, and I can't help but laugh.

'You see, your mum is a very good friend of mine. She's very important to me.' He clears his throat. 'So I wanted to come out here and see if you ladies needed anything, and also to remind her that her friends are here for her. And you. Because, sometimes when we have rough weeks, it's nice to have some friends around to keep us company, isn't it?'

I give him a look I hope conveys exactly what I think of his sudden transformation from demanding boss to concerned "friend." That's quite a change of heart from the man who treated me like his plaything a few days ago. That said, this isn't the guy who tried to get me to suck off his random mate in front of a roomful of leering, jeering blokes. This is the real Brendan, the one I've seen glimpses of. The one he does a very good job of keeping hidden most of the time.

Honestly, he gives me whiplash.

'Did he really steal it, though?' Tabs asks me.

'I think it's supposed to be for business use,' I tell her. 'So it might have been a bit cheeky of him to use it for a personal visit, but he's the big boss, so I don't think he'll get into too much trouble for it.'

'I don't care if I get into trouble,' Brendan says, looking straight at me. 'Because your mum is a very special friend of mine, and she's worth it. That's what friends do.'

I stare at him wordlessly for a moment, drowning in his

big blue eyes and trying to work out whether he's genuine or full of shit. Maybe he doesn't want me seeing into his soul, because he averts his gaze and clears his throat.

'Why the hell are you on a ward, anyway? This place is horrific. Tabby can't get better in here. You should be in a private room.'

Ahh, there he is. The belligerent boss-hole, intent on looking down on everyone and everything.

'Why do *you* think we're not in a private room?' I ask him, keeping my voice neutral. There's no way I'll let Tabs know I'm counting every penny of this already extortionate experience. That's what it feels like. Extortion.

He frowns, message received. 'Yeah, well not for much longer. Give me a minute.' He turns back towards the entrance of the ward, but Athena stops him.

'How about this? I'll speak to the nurses and get your accommodation sorted. Brendan's right. You can't heal in here —either of you. Now, I would very much like some time with my goddaughter.'

She bends and tenderly tucks a matted lock of Tabby's bedhead behind her ear. 'Maybe we can play hairstylists? Tabs, how do you feel about Brendan taking your mum out for a couple of hours for a little break? We're staying in a lovely hotel nearby. I think she deserves a shower and a square meal —how about you? And then you and I can have a proper catch-up and you can tell me all about your operation.'

I'm about to protest, because I don't want to leave Tabby here in this strange hospital, even with Athena, and I definitely don't want to be alone with Brendan, whose presence is causing all sorts of unwelcome hormonal upheaval in my body and with whom, I remind myself, I'm very, very cross.

Even if the concept of taking a shower might be the most decadent thing I've ever conceived of. Right now, even clean underwear would be decadent.

Tabby, however, interjects before I can speak. 'Yay! Can we, Mummy? I want to play with Athena.'

'I'll stay here,' I say firmly. Personal hygiene is overrated, I'm sure. Besides, there's a crappy parents' shower somewhere that I can brave while Athena watches Tabs.

'Please come and take a break with me,' Brendan says, his face beseeching. 'God knows, you deserve it.'

I can't have a frank conversation with him here. Not in front of Tabs. I can't tell him where he can stuff his hot shower and fluffy towels and real food.

'I don't want to go anywhere with you,' I say as quietly and menacingly as I can pull off in a noisy children's ward. '"Good friends" wouldn't try to ambush their mates, would they?'

'I get that,' he pleads, 'but I'm not trying to ambush you, honest. I have—there's a *lot* to say, I know that, but this is about you. If you want me to give you my keycard and wait for you in the lobby, I will. Just do yourself a favour and take a break, please.'

I consider. He doesn't seem to have an ulterior motive, but it's hard to tell with Brendan. He's fully capable of manipulating people for his own ends even without realising he's doing it.

And there's the shower factor. I bet the parents' one is grim AF.

'Fine.'

He grins. Smug bastard. 'I'll get you back here by dinnertime.'

'Bring sushi, please,' Athena tells him. 'I'm not eating a single thing in here.'

I sigh, feeling outnumbered and vulnerable and even shy. 'If you're sure?' I ask Athena and Tabs.

'Positively,' Athena says.

Tabs grins. 'Go, Mummy.'

'You need a break, Marlowe.' Brendan sounds weary, and I realise he and Athena must have had a pretty early start to have got themselves here by lunchtime. He reaches into his pocket and slides a platinum Amex from his wallet. 'If you can sort out the room situation, I'd be grateful,' he tells Athena. 'Whatever it takes. I want a decent bed for Marlowe too, okay? None of this armchair sh—rubbish.'

She takes it from him and nods briskly. 'Leave it with me. Now go. You're no use to anyone if you run yourself into the ground. Brendan—take good care of my girl.'

'I will,' he promises, his face solemn.

I've definitely been ambushed, but I'm not sure it's a bad thing.

# CHAPTER 45

# Marlowe

Brendan holds my hand as we weave through the bowels of the hospital, and I let him. He holds it in the fancy car that's waiting outside for him, complete with driver, and I let him. He doesn't mean anything romantic by it—I'm pretty sure it's just that I'm clearly not with it and in need of a little guidance. A little friendly comfort. That's how it feels. Friendly and supportive. I may have given him short shrift in there, but I'm too exhausted to keep on pretending a piece of me isn't glad to see him.

On the short journey to his hotel, he asks me in great detail about the surgical procedure Tabby's just undergone. Some of his questions are too complex for me to even answer. Neither of us touches the elephants in the room: the fact that I've lied to him consistently since applying for the job and that he treated me like dirt last time I saw him.

Instead, he asks me about me. About how I'm holding up. How long it's been since I slept in a bed. Since I've showered. Eaten a square meal. Judging by the set of his jaw and the thin line his lips make, he doesn't like my answers one bit.

He's staying in a luxurious suite that's about four times

bigger than my flat, with a vast living area and a beautiful terrace. After several days of being holed up in hospital hell, it feels like I've died and gone to heaven.

'Do you want me to leave?' he asks, stopping to look at me, his expression unsure. He's still gripping my crappy little suitcase. This is a far less confident version of Brendan than the one I'm used to seeing.

I sigh. 'No. You're fine.' It's his hotel suite, after all.

'Okay, then. What do you need first? Shower? Nap? Food?'

I groan. This is like those times when you get home and you're parched and also dying for a pee, and it's impossible to know which to tackle first. They all sound amazing, but the thought of falling into Brendan's wonderful, clean bed while I'm this crusty is too revolting. I'll feel amazing if I have a good wash.

'A shower would be amazing.'

He jerks his head. 'This way.'

I follow him through a set of double doors into a master suite that's all slick neutrals and fresh flowers. The bed is untouched, his bag still sitting on it. They must have checked in and headed straight to the hospital. Beyond that is a glorious white marble bathroom with a tub I could happily drift off in and a shower cubicle the size of a football pitch.

He heads straight for it and opens the glass door, cranking on the shower so that a torrent of water bursts instantly to life. I glance around the bathroom, second-guessing myself. Now that I'm away from the hospital and in this place of luxurious stillness, I've hit a brick wall. I don't even know if I have the strength to wash my hair. Everything feels like so much effort. Maybe I should just go to bed first, crustiness be damned.

'Hey,' Brendan says, coming towards me. 'You okay? You're white as a sheet.'

I nod. 'Just tired. I'm fine.' Saying the words takes so

much effort. I sway slightly on the spot, and he grabs my biceps.

'Woah. You're on your last legs, aren't you? Okay, look. I know I'm probably not your favourite person at the moment, given my little stunt last week, and I won't try anything funny, I promise... but let me take care of you, please. You can lean against me while I wash you, at least.'

The thing is, I trust this version of Brendan. I trust *most* versions of him. There's no swagger today. He's here, and that speaks volumes. I don't know if it's guilt or a misplaced sense of duty, but I know in this moment he has my back.

That, and I'm not sure I can make it through a shower in one piece without some help.

'Okay,' I say, and he nods.

'Okay. Good. Here. Sit here.'

He settles me on the toilet seat as he strips off his clothing, tugging on the back of his t-shirt and pulling it over his head before losing his shoes and socks and shoving down his jeans and boxer briefs. It's a testament to how exhausted I am that I can't muster up more of a reaction than vague appreciation, even when he walks towards me in all his naked glory.

'Your turn, love. Up you get.'

I rise, and I shamelessly allow him to peel off my skanky clothes and probably stinky underwear as if I'm a helpless child. With great care, he releases my hair from its knotty bun. Then he takes my hand, leading me gently into the shower and under the torrent of water.

Oh wow. It's gloriously hot and the pressure is amazing. I stand under it like a zombie. I just want to sink to the floor and let it wash over me. Brendan is eyeing me with concern, and I gaze back at him exhaustedly. I swear there are two of him.

Mmm. Two Brendans.

'Jesus, Marls, I can't bear this,' he says finally. 'Come here. Let me give you a hug, for fuck's sake.'

My tiny nod is all the permission he needs. He closes the space between us and joins me under the spray, banding an arm around my back and tugging me close. With his other hand, he cradles my head, pressing it against his chest.

The relief is instant. His body is huge, the most physical reminder of how much I've missed having any kind of support. I bury my face in his chest and luxuriate in the incredible sensation of hot water and warm, solid man. If he wasn't holding me up, I'm not sure I could have stayed upright for another second.

He holds me more tightly, crushing me to him, his body a cocoon. He drowns out everything else: the exhaustion, the worry, the isolation, the *noise*. I wrap my arms around his torso and hold on tight, an overwhelmed child clutching her giant teddy bear for dear life. Whatever fuckwittery he's been guilty of recently, right now he's undoubtedly my safe space, my port in a storm.

Gently, silently, we sway together, his hand smoothing my hair as the water soaks it. After a few moments like this, he speaks.

'I'm so fucking sorry you've had to go through this, sweetheart. I'm just—I'm so blown away by you. Athena's filled me in on a lot of stuff.' He pauses. When he speaks, his voice is gruff. 'I think you might be the best parent I've ever met.'

I give a little laugh-sob then, because what he doesn't know is that anyone would do this. In my place, anyone would fight for their child's health and wellbeing like I have. It's all part of what you sign up for when you have a kid.

'I can't imagine how tough it's been on you, especially this week,' he continues. 'You're bearing up so well. And I'm not here to waltz in and save you—Athena made it very clear on the way over that you're far too strong to need saving, and I agree.' He twists my hair idly into a soaking rope before resuming his stroking. 'You've been saving yourself and your little girl for longer than I can bear. But I'm here to support you for as much as you need, okay? Let me take some slack off you, whatever I can, even if it's doing laundry runs for you, or sitting with Tabs every day while you come back here and shower. I'm not going anywhere.'

'What do you mean, you're not going anywhere?' I mutter against his skin.

'I mean, I'm staying here till she gets discharged.'

I summon the energy to lift my head so I can gape up at him. He looks down at me and nods sternly.

'Seriously. I'm not leaving you.'

'But you can't do that,' I protest. 'We could be here another week! You have work—oh my God, isn't it the summit this week?' I wade through the treacle in my brain. 'Wednesday?'

'Today is Wednesday, love. I canned it.'

I gasp. This summit has been Brendan's sole professional focus for weeks. I know what a massive deal it is for him. It's *today*? And he's here, casually hugging me in the shower like he has nowhere else to be?

The horror on my face makes him smile. 'It's just work. Whatever. No one's saving lives. Not like you.' He gathers me close again, and I lay my cheek against his chest. 'Through that lens, it's completely unimportant. *Everything* is unimportant compared to you and what you're going through right now. Do you understand what I'm saying?'

His heart beats steadily against my cheek as he resumes stroking my hair. I can't hear his heartbeat under the thunderous water, but I can feel it. I've spent the past few days monitoring the beat of my daughter's heart, obsessing over it. The steadfastness of Brendan's tells me he's healthy. Strong enough to take some of this cup of suffering for me.

He fucked up big time last week with his nasty, degrading behaviour, and I honestly don't know where that leaves our unique professional relationship. But right now he's here. He's sacked off a huge career opportunity and chartered a jet and crossed an ocean to be here with me. *And he's telling me he's not going anywhere.* That he's staying here, of his own volition, for me and for a child he doesn't know, for whom he bears no parental responsibility.

The gravity of his gesture hits me like a freight train, and I screw my face up as I turn to bury it fully in his lovely pec.

Stress has built this week, just as surely as exhaustion. I've had no outlet, no ability to fall apart. Not when I'm the sole adult present for Tabs. A heart operation is exhausting and terrifying, an enormous strain on not just her heart itself but on her whole body. She's the brave one. She's the one who's had to put her life in strangers' hands. She's so full of courage that it blows me away.

I've been helpless to do much except be there for her.

Comfort her when she's scared.

Distract her when she's in pain.

Stay strong.

So no. Falling apart has not been an option, but it's come at a hell of a price, because my entire head feels like it's going to explode. I'm so full of unresolved stress and anguish and fear that my eyes and my sinuses ache with the tears I have not been able to shed for my little girl, the suffering I haven't been able to take from her.

Something was always going to have to give.

Something was eventually going to push me over the edge.

And it's this. The kindness of a man with whom I'm supposed to have a purely transactional relationship. The very fact that he is here, offering to help me carry this burden *for as long as it takes.*

I've been holding the vaguest appearance of sanity

together with the emotional equivalent of a rusty old lock securing a dam, and Brendan's unexpected acts of compassion have that lock giving up the ghost and the floodgates bursting open, obliterating every last drop of composure in spectacular style.

The tears aren't decorous tears. I don't sob prettily into his chest.

I bawl.

I wail.

I howl.

I actually *keen*.

I cry on Brendan like the world is ending, like I've lost everything there is to live for, which is ridiculous! Because Tabby's had her lifesaving op, and she survived it! It's as though my body hasn't got that message, as though all of that embodied trauma of the past hours and days, years even, is making a break for freedom, as though my body has been a pressure cooker all this time and now, at the kindness of my boss, it's completely unleashed.

I cry like I've seen mourners cry on the news at bomb sites. I cry in a way we Brits tend to find overly dramatic, incredibly awkward, and not a little unseemly. If he didn't band his arms even more tightly against me, I would certainly fall to my knees. I'm practically bent over with the relief of it all and the grief of it all, with a tidal wave of emotions I can barely make sense of. Emotions I've pushed down and down and which now have me in their chokehold. Emotions, it seems, that have no intention of going back in that very effective bottle of mine.

As I fall apart in spectacular, horrifying style, Brendan holds me under the water, rocking us gently, whispering words of reassurance and praise, the same words I've whispered to Tabby over and over this week, words with whom parents have comforted their children through the ages.

*That's it. Let it all out.*
*Such a brave girl.*
*I'm so proud of you.*
*You did it.*
*It's over now.*
*Everything's going to be okay.*
*You don't have to worry.*
*I'm here now.*
*You're not alone anymore.*
*I'm not leaving you, I promise.*

# CHAPTER 46

# Brendan

I don't know whether to be terrified or relieved that Marlowe has broken down so spectacularly. I think I'm a bit of both.

I've never seen her like this. This isn't a chink in her armour: it's as if every last wall has come crashing down, allowing the beautiful, brave woman within to bare herself. To recognise her needs and to let them sing. Her physical nakedness seems symbolic of this emotional collapse.

Impulse control has never been my thing, but the force that propelled me to get on that plane, to go to her, wasn't a mere impulse—more an instinct of rightness. And while I may have second-guessed that instinct most of the way over the Atlantic, I couldn't be more relieved that she's unburdening herself on me so freely.

I won't flatter myself that she trusts me now, that she's forgotten the things I tried to make her do—things that make me burn with shame now that I know the full picture. It's more that I'm here, that she needs *someone* to parent her after going through God knows what without any real support. But I'd like to think it's also a testament to the relationship we'd built before I got the fear and behaved like a twat. Transactional it may be, but it's given us a level of familiarity, of intimacy that stands us in good stead now.

I'd like to think she wouldn't jump into the shower with just anyone.

It may be harrowing to see her like this, to bear witness to such a raw and painful outpouring, but I know better than to try to distract or deflect. She needs this, and frankly it's better than seeing the brittle, exhausted version of her we encountered at the hospital.

Besides, I'm only human. Having Marlowe naked in my arms, leaning on me, both figuratively and literally, is indecently pleasurable. So pleasurable, I'm having stern words with my dick, because now is not the time to sexually harass this woman who's sought refuge in my arms.

Instead, I hold her, and I sway with her, and I comfort her. I stroke her hair, and I tell her how proud I am, how amazing she is. I observe as the animalistic wailing turns to sobbing and then shuddering. Eventually, she's still, aside from the occasional hiccup. I keep a tight hold on her. I don't want her having some sort of vulnerability hangover after this.

'Will you let me wash you?' I ask, and she nods against my chest. So I do. I pump shower gel into my hands and I lather up her beautiful body, sliding my hands over her and doing my damnedest to make my touch soothing rather than creepy.

'You're hard,' she says.

'Sorry. Ignore it. Hard not to be with you around.' I bend, and she raises one leg and then the other for me to wash.

'You should wash your bits yourself,' I tell her in a voice more strangled than I'd like.

She hums her agreement and turns away from me so she can tend to the space between her legs.

'Can I wash your hair?' I ask.

She turns back to me. 'I'd love that.' Her eyes are reddened and puffy, but her expression is dreamy, as if I've just promised her a full spa day and not a perfunctory act of hygiene. This is the woman who gives of herself all day long. She serves me all day like I'm some vile little emperor, and then she goes home and cares for her sick, fragile little girl. I decide that this is going to be the best damn hair wash she's ever had.

'Good. Hands on my shoulders.'

With my hands full of shampoo, I slide them over her scalp and get to work. She lets her eyes drift shut and I take her in like never before. I really *see* her. I see the stresses and the sacrifices; I see the vulnerability and the bravery. I marvel at her, at the hidden depths I didn't even know to plumb. And as I do, I use my thumbs and fingertips to rub at her temples and massage her scalp.

She lets out a little moan. 'Oh my God. So good.'

'Good,' I say curtly. I have no idea if I'll ever get to hear those moans again for sexual reasons, and just now, I'm not even entitled to entertain the possibility. I haven't earned the right.

My dick is getting harder. Perhaps it is time for a little distraction, after all.

'So if Tabby is actually a human, who the hell is that dog you showed me?'

She opens her eyes a little and laughs weakly. She's still pretty shaken up. 'I'd forgotten about that.'

'Well?'

'Daniel the Spaniel.'

'Daniel the—good Lord. Okay, I think I see why you didn't want to bring him into the office, in that case. He yours?'

'He's my parents', actually.'

'Strong name. Maybe I should have gone that route for Mark. Daffy the Staffie? Raffy the Staffie?'

She laughs a little, then hesitates. 'I'm sorry I lied to you about so much. For what it's worth, I hated every minute of deceiving you.'

'Head back.' I swallow as I angle her head so that I can rinse out the suds. I'm not about to make her feel bad, but the truth is that I wish she and Athena had had enough faith in me to let me in on their secret from the outset. 'You don't need to apologise for anything,' I tell her, 'but I wish you'd trusted me to tell me. It wouldn't have changed anything for me.'

She opens one eye to peer at me. 'With all due respect, Brendan, that's bullshit and you know it. You would never have hired me if you'd known I was a single mum.'

Hearing her swear makes me a little relieved. It's a small sign that this crisis hasn't completely wiped out her life force energy.

'What, you thought I'd take one look at that beautiful little girl who has your eyes and your smile and run for the fucking hills? Is that it?' The vehemence in my voice takes even me by surprise, but she just rolls her eyes before closing them again.

God, she's exhausted. She needs a nap, and now. I pump a dollop of conditioner into my hand. I have no idea how much is enough, but I pull her out from under the spray so she's leaning against me again. Once I've covered both my palms in conditioner, I begin to smooth it down her hair. It might not be perfect when I'm done, but it'll be clean, at least.

'I think you're rewriting history a little,' she says sleepily. 'It must have been quite emotive to turn up here and see us like this. But yeah, if you'd found out I had a sick little girl at home and you hadn't seen her hooked up to machines in a hospital ward, then I think you would have run for the hills.'

The resignation in her voice kills me. I can't tell if she's right, can't think back to the Brendan I was before I met her. I don't even know who I was before yesterday. I hate that she could be correct, that her problems would have meant nothing to me except for potential inconvenience or disruption to *me*.

'I'd like to think I'd have taken a chance on you anyway,' I say. It's the most truth I can feasibly give her. 'I was pretty obsessed before you even interviewed, remember?'

'But *I* couldn't take a chance on you knowing,' she says. 'Seraph was the only way I could get my hands on that kind of money. And I was so, so terrified of the prospect of selling myself to some arsehole. I was petrified. So when Athena suggested we approach you, I did everything in my power to sell the dream. Telling you I was doing it for a gravely ill child was definitely not part of the plan. You were the only one I could trust, Bren. I couldn't jeopardise that. I'm so sorry.'

That's the thing that kills me. She went into this whole Seraph thing terrified, and she trusted me to handle her with care. I was the *one* guy she felt confident enough working for in this fucked-up dynamic, and I certainly did *not* handle her with care. I didn't treat her with the respect, the decency, that I should have. On the contrary, I treated her like a fucking blow-up doll and not much more.

Dressing her up.

Ordering her about.

Wheeling her out to show her off to my mates.

But after everything I've done, she's the one who keeps saying sorry.

And I can't bear it.

# CHAPTER 47

# Marlowe

When I'm all clean, Brendan leads me out of the shower and dries me off with brisk movements. I notice that he keeps his eyes off my body as much as he can, even if he's still impressively hard. It's a considerate gentlemanly gesture, and I appreciate it. It couldn't be more of a departure from how he treated me last week.

He holds up a fluffy robe and I thread my arms through it. Only after he's tied it tightly around me does he manage eye contact. 'You got a hairbrush on you?'

'In my bag, but I can—'

'Nope.' He takes my shoulders and walks me through to the bedroom. 'You're not doing a bloody thing.'

I have to work on stifling my smile as I sit at the fancy dressing table and surreptitiously watch this big, hot guy, wearing nothing but a white towel fastened around his waist, brushing my hair as carefully as if it's made of spun gold. He really can be very sweet when he wants to be.

My eyes wander around the mirror image of the room behind him. It's as impersonal as it is luxurious. I could be anywhere in the world. It feels so, so wrong to have left Tabby at the hospital, even if she's in the care of the most capable person I know. I'm afraid our relationship is pretty co-dependent, and our anxious attachment to each other has ratcheted up this week, amid the stress and uncertainty and unfamiliarity. For all its faults, GOSH is practically a second home to us. This hospital is massive.

Brendan takes a towel and squeezes out my hair when he's done brushing it. We gaze at each other through the mirror.

'Food first, or sleep?' he asks gruffly. There's an undoubted awkwardness between us. For my part, I'm mortified by my little breakdown back there, and I suspect he has no idea how to behave towards me in a hotel room he hasn't dragged me to for sex.

I'm considering my options when my stomach growls loudly, and it gets a smile out of him.

'Some real food would be amazing,' I admit with a sigh. 'I've been living off protein bars and disgusting sandwiches.'

Brendan's idea of *real food* is pretty epic. He puts me in a huge white *Sullivan Construction* t-shirt, props me up on a mound of pillows in his huge bed and proceeds to feed me a platter of fruit that's far riper and tastier than the imported shit we get in London supermarkets. I've never tasted mango like it. And when I say *feed*, I mean that he sits on the edge of the bed and feeds me forkfuls like I'm an invalid.

He's so solicitous, so tender, that it moves me. He's put on running shorts and a t-shirt, and I'm not above perving over him as he serves me. He's such a beautiful man, and when he's quiet and thoughtful like this, he's almost irresistible.

If only this was his sole personality.

After the fruit come perfectly poached eggs and fans of sliced avocado on some delicious seeded bread, which he again holds to my mouth as if I've lost the use of my hands. And tea —really good loose-leaf breakfast tea served in a silver pot. It's unrecognisable from the shit the hospital vending machines spit out and so exactly what I need that I consider requesting an IV full of it.

'Thanks,' I tell him, wiping my mouth with my hand when I'm done mainlining the hotel's entire food supply. 'God, I needed that.'

'And now you need a nap,' he says, standing so he can move the huge tray away. 'As do I. I'll grab the sofa outside.'

I sit bolt upright. 'No you bloody well will not. This is your bed. Come and lie with me, you doofus.'

I'm not used to seeing him so uncertain. 'Really?'

'Really. We've been in far more compromising positions than this, haven't we?'

'That's what I'm worried about. I might get confused in my sleep. What if you wake up to find me dry-humping you?'

He looks so worried that I laugh. 'I'm sure whatever you do to me, I'll sleep right through it.'

'Rude,' he grumbles, but he pulls back the covers on his side and climbs in.

The memory of the last time I was in bed with Brendan is such a happy one. I may have been horrified when I woke up to find I'd slept through the lunchtime rendezvous he was paying me for, but I also rejoiced in the amazing, unfamiliar feeling of having a gorgeous man's warm limbs wrapped around mine.

That can't happen today.

We settle on our sides, facing each other. I tuck my hand between my cheek and the pillow.

'I have some things I need to say,' he says. 'I wanted to say them as soon as I got you alone, but I also didn't want to dump on you. I need you to know how sorry I am for the way I behaved last week—the way I treated you. It was fucking disgusting.'

I stare at him. The regret on his face is undoubtedly genuine.

'Thank you,' I whisper.

'Do you know what the worst bit is?' He screws his face up. 'I didn't even feel bad afterwards—I was pissed off with you for not playing along. Really pissed off and self-pitying and immature. I was so shitty to you all last week, but I didn't regret it until I found out the truth about Tabby.

'Since then, I've been recalibrating every single interaction with you in my mind and I've felt sicker and sicker and sicker. Jesus. When I think about the things I made you do, knowing that all the time you had no choice—no real choice, anyway, that you just had to suck up all my shit and demands so you could get your hands on that money to save your daughter's life... God, it makes me feel sick to my stomach. I actually puked at Gabe's when Athena told me the truth, you know? I've never, ever felt so despicable in my life.' His voice drops to the quietest whisper. 'I'm so fucking ashamed, and I'm so desperately sorry, love.'

We stare at each other across the sea of pillows.

'I didn't just suck it all up,' I tell him. 'I may not have entered into it by choice, but most of the time it was amazing.' I give him a shy smile. 'Obviously you know I had fun. You were there. I just—I don't understand why you were so mean to me last week. It was like a switch had been flipped—you were so nasty and contemptuous. It felt like you hated me, or something. I've never seen you be misogynistic before, but last week you were.'

His face is so stricken that I almost feel bad, but it has to be said. He has to know that the particulars of our working relationship don't give him the right to treat women like that.

'I know, believe me, and like I said, I'm disgusted with myself. But I definitely don't hate you, love. Far from it.'

I wait, because an explanation is still forthcoming.

He sighs. 'Are you sure you're up for this conversation? You're exhausted. I don't want to dump my shit on you if you'd rather wait till later.'

'I'd rather clear the air,' I say firmly. 'I think it's important.'

He nods. 'I got scared, which sounds even more pathetic when I say it out loud. *God.* I felt us growing closer, and it freaked me the hell out, so I thought I'd put some distance between us. I was livid that you were buggering off on jury duty, because I knew I'd miss you, and it made me act out. I told myself I should put up some boundaries and remember what our relationship was supposed to be.' He pauses. 'Rather than what it was actually becoming, which was something real.'

We're both quiet for a second. While I appreciate his candour, I can feel myself getting angry. I may have deceived him to the extreme, but the choices he made last week were frankly disgusting. He needs to know that when he lashes out thoughtlessly, the effect on others can be devastating.

'So you thought treating me like the whore you bought would be an effective antidote,' I say, my voice quivering. 'You shot your load in my mouth and then told me to, I quote, *clear off.* You bent me over your desk and just left me there.'

He flinches, but I'm not finished.

'I know we have a contract, and I've always tried to give you what you need to compensate for all the deception, and I know we both find aspects of the dynamic really hot. But there's dominating me, and then there's treating me like I'm a worthless piece of shit, like I'm not even human.' My voice breaks, my face crumpling like a child's. 'And that was how you made me feel, even before you called me into that lunch meeting and ordered me to suck your friend off. You made me feel like I had no value whatsoever, aside from my holes, and I can safely say I've never, ever felt so devalued in my life, not even when Tabby's father told me to go fuck myself.' I can barely get the words out. 'Last week was so horrible that I wanted to curl up into a ball and die. I couldn't, though, because I had a very sick, very scared little girl to look after. But I will tell you this—I've never been so glad to get away from anyone as I was from you that day.'

It's all flooded back to me. The emotions I'm reliving towards this man are so different from the ones he's elicited today. I want to punch him and hug him at the same time. How can the same man shove his hands between my legs in front of a roomful of his friends and then wash my hair so tenderly?

'Fuck, I'm so sorry.' The tears course over my nose and down my cheek, soaking my pillow. He reaches out and drags his thumb over them, but it doesn't do much. 'I can't bear it. I'm so disgusted. I don't—I don't know what the hell came over me.'

He swallows, but he doesn't look away. 'I've been an entitled shit who values the wrong things my whole life. Ask my brother. I didn't get Gabe's strength of character. It's no excuse, but everything I did last week was out of self-preservation. You were collateral damage in the worst possible way, and I chose not to see what a dick I was being to you because I purposely blocked out any thoughts about anyone other than yours truly.

'I had this fucked-up idea that you were there for *me*, and that I deserved to get my pound of flesh, and I did all those things knowing what a truly special person you were.' He grimaces. 'I think that made me worse. And I think that if I had a therapist, which I probably should, they'd say I was self-sabotaging as much as anything else, by driving away the only real thing of value in my life.'

It doesn't take a therapist to work out that Brendan abusing me is more about his issues than my value, but it's so fucking childish. And it's exceedingly hard to lie here after the week I've had and sympathise with his poor-little-rich-boy issues. For fuck's sake. The guy has too much time and too much money and too few responsibilities, and this is the result. Total self-absorption.

Well, maybe not *total*. He's here, after all. But a *lot*.

I don't think I could have stopped my scathing rejoinder if I tried.

'And you wonder why I didn't trust you with my secret.'

I may as well have slapped him across the face.

'Wow. Yeah. That's fair. Harsh, but fair.'

'You know what,' I say, warming to my theme, 'you have so many redeeming qualities. You're so generous, and I still can't believe you flew all the way over here. But it shouldn't take a crisis like this for you to put yourself in someone else's shoes. You were a dick to Elaine when her son was ill, too. Everyone has issues, and everyone's struggling with something. When you're in a working relationship like you and I are, you owe it to the other person to have some basic empathy, to wonder how your actions will affect them. I'm not just a Non-Player Character in your life, you know.' I'm secretly proud of that analogy—thank you Tabs for the video game reference. 'I'm a human being, and I have feelings.'

He's crying now, too. He nods violently. 'I know. I know. And, like I said, I think deep down I was trying to punish you. I was pissed off, and I acted out, and by doing that I hurt you and made you feel the absolute opposite of how you deserve to feel, which is valued and adored.'

He can rationalise it all he likes, but the bottom line is that he has that nasty, infantile streak in him. It doesn't mean I hate him—not even close—but it does make it very hard to trust him with the stuff that counts.

'Look,' I say, because this has been bothering me, 'I realise I agreed to stuff in that questionnaire that I wasn't actually ready for, and that was incredibly irresponsible. I did it to get the job, but that's on me. Like I said, most of the stuff we've done, I've loved, even when you've pushed me out of my comfort zone. I even enjoyed that threesome, weirdly.' I give him a watery smile, but he doesn't return it. He's still crying. 'I knew you wanted to do certain things with me that I was never going to be comfortable with, and they're probably things that Athena would do without batting an eye, but—'

'You're not Athena,' he growls. 'And you should *not* have to apologise for your limits because they're different from other people's.'

'Okay. But what I mean is... it wasn't just the things you wanted to do at that lunch that bothered me. You blindsided me on purpose. You were arrogant and callous and so dismissive, and you wanted to make me feel vulnerable and humiliated. It was very deliberate.'

'I agree,' he says, sounding like a broken man. 'It was deliberate. And I told myself it was about showing off my trophy EA to my mates, but it wasn't even about that.' His eyes flicker downwards, away from me, and he mumbles, 'It was about showing you who's boss.'

There it is.

The truth.

He didn't like his reactions to me, his feelings about me, so he decided to pull rank in the nastiest way possible.

I'm not convinced this is remotely the right time to have this conversation, nor do I have the energy for it. But I may as well build on the momentum we've made here and advocate for myself. If this long, lonely week has reminded me of anything, it's that I owe it to Tabs and myself to advocate for the both of us with every scrap of agency I have.

'I'd like some assurances that you won't pull a stunt like that again when we go back to London,' I say stiffly, and his eyes fly to mine in shock.

'What do you mean?'

'I mean, if it's okay with you, that we should sit down together and redraw the rules. I'm really not comfortable in group sexual situations, so I'd rather not do any of those anymore, and if you're in a bad mood then I'd rather you didn't take it out me.' My voice quivers, but I forge on. 'I think on days like that, we should set firm—'

His protest is explosive. 'Jesus Christ, Marlowe!'

'What?' I ask, taken aback by the abject horror on his face.

He gazes at me through his tears, his expression pleading. 'You honestly think I'd let you take a penny for sex from now on in? No way. I'm never laying a hand on you in that office again. We're done with the Seraph thing.'

# CHAPTER 48

# *Brendan*

er face crumples, and my first thought is *oh Jesus, I've made her cry again.* But this is important.

'No, please,' she begs, pushing up onto her elbow and staring down at me, her brown, tear-filled eyes beseeching. 'Seriously, Brendan, I know we've both fucked up, and I knew I was playing with fire by lying so much, but I need this job. I've still got—we're not done with the expenses, you see. I need to save more, I need to know we have an emergency fund in case Tabs has any complications. I can't go back to relying on the NHS again. I've never felt so powerless in my life. Forget I said anything. If you'll—I just need a couple more months.' She hesitates. 'I'll do whatever you want.'

She's breathing heavily, and I feel sick to my stomach once more, because Jesus fuck. She thinks I'm firing her, and *she thinks she can tempt me to change my mind by offering to overlook her own sexual boundaries?*

I have never heard such fucked-up horseshit in all my life.

I pull her right back down onto her pillows and haul myself up so I have the advantage. 'Fucking hell, Marlowe. Don't you ever, *ever* offer to prostitute yourself like that, understand? I'm not firing you, love. The contract stays. I still want you as my PA, and God knows, I'm not about to cut your pay either. I'm telling you I won't touch you. I'm not in the habit of exploiting struggling single mothers who do desperate things to save their kids' lives. Not consciously, anyway,' I add, because I've been unwittingly doing just that.

She glares at me. 'I can't take that obscene salary every month and not hold up my end of the bargain,' she spits, and I hate this. I really fucking do. I hate that there's any transaction between us, and I hate that she feels some obligation to "uphold" it, and I hate most that I've ruined the tentative trust that was blossoming between the two of us.

'Well you have to, because I have no intention of going anywhere near you sexually in the office, and if you try something then that'll be harassment,' I argue.

We eye each other mulishly.

'I could quit.'

'You need the money, and there's no fucking way I'd let you go back on Seraph's books. Over my dead body. Look, you have two options. You can take a pay cut and I'll fund all of Tabby's medical bills going forward, no questions asked. Or we can continue everything about our working relationship, minus the sex part, which gives you the chance to save whatever you need.'

She hesitates, and I know she's close to caving. The perverse benefits of negotiating with a broken, exhausted woman, I suppose.

'You have one priority, and that's Tabby,' I continue. 'Now is not the time to be settling into any new job while she recovers. You and I work well together. You know my systems and my business and my idiosyncrasies. I don't want a new assistant.'

'Why are you doing all this?' she whispers.

I'm still up on one elbow, gazing down at her. She looks so

small and alone and uncertain that it slays me. I wish I could run my fingers through her still-damp hair and tell her what I've grown to accept over the past twenty-four hours—that she is my whole world, and it terrifies me. That I will move heaven and earth to make her happy and to keep her daughter safe. That she holds all the power, every last drop of it, and I never stood a chance with her, only I was too scaredy-cat to admit it to myself.

I wish I could tell her that keeping her on as my regular EA-with-no-benefits isn't an altruistic or financially reckless move on my end but a desperate ploy to keep her close, to buy myself time while I embark on several monumental tasks.

To regain her trust.

To build a relationship with the most important person in her life.

To prove myself worthy of playing the part I know I want to play in both their lives.

It may sound rash. After all, I'm not known for my impulse control. But it's not. On the contrary, it's very bloody overdue. I fucked up once, and I'm not going to let this opportunity slip through my fingers again.

Because I have no intention of *ever* losing this woman again.

But I can't divulge the wishes of my heart now, because she won't want to hear them, and she's not ready to hear them, and, most importantly, I haven't earned the right to voice them.

Instead, I shrug. 'Partly it's self-serving. I'd rather keep you around than train up a new EA. But mainly it's a way for me to make amends. I didn't support you. On the contrary, I failed you, big time. I told you in the shower that I'm not here to save you, but I *am* here to support you. I've put so much extra strain on you at a time in your life when you needed to conserve all your strength for Tabby, and I've caused you so much hurt, and I'll regret it for the rest of my life. So let me show you my support in the way I know best.'

She bites her lip, then nods. 'Okay… thanks. If you're sure —I mean, it's so generous. But only for another couple of months, alright? Then I should have enough saved up.'

I'm sure it will seem to her as though I'm throwing money at the situation. *Good old Brendan. He's never one to inconvenience himself, but God knows he's adept at putting his hand in his pocket.* But that's not the full truth.

I'm not trying to buy her. I'm trying to buy *time*.

The money buys me a way in, and I'll take every second as a chance to show up for her. To show up for Tabby. To prove to them, through consistent action rather than my usual charming words and easy smiles, that I'm someone they want to keep around.

I should probably reacquaint my dick with my fist.

It's going to be a long, dry couple of months.

# CHAPTER 49

# *Brendan*

I'm a grand gesture kind of guy, which is probably a nice way of saying I tend to throw money at problems in the hope that they'll go away. I'm far more generous with my money than I am with my time and energy. If I piss off any of the women in my life—Mum, Mairead, Elaine—I'll send them a huge bunch of flowers and pray that does the trick.

But as I watch Marlowe sleeping, I realise that grand gestures aren't going to work with her. One, because she's not impressed by them, and two, because they're not what she needs. She's brought a very sick kid up alone and borne the sole weight of that burden for years. What she needs is support and companionship and commitment, not a bunch of fucking roses.

There are no shortcuts here. I'm relieved she bawled me out before she finally fell into a deep, exhausted sleep. It tells me she's not completely broken. But it was a tough listen. I won't kid myself that the intimacies she's permitted this afternoon are born out of anything other than necessity. Her tank is empty; I'm around to help her replenish it a little. I'm a body, if you like: someone who can relieve her stress and pull his weight and just generally make himself available.

I'm not stupid.

The symmetry of this situation isn't lost on me. She'll be able to use me, just like I thought I was using her. She already has used me. I kind of love it. If it levels the playing field even the tiniest bit, then I'm thrilled.

And do you know what? I may be an analytical genius, because if I have my way, the dynamic will be exactly the reverse of what we had. I used her, took her for granted. I thought I had boundaries up. Thought I was clear in my head about what I'd allow and not allow from this relationship.

Was I fuck.

The whole time, I was falling. All that proximity, all that carefully prescribed intimacy, was fucking kryptonite. I didn't stand a chance.

Neither will she. She'll get used to having me around, and she'll begin to trust me, bit by bit, and she'll see I'm not going anywhere, and, despite herself, she'll soften. It might take months, but she'll soften, and she'll fall, and she'll grow to understand that I'm good for her and Tabs. That I can make them happy.

Maybe I'm not an analytical genius so much as an evil genius, because I have an endgame.

Marlowe doesn't need to know about it just yet, but I have one nonetheless. I think it's been percolating, dripping into my brain like coffee through a filter, since that awful moment I discovered she had a sick daughter.

My endgame, you see, is that she and Tabby never experience worry or fear or anxiety ever again. Not over money, not over health.

It all ends here.

They've paid their dues. They've had so much more than

their fair share of suffering over the years and, while they may not know it yet, they are fucking *done*.

Yeah, I realise Tabby will need another replacement valve or two before she's fully grown, but it will be a different story this time around. She'll have everything she needs, even before she needs it. She'll be monitored so vigilantly that a replacement will be a formality, not a calamity.

Obviously, I'm getting ahead of myself.

I don't even know the kid yet.

That changes now, too.

If the poor little thing is stuck in a hospital room, hooked up to machines, then that's what I'd call a captive audience.

## MARLOWE

Waking up next to Brendan is less charged than last time. There's no cuddling, for one—it looks like he stuffed a bolster between us after I fell asleep—but I'm hoping that means there won't be any of the previous fallout, either. No callous words or dismissive behaviour.

I take my bag into the bathroom and change back into a clean set of clothes. Before we left the hospital, Brendan ordered me to bring all my and Tabby's dirty clothes along for the hotel to launder. I stuff them into the cotton laundry bag in the wardrobe. My pride is not above accepting more clean underwear.

'How are you feeling?' he asks, looking me over. He's back in his pristine t-shirt and blue jeans.

'Like a different woman,' I answer honestly. 'I can't thank you enough.'

He looks away. 'You never have to thank me.'

It strikes me that we're in a weird hinterland. I'm still his EA, but my job description has just been ripped down the middle. I'm technically on leave, but if Brendan insists on staying here for the next week or so, which frankly strikes me as ridiculous, then he'll have to work from here and I have no intention of letting him do that alone.

'Can I ask you a question before we head back?' he asks. The solemnity on his face gives me pause.

'Of course.'

He sits on the bed and pats the space next to him. 'Come here.'

I sit. 'What is it?'

'It's a personal question. Are you comfortable telling me what the score is with Tabby's father?'

'He's not in the picture,' I say quickly. While I haven't missed Joe as a lover for a very, very long time, weeks like this make me curse his irresponsible, unfeeling soul for leaving his daughter in the lurch like that. 'Never has been.'

'Athena said that. She wouldn't tell me anything else, though, except to suggest it happened at uni.'

'That's right.'

He sighs. 'It's no excuse at all, but I imagine a lot of teenage guys are pretty useless when you ask them to step up to a pregnancy.'

'He wasn't a student. He was my professor.' My voice is small. Flat. I know how it sounds to be the girl who got knocked up by her professor, like I was either a seductress or a clueless ingenue. I look down at my hands on my thighs. My fingernails are wrecked from chewing on them the whole way through Tabby's op.

There's only silence, and I glance at Brendan. He's looking at me, stunned.

'Your professor got you pregnant and bailed on you.' He grits out the words.

I shrug. 'Basically.'

'That fucking *wanker*. Jesus Christ, love. I'm so bloody sorry. Was it a one-off? Do you mind my asking?'

'No, it was a... relationship. Well, not a proper relationship, it turns out, because he was married, which I knew, and he had no intention of ever getting serious with me, which I didn't know. It was all very cliché.' I give an awkward little laugh. 'He was my personal tutor and a lecturer in baroque music. Very cerebral, cultured, charming... and very married.'

Brendan exhales like he's in pain and puts his hand on top of mine on my thigh. 'This okay?'

'Yeah.'

He wraps his fingers around my hand, and it gives me the strength to continue. 'He didn't hide it. Wore a ring. Said he was unhappy, yada yada. He targeted me, sought me out, and it didn't exactly take long for me to roll over. I'd only slept with one person before him,' I whisper.

'Hang on. I'm only the third person you've slept with?'

'Not that it's about you, but yes,' I say, embarrassed.

'Jesus Christ.' He groans and rubs his free hand over his face. 'Sorry, love. Go on.'

'There's not much to tell, really. It went on for about four or five months—all very secretive. I was head over heels, and he seemed really taken with me.'

'Of course he was,' Brendan grumbles. 'Some crusty old academic, festering away with all his turgid music, and then eighteen-year-old you comes along and blows him away. Of course he was fucking "taken with you".'

I nudge his arm with my shoulder. 'Thanks.' Even years after the death of the relationship, a little posthumous validation is always nice.

'So he fucked you in private, led you on, knocked you up, and...' Brendan prompts.

'... And when I told him I was pregnant, he just shut the

whole thing down. Made me feel stupid. Made me feel like it was my fault for having false expectations and getting knocked up.'

'Good job he wasn't a biology professor. Stupid cunt.'

I grin. 'Yeah. He really, really was a stupid cunt.'

'So he buggered off and left you to it?'

'Quite literally, yes. He told me to get an abortion, froze me out, and then moved his family to a different city that summer—he got himself a new tenure. And that's it.' I shrug. 'I took a year out to have Tabs. I didn't put his name on the birth certificate. He's dead to me, basically.'

'Good. And where does he live?' Brendan growls in a way that makes him sound like a mob boss. I fear for Joe's kneecaps too much to divulge that he, in fact, is still lecturing at Nottingham University, so I shrug. 'Dunno. Don't care.'

'Good girl.' He looks down and brushes his thumb over the back of my hand. 'So you're telling me you've done all this on your own.'

'I have Athena, obviously. And my parents are amazing. Just incredible. They sold their home in Kent after I finished uni and bought a crappy flat near me so they could help me bring up Tabs.'

'I'm glad you have them. But still. This is a lot, love. It would be a lot for any parents, let alone someone without a partner.'

The word hits me harder than usual. *Partner*. Buddy. Support System. *Person*. Yeah, it would be really nice to have gone through all this having someone in my corner. I make a non-committal noise, and he squeezes my hand again.

'Come on. Let's get you back to your little patient.'

# CHAPTER 50

# Marlowe

I've been away from the hospital for three hours, which is a long time to be away from Tabs but a very short amount of time for Athena to have pulled off an epic room switch.

When we get back to the Heart Heroes ward, a smiling nurse directs us down the corridor to a private room. The late afternoon sun is shining through the window and onto a very smiley Tabby. Athena's sitting beside her, looking entirely at ease, while between them are scattered most of a deck of playing cards.

I stop just inside the doorway and gape. These four walls represent a space so quiet, so peaceful, that they may as well house a Tibetan monastery. Sure, Tabby's still hooked up to her machinery, so we still have to suffer through some beeping, but we're alone. We're alone!

'Hello, ladies,' I say, looking around in amazement. 'You've been busy. Look at this!'

'Hi Mummy!' Tabby practically shouts. I haven't seen her this animated since her operation. 'We have a new room!'

'Your boss has been busy.' Athena brandishes her mobile. 'He put me on a three-way chat with the hotel concierge and he was *bossy*. Only the best for his assistant.' She winks at me, and I spin around to Brendan for clarification.

'When could you have possibly done that?'

'When you were asleep,' he says, looking sheepish.

'I thought you slept too!'

'Not with that snoring.' Tabby giggles, the little traitor, and he shoots her a grin over my shoulder. 'Anyway, I had a clear vision, and I wanted to make sure Athena was executing it fully. Which she has, obviously,' he adds hastily.

'We're a good team,' Athena says blithely. 'His Amex and my bullying tactics work together like a charm.'

'Look at your bed, Mummy!' Tabby cries, pointing over towards the window.

'Oh my God.' I set down my bag and go to check out the full-sized divan on the far side of Tabby's bed. Now this really *must* be a mirage. It's beautifully made up with white linen and piled high with fluffy pillows whose cases I could swear bear the same monograms as the ones in Brendan's hotel suite. The top of the duvet is turned back with all the precision of a hotel turn-down service. I swing around. 'Is that...?'

'A lady came and maked it for you, Mummy,' Tabby pipes up.

'Brendan strong-armed the concierge into selling us an entire set of linen and then sending it over in a cab with one of the maids who set the whole thing up,' Athena clarifies. 'Right down to the memory foam mattress topper. Oh, and get this. He made the concierge send through *a PDF of the pillow menu*. He went for Norwegian goose down, if you must know. It seems our Brendan is the real life equivalent of the princess from The Princess and The Pea.'

Tabs covers her mouth, peals of delighted giggles pouring forth in the most magical way. I drag my eyes away from my princess bed for long enough to see something akin to awe pass over Brendan's face at the sound of it. He recovers quickly.

'That's because your mum needs her sleep, doesn't she sweet pea? Though I should have bought her some snoring strips for her nose too, shouldn't I?'

Okay, the snoring jokes are getting a little tedious now. I don't snore.

I turn back to the bed and reverently stroke the heavenly sateen cotton of the duvet cover before pressing down to reveal that yes, there's definitely some memory foam under there. I can say I've never, in my entire life, been so delirious at the sight of a bed.

Well, not since Tabs's newborn days, anyway.

'This is incredible,' I say to Brendan. 'Thank you, thank you. Honestly, I'll sleep like a dream tonight. I feel like Sara Crewe after Ram Dass gives her garret a glow-up.'

Athena and Tabby both give *ahhs* of appreciation at my analogy. Brendan frowns in confusion.

'In *A Little Princess*,' Tabs tells him, 'Sara is so poor and has no mummy or daddy. She sleeps in an attic with her pet rat. But one night the nice servant Ram Dass breaks into her room and leaves loads of hot food and fluffy pillows for her, and when she wakes up she's all warm and cosy.'

Brendan's frown intensifies. 'Sounds very, very creepy to me,' he says. 'And do we think your mum's being a bit overly dramatic, perchance?'

Tabby giggles again in delight. Oh, dear God. He's winding me up to score points with her, and she's already falling prey to his charms. Not that she can help it—she's only human, and she hasn't seen his arsehole side yet.

That said, I am very, very touched. I know Brendan admitted back in the hotel that he'd be supporting me in the only way he knew how, by throwing his money around, but this is another level of thoughtfulness.

'You try sleeping in a plastic armchair for two nights and then see how dramatic you're feeling,' I retort, but then I smile at him. 'That's the best present I've ever, ever received. Thank you. And thanks for being his Girl Friday, Athena.'

'It's nothing,' he says, then turns to Athena. He seems embarrassed by my gratitude. 'Food all sorted?'

She stands and smooths down her lightweight sweater. 'Yep. A local chef will deliver meals for both of you three times a day, starting in about—ooh, an hour. Tabby helped me choose the menu. It's weirdly heavy on both watermelon and sweet potato fries, but there are ginger shots in there for you.'

Okay. This is getting ridiculous now. We're in a hospital, not the Four Seasons. 'You've been very kind, but we can slum it for a few days.'

Brendan closes the gap between us in a few easy strides and looms over me, putting his hands on my upper arms. I stare up at him.

'It's not up for debate. She's ill and you're exhausted. You know full well you need good-quality rest and nutrition if you want to survive this. Don't argue.'

'Thank you,' I mutter again.

'I'm going to head back to the hotel and shower,' Athena announces. 'It's no fun being thrashed at cards by a clever little monkey. You coming, Brendan?'

He sticks his hands in his pockets. 'I think I'll hang around for a bit, if that's okay with Marlowe and Tabby. Nice to have a change of scene from the hotel.'

'Of course,' I murmur, but I can't quite work out what his game is. I suppose, if he's sticking around all week, then he doesn't intend to hide out in his hotel the entire time, but I can't imagine it'll be fun for him to hang out in a hospital room for hours on end.

Athena takes her leave after a big hug from me and Tabs

and saunters off. Brendan sits himself down next to Tabby's bed, crossing one ankle over its opposite knee.

'A lot of machines,' he comments. 'Do you know what they all do?'

She looks puzzled, like she's not quite sure what he wants from her. 'Some of them?'

'How about this one?' He points to the oximeter on her left index finger. 'What's that one for?'

'That's an oximeter,' she tells him shyly. 'It measures my sats.'

'SATs? Aren't they the tests you take in school?'

She giggles. 'They're different SATs, silly! These ones are my oxygen sat-ur-a-tion levels.'

'And what are those when they're at home?'

'They are how much oxygen is in my blood.'

'Ahh, I see. Wow, that's clever.' He's acting as though this is a fascinating revelation. 'And is ninety-nine per cent good?' he asks with a straight face.

'It's brilliant! That's why Nurse Shondra gave me a star.' She points to her chest. She's still in a surgical robe for easy access to her heart electrodes.

'So you're top of the class, just like your mother.' He glances up at me, and something soft in his blue eyes makes me feel a bit fluttery inside. Damn him and his sexy eye contact and his dangerous knowledge of my praise kink. Silently, I pull another chair up so I can sit on the other side of Tabby's bed. 'And how are you feeling? You've had a pretty busy few days.'

She sighs. 'I'm a bit bored and a bit tired.'

'Yeah, sleeping through your mum's snoring is probably pretty difficult,' he muses. 'At least you've got rid of all the other kids now. You should sleep better tonight. Does it hurt where they operated on you?'

He's talking to her easily, I realise. He's shooting the breeze like he chats with kids every day. I find that some childless adults freeze around children, that they have no earthly idea what to say or how to act.

'My heart is a bit sore,' she admits, her lower lip sticking out. 'But they give me medicine to help.'

'I think you're really brave,' Brendan says, gathering up the scattered playing cards. 'I could never, ever be so brave as you. I broke my wrist playing rugby when I was a grown man and I screamed so loudly for my mum that they had to give me morphine just to shut me up. It was really embarrassing.'

I shake my head. This man. I'm ninety-nine per cent sure he's making this shit up for Tabs' sake, but it's working, and it's seriously sweet. I sit and watch as they interact: my tiny blonde daughter and this big, dark-haired brute of a man chatting away easily. Brendan is a giant kid, after all, so I shouldn't be surprised.

He splits the deck of cards and laying them on the overbed table before performing a flawless dovetail shuffle that has Tabby's jaw dropping.

'Wow.'

'Someone clearly spends too much time in Vegas,' I mutter. Elaine has mentioned his penchant for boys' weekends in Sin City.

'Maybe I can teach you how to play poker while you're stuck in here,' he says, ignoring my jibe. 'Then you could drop out of school and make millions at illegal poker games.'

'Helpful, thanks,' I tell him.

'But I like school,' she says, and my heart breaks a little. From the way his face softens, so does his.

'Fair enough. Do you know what else this table would be amazing for?' He slaps it. 'LEGO. Do you like LEGO?'

'I love it! I have some LEGO Friends at home that I got for my birfday.'

'Which ones do you have? I have a niece, Elsie, who's your age. She loves them.'

This is news to me, but it helps explain his ease with Tabs. Elsie must be the kid of Gabe and Brendan's sister, Mairead.

'Which ones does she have?'

He grimaces. 'Not sure. Sorry. A diner, maybe? And, hang on—a villa, I think? She made me buy her that one for her last birthday.'

Tabby's face lights up. She's wanted a LEGO Friends villa for ages. 'Does it have a yellow slide?'

'I think so? Do you have that one?'

Her face falls. 'No. It's really 'spensive.'

Brendan's gaze flickers to me and back again. 'Well, do you know that LEGO is *way* cheaper in the US than in the UK? Maybe I'll see if I can pick one up and we could build it tomorrow. It would be a fun bed project. What do you think, hmm?'

I suspect the cheapness of LEGO in the US is a downright lie, but I know what he's doing. He's warming me up to him splurging and assuaging any potential unease Tabby might feel about accepting such a gift. It's on the tip of my tongue to protest, but Tabby's face is positively alight.

'Can we, Mummy? Would that be okay?'

I force a smile. 'Of course, darling, if Brendan's sure.'

'I'm definitely sure,' he tells her. 'I'll get the hotel concierge to sort one. It'll be epic.'

'Thank you,' she whispers. She's looking at him as if he's her fairy godfather. Then she turns to me and tugs on my sleeve. 'Mummy. I need the loo.'

We get a nurse in to disconnect Tabs from her endless wires so she can make the short trip to the ensuite bathroom.

'Let's play a game,' Brendan says. 'We'll both guess how low your sats will go while you walk to the bathroom, and the person who gets closest to the right number wins.'

I smile to myself. Clearly this guy knows exactly how an oximeter works.

'Okay,' she says, beaming as I lift her gently off the bed.

'Eighty-five,' Brendan says, and she scoffs.

'Ninety-six.'

'Punchy. No way can you keep them up that high. But you need to be honest and tell me what the number is when you get to the bathroom. No cheating, okay?'

'I don't cheat,' she says, scowling at him.

He laughs. 'We'll see.'

'You feeling okay to walk, angel?'

'Yep. I need to walk so I can play the game.' She slides her hand in mine. She's always had such tiny hands with delicate fingers. She'd make a great pianist if she ever had a piano to practise on.

'Nice and slow, Tabby,' the nurse tells her as we set off at a gentle pace. Tabs keeps her hand up in front of her so she can watch the oximeter. We take a few slow steps. 'Ninety-eight,' she says. Four more steps take us into what is a big, spotless bathroom with a proper shower. I lower her onto the loo, and she sighs. 'Ninety-seven,' she calls out.

'You're cheating!' Brendan shouts back, and we both laugh.

I shake my head at her. 'He's very silly, isn't he?'

She beams, and my heart constricts. 'He's fun.'

'Yes he is.' One thing no one could accuse Brendan Sullivan of is lacking in the entertainment area. I'm grateful that he's here and trying to gamify what could be a tedious week for us. Usually, it falls to me as the sole parent to keep Tabby's mood up, even when I'm feeling totally devoid of personality myself. I don't want to admit just how much of a reprieve his being here might mean for me.

'Ninety-eight!' Tabs calls out to Brendan as she sits on the loo and does her business. 'Ninety-nine!' I stare at the number in disbelief as it ticks back up to resting levels. She may only have taken a few steps, but this light physical exertion has barely moved the needle on her sats.

'Liar, liar, pants on fire!' Brendan yells back, and I hear the nurse laughing softly.

But she's not lying.

The valve is working.

It's really, really working.

# CHAPTER 51

# *Brendan*

If I say so myself, the LEGO Friends villa was a genius move, and, as I predicted, a great way for me and Tabby to spend the day. It's the perfect project for someone stuck in hospital: fun; clear end goal; lots of smaller satisfying milestones along the way. Something Marlowe doesn't know —or need to know—about me is that I *adore* LEGO to the point of having an actual LEGO room at home. It has a big square table for building and solid glass shelves for displaying the finished items.

Unsurprisingly, my main focus is on the really cool, expensive pieces of kit—the Millennium Falcon, the Eiffel Tower, the Titanic. You get the idea. I can get really, really obsessive about it and find it impossible to step away. My LEGO room is where I get a lot of solutions to my most vexing business problems. I've even had my marketing team reach out to LEGO several times to suggest they create a version of some of Sullivan's more iconic buildings, and I couldn't be more peeved that they've yet to take me up on my offers.

I rock up at the hospital after breakfast with a big box

containing the LEGO Friends villa. I slept great, hugging the pillow that Marls had slept on that afternoon and revelling in the faint scent of her. This morning was an early start—thanks, jet lag—but it gave me a chance to get out for a run and clear my inbox in preparation for being laser-focused on Tabby. There were several passive-aggressive messages from competitors saying what a shame it was that I couldn't make the summit. Who fucking cares. I'm right where I'm supposed to be.

Athena flew home this morning. She and I had a quick chat last night when I got back from the hospital. She understands that, rather than using her as a childminder while I try to get Marlowe to sneak around with me, I'm intent on putting in the hours with Tabs this week. I'd go so far as to say she approves. So she's got out of my hair and gone back to my brother.

When I get to the hospital, my girls seem in good shape. Marlowe is in yoga pants and a simple white vest and looks good enough to eat. While she still seems tired, she's lost that awful, pinched look of exhaustion. Tabby has her hair in two very tidy French plaits with little green bows at the bottom of them, and I find myself wishing I'd been a fly on the wall for that quiet mother-daughter moment. I wonder if Marls has any idea how beautiful each and every act of service she performs for Tabs is. I bet she does the vast majority of them privately, with no recognition, no validation at all, which is pretty alien in my book.

'How'd you both sleep?' I ask her.

'Like a dream. You know, they still come in every hour to check on Tabs' vitals, which is disruptive for her, but the private room and the amazing bed made all the difference in the world.'

'I had pancakes,' Tabs pipes up cheerfully, and I turn the full wattage of my smile on her.

'Pancakes? Is that what you ordered from the chef? Did you leave any for me?'

'Nope, all gone,' she tells me in delight, patting her stomach.

'Right, well I'm glad you got some fuel into you, because we have some hard labour to accomplish this morning.' I set the box carefully on her overbed table so she can get a good look at it. Poring over the photos of the tiny details is always one of the most fun parts of a new LEGO set.

I turn to Marlowe. 'And you, missy, have a date with my hotel's rooftop pool.'

She gapes at me. 'I can't. I need to stay here.'

'No offence, but there's no way you're better at LEGO than me. I've worked in construction my whole life. And we have a fleet of medical experts just a button away, all of which makes you officially redundant. Go on, go. You need some vitamin D badly. You're still white as a sheet.'

'Tabs isn't ready to be left with a stranger, are you, Tabs?'

'I want to make it with Brendan,' Tabby replies, and I swallow a smile. Kids are such disloyal little shits. So easily bought.

'But I don't have a swimming costume with me,' Marlowe protests.

'All sorted. The concierge had a bikini delivered to the room for you.' I lean right in. 'Make sure you send me a selfie. It's the least you can do.'

When I pull away again, I see with immense satisfaction that her attempt at looking outraged has flat-out failed. She looks a mix of pleased and flustered. I wink at her.

I promised I wouldn't lay a finger on her at work.

I never said I wouldn't play dirty while we weren't at work.

'So which bit do you want to build first?' I ask, laying out the two main instruction booklets between us. 'The swimming pool or the main house?' I'm hoping she opts for the pool. The transparent blue bricks are begging to be assembled.

Tabby studies the booklets with the seriousness of a structural engineer.

'The house book says number one. The swimming pool is number two. I think we should do them in order.'

Such a good little rule follower, just like her mum.

'That's a good point, but it's just us. Sometimes you need to build LEGO stuff in order, but not with this one, because they're both separate. So you should choose whichever one you're most excited about. Life's too short to leave the good stuff for last.'

She purses her lips as she focuses on her decision, then nods. 'Then the swimming pool. Definitely.'

'Excellent choice. Swimming pools are my speciality.' I wink at her as I rip the first bag open and shower the table with bricks. 'You know, I've probably built at least ten LEGO pools in my life, and God knows how many real ones.'

'Ten?' Her eyes widen. 'That's a lot.'

'Well, I'm practically ancient compared to you.' I start sorting the blue pieces while she organises the tiny deck chairs. 'Hey, when you're all better, I'll show you my LEGO room. It's my secret happy place.'

'You have a whole room just for LEGO?' She looks genuinely impressed.

'Yep. Some people think grown-ups shouldn't play with toys.' I lower my voice conspiratorially. 'Those people are very boring.'

She giggles, and I notice her laugh has the same musical quality as her mother's.

'My friend Emma says her dad doesn't play anymore. He

just works and sleeps.' She's making quick work of sorting the blue, transparent pieces away from the others. 'I think that's sad.'

'Super sad,' I agree, handing her another one. 'What's the point of being a grown-up if you can't buy all the cool toys you want?'

'I can't wait,' she says. It's funny and wise and sad, because if feeling powerless is a pretty fundamental part of being a kid, God knows how powerless her health and financial woes have made her feel.

We work in comfortable silence for a few minutes. I'm surprised by how patient she is—no rushing ahead, carefully following each step.

'You're really good at this,' I tell her. 'Most people get the steps mixed up, or they rush and then they get in a mess.'

'Mum says I'm mef-od-ical.' She pronounces the word carefully. 'It means I do things in the right order.'

'That's a big word for someone your age.'

She shrugs. 'I learn lots of big words in hospital. Like "pulmonary" and "cardiothoracic".'

Something catches in my chest. She shouldn't have to know those words.

'You know what I think?' I say, connecting the pool filter piece. 'I think you're the toughest person I've ever met.'

She looks up, surprised. 'Tougher than you?'

'Way tougher. Look at these muscles.' I flex my arm, making her giggle again. She's so tiny. So slight. Way smaller than Elsie, who's the same age as her and sturdy as fuck. 'But you? You've dealt with more hard stuff than most adults I know, but look at that smile! That takes real strength of character.'

Her small fingers pause on a LEGO brick. 'Sometimes I get scared though.'

'Of course you do. Being brave doesn't mean not being

scared. It means doing what you need to even when you're terrified.'

'Like Mummy,' she says quietly. 'She gets scared a lot that the doctors won't be able to help me. When I waked up after my operation she cried. But she always pretends she's happy.'

I swallow hard. 'Your mum is the second toughest person I've ever met.'

'Is she going to go swimming at your hotel?'

'I hope so. She definitely deserves a swim, doesn't she?'

'I wish I could go swimming,' she says idly, like it's a faraway dream.

I frown. 'Can you swim?'

'Yeah, but it's really tiring, so I'm not allowed to do it,' she says. My heart bleeds afresh for the basic fucking parts of childhood that she's missed out on.

'Well, my apartment block has a pool, so you can definitely come swimming any time you like.' Her smile of astonishment is like crack, and it has me forging on impulsively. Fuck me, she's so like her mother. They're peas in a pod. And, just like her mother, her smile makes me want to jump through every hoop there is. 'And my sister and parents live in the country-side, and they have outdoor pools and lots of ponies, so maybe you can come out and have some fun before the summer holidays are over. You have to put that swanky new valve of yours to good use, after all.'

In the back of my mind there's a niggling worry that Marlowe would call promises of pools and ponies "buying Tabby's affection", but she can go take a running jump.

This isn't about me playing games or using my money to worm my way into her or her daughter's hearts.

It's about the privilege of helping an incredible little girl play catch up on all the shit she's missed.

It's about doing the right thing.

# CHAPTER 52

# Marlowe

'You have got to be kidding me.'

I mouth the words at my boss as I shoot him a look of disbelief that I believe is warranted, given I've just walked back into my daughter's hospital room to find an actual troupe of Disney princesses lined up in front of her bed, singing *We Don't Talk About Bruno*.

When he sent me packing to the hotel a few hours ago, after Tabs passed her six-minute walking endurance test with flying colours, he told me he had "some fun stuff" planned for her.

This is more like a full-on Broadway show. I could hear it the whole way down the corridor.

He jumps to his feet at the sight of me and scurries over, holding his silver tiara so it doesn't slip off his head. It's a twin of the one Tabby's wearing as she stands at the end of her bed in her hospital gown, beaming and swaying and holding hands with Elsa, and he looks so adorable, so fucking *fatherly* in it, that a visceral pain shoots through my heart.

'I know, I know,' he says, catching up with me as I stand in the entrance, having pushed through a gaggle of rapt nurses to enter the room. 'It's a lot.'

'Yes, it is,' I say quietly, giving him a meaningful look. It's a lot on every level. It's financially indulgent and very overstimulating and emotionally confusing and just—everything.

'You can bollock me later,' he says. 'Just, please, come and hang out. Enjoy seeing your little girl singing her heart out.' He flinches at his turn of phrase. 'I didn't mean that. But she's wearing her oximeter, and the nurses are keeping a close eye, and she's in seventh heaven.' He clasps my hands in his and squeezes. 'Just come and enjoy it, love. It's really special. We've even got a princess crown for you.'

Apparently, Brendan, Athena and the hotel concierge have been cooking this up with the Heart Heroes nurses for days. The nurses signed off on this particular visit on the understanding that it would only happen if Tabs got the all-clear from her walking test and if the troupe visited the rest of the children's wards, too. It seems they've done some charity work here before and are always a huge hit.

That's no surprise. They do an incredible job. When Tabby gets tired, which she inevitably does, I sit on the bed with her and hold her in my arms as we watch Cinderella and Ariel wrangle Brendan into a conga.

I wish I could tell you he took some persuading.

And so I sit there cuddling Tabs and allowing myself to do what I've promised Brendan—to enjoy it, to soak it up, to marvel that we've come so far only six days post-op, and to also face some very confronting facts: namely, that I'm enjoying having him around far too much.

It's as though that last week at work was a horrible nightmare, and this week in the hospital has been a weirdly lovely bubble. It should have been brutal, but it hasn't been. It's helping that I'm sleeping in five-star hotel bedding and eating delicious meals and enjoying enough poolside downtime to make parts of it feel like an actual holiday, but I'd be lying to myself if I said it was just that.

Because it's not.

It's having Brendan around. It's him making everything seem fun and easy and achievable rather than terrifying and difficult and exhausting. It's having another adult to lean on, to pick up the slack, to provide me with physical and emotional support.

And all of that is confusing and unwelcome and scary, because Brendan doesn't actually have a place in my life aside from professionally, and even that is a bit of a shit show. So when he spoils me, when he dazzles Tabs with these crazy, grandiose schemes and, worst of all, when he's just *there*, being funny and steadfast in all the quiet, normal moments, I can't for the life of me shake that feeling that I'm waiting for the other shoe to drop.

Because the absolute worst thing about this week is that we've felt like a team, and that is very, very dangerous. A team-mate, a partner, is something I've never had the luxury of. I'm the parent sitting white-faced and alone in A&E at 3 am, and I'd do well not to get used to anything else.

Brendan stays all afternoon, eats dinner with us in our room, and then pulls me out into the main corridor while a happy, exhausted Tabs is having some downtime on her iPad. I collapse onto a hard plastic bench, and he produces two bottles of water.

'Date night. Cheers.'

I smile tiredly and clink his bottle against mine.

'Are you cross with me?' he asks, looking adorably boyish and annoyingly hot.

'About Disney-gate, or in general?'

'Disney-gate, for now.' He cracks open his water and takes a long swig of it, and I marvel like a filthy pervert at the manly way his throat muscles contract as he swallows.

I tear my gaze away before he can see me. 'No. I'm not angry at all. I'm grateful, and I'm so thrilled for her to have had such a lovely treat. I'd hate you to think otherwise. But—'

I screw the lid off my water and fiddle with it. He waits with uncharacteristic patience. I blow out a huge breath.

'I just don't want her getting used to that kind of thing, because that's not who we are—that's not our kind of lifestyle. I don't want her being sad when everything goes back to normal.'

When he speaks, his words are halting. Considered. 'That was a treat. A one-off. And yeah, hopefully it was more fun than most of the stuff in her daily life. But if you think about it, this week—and well before that—has been much worse than what the vast majority of kids have to deal with in their daily lives. What Tabby's been through has been fucking hideous, love, so she deserves to have something far better than most kids get to enjoy, too.'

'I get that, but—'

He cuts me off, gently but firmly. 'It's not obvious that you do. If all the bad shit hasn't ruined her, then a couple of treats won't spoil her, either. It's all about redressing the balance, love, giving her something to make it all worthwhile.

'If a good day for her is not being in pain or not turning blue, then fucking hell. That's no childhood. But wouldn't it be nice if she knew that after the lows come some crazy highs, too? She's not my kid, but wouldn't it be lovely if she built her capacity for those things, too? Because her capacity to handle the bad stuff is far too good, in my view.'

I stare at him, wondering if Yoda has somehow embodied my hot boss. 'Athena said something similar a while back, when she played Father Christmas with this crazy tent,' I muse, recalling how hard her words hit me at the time. 'She said it was about building an abundance mindset for Tabs, so she knew to believe the magical stuff was possible.'

He smiles at me, and to my surprise, reaches up to stroke my face with his fingertips. 'Yeah. Well, she's a lot more articulate than me. But that's exactly right. Surely a bit of magic can only be a good thing for a little rockstar like Tabs.'

I stare at him, drinking him in, every bone in my still-weary body aching to slump against him. To give up the fight and collapse.

He must be a mind reader, because he takes my bottle and puts both of them down by his feet. 'Come here. You look knackered.' He wraps his huge arm around me and pulls me into a sideways hug against his shoulder, and I go with the flow. I allow it, because this is a bubble, and weird stuff happens in bubbles.

'You're a rockstar too, you know,' he says, planting a kiss on the crown of my head. 'You deserve some magic, too.'

I snort inelegantly to conceal my awkwardness at the very inappropriate thought I've just had: that a part of me would very happily spread her legs and take some of Brendan Sullivan's particular brand of magic.

Where the hell did that come from?

Probably from the pheromones that I'm sniffing through his t-shirt—pheromones I'm all too familiar with—and from the warm solidity of his muscular body against mine, as much as from the sweetness of his words.

'Seeing Tabs well and happy is enough magic for me,' I say, which is the truth but possibly not the whole truth. I allow myself to nestle further into his body, because this really is very, very nice.

'I have a confession to make, sweetheart,' he says after a

moment. His voice sounds strained. Reluctantly I ease myself out of his grasp so I can look up at him.

'You have the entire cast of *Hamilton* coming in tomorrow?'

'No, thank fuck.' He pauses. 'But I want to make my intentions clear so you can't try to claim down the line that I pulled the wool over your eyes.'

*Intentions?* How very Mr Darcy of him. My poor, bruised heart gives a little thump. 'Okay...'

'I told you I'm not going to lay a finger on you at work. That's because I want a clean break from the kind of relationship we had before.' He blows out a breath. 'And that's because I want a *different* kind of relationship with you.'

Thump, thump, thump goes my heart, like Daniel the Spaniel's tail on the floor when he's waiting for a treat. Brendan reaches down and takes hold of my hand, and I don't know why the warmth of his huge hand around my smaller one feels so life-affirming, but it does.

He smiles at me, but it's not cocky or expectant. It's pleading. Apprehensive. 'I'm not going to tell you how I feel just yet, because I've done such a shitty job of showing you so far. But remember how it was in my bed after we played the piano?'

I nod wordlessly.

'That's how I feel. But you don't have enough datapoints yet, you just have a few moments of me not behaving like an absolute dick. So I'm going to give you more, a lot more, because I want a future with you, love. And with your permission, I'd like to spend time with Tabs too when we get back. I want to get to know her better and prove to you that I'm worthy of giving you both the future you deserve.'

I'm so overcome, so moved by his beautiful words and halting delivery and intently burning eyes, that I barely know where to begin. The enormity of what he's pledging is so hard to comprehend. Yes, he's here, and yes, he's been fantastic with Tabby. But if I understand him correctly, he wants a future *with me and my daughter.* He's not asking me to take a chance on him. He's asking *us* to take a chance on him.

'Bren,' I murmur. 'I don't know what—'

He drops his forehead to mine. 'Please don't say anything,' he begs. 'Don't write me off before I've had a chance to prove it to the two of you. There are no shortcuts here, I know that. But I promise I'll put the work in, because it won't even feel like work. It'll feel like a privilege. I know how I feel about you, love, but I know you'd never let a man in if you weren't completely convinced that he'd make a good father figure to Tabs. And quite right, too.

'But I know what I want, and what I want is to give the two of you everything you deserve. Forever. So please, just give me a chance.'

I want to believe him. After all, it's a hell of a sales pitch. It's every single mother's dream to have a beautiful man tell her he wants to carry her and her child off into the sunset, to make all their problems go away.

But he told me in my first audition at the club that he was a hell of a salesman. That he could close anyone.

Only time will tell if he can come up with the goods to back up these pretty promises.

CHAPTER 53

*Brendan*

I feel like a schoolboy as I sit in my office waiting for Marlowe to show up. I wanted to get in before her today, on this first day of our "new normal". I've made an effort. I'm wearing a tie today, a favourite sky blue Hermès one with dolphins on it that far too many women have told me makes my eyes pop.

I'm nervous, and I'm not sure why. I suspect it's because I'm worried about fucking up. Not only is this a big change from the past week we've spent together in North Carolina, but it's a huge shift from our previous office dynamic.

I'd gauge her reaction to my impassioned speech the other day in the hospital as "hopeful but seriously fucking dubious". I'd like to think she has feelings for me, but those feelings come way, way below her concern for Tabby's welfare and have been badly tarnished by my behaviour.

The way I see it, it's my job to show her that her welfare and that of her daughter are entwined. That what's good for Tabby will also be good for her.

It's a tall order.

Oh, shit. She's here, and she's wearing that white sleeveless dress I love so much. I watch like a lovesick fool as she dumps her bag and indulges in a big, messy hug with Elaine. Yeah, yeah. I'm glad Elaine's in her corner, but I would really like her to just get her arse in here and come give me some attention. Elaine didn't drop everything and fly out to the US to be with her, after all.

Elaine says something, and Marlowe nods effusively and squeezes her arm before finally, finally turning towards my office. I scoot my chair back in a panic and go to greet her, but I'm not sure what to do with my arms. I shove my hands in my pockets, finding my fidget toy.

We took a daytime flight home on my jet a couple of days ago, having decided together that it would be less exhausting for Tabs than a red-eye. Look at us making joint parenting decisions! It was a great call, affording the three of us some quality time together and giving Tabby one hell of a kick. I insisted Marlowe take yesterday off to get her and Tabby back on London time. I, too, took a day for myself and spent most of it in the gym. Being in the office without Marlowe is no fun at all.

'Hi,' she says from the doorway. She looks exactly like she always looks at work—glossy and gorgeous and like every CEO's wet dream—and not at all like how she's looked this past week. I feel extremely conflicted. On the one hand, I could stare at Work Marlowe all day long. On the other, I now know that she uses her workplace appearance as a type of armour, shielding the real her.

I had a week with Real Marlowe, all messy buns and pale-faced exhaustion and soft, cheap clothing. I know how it feels to be with her in a way that's raw and vulnerable and human, and I don't know if I'm ready for us to be Work Barbie and Work Ken again. I really don't.

'Hey.' I stop a few paces in front of her. 'You look, um, rested. How's Tabs?'

Her lovely face softens at the mention of her little girl. 'She's pretty good. Still talking about the jet.' She smiles.

'It must have been hard leaving her this morning.'

'Yes and no. It's always hard leaving her, but I felt better about walking away this morning than I would have done if she hadn't had the op. Her sats say it all. The valve is working like a dream. Now she just needs to focus on recovering her overall health and gradually upping her fitness levels.'

It makes sense. Marlowe told me that Tabby loves sports but that she's had to play it very safe on the exertion front over the past year or so, as her old valve came under more and more strain. Even for an otherwise healthy little girl, I guess it'll be a journey to rebuild her cardio fitness.

'So you won't be signing her up for the five different dance classes she was talking about on the flight?'

She laugh-groans. 'Not just yet. At least we still have a few weeks before term starts. God help us.'

'Is her school good for extra-curricular stuff?' I ask as casually as I can.

'Please. It's a standard state primary, so no. I'll have to look at getting her a couple of classes elsewhere—on the weekends, maybe.'

I have some thoughts about that. I have some ideas that involve Tabs going to a gorgeous private school with tons of pastoral care and endless extra-curricular activities to choose from, but I won't play that card just yet. I can't imagine Marlowe would appreciate that *at all*.

'Sounds sensible,' I say noncommittally. 'Come and have a seat. There are a couple of things I want to put in the diary.'

She visibly springs into professional mode. 'Of course. Should I get my notebook?'

'No, you're good.'

We take a seat on the sofa that runs along one side of my office. I've fucked Marls on it plenty of times, and the air feels full of all those sexy little ghosts. She crosses her legs elegantly and I make a herculean effort not to watch.

'So the first item,' I say crisply, 'is that I want to see Tabs again. When can we make it happen?'

She blinks in surprise. 'Oh—I don't—'

I push on. 'I had an idea. Hear me out. Gabe and Athena are heading up to my parents' place this weekend. I was wondering if you guys fancied joining. I thought we could take Friday off and head up early—it might be nice to get out of London and give the little invalid some fresh air?'

'Oh, wow.' She looks taken aback. 'I don't know—wouldn't we be in the way?'

'Absolutely not. My parents should have *the more the merrier* tattooed across their foreheads. I can't promise it'll be relaxing, but it'll definitely be fun. They love a full house.'

She worries at her lower lip. 'What if they figure out that I work for Seraph? If Athena barely survived that scandal, I definitely couldn't.'

I laugh. Athena got outed in front of my family by a total twat at a gala dinner. It was horrific, but my parents got over themselves eventually. 'Sweetheart, you look like a fucking chorister. You're the most wholesome woman I've ever seen. There's no way on earth they'd ever, ever suspect. Besides, there's no funny business going on here, is there?' *Not anymore.*

'I suppose you're right. But they really wouldn't mind?'

'Quite the opposite. They'd be thrilled to bits. We'll tell them the truth—you're my assistant and Athena's friend and you and Tabs could do with a bit of R&R. They know about you already—they know I was in the US with you. It'll do you both good. There's a pool and tennis courts, and lovely woods for a stroll... it would be a good place for Tabs to find her feet again, physically speaking.'

I'm pitching it as a casual weekend in the countryside, but

there's more to it than that. There's the fact of getting time with Marlowe and Tabby for an entire weekend, obviously, but there's also the matter of showing them that I don't come in a vacuum. I'm part of a warm, noisy and incredibly influential family who look after their own. If they were to become part of my family at some point, they'd never want for anything again.

It's not a case of flaunting our wealth but of painting a picture of a life where everything feels easy, where nobody suffers from a lack of means, where anything is possible. I'm aware that my parents' pad will seem like Disneyland to Tabs, and I'm not trying to manipulate the situation. I'm really not. If Marlowe, for whatever reason, decides to walk away from this, from me, I don't want to break an eight-year-old's heart by giving her a glimpse of all she might have had.

But I *do* want to show them both that all the magic, the abundance, that we spoke about in the hospital aren't one-off "treats". They're not flukes.

They can be their future, if they make room for me in their lives.

'Okay,' she says hesitantly. 'If you're sure. It sounds amazing.'

'It will be. And I'm sure. So that's settled, then. Now, next agenda item. When can I take you on a real date?'

# CHAPTER 54

# Marlowe

Brendan warned me on the drive up to Newmarket that his parents' house was like something out of a Jilly Cooper novel, and having binged on the TV adaptation of *Rivals*, I can concede that the guy has a point.

The house itself is absolutely gorgeous—a huge square Georgian pile sitting in perfectly manicured gardens that spill over into extended grounds. There's a pool, two tennis courts, an actual *maze*, and endless lovely spots for losing yourself in a book. Inside, it's luxurious if somewhat over-furnished, accessorised to the hilt with festoon blinds and curtain tassels and horsey oil paintings.

Every single surface—walls, beds, soft furnishings—of the airy twin room that Tabby and I will share is covered in a cheery rose print that continues into the ensuite bathroom. It's full-on but decidedly charming. It's clear that, despite the extreme wealth the Sullivans have, their house is a proper home. I allow myself a small private giggle at the thought that perhaps it was the aggressive florals that drove Brendan to furnish his penthouse in floor-to-ceiling taupe.

We're a party of thirteen this weekend: Brendan, Tabby

and me; Athena and Gabe; Brendan's parents, Ronan and Maeve, who are lovely; Mairead, her husband Peter and three kids; and a guy Brendan introduces as "my mate Dave". Dave seems slightly out of place, and I struggle to work out why until Brendan pulls me aside and explains that Dave is, in fact, a highly trained paramedic with a fully equipped private ambulance parked discreetly in one of the many garages. If Tabby suffers the slightest setback, Dave will spring into action and, worst case, transfer her to the nearest A&E.

I'm absolutely blown away that he's thought of this—that he's gone to this much effort and expense to guarantee Tabs' wellbeing while keeping the setup discreet enough to ensure she doesn't feel self-conscious. It's a level of detail that would totally have evaded me. That said, I'm relieved to know a trained medic is in our midst in this rural location. Brendan's bought me peace of mind this weekend, and it's as wonderful as it is alien.

Brendan was fab on the drive up here, putting on a Disney playlist to which the three of us proceeded to sing our hearts out. I had one of my moments when the other two were singing *Hakuna Matata*, and I'm not sure if it was dissonance or downright fantasy, but it was sweet and cruel all at the same time.

*This could be your future*, the little voice in my head said. *A gorgeous man to share these moments and make everything better. Brighter. A father figure for Tabs and absolutely every-thing for you—best friend, lover, confidant. Partner.* As if he'd read my mind, he looked over at me mid-song and smiled like he was having the time of his life.

Brendan Sullivan, billionaire playboy, singing along to *The Lion King* with a single mum and her little girl and looking perfectly content.

The weekend officially kicks off with a lavish lunch on the huge terrace. The spread is an epic ploughman's—indecently good pork pies, brightly coloured salads, a wooden cheese-board groaning under the weight of all that lovely, runny cheese, and scotch eggs so well-crafted that I declare them a delicacy.

I'm more interested in the people-watching, though. The dynamics. Athena's not one to struggle in any social situation or let insecurities get to her, but she doesn't seem entirely comfortable with Maeve yet. I know Brendan's parents took it hard when they discovered the true nature of Athena's rela-tionship with Gabe. Athena and Maeve are very polite—almost too polite—and it feels forced.

It's only when the conversation moves onto the Audacity Foundation, the family's foundation which Athena now runs, that Maeve warms up a little. It's a relief. Athena's amazing, and Gabe couldn't have found a more wonderful partner, but I know mothers can struggle to see their sons move on with another woman.

Brendan and his parents have a different dynamic, I notice. They seem to defer to Gabe a lot. He used to be a priest, so I suspect they still view him as a font of wisdom (even if his mother will never quite forgive him for leaving the priest-hood). But they don't seem to view Brendan with quite the same respect, which frankly dumbfounds me.

Gabe may look after the family's wealth, but Brendan runs their core business. Sullivan Construction is a behemoth in UK industry, and he's a highly respected CEO. There was absolute devastation when he dropped out of the summit to go be by my side. And still, they seem to treat him as a hapless, bumbling kid. When he put something in the wrong place on the lunch table his mum called him *a big eejit*. I think she meant it teasingly, but his reaction hit me hard: he instantly mumbled an apology, his huge shoulders slumping.

Jesus. Is this why he's obsessed with image and trophies and playthings—because his parents still don't take his success seriously? Because *he* doesn't allow himself to take it seriously? Maybe it's easier, safer, if it all feels like a game.

After lunch has been cleared away by several discreet members of staff, Brendan's parents go off to view a horse they're considering buying (as you do) and the rest of us set up camp around the pool. It's a lovely long pool in a secluded part of the garden that's walled off for safety reasons by tall laurel hedges and a wooden gate. There's a long row of solid wooden sun loungers with thick mattresses on the flagstone area, and a generous border of grass around the edges. At one end is a bar whose row of glass-fronted fridges is stocked with every drink imaginable. It's so hard to comprehend this kind of wealth. Even the cash sitting in all those purchased beverages must be hundreds or thousands of pounds.

'How are you feeling, sunshine?' Brendan asks Tabs as he clips her oximeter onto her finger.

'I'm good,' she says. 'I want to swim.'

'That's absolutely fine as long as you—oh, would you look at that. It's all running like a Swiss watch in there.' He pokes her in the breastbone.

It is. Her sats are at ninety-eight. I'm not sure when the thrill of seeing those numbers will fade.

'Just take it easy,' I tell her gently. 'You can have fun, just remember to take breaks if you feel tired or breathless.' I'm so used to managing her levels, to preempting every moment of exertion, that it will be a long time before I relax enough to let her activity levels run riot. Still, she looks to be full of life and raring to go, and Dave has taken up residence at the far end of the pool with a soft drink from the bar and a newspaper.

'I'll look after her,' Brendan tells me. 'Come on, sunshine. Let's go make a splash.'

We put our swimming costumes on in our room after lunch. I help Tabby take off her sundress and hand her her goggles. Her little body is vibrating with excitement. The plaster over her scar is barely visible under her swimming costume—the joys of laparoscopic surgery.

'We're going to do cannonballs,' Elsie, Mairead's eldest, tells Tabs. She has a shock of ginger hair and is, according to both Gabe and Brendan, a total terror.

'I hope no one wants to go swimming today,' Brendan says, reaching behind him and tugging his t-shirt off in one fell swoop, 'because I'm going to cannonball so hard that I'll empty the whole damn pool of water.'

'Nooo, Brendan!' Elsie pushes him ineffectually on the thigh. 'Not fair!'

I forget to be amused, because he's now wearing nothing except for a pair of sky-blue swim shorts whose low cut show-cases that happy trail I used to lick down. His body is smooth and bronzed and cut, and I'm hit with a shot of lust so potent that it makes my breath hitch. I haven't seen him naked since... probably that day I fell asleep on him at the Kingsley. I've tried very, very hard not to think about what I'm missing out on in my "new normal" with Brendan, and this reminder is very fucking unhelpful. I can just about keep myself together at work, but I'm only human. This level of exposure he has going on is frankly indecent.

Right now, I would gladly empty the pool area of every-one, including my beloved daughter, so I could yank those shorts down and get my mouth on that cock of his before pulling him down onto the lounger and grinding on him so shamelessly that—

Brendan throws his t-shirt at me. 'See something you like?'

I glare at him, feeling totally busted. 'That is very inappropriate,' I spit.

He bends down so he can whisper in my ear, and I can smell his sun-warmed skin. God, his shoulder is so close to me. So tanned and huge. I just want to sink my teeth into it. 'That eye-fucking you were giving me was even less appropriate,' he whispers, his breath warm against my jaw. His fingertips skim discreetly over the skin of my back, and I shiver. 'There are children around. Try to have some self-control. Nice bikini, by the way.'

When he straightens up, he's grinning at me. I shake my head at him, trying not to smile and failing miserably. The man has far too much swagger. He's a danger to himself and to society.

He turns away. 'Cannonbaaaaaall!' he shouts, leaping off the edge and tucking his legs in so tightly that, when he hits the surface of the water, he soaks every last one of us.

Cocky little shit.

Tabs may have a fully functioning pulmonary valve now, but she's just had major surgery, a fact of which I grow increasingly aware as the antics in the pool escalate. Still, the fear can't detract from the sheer joy I feel at watching her splash and swim around like a normal little girl. Just when I'm thinking she should get out and rest, Brendan procures a large watermelon-shaped floatie and has her get up on it. He drags her around the pool in it for a few minutes, sprinkling her with a tiny pink watering can until she squeals, and I realise it's his way of getting her to take some time out without missing out on the fun.

'He's very devoted,' Mairead observes. She and Athena are flanking me; Gabe and Peter are in the pool with the four kids.

'To Tabs or Marlowe?' Athena quips, and I glare at her.

'Both.' Mairead turns and slides her sunglasses down her nose so she can give me a pointed look. Unfortunately, I suspect this woman doesn't miss a thing.

'Agreed,' Athena says decisively.

'I don't think so,' I protest, embarrassed. 'He's very sweet, but he's just having fun with her. He seems great with kids.'

'Probably because he's been a big kid all his life,' Mairead agrees. 'It's not weird for him. He treats them like equals.'

I think of the hours this restless, distractible man spent closeted in a hospital room last week, painstakingly building a LEGO villa with my daughter while chattering away with her easily.

Mairead cuts through my thoughts. 'You know, he's never brought a woman home with him before. *And* he messaged me earlier this week to ask what kind of food kids Tabby's age like.'

My cheeks are growing hot, and not from the sun.

'He's very sweet,' I repeat lamely.

'He's not, though,' she muses. 'Not really. He doesn't do things he doesn't want to do. Ditching the summit and flying out to be with you in the hospital? That is *not* in character for Bren. He's been harping on about that summit for months. I thought Dad would blow a gasket when he found out he'd bailed.'

'To be fair,' Athena says, 'he's been pretty shitty to Marlowe. He owed her one big time, so when he found out about Tabs, it really shook him up.'

'Yeah,' Mairead says. 'Gabe filled me in on how it all went down. I have to say, I can see how that would have been a huge bombshell for Bren to process. It's all sunshine and roses in his life. His biggest headache in life is which of his cars to take for a spin.

'And then he starts falling for you, freaks out, *acts* out, and then finds out that while he's been behaving like a spoilt toddler, you've been dealing with some real-world shit that's so horrific as to be unimaginable.' She takes a sip of her iced rosé. 'I think that's what we call a *come to Jesus* moment—am I right, ladies?'

She may not be aware of the Seraph piece of this entire puzzle—at least, I hope she isn't—but she's nailed it, basically.

'You are,' Athena says. 'Do you think it's fair to say it might be the kick up the arse he needed? Not just with Marlowe, but for his life in general?'

'I think,' Mairead muses, 'that our little Bren has wanted more meaning, more purpose, in his life for quite some time, even if he was completely unaware of that fact, bless him. I have a feeling that you and Tabby are exactly what he needs, and that's why he's risen to the occasion so readily. He'll probably be telling himself that he wants to be your knight in shining armour, to swoop in and save you both. But don't be fooled for a moment, because I'm quite certain it'll be you two who save him.'

When I put Tabs to bed, it's clear she's tired in the best possible way, in a way that kids should be after a day in the countryside. She's swum and laughed. She's made new friends and learnt new games. Her body is working as it should, and it's a revelation.

'Elsie's really naughty, Mummy,' she tells me as I sit on the edge of her bed, stroking her hair. 'She poured her daddy's gin and tonic into the hedge and filled the glass with water from the swimming pool. When he got out of the pool, he took a big gulp and spat it all out.'

I laugh. 'Oh dear. That is very naughty. Poor Peter. What a horrible prank to play on her daddy. Have you had a good day, my love?'

'I've had the best day ever.' She sighs sleepily. 'Can we swim again in the morning?'

'Of course, as long as you're feeling up to it.' Dave has retired for the night, to one of the guest cottages (yes, that's a thing here) and has given me his number. I'm to call him if I have any worries in the night.

I'm peppering her face with kisses when Brendan appears in the doorframe. He may be in a linen shirt and shorts, but I'm struggling to erase the image of him in swim shorts from my mind.

'Hey,' he says softly. 'Okay if I say goodnight?'

'Of course.' I stand to make room for him by the bed.

He closes the distance and runs a huge hand over Tabby's hair. 'You did great today, sunshine. Did you have fun?'

'I had lots of fun,' she says. 'Can we play more Marco Polo tomorrow?'

'Yeah. Definitely. Though I may have to cheat a little and open my eyes. It was pretty embarrassing when I grabbed Peter thinking he was you.'

Tabs giggles, and it's a magical sound. He leans over and kisses her on the forehead.

'Goodnight, sunshine. Well played today. Get some rest, yeah? You'll need it for tomorrow.'

We walk downstairs in comfortable silence. 'Come outside with me?' he murmurs as I head towards the living room, and I nod.

'Sure.'

He takes my hand and walks me out of the French doors, across the terrace, and down the steps to the lawn. It's almost dark, but the gardens are illuminated by the light flooding out from the windows of the house.

'Thank you for today,' I begin, but he turns and pulls me into his arms, tugging me close and burying his face in my neck.

'God, I miss you. I miss you so fucking much.'

I've seen him every single day since we got back from the US, but I'm in no doubt about what he means. No doubt at all.

I wrap my arms around his back and I allow myself to breathe him in, to luxuriate in the unparalleled joy of being engulfed in his huge body. For two people who used to fuck like rabbits, deliberate celibacy is a real effort. And yet I'm quite aware that, moments like this, days like today, are more intimate in other ways. More meaningful.

'I miss you too,' I murmur, and he hugs me more tightly.

'Today was no effort at all. Spending time with Tabs is a joy. She's bloody amazing.'

'You're great with her,' I tell him. 'She has the time of her life with you.' It's the truth, and I'm not about to deprive Brendan of that truth, no matter how uncertain our future is.

'And I with her. But I know this kind of stuff is the fair-weather side of parenting. Anyone can have fun in a pool on a sunny day.' He kisses my temple. 'I promise you, sweetheart, I'm going to prove to you that I'm capable of sticking around for the tough stuff, too. I'm not going anywhere, and I'm willing to wait for as long as it takes to prove to you that I will never let you and Tabs down. *Ever*.'

# CHAPTER 55

# *Brendan*

Organising a first date with the woman you've given your heart to should be easy when you're a billionaire. We've all seen *Pretty Woman*, right? Take a jet to another city for an evening at the opera. But while Marlowe would love a night at the opera, she'd hate the flashy side of that gesture. The unnecessary expense. So I have to tread carefully here.

Here's the thing, though. I want to spend money on her. She's squirrelling every last penny away for Tabby's future medical needs, a fact that breaks my heart and terrifies me in equal measure, because once she's happy that that pot is adequate, she'll be handing in her notice and running for the hills. She's far too proud to keep taking her current salary for a regular EA role.

My only hope is to win her trust so fully in the meantime that she agrees to enter into an official romantic relationship with me.

After extensive mulling over it, I decide to call in a hefty favour from my good mate Santi to make this an evening for Marlowe to remember, and so it is that she and I meet outside

London's iconic jazz club, Ronnie Scott's, one Friday night. She refused to let me pick her up, so I make sure I'm waiting on the street when she turns up.

'You look absolutely beautiful,' I tell her sincerely before planting a chaste kiss on her cheek. It's true. She looks knockout in heels and a little black dress that shows off her toned arms and legs. Her hair is long and straight, and I wish I could bury my nose in it.

'Thank you,' she says a little breathlessly.

'Tabs doing okay this evening?'

I've seen Tabby with Marlowe four times since our weekend at my parents. Given it's the end of August and the construction industry is as dead as a dodo, I've enforced early departure times for the two of us whenever I can. Just this week, we've taken Tabs to play mini golf one evening and do roller skating on another. She was excellent at the latter, Marlowe looked like one of the newborn foals at my parents' stables, and I was pretty fucking awesome. At least it gave me a chance to hold Marlowe's hand a *lot*.

I also gave her the afternoon off to take Tabs back-to-school shopping.

'You've both been through a lot,' I pointed out when she protested. 'The summer holidays have been seriously rough for both of you. She'll be back at school next week. Take some time with her while you can.'

She kissed me on the cheek then, which sustained me through her absence for the rest of the afternoon.

'She's okay,' she says now. 'A bit tired, maybe, but her sats are normal. She's with a sitter tonight.'

I'm instantly on alert. 'Are you worried? Do you want to go home?'

'No, I'm good.' She lays a hand on my arm. 'Robbie has her in hand. I use a babysitting agency that's staffed by paediatric nurses. It's probably just that she's had a hectic week—far more active than she's used to.'

'Okay. If you're sure. We can leave at any point, you know.'

She smiles at me. 'I hope not. I'm excited. Who's playing tonight? It didn't say anything on the website.'

I tut. 'Such a nosy girl. It's a private event. You'll see soon enough.'

In reality, I'm thrilled that she's excited about being out with me. I made it very clear that this was a date. Not my usual kind of "slutty first date" where I try to get in my date's knickers, and definitely not like our first "date" at that club. But I wanted her to acknowledge verbally that this was a romantic date. It feels to me like we're making progress, and I need her on board with that. I've told her I'll wait as long as it takes to prove myself to her, but in reality, I am not a patient man.

And definitely not when I know exactly what and who I want.

We'll be sitting at one of the best tables in the house tonight with a great view of the stage. But before we take our seats, there's someone I need to introduce Marlowe to.

Santiago Vale, AKA Santi, is an old mate of mine. We were at uni together and have always stayed tight. He's achieved great success, not only as the CEO of his family's multi-billion pound classical music label, but also with his career as a tenor. He tours with Andrea Bocelli and regularly sells out the biggest arenas in every city around the world. Tonight's intimate audience isn't a money-spinner in the slightest; it's a way for him to indulge his great love of singing in an intimate setting and a way for punters like me and Marls to enjoy a truly unforgettable evening.

I just hope the surprise I have planned for her proves the icing on the cake.

MARLOWE

'So,' Brendan says as he leads me by the hand between the tables in the direction of the stage, 'tonight's performer is Santiago Vale. I hope you're a fan.'

I stop still and tug on his hand, my jaw dropping. '*Santiago Vale* is performing here this evening? What the hell?'

He grins at the look on my face. 'So she *is* a fan.'

'Of course I'm a fan,' I hiss. Hard not to be. The man is a dead ringer for Tom Ellis and has a voice like an angel. 'But he usually plays massive venues, and he's not a jazz singer. What on earth is he doing here?'

'He likes to do the occasional small venue, just to keep it real, you know? And I'm glad you like him, because we're going to go and say a quick hello.'

I stare at him in horror. There's no denying Brendan is an entitled git, but thinking he can waltz backstage and say "a quick hello" to one of the most famous tenors in the world is another level of cockiness.

He laughs. 'Relax. Santi and I are old mates. I'm his daughter's godfather, actually. Violet.'

My jaw is officially on the floor. I will never get used to this strange, incestuous world of the super-rich. They all seem to know each other. It's seriously weird. But I allow Brendan to tug me through a door by the stage. When he drops his name, we're waved on. It seems "Santi" is expecting us.

By the time we enter Santiago's dressing room, I have serious butterflies in my stomach. This man is a living legend. I don't know how many times I've played his album *Reflections* in various hospital wards over the years. Sometimes, his voice is the only thing that calms my soul. But in the flesh he's all white teeth and devastating, black-eyed charm, his lean, rangy body shown to elegant perfection in a black shirt and black suit.

'Sullivan!' he shouts, jumping to his feet at the sight of us. 'Mate, it is so good to see you.' They hug and slap each other's backs before Santiago pulls away and flashes me his gorgeous smile. He broke hearts everywhere when he announced that he was marrying his family's chef. 'And you must be Marlowe,' he says with a wink. 'I've heard so much about you.'

Before I can even speak, he grabs me and kisses me on both cheeks.

'I'm such a huge fan,' I stammer. 'I really am.'

Brendan grins at me. 'I think I'm getting jealous.'

'I'm delighted to hear you're a fan,' Santiago drawls, 'because I hear you and I are doing a little number out there tonight.'

I think I may have fainted. That's the only explanation for my hallucination. I stare blankly at Santiago.

'I asked him to invite you up to sing with him later,' Brendan explains in a kindly voice, like I'm a dim-witted toddler.

I. Am. Mortified.

'No you didn't. You did not.'

'He did,' Santiago tells me cheerfully. 'He said you're amazing. And classically trained. You trained at King's College, correct?'

'Yes, but—' I have to make him understand. 'I'm out of practice, Santiago. I haven't performed for years, and even then, only as a student. I—'

Santiago cuts me off smoothly. 'Call me Santi. I thought

we could sing *Summertime* together. Everyone likes a bit of Gershwin on a warm evening, even if we are stuck indoors. Don't worry, we're going to rehearse it right now.' He gestures at the piano.

If I were a multi-platinum-selling artist and my mate was suggesting I bring some random woman on stage to sing with me, I'd be freaking out. But not Santiago. *Santi*.

Oh my God, what is this rabbit hole I've fallen down?

Brendan doesn't stop grinning as Santi leads me over to the upright piano and opens a *Porgy and Bess* sheet music book.

'Let's have you sing the soprano part like normal first time around and I'll just fit in around you,' he explains, as though there's anything normal about this situation. 'Second time, feel free to ad lib. This one is just the *best* for playing around with—especially those second and third verses where you can really sock it to 'em.'

He's so casually, easily charming. The star quality positively shines out of him. I'm sure he's used to people doing everything he tells them to do.

'Okay,' I manage, shooting Brendan a last *save me* glance, but he just grins at me and squeezes my arm.

'Break a leg.'

I roll my eyes at him and stand behind Santi, looking over the sheet music.

He begins to play, and the part of me not currently shitting herself thrills at being in a room with *the* Santiago Vale as he plays the piano.

'We've got a nice little jazz sextet tonight,' he tells me, his fingers flying over the keys, 'but I'll lead us in for now.'

I've already made the split-second decision to give this one a very languid, jazzy arrangement. I've seen it sung in operatic style, but that's not right for a jazz club with as devastating a performer as Santi. I'd rather give it a sexy, sultry delivery that speaks of that lazy drift of a summer's day.

When I open my mouth, to my surprise, that's exactly what pours out, the very first word setting the scene for what's to come. Santi joins me, and we find our rhythm. It's a short song, the third verse a repetition of the second verse (a fact that makes it far easier for me to remember the lyrics). What's incredible is how evocative it is from that very first note.

I have an *oh holy crap* moment when I realise that *I am singing with Santiago Vale.* His voice is low and rich and decadent and just so fucking gorgeous, and it would be an absolute crime not to embrace this moment. I decide to ditch the idea of sticking to the notes on the first round, and I really go for it on verse two. When I do, Brendan lets out a positively orgasmic groan, and Santi shakes his head in a *damn, girl* way as his magical voice and fingers do their thing.

I let rip at the end. I may be out of practice. I may be a rusty amateur at best, but I can tell when two performers make magic together.

*And we just did.*

Santi laughs aloud. 'Fucking brilliant! That was immense! You could hear that, right? We were good.'

I can't stop smiling. 'Yeah. We were.'

'Your voice is fantastic. Rich and so fucking sexy. Where the hell have you been keeping this one hidden, Sullivan?'

'Locked up in my office,' Brendan says, 'which is fucking criminal.' He doesn't take his eyes off me as he says it.

'Amen to that,' Santi says. 'Okay, one more time, from the top.'

We're sitting at our table, and I'm clutching my champagne coupe like it's a life raft. I'm trying really hard to enjoy Santi's incredible set from this excellent position right in front of the stage, but the nerves are real. I'm glad we're doing drinks and not dinner. I'd never be able to get anything down.

Then Santi's talking and winking right at me. 'Ladies and gentlemen. I have a special treat for you tonight. To sing Gershwin's *Summertime* with me, please welcome to the stage Ms Marlowe Winters!'

Oh fuckity fuck. I give Brendan a panicked glance, and he grins back. 'You'll kill it. Go show everyone you were born to be a star.'

That's ridiculous, but I can't keep Santi waiting. I rise and walk as elegantly as I can to the low stage. A roadie helps me up the steps, and then I'm joining Santi onstage and taking my seat on a bar stool next to his. He flashes me a warm grin as the audience applauds me and the same roadie hands me a mic.

It feels so different being up here, so atmospheric, with the stage lights and the sublime jazz band and all the eyes on me. I look down and see Brendan leaning forward, his expression rapt, phone held up to record this historical moment. He's gunning for me one hundred per cent, and it gives me the shot of confidence I need. I glance back at Santi, who raises his eyebrows. *You ready?* I nod. *Ready as I'll ever be.*

And then the gorgeous jazz intro kicks in, and we go for it. I don't know if it's the orchestra, or that I'm playing to a crowd, but this performance is far more charged than it was back in the dressing room. We riff off each other, but I get the sense that he's holding back, maintaining the melody so I can shine. I act on instinct, embracing the improv nature of jazz as much as the uniqueness of this opportunity, my body producing trills and flourishes in real time from seemingly nowhere. I go a little crazy on the final notes, and when I still, the crowd and Santi are on their feet, clapping and stamping and yelling and wolf-whistling.

It's the most astonishing hit of adrenaline. The performer in me, deliberately dormant for so long, is still there. She loves this. She thrives on it. It's what makes her feel alive.

And that's dangerous.

# CHAPTER 56

# Brendan

Marlowe can't stop smiling all the way home.

Neither can I.

I've held this broken, exhausted mother in my arms as she emotionally collapsed in the safe confines of a shower. That image is indelibly printed onto my brain. So seeing her like this, vibrant and grinning and still high from her epic performance does things to my heart that I can't articulate.

*I* knew that Marlowe was inside her.

But whether *she* knew is another matter.

The best bit? Santi dropped by our table for a drink after his set and slipped Marlowe his business card, telling her to give him a call if she ever wanted to pursue a recording career. He's a good guy, but not that good. He wouldn't have made that offer if he didn't think she had serious potential.

'I still can't believe you pulled a stunt like that,' she says, shaking her head and beaming at me.

'It was a gamble,' I admit, taking her hand. She lets me. 'Not because I thought you'd fuck it up—I knew you wouldn't—but because I thought you might actually strangle me for putting you on the spot like that.'

'I was tempted to. But it was also the most incredible thing anyone's ever done for me. So thank you.' She looks down at our hands. 'It means the world to me that you have that much faith in my singing abilities.'

'I may be besotted with you, love,' I tell her, 'but I'm not stupid. I know talent when I see it, and your talent basically punched me in the face. You looked like a star up there. You held your own on stage with a global megastar—that should tell you how much fucking potential you have. All you have to decide is whether you're going to call him.'

She gives me an *oh, please* look. 'I have a job. And a daughter who needs me.'

'I'll happily fire you,' I retort. 'And you have a daughter who's going back to school next week and is now perfectly capable of leading a normal life.'

What I don't spell out is that, if I win her over and she becomes my girlfriend, she'll never have to work a day in her life to pay the bills. Instead, she'll be free to follow her dreams. I want that for her so badly. I want to be able to give her that freedom she deserves after years and years of thankless fucking toil, but I can't say that.

Because she'll accuse me of buying her right as I'm trying to set her free.

I've insisted on dropping Marlowe home. She's tried so hard to dissuade me that I suspect this goes way beyond her dislike of inconveniencing others. I have a feeling she doesn't want me to see where she lives.

Well, tough shit, sweetheart.

Yan eventually turns into a large, shitty housing estate and immediately my hackles go up.

'Is this where you live?' I ask her.

'Yeah.' Her voice is quiet.

'Is it a council estate?'

'Some of it, but quite a bit of it is privately owned now. Our landlord's a rental agency.'

I inwardly grimace as we drive by a wall of graffiti. That might be, but nothing about this estate screams *secure environment for a child and her single mother.*

'Did you ever think about living with your parents?' I ask in a neutral tone, my thumb stroking her knuckles.

'Not really. It would have been the practical option, but they need their space and so do I. I'm twenty-seven. I chose to bring up my daughter on my own, so at some point I was just better off standing on my own two feet and getting on with it, you know?'

'Yeah,' I tell her. 'I get that.' My circumstances couldn't be more different from hers, and I'm a decade older, but being overly reliant on our parents in adulthood is seriously rough. There comes a time when we need to spread our wings and forge our own path.

'It's just round to the left,' Marlowe tells Yan. 'Second block on the left. It's a bit of a shithole, I'm afraid,' she adds, turning to me.

I hate that she's embarrassed about where she lives almost as much as I hate that she lives here. I hate that she's so much better than me as a person and yet life has dealt me a far better hand.

It's not fucking fair.

Yan pulls to a halt outside a grim-looking block of flats with a grey pebble-dashed exterior. My professional guess is that these blocks were built in the seventies and should have been pulled down instead of being sold on privately. They're not as bad as some of the worst estates in the Docklands, but they're not the best, either.

'Thanks so much for this evening,' she says. 'I'll see you on Monday.'

'You can thank me inside,' I say firmly, releasing her hand so I can unfasten my seatbelt.

'No, that's not—you don't have to—'

'Nice try, sweetheart, but I'm walking you to the door. Come on. Out you get.'

She obeys reluctantly, and we start towards her block of flats. The air outside is thick with the smell of weed. It's noisy —TVs blaring, music thumping, voices raised in anger. It's the soundtrack of people who don't give a fuck about anyone else. Case in point: the fly-tipping. Right by the front door someone's left an old, stained mattress, a rusty pram and fuck loads of old baby clothes. For fuck's sake.

'It's very different from your place,' Marlowe says apologetically as we walk up the path.

'I'm not a snob, love. I just care that you're safe.'

She enters a code and pushes open the front door, and Jesus Christ. It's like I've been teleported into some gritty TV crime drama. This place is a dump. The first thing I clock is that the smell of skunk intensifies, along with the stench of stale piss. It smells like a public gents' toilet in here. The next thing, once I follow her in, is the gang members lurking in the dingy lobby. The metal and concrete staircase is to their right, just visible behind them a bank of lifts. They're all in black hoodies or balaclavas, and they're loitering in a way that smells trouble.

I'm instantly, horribly, conscious of the chunk of metal on my left wrist, courtesy of Patek Philippe. I'm pretty sure the cuff of my shirt is hiding it, but I daren't glance down and risk drawing attention to it. They stop talking as we enter and stare at us. Marlowe, I notice, doesn't engage with them at all. She bows her head and makes herself as small, as invisible as possible, scuttling towards the stairs. They ignore her, but they don't fucking ignore me.

'What you staring at, fam?' one of them asks as I put my foot on the bottom step. He's a skinny white guy with a spider tattoo on his face. Charming. I shoot him a look I hope will communicate my derision. 'I'm looking at you, dickhead.'

Probably not my smartest move, but I'm a fucking leader in business. I've got more petty cash in my sock drawer than these losers will ever see in their pathetic, crime-ridden lives. I have no intention of letting these little shits intimidate me.

'Brendan,' Marlowe hisses without breaking stride. 'Come on.'

'You 'ere that, Baz?' Spider says. 'He called me a dickhead. That's not very nice, is it?'

His mate steps up, a massive Asian bloke. At least a foot taller than Spider. Built like a brick shithouse. 'No, it's not. We don't like posh, cocky wankers around here. And we have our ways of showing them they're not welcome.' He pulls out a knife and flicks the blade open. When he holds it up, it glints in the dim light.

What a prick. My PT is a former marine. I have moves these guys have never seen. So no, I'm not scared of a crappy little blade, but I have no intention of exposing Marlowe to a knife for a second longer.

'There's no need for any of that shit,' I tell the guy. 'You and I both know it'll only land you in prison, so don't do anything stupid, yeah? I'm not here to make trouble.' I turn to Marlowe as calmly as I can. 'Let's get out of here, love.'

She nods, stricken, and begins to take the stairs two at a time. I follow her, hoping my body provides enough of a buffer between her and them. When I look behind me, the gang members aren't following us, thank God.

'How far up are you?' I ask as we climb.

'Fourth floor. Come on.'

*Jesus.* I'm more winded than I'd like by the fourth floor. With those wankers blocking the lifts, I suspect Marlowe and Tabby have to use the stairs more often than they'd like.

Marlowe puts her key in the lock and opens the door with a warning *shh* in my direction. I slide in behind her lest she try to shut me out. But the instant I'm in her flat, my stomach sinks like a stone, because, fuck. *This* is where she lives?

I mean, compared to the lobby it's practically the Four Seasons, but it's so small and shoddy. Not her furnishings or cleanliness level, but the actual build. You can tell just by looking at the walls that a well-aimed fist could punch straight through them. Her front door is flimsy as fuck. I can see damp from here on the ceiling over by the balcony, and I bet those windows are poorly sealed. They must let so much heat out in winter.

My internal property survey screeches to a halt, because next thing you know, a big Black guy in shorts and a t-shirt emerges into the living room. He has a smile as wide as his face and a body that says *I lift old people in and out of bed all day and push serious weights all night.*

'Hi Robbie,' Marlowe whispers, ignoring me. 'How was she?'

He smiles. The guy is a walking dental ad. 'Not too bad. She seems a bit under the weather, but I took her temperature a couple of times and it's in the normal range. She complained of a headache and feeling a bit rubbish in general, so I administered a dose of paracetamol at seven-thirty. Otherwise, she was very sweet. Sounds like you guys have had an adventurous month.'

'You can say that again,' Marlowe says, digging in her handbag for some cash. I know she'd go ballistic if I tried to cover the sitter, so I don't even try. She hands over a few notes.

'Here you go. Thanks so much for looking after her. I'll keep a close eye on her.'

He nods and takes the cash. 'Cheers. And I wouldn't worry too much. Probably just a summer cold. I'm sure she'll work through it pretty quickly.'

'Be careful, mate,' I tell him. 'There are a few unsavoury characters hanging out in the entrance hall. They just tried to pull a blade on us.'

'Take the fire escape stairs,' Marlowe suggests. 'It's left out of the door, at the end of the hall. It'll take you straight out onto the street.'

When he's gone, Marlowe jerks her head towards the door Robbie emerged from. 'I'm just going to…'

I follow her in. Tabby's room is larger than I would have expected. Best guess: Marlowe gave her the biggest room. She's probably sleeping in the shitty box room. This is definitely a haven, though. My heart aches at the effort Marlowe must have put in here. Strings of flower-shaped fairy lights cast their rose-pink glow, and in the corner is, I assume, the epic tent Athena organised.

But the real attraction lies in the middle of the room, where the little girl who's already stolen my heart sleeps peacefully. Her blonde hair covers most of her face, and I wish I could stroke it. I remember how soft it feels. I'm glad she has this sanctuary, even if the illusion of safety in here is just that.

An illusion.

I watch as Marlowe bends to kiss her head and then I follow her out to the main living area. It's clear she takes pride in keeping her home clean and cheery, but the colourful prints and the bunch of cheapo supermarket flowers can't detract from the stark reality: that this is a tiny, badly constructed flat in an unsafe block in a rough neighbourhood. Marlowe doesn't belong here.

Even if she's not ready to step into the professional glory

that could await her, she should at the very least have a life where her safety, and that of Tabby's, is a certainty.

'Thanks for an amazing evening,' she says to me distractedly. 'It meant so much to me. I'm going to hit the sack, so you can go now—'

'Not on your life. I'm not going anywhere. Not while those stabby little shitheads are around. I'm calling the police.'

'You can't call the police,' she hisses. 'They never give me any hassle, but you just went full alpha male on them. Of course they're going to act out if they're provoked. But if you call the cops it'll raise a whole load of trouble for me and everyone else in here.'

'They can't get away with shit like that—holding court down there in a public space and threatening other residents.'

'It was very clear to them that you're not a resident,' she argues, and I glare at her. 'Semantics. I'm calling the fucking cops.' I pull my phone out, and she grabs it.

'Brendan. *Don't*. I'm begging you. It'll just make things a million times worse for me. They'll just get a warning and then they'll know it was us who caused trouble for them. And you're not the one who has to walk past them every day with a kid.'

I stare at her, feeling sick. I can't bear the idea of Tabs and Marlowe feeling scared every time they enter their own fucking building. And what about Marlowe's parents? They must feel desperately unsafe when they come here.

'Fine. You can move in with me. I have loads of space, and Mark will be thrilled, and you can play the piano whenever you want, and—'

'Bren. We're not moving in with you. Don't be ridiculous,' she says, but her face is soft. 'We're not in a relationship. I'm your employee, and yes, you've been a very good friend to me and Tabs these past few weeks, and we're so grateful. But no one is moving in with anyone.'

This is crazy. I understand somewhere deep down that Marlowe is her own person and is entitled to call the shots in her own life, but it's beyond frustrating that she refuses to listen when I so clearly know what's best for her.

'For someone who's as amazing a mother as you are, you're very cavalier about Tabby's safety,' I spit out. I regret the words as soon as I've said them. 'I'm sorry. That was a dick move. I'm so sorry, love.'

Her eyes prick with tears, and I hate myself. My only goal this evening was to bring happiness and hope to her, and I've gone and ruined it by being a giant bellend.

'I do everything I can to keep her safe and well, and you know it. But I'm a normal person with limitations on what I can provide for her. Right now, I'm prioritising her health, which, thanks to you, has turned a corner. But I'm not in a position to sweep her off to some fancy enclave in Chelsea or other places that feel like fantasy lands. I live in the real world, with dangers and shitty neighbours. Like everyone else, I just have to suck it up and do my best and hope the universe doesn't hate me enough to throw a mugging onto the shit show I'm already dealing with.'

I can't bear it. I wish I could tug her into my arms and squeeze her as hard as I can. 'You're amazing. You're doing amazing, and I'm an entitled prick. But it fucking kills me to see you living like this when you work so hard and deserve so much.' *And when I could give you the moon if you let me.*

'I know you mean well,' she admits through gritted teeth. 'Just try not to be so heavy-handed, alright? My life is not your problem.'

*My life is not your problem.* Truer and more devastating words were never spoken.

'You can say that, but those guys downstairs might come up and make trouble for you, and this front door of yours is a fucking joke. I'm staying here tonight.'

Her jaw drops in horror. 'Not on your life. Don't you try to pull that card. I wasn't born yesterday.'

'I'm not trying to get into your knickers, love. This isn't some sleazy ploy. I'll sleep on the sofa.'

We both look at the sofa, which is a modest two-seater and a good foot or two shorter than me.

'Go home, Bren,' she says wearily. 'We'll be fine.'

'Who knows how much I've pissed them off. I don't want them to come looking for trouble and break this fucking door down. Your locks are shite, by the way.'

'You can't sleep on the sofa,' she protests, 'and you're not sleeping in my bed.'

'Fine.' I stride over to the sofa and pull the seat cushions off, throwing them in the direction of the door. I do the same with the various scatter cushions. It will be woefully inadequate, but it'll have to do.

It's only one night. How bad can it be?

'What the hell are you doing?' Marlowe asks, looking at me as if I've finally lost the plot.

Maybe I have. The Brendan Sullivan I know doesn't walk away from the career opportunity of a lifetime to hang out on an airless paediatric ward for a week. He prefers living it up in the South of France to playing endless rounds of Marco Polo on the weekends.

And he's sane enough to choose to go home to his bespoke Hästens mattress instead of playing build-a-bed with some foam blocks.

Churlishly, I shove the big square cushions against the wall so they form a makeshift mattress in front of the door. If these dickheads want to threaten Marlowe and Tabs, they'll have to get past me first.

'Isn't it obvious?' I ask crossly. 'I'm sleeping on the floor.'

# CHAPTER 57

# *Brendan*

I t's stupid o'clock and I can't sleep. Not surprising, given this flat is like a furnace and every time I turn over, the cushions skid on the laminate floor and separate.

I should probably just sleep on the floor itself.

As soon as Marlowe took herself off to her room I called Yan to tell him to go home. Then I called a mate of mine, Adrian, who runs a seriously hardcore private security firm. I met him through the guards who patrol my apartment block and he now does quite a bit of work for us.

I smile to myself as I imagine one of his most badass guys turning up sometime tonight to kick off what will be a permanent security presence downstairs from now on. While private security guards can't carry weapons, Adrian's guys don't need them. They're all trained killers, former mercenaries who require nothing more than their wits and their bare hands to make short shrift of anyone.

Those little turds will have to find somewhere new to hang out.

This is useless. I kick off the sheet Marlowe gave me and get to my feet. I'm only wearing boxers—my plan is to be up and out of here before Tabs wakes up. Much as I'd like to see her, Marlowe wasn't exactly thrilled about my "ridiculous caveman antics" (her words) and I can't imagine she'll want to see me in the morning. I'm not here to earn brownie points. I'm here because it's the right thing to do, but I don't want to undo the momentum we achieved last night.

I pad around her living area as quietly as I can. There are no curtains at the kitchen window, so the street lamps provide adequate light for me to see. What this place lacks in comforts and basic security requirements, it makes up for in love. There may not be an Hermès throw in sight, but the fridge is covered in Tabby's artwork and photos of the two of them. It makes my heart hurt to think of what a special bond these two have, and how much pain and suffering that bond has caused Marlowe over the years as she fights so hard for Tabby's health.

There's a card spelling out *I love you Mummy xx* with a selfie of Marlowe and Tabs in a park somewhere, minus Tabby's two front teeth. Marlowe looks so beautiful. Her hair is blowing around her face, her cheek squished against Tabby's.

I drift towards the bookshelves. They're cheapo ones whose ability to hold the shitload of books Marlowe has doesn't inspire confidence. I glance through the books. She really likes cookery. There's a lot of sheet music at the bottom, which I assume is left over from her degree. I find myself wishing I could just drag her and Tabs and all this music over to my place and be done with it. There are also some photo albums.

Bingo.

They're the ones you compile online before receiving the printed version in the mail. It looks like Marlowe does one each year.

I pull four or five out of the stack and return to my makeshift bed, opening the first book up. I'm not great with kids' ages, but Tabby looks to be two or three at a guess. It's amazing that Marlowe finds the time to put these mementos together amid the stress of working and parenting and dealing with hospital visits.

I drop down to one elbow and proceed to take a trip through the memories of the two people I've fallen for, memories I play no part in. Right now, the best I can hope for is that they allow me to be a part of their future memories. I may be the one with the ten-figure net worth, but there's no denying that Marlowe is richer than me in the ways that count.

I must have passed out eventually, because when I wake, the sun is streaming through the room. The floor beside me is strewn with photo albums, and my phone reads just after seven. Shit. I sit up in a panic before realising that the sound that's woken me is gentle crying.

Tabby's crying, to be precise.

I pull my shirt and trousers on hurriedly and pad over to Tabby's room. Marlowe's already in there, sitting on the edge of her bed.

'Hey,' I say as softly as possible so as not to startle Tabs. 'What's up, sunshine?'

Tabs gapes at me through her tears. 'Hi, Bren. What are you doing here?'

I glance at Marlowe. She's in shorts and a thin tank top and no bra, none of which is remotely helpful. I avert my eyes and focus on Tabs. 'I took your mum out last night, and I wanted to have a sleepover so I could see you this morning.' There's definitely no upside in mentioning any security issues to a kid her age. 'What's up with you? You not feeling too good?'

'She's got a fever,' Marlowe says, sticking a little plastic cup on the end of a thermometer. 'It doesn't feel too bad, but let's see...'

She sticks the device in Tabby's ear and it beeps. 'Thirty-eight-point-two.' She grimaces.

'Is that bad, Mummy?' Tabs asks with an adorable little hiccup-slash-sob.

'It's not too bad,' Marlowe tells her with a kiss to her temple, 'But it tells me your body is heating up so it can try to kill some germs.' She chews the inside of her cheek. 'I don't know if the GP surgery is open on the weekend, though...'

I immediately spot a way to add value. 'Sod that. I'll organise a house visit.'

'But...' she begins, and I shake my head at her. Now is not the time for pride. 'Consider it sorted.'

I pull up the number for the private on-call GP service I use. It's part of the obscenely top-end health cover I have. They guarantee house calls within the hour—in theory, anyway.

'I need an urgent visit for an eight-year-old,' I tell them. 'She's running a fever and she had a pulmonary valve replacement operation around three weeks ago. How soon can you get someone here?'

I hand the phone over to Marlowe to provide more medical and location details and run my hand through my hair as I blow out a breath. How quickly these terrifying medical terms insert themselves into our vernacular. Marlowe sounds like a cardiothoracic surgeon right now.

In the hour that we're waiting for the doctor to show up, I call the concierge in my building and ask him to bike over a few bits and pieces for me to wear so I don't have to spend the day in last night's clothes. I look like I'm about to do the walk of shame, which is very fucking ironic given I had precisely no action last night.

Tabs wanders out of her room as I'm putting the cushions back on the sofa. 'Where did you sleep?'

'On the floor. I was too big for the sofa.' She smiles, and I consider it a win. I scoop her up into my arms. That's better. She's light as a feather.

'How's your tummy? Is that sick too? Do you think you could eat some pancakes?'

I have just enough time to make us all some pancakes, take a shower in Marlowe's bathroom, which is spotlessly clean but has Third World levels of water pressure, and throw on the shorts and t-shirt my concierge team has delivered when the doctor shows up. She sits at the kitchen table with Marlowe and Tabby while I hover uselessly, sipping on my cup of tea. It was that or instant coffee.

'How are you feeling, Tabby?' she asks.

'Yucky and shivery,' Tabs says. 'Everything hurts.'

The doctor hums sympathetically. 'That's no fun, is it? And you had a big operation a few weeks ago, didn't you? How long ago, precisely?'

'Twenty days ago,' Marlowe supplies. She has Tabs on her lap. She gives the doctor a brief, calm rundown on the details of the operation.

'Okay, Tabby, I'm going to listen to your heart now,' the doctor says. She takes her stethoscope and listens for a few moments before frowning. 'Can you show me your hands?'

The room is silent as she inspects Tabby's fingernails—for what I don't know.

'I can't be sure, but given Tabby has recently had a valve replacement, it could be endocarditis.' She pauses. 'Did the surgical team mention this as something to watch out for in the weeks following the operation?'

Marlowe and I glance at each other. I was with her and Tabs for the entire discharge process.

'An infection?' I recall.

'Exactly.' She pauses. 'Her fever's not too bad, but I'm detecting a slight murmur in her heart.'

Marlowe lets out a strangled sigh and holds Tabby tighter.

'She's also showing some tiny splinter haemorrhages under her fingernails,' the doctor explains. 'There can be other reasons for them to appear, but given Tabby's recent operation and this little murmur, they would indicate endocarditis.'

'Okay, so…' Marlowe shifts Tabs on her knee and I step forward, bundling the little girl into my arms so Marlowe can talk to the doctor properly. 'She has an infection. What now—antibiotics?'

'I know this won't be welcome news,' the doctor says gently, 'but if—and currently it's an *if*—the new valve is infected, then it will need to be replaced. I'm so sorry.'

'But we had it in the US,' Marlowe stutters. 'We can't—I can't—'

'I know it's a lot to take in. The first thing you should do is get Tabby seen by her cardiologist immediately. He or she will be able to take some blood cultures and evaluate further.'

'What does that do?' I pipe up.

'They'll monitor the cultures for a day or two. If they start to grow bacteria, that's your sign that there's an infection, in which case I'd expect them to push to replace the valve as soon as possible.'

Marlowe stares at her, and I see every ounce of the grief and disbelief and shock in her beautiful face. There's defeat, too. Because she has moved heaven and earth to get this little girl a new valve, and this doctor is telling us it could all have been for nothing. Tabby might have to go through the exact same rigmarole *again*.

It's unthinkable, but there's one massive difference.

This time, I'll be by Marlowe's side every step of the way.

# CHAPTER 58

# Marlowe

The past seventy-two hours have been the worst kind of blur.

I say that, but it's not true. Because if Brendan hadn't been here with us, for us, it would have been unbearable.

As soon as the doctor had left on Saturday, I pretty much collapsed.

All that money.

The travel.

The recovery time.

All for nothing.

I couldn't bear it. I couldn't go through it again. I just wanted to lie down on the floor and sink into an exhausted puddle and fall asleep and never wake up.

But Brendan wouldn't let me do any of that.

I've always known he was an impressive guy, but boy did he show his true colours that day in the kitchen. And yeah, he's teased me before that he's good at throwing both money and his weight around, but this was far more than that. This was the kind of power flex that came from a parallel universe.

My plan was to call GOSH and see if they could squeeze Tabs in for an emergency appointment that day to conduct the follow-up tests the doctor had told us would be needed to diagnose an infection in the valve itself. But Brendan's proposal blew that out of the water.

First, he insisted that this would all happen privately and at his expense.

'You're not jumping through NHS hoops,' he said. We were all sitting on the sofa together, Tabs on his lap and his arm around me. At that point, I'd take his physical comfort over any concerns about what Tabs might think.

When I tried to push back—because the money involved would be *crazy*—he shut me down.

'It's the best thing for Tabs,' he said tersely. 'End of story. And nothing else matters but that.'

So he called his swanky health insurance provider and had Tabs added to his coverage. Just like that. Then he got them to hook us up with the Portland Hospital, a private women's and children's hospital where celebrities give birth, and their cardiology team said they would meet with us that day. His health concierge then got on the case with pulling Tabby's files from both GOSH *and* Duke to send over in time for our appointment.

Apparently, when Brendan Sullivan tells people to jump, they ask *how high*.

We saw the consultant there and she took some tests, including those blood cultures. After a tense forty-eight hour wait, during which Brendan refused to let me go into the office at all, she confirmed that Tabs did indeed have endocarditis and would need a full valve replacement posthaste.

It was nobody's fault.

It was just one of those things.

This was where it got stressful. I had chosen Duke for a reason. The private London hospitals have fancy equipment, but Dr Elliot and his team are the world's leading experts at valve replacements for children. A transatlantic trip wasn't an option for us.

Most normal people would admit defeat and settle for Plan B. Not Brendan. To say he behaved like an emperor was an understatement. He called and called and hustled and hustled, with two outcomes.

One. Brendan formed a multi-million dollar endowment to establish the Tabitha Winters Fellowship in Pediatric Cardiac Innovation at Duke Children's Hospital.

And two. Poor old Dr Elliott agreed to take a jet—chartered by Brendan, of course—to London yesterday.

I was as mortified as I was horrified.

And I've never been so grateful to another human being in my life.

It wasn't just the money. Brendan pulled strings to expedite practising privileges for Dr Elliott at The Portland, and he had his people handle all sorts of stuff for us, right down to matching monogrammed PJs for him, me and Tabs. We're going to wear them when she's out of the High Dependency Unit and back in her private room.

I should add that they all have huge pink hearts all over them.

Another surgery kicks off.

Another painful morning for Tabs of having to fast.

Another heartrending farewell before she goes under.

Another endless, terrifying wait while Dr Elliott works his magic for a second time.

Only this time I'm not alone.

This time, I am wrapped up in the arms of a man, a man strong enough, brave enough, committed enough, to be here for me.

A man who, despite first impressions, doesn't scare easily when life gets real. His money, his reach, may have salvaged this medical disaster from a shit show of NHS emergency surgery, and I'll never be able to thank him enough for that. But it stops there.

What happens behind those doors is down to Dr Elliott and the surgical team from The Portland now, and money can't affect the outcome I need so badly.

Only the universe can do that, and we both know it.

Still, he's not going anywhere. Not during the surgery, not after.

He's told me over and over again.

I cast my mind back to all those times over the past nearly nine years when I've sat in waiting rooms alone, frozen with fear and what-ifs, paralysed by the unconscionable knowledge that this time, it might not work. This time, something might go wrong.

This time, Tabby might not wake up.

I'm playing a different what-if game.

'I can't believe I let her catch an infection,' I mutter into Brendan's chest. It's so wonderfully, warmly solid. I don't ever want him to let me go. 'I can't believe it. All I had to do was keep her safe for a month or two after the operation. I can't *believe* she's having to go through all this again on my watch.'

'You can't blame yourself,' he says into my hair. 'You know that. She's a kid! They're grubby little fuckers. You can't wrap her in cotton wool.'

'Try me,' I say, and he chuckles softly. 'I shouldn't have let her go swimming at your parents' place. God, that was so irresponsible.'

'You heard what they said. It was far more likely to have been that tooth she lost last week.'

I know he's right. The consultant said as much. Apparently, poor dental hygiene—or an ill-timed wobbly tooth, as luck and shitty timing would have it—is a common entry point for bacteria.

I sigh.

'Listen to me. It's all going to be fine. Elliott's the best in the world at this stuff. He could do it in his sleep. And she won't get an infection next time.'

He's right, I hope. The surgical team have already put in place a rigorous post-op protocol for Tabs, consisting of preemptive and highly specific antibiotics, weekly blood tests to spot infections early, and more regular follow-ups. Tabs will probably need antibiotics ahead of any invasive dental treatments for the rest of her life. None of it's ideal, but it reassures me that this level of infection won't happen again.

It can't happen again.

'Come here,' Brendan says, scooping me up and lifting me sideways onto his lap. We're alone in the absurdly comfortable waiting area. 'I've got you. I've got Tabs. This won't happen again, and you'll never again have to face anything that *does* happen alone, no matter how routine.'

I stare down at him. His face looks creased and exhausted, and the tough part hasn't even started yet. He's been sleeping at his place but spending every waking hour at mine as we—he —put together this medical intervention of sky-high stakes and costs. I've had a front-row seat to not only his brilliant strategic brain, but his action orientation. Brendan is a doer. He gets things done to an extent that blows my mind, and I've never been more grateful for that particular skillset.

'Listen to me,' he whispers, his fingers playing through my hair. 'The only way I'm going anywhere is if you tell me to. In case you haven't noticed, I'm all in. I know I messed up really,

really badly and treated you like—well, like you never should have been treated, and I'm so fucking sorry. I'll never stop being sorry. But I need you to know that the only thing I care about in life is your wellbeing and Tabby's, and I want to stick around. I want to be there for you at times like this, and at happy times too. The whole shebang.' He pauses, his face beseeching. 'Because I am stupid levels of in love with you. Stupid levels.'

I gasp and go to speak, but he puts a gentle finger over my mouth. 'Don't say anything. I just wanted you to know. It's probably shitty timing, but I couldn't risk you sitting here, all wrapped up in your worry and not knowing how very much I love you and how desperate I am to be here for you in any way that I can be.' His voice drops to a whisper. 'And I'm head over heels for that little daughter of yours, too.'

He's had his moments, but I can't think of those right now. All I can think of is that, from the moment he discovered the truth about Tabby's existence, Brendan has been thrown into the car crash of our lives in the most epic style, and the man hasn't batted an eye. Not only has he stumped up unthinkable sums of money to secure her good health, but he's spent a good half of his time pulling his weight in doctor's offices and on hospital wards in recent weeks.

Showing up for someone doesn't get more powerful than that.

I let my head fall to his lovely broad shoulder, and I proceed to soak his shirt with my tears.

BRENDAN

'How are you doing, sunshine?' I ask Tabby as I reach out to clasp her little hand. Marlowe and I were both there when she came around about half an hour ago, but Marlowe's just popped to the loo.

Tabby is groggy but lucid. She smiles goofily at me, and my heart constricts.

'I'm good.'

'That's excellent to hear. You feeling sore?'

She shakes her head. I'm sure they still have her on strong painkillers. Some discomfort will be inevitable, but the important thing is that the operation went perfectly.

Thank God.

I glance down at her hand. 'Do you know what your sats are right now? You'll never believe it.'

Her eyes go big and round. 'What?'

'A hundred per cent. How about that? Little overachiever.' I bend over the hospital bed so I can press a kiss to her forehead. 'I'm so proud of you, sweetheart.'

Her brown eyes dance over my face. 'You sound like a daddy.'

I go completely still. Tears well in my eyes instantly. Like, immediately. I brush my thumb over her knuckles.

'Do I?' I manage.

Her smile is shy. 'Yeah.'

'Do you think I'd make a good daddy?' I press. This might just be the highest-stakes conversation I've ever had in my life.

She cocks her head. 'Yes. A lovely daddy.'

Okay, this next question is seriously fucking out of order, but there's no sign of Marlowe, and I may as well ask it.

'Do you think one day you could imagine me being your daddy?' I ask, my voice thick with emotion.

Her pale little face lights up, and it's all the answer I need.

# CHAPTER 59

# Marlowe

When I knock on Brendan's office door, his face is a picture. I watch with delight as his expression goes from shocked to downright feral. His eyes skim over my face and drop down, down, down. This dress is made from silk in a soft blush colour, with a swooshy skirt that ends just above my knees. It's one of my favourites from the selection Brendan bought for me at the start of the summer.

I think he likes what he sees. Then again, he's seen me at my most exhausted and crusty over the past few weeks, so the bar, I suspect, is low for the poor guy.

'What are you doing here?' he asks, sounding not the slightest bit displeased.

I shrug. 'Tabby got off to school fine this morning, so I thought I'd come in and make myself useful.'

'You don't have to, you know.' He pushes his chair back from his desk. 'You should have just taken the day for yourself. God knows you could have done with a break.'

He's ridiculous. He pays me to do a job and I'm only doing around a quarter of it at the moment, between the enforced celibacy and a sick little girl.

'I had other ideas about how I wanted to spend it.' I turn and lock the door before sashaying over to him. His hungry eyes track my every step.

I stop in front of him, looking down at this beautiful man of mine, this man who is every bit as flawed as the rest of us but who has shown up for me and Tabs, over and over, in every possible way, with frankly very little from me by way of reassurance.

He may have taken things from me this summer, but God knows I've taken from him in a way that I haven't allowed myself to do with anyone else aside from my parents. I haven't even allowed myself to lean on Athena as much as I'd like to over the past few years.

But Brendan has been there for me the whole time: this big, gorgeous, steadfast rock. He's held me and comforted me and fed me; he's sent me packing when I've needed a break; he's showered my little girl with attention and compassion. Above all, he's been the respite we've both needed, the person through this entire shit show who's been able to retain their sense of humour and hold onto their perspective.

I honestly don't know if I would have survived without him.

I can't bear to think about how it would have been without him.

And through it all, he's asked for nothing. *Nothing*. Everything he's given us, he's given it freely. No agenda. And definitely no recompense.

So now it's time to thank him. To tell him how I feel. To *show* him how I feel.

He stares up at me with those big blue eyes. 'You look so beautiful,' he stammers. 'I mean, you always look beautiful, but...'

'Thank you,' I whisper. I lay a hand on one broad shoulder for balance and swing my leg over so I can straddle him. As I lower myself down on him, my skirt flowing around me, the disbelief on his face grows. He looks like all his Christmases have come at once, poor guy. He bands an arm around my waist while his other hand slides through my hair to find the back of my neck as if in a dream.

'What are you doing?'

I pause, gazing down at him. My fingertips skate over the dark, neatly trimmed beard I adore so much.

'Showing you how much I appreciate you.' I swallow. 'Showing you how much I love you.'

He stills beneath me. His mouth opens, but no words come out.

'I love you,' I repeat, growing teary. 'And I'll never, ever be able to thank you for the way you've looked after me and Tabs.' A pause. 'And I miss you.'

I know he'll get my meaning. I mean it how he meant it when he said it in his parents' garden.

'I miss you too,' he whispers. 'I love you too. And you don't ever have to thank me. I did it because I love you. Both of you.' His fingers drift absently through my hair, setting off a trail of goosebumps over my neck. His eyes are almost all pupil now, and they're astonishing. 'I think I've been in love with you since that very first time I laid eyes on you at the RA. I've never had that reaction to a woman. Never. And it's just got stronger and stronger since then, sweetheart.'

I believe him. He may have had a funny way of showing it at times, but I believe that he loves me. I believed it when he told me in that waiting room, too.

And I can't wait a second longer.

I dip my head and I kiss his lovely mouth, and oh my God, the second my lips touch his, the second my chin brushes against his soft beard, I'm spinning, soaring through the air, because *I missed this so much.* He's provided me with so much physical comfort during 'Tabs' medical marathon, but nothing beats *this*.

The drag of my lips against his.

The satisfaction of him opening for me.

The filthy slide of his tongue into my mouth as he gets the memo that I want this. I need this.

I shunt myself further forward and hit a serious bulge as he drags his hand lower and grabs my bottom, tugging me more closely against him. I moan into his mouth and claw at his short, silky hair with one hand as I let the other roam over his bicep. His shoulder. He's *so much*, and I am fucking *starving*.

'Did you come here to tell me you loved me or to get railed, love?' he rasps in the low, dirty voice of a man rapidly losing control.

'Both,' I admit, grinding against him. *Definitely both.*

'*Fuck.*'

We're groping each other like horny teenagers, and it's amazing. I frantically undo the top few buttons of his shirt so I can slide my hand in and remind myself how fucking fantastic his pecs feel. Then I'm pulling on the concealed zip down the side of my dress so I can tug it off. It lands in a silky pile somewhere off to the left, leaving me straddling Brendan in nothing but heels and white lace lingerie.

'Jesus,' he says, leaning back so he can take me in, his jaw flexing as he smooths his warm palms down the sides of my body. His eyes meet mine. 'I'm speechless, sweetheart. Just speechless.'

A wave of intense frustration crashes over me. We had it so good before—on the physical side, I mean. Given everything that went down, I know we needed to halt our sexual relationship while we worked on everything else. These past few weeks have been a time of healing for me and Brendan as much as for Tabs.

Still.

A girl has needs, and it's been way too fucking long. We've wasted quite enough time.

I grind my lace-covered pussy against his trouser bulge again and pull at his hair. 'I need you inside me yesterday. I need you to fuck me, Bren.'

He chuckles, and it gives me pause. I stare at him. The Brendan Sullivan I know and love does *not* turn down a practically naked woman straddling him at his desk. 'What?'

'Remember your first audition?' His hands move languorously over my skin. He seems to be in far less of a hurry than I am.

I smile down at him. 'Yeah.'

'You were so shy. So nervous.' He swallows, his face growing serious. 'And now, of course, I know exactly why you were so nervous. Because you were practically a born-again virgin, showing up to fuck some rando to save your little girl.'

'I was,' I concede, 'but I loved every second of that evening, honey, in case you didn't notice.'

'I did notice.' He drags his hands lower, over my spread thighs. 'I was just thinking how far you'd come from then.'

I grin at him. 'You mean by marching in here and straddling you and stripping?'

'Basically, yes.'

'You said in your questionnaire that you liked the whole innocent thing,' I say haltingly. 'Do you think you can handle this?'

'The woman I love showing up and telling me what she needs? Yeah, I can handle it. This confidence of yours is the sexiest thing I've ever seen.'

We smile at each other dreamily.

*He did this.*

*He gave me this gift of sexual confidence.*

'It's quite fun being in charge for once,' I muse. 'Look who's calling the shots now.'

'If you're going to treat me like your little office fuck toy, you should know I can get on board with that,' he tells me. Fuck, he's sexy with his shirt half undone and his hair messed up and that cricket bat in his pants.

I run a fingertip down the exposed skin of his chest. Now, there's an idea. 'Really?'

'Really.'

I sigh for effect. 'I could use a few orgasms. It's been a stressful few weeks.'

His grin is filthy. 'Then use me.'

It's the hottest thing I've ever heard.

'Okay... then take off my bra. My nipples need some love. They're so achy.'

They really are—tiny, aching nubs that require some serious attention.

'Done.' A quick one-handed snap behind me and the bra falls away from my body.

'You're way too good at that.'

'Well, I am a professional.' He looks far too pleased with himself.

'Then what are you waiting for?' I demand.

He shakes his head with pride. 'Fuck me, you're cocky.' Then that same dark head is dipping to my left breast so he can suck one greedy nipple into his mouth. His pull is strong, the shot of arousal instantaneous.

'Oh my God oh my God,' I chant as he finds my right nipple with his fingers and pinches it hard. I grind against him, shoving my breast into his mouth, desperate for as much sensation as I can chase. Jesus Christ, I've missed this. Missed Brendan's dangerous mouth and skilful fingers. I luxuriate in the unearthly pleasure of writhing in his lap as he tends to me.

'I need your fingers,' I gasp as the devilish things he's doing to my breasts threaten to undo me. 'And your dick.'

He pops off my breast with an agonised groan and comes up for a hard kiss, his ravenous tongue devouring my mouth, his hand sliding down over my stomach like an obedient little fuck toy, fingertips brushing the thin lace strip covering my outrageously needy pussy only to stop dead. He pulls away from the kiss, and I freeze.

'Bren? What's wrong?'

His mouth twists in distress. He meets my eyes hesitantly. 'Last time I tried to pull this stunt, I—'

Oh shit. He's thinking back to that moment in that lunch meeting, the one I've tried my hardest to bury.

'Jesus, this is nothing like that,' I tell him. 'I didn't even make the connection.'

'I did, though. I'm not sure I've earned this.' He looks so devastated that I cup his cheek, stroking the soft hair of his beard.

I attempt to focus on the issue at hand and not on my screaming, weeping pussy. 'Honey, listen to me. You have earned this with every single hour you've spent by a hospital bed, these past few weeks. You've earned all of it.' I drop my voice to a whisper. 'It's just you and me here, doing what we do best. I want this. I want all of you, and I promise when you touch me down there, you'll see *exactly* how much I want it.'

'I can't get rid of the memories, though,' he says, shaking his head as if hoping that'll loosen them. 'The things I did to you that week, the way I acted—it makes me sick to my stomach.'

'There are a lot of memories from the past couple of months that I wish I could erase forever,' I tell him now. 'Believe me. But they're behind us, and we've both grown.' I look into his beautiful blue eyes, as tortured as they are aroused. 'I love you,' I whisper. 'I trust you. I know that if I tell you to stop, you will always, always stop. But you promised me once that if I begged you not to stop, you wouldn't. So please, *don't stop*, because I need you.'

Slowly, so slowly, he hooks his fingers into my thong and drags it to one side. I shiver at the fleeting brush of his touch where I need it. Then he holds my gaze as he slides a couple of fingers through my wetness and pushes them deep inside me. He keeps me in place with a hand clamped around the back of my neck.

'I love you so much,' he rasps. 'If you need me, I won't stop, I promise.'

I let my head fall back as he finger-fucks me good and hard, my body noisily sucking him in each time. But it's when he presses his thumb to my clit, exactly where I need, that I spiral heavenward. It's been too long, and I'm so in love with him, and he's too good at this, and I don't want to be strong or self-controlled; I just want this first orgasm to zip through me like the life force that it is. I want it to consume every cell in my body.

'Harder,' I beg. 'Harder, please.'

And my beautiful man obliges. His thumb rubs decadent circles over me as his fingers thrust as deep as possible. I arch back, taking it, taking every last, filthy ounce of this pleasure he's giving me, I douse myself in it like a rag soaked with lighter fuel.

And I allow it to set me on fire.

I come so hard on and around Brendan's fingers that I have to squeeze my eyes shut against the black voids where my peripheral vision should be. Sight is overrated, anyway, because the only thing that matters is this feeling, this astonishing pleasure whose flames are licking at every last inch of my body, inside and out. I ride his hand so damn hard I'll probably dislocate the poor guy's fingers.

As my orgasm floats away and I open my eyes, Brendan's face is a picture. Never have I seen a man look more awe-filled.

'Take me out,' he says, and I oblige, harnessing whatever shambolic remnants are left of my fine motor skills to undo the rest of his shirt buttons and fumble with his belt buckle and get his trousers open. His dick, huge and angry and weeping precum, is making a break for freedom over the waistband of his boxer briefs when I unearth it.

Honestly, my main coping mechanism these past few weeks has been studiously *not* thinking about what Brendan's packing, but holy fuck.

The damn thing is even bigger than I remembered.

## BRENDAN

'Wait,' I bark gruffly, attempting to reach past Marlowe to my desk drawer so I can grab a condom. I've scooted my chair back too far, and I can't—quite—reach—

She stops me with a hand on my arm. 'No.'

'No?' I stare up at her stupidly. Her nakedness, and gorgeousness, and declaration of love, and her orgasm, that fucking *orgasm*, have all addled my brain to the point that I'm officially more chimp than man right now. Has she changed her mind, or...

'No condom,' she says. Her face is flushed, her eyes are still glassy, that blonde hair of hers is tumbling over her spectacular tits, and I've never in my pathetic life seen anything so perfect.

And—no—she wants to—

'I had a coil put in when I started working for you.' She smiles at me, but it's not the smile of bashful disbelief she used to give me after I made her come in the early days. This one is powerful. Knowing. Like she's fully aware of how much this revelation will slay me. 'I don't want anything between us.'

*She wants me to go bare.*

That she trusts me with this after all my fuckwittery is almost too much for my heart to handle. She knows I didn't do anything with Fernanda. She knows I went to Alchemy but didn't—*couldn't,* if we're being technical—do anything. She's aware of it all. I divulged every pathetic detail to her one night in the US.

An unsheathed dick as a clean slate.

This is—this is the ultimate gesture of trust. It's the mother of all invitations, and my dick twitches at the thought.

'I'll make it worth your while,' I tell her, and she presses her forehead to mine as she rears up in my lap. She takes my dick in a strong grip and slides it through her soaking cunt. *So confident.* My girl knows exactly what she wants.

That it's me she wants is the greatest privilege of my life.

She feels incredible. She feels like home, and I can't wait to get inside her. 'Put me in, love,' I grit out, gripping her waist with both hands in an attempt to regain some kind of control, because she's taking too long.

She straightens up and smiles at me as she operates me like a joystick, directing me to exactly where she needs me. As she lowers herself down and takes the first inch, we both hiss with the pleasure of it.

'Fuck,' I groan. 'Not sure how long I'll last.'

'If you come before me, I'll need a refund,' she says sweetly. Despite my physical anguish, I throw my head back and laugh.

'Touché, sweetheart. Sex work's a tough gig, isn't it?'

'You bet your life it is.' She lowers herself down another inch and I groan.

'I could die a happy man right now.'

'You're not allowed to die. I love you far too much.'

'I'm not going anywhere. I promise.'

She pushes all the way down onto me. This feeling of bottoming out so deep inside her is so sublime, so other-worldly, that it is literally melting my brain. She does a little shimmy of her hips, and I utter a shaky groan. I simply won't survive this.

'Give me a sec,' I beg her, and she stills. We gaze at each other, finally joined in that unique way I took so much for granted in our early days together and at which I now marvel, because there is nothing on earth like this.

I stare into her huge brown eyes, so close to mine, so full of love and desire. In their depths, I see my entire future.

My happiness.

My life's meaning.

My *children*.

'You can move now, love,' I tell her hoarsely. 'Fuck me. *Use* me. I'm yours to do whatever you like with.'

She cups my jaw with both hands and watches my reaction as she drags herself up my dick. 'Say that again.'

My voice breaks with emotion. 'I'm good for absolutely nothing in this life but making you happy. Nothing. So let me do that for you. Because *I'm yours.*'

*Epilogue*

MARLOWE

I'm chuckling to myself as Brendan reenters the bedroom, but the sight of him has me instantly distracted. It's the low-slung cotton pyjama bottoms and all that bare skin and muscle up top. He's carrying two mugs of steaming hot coffee, and his dark hair is sticking up in several directions.

He is quite simply the dream.

If sleeping with Brendan Sullivan is heady, then actually *sleeping* with him is sublime. He's a huge, hairy, cuddly teddy bear, and falling asleep and waking up in his arms is the safest, the most loved, I've ever felt.

I simply don't know how I slept alone for so many years.

Tabs and I are having a sleepover at his place in Battersea. I call it a sleepover, but we haven't actually slept in our flat for a month. It's more of an *extended* sleepover. After I threw a tantrum over the ridiculous security presence Brendan had implanted, he told me firmly that as long as I was living there, his scary guards would be there too, keeping the stabby gang members away.

As a compromise, we've been staying with him and Mark more often. And who am I kidding? This place is a palace. Tabby adores the room Brendan has had set up for her, and I adore coming home from work, kicking off my shoes, and sitting down at that gorgeous Steinway to let the day pour out of me through the healing power of song.

It's not ideal for Tabby's school, but with the lovely and very attentive Yan on school run every morning and afternoon, it's doable for now. That said, it's a temporary solution. The three of us are finding our feet in this new relationship dynamic. We went through a lot this summer. Tabby's only been back at school for a few weeks, after all. So this new period of good health and tranquility, of feeling like we're floating gently downstream instead of drowning in the rapids, is very new to all of us.

'What's so funny?' he asks, setting a mug on my bedside table before planting a soft kiss on my hair. He wanders around the bed and climbs in, tugging me back against him. I brandish my phone at him.

'It's Soph. Seems she finally interviewed with Ethan Kingsley yesterday.' I try to keep my voice natural, but it still feels weird mentioning him to Brendan. He seems to think so too, because he frowns.

'Go on.'

I glance down at my phone and giggle again. This girl is hysterical. 'So, she thought he was an arrogant wanker, which she made abundantly clear to him during the interview, and they had a big fight.'

Brendan groans, but his mouth is twitching.

'Nice one, Kingsley. Yet another woman alienated. So she walked?'

'Not quite. Apparently the fight got them so worked up

that they decided to go ahead with the audition part there and then, and he called Camille and told her to release the twenty-five grand.'

He grins. 'Classy. So they hate-fucked right there?'

I'm almost giggling too hard to speak. 'Yep, but after he made her come, he was being so smug that she turned around to him and said, "Look, dickhead, my last boss was sixty-five years old so the bar is really fucking low, okay?"'

'I want to shake that woman by the hand. What a fucking queen.'

'Seriously. She's amazing.'

'So did he kick her out or offer her the job?'

I throw my phone down on the bed. 'He offered her the job.'

The people I love seem to have a habit of approaching me cautiously, glossy brochure in hand, when they want to change my life.

Athena did it ten months ago, when she first planted the intoxicating idea of having Tabs treated at Duke.

And Brendan is doing it now. Except that, when he pulls open the drawer of his bedside table and turns back to me, he has *two* glossy brochures in his hand.

'Don't fly off the handle,' he says, snuggling closer. 'Just—consider it, okay?'

'Okay,' I say, raising myself up on one elbow and taking a moment to eye-fuck my boyfriend. He may be the handsomest guy in the world, but that's not what's holding my attention. Not when he's looking at me with so much love and adoration and tenderness.

I tear my eyes away from his bare chest with difficulty and look down at the two brochures.

One is from a fancy estate agent. Its cover depicts house porn of epic proportions: a huge white Georgian mansion whose perfectly symmetrical front is festooned with wisteria. It is bloody stunning. *Winsford House, Ham, Richmond,* the caption reads.

The other is a school brochure bearing a photo of happy children outside a spectacular redbrick Queen Anne building with verdant lawns in the foreground. *Chancery School, Richmond.*

I glance back at Brendan, who clears his throat.

'My brother was telling me they're thinking of buying in Richmond at some point now that they're engaged, and, um, I thought it might be a nice place for us to settle, too. I'd like Tabs to have a proper garden to run around in, now that she's actually allowed to exert herself, and Chancery School is supposed to have incredible extra-curricular activities.'

At some point, the billionaire playboy who hired me for on-tap office sex has become a family man. I hit him with a secret, supremely unwell child and he didn't even flinch. He's been there for Tabs and me every single day since he jetted out to North Carolina to support us, and now he's planning houses and schools and futures around what will best suit her wellbeing.

'Hey,' he says, looking alarmed. 'What's up?'

I shake my head and sniff. 'Nothing. Just being a bit silly. I still can't quite get used to you making every single one of my dreams come true.'

'Well you'd better believe it.' He wraps an arm around my shoulders and pulls me in closer. 'I need you to get on board with this, love, because I'm never letting you go. This is it. You guys have endured more shit than anyone else I know, but that's all over now. This is going to be the phase that makes all the other crap feel worthwhile.'

I nod tearfully, twisting my head so I can bury my face in the crook of his neck. This is my favourite way to be: in Brendan's arms, his immense physicality the most effective reminder that I've found a safe place to land. That I don't have to do it all by myself anymore. That I have a true partner in every sense I've ever wished for and many, many more. I'm still working for him, mainly because we hate being apart from each other all day.

There are a lot of happy endings for both of us in the office.

'I love you,' I say, because it's easier than launching into a tearful monologue about the million ways in which he's touched my and Tabby's lives.

'I love you. So much.' He pauses. 'So... we can go visit the school any time we want, and we could look around the house this weekend. Or we can look at any houses you choose. It's just that this one jumped out at me. I could see it fitting us.'

I sniff back my tears. 'Why's that?'

'There's a hollow at the end of the garden,' he says slowly, 'that I think would make the most amazing spot for an adventure playground. Also, there's a pool. From what I can see online, the main drawing room has a big south-facing bay window where you could play the piano. And the basement is vast. It could easily accommodate a recording studio for you, if you wanted one.' He pauses. 'If we got our skates on, we could be in before Christmas and then Tabs could start at Chancery in January.'

'That all sounds amazing, honey,' I tell him. 'I can't wait to see it.'

'There's also a smaller investment property nearby that I was thinking of buying,' he says casually. 'It's a good price, but it's a lot of upkeep. Huge kitchen garden. I thought your folks might like to live in it for me, and I could pay them to maintain it.'

I stare at him, my eyes filling. He doesn't fool me for a second. He's been plotting for a way to get my parents' futures secured without making it feel like charity, and he's all too aware of how much they love growing fruit and vegetables. 'I don't know what to say.'

'You don't need to say anything.' He slides a hand around the back of my neck and tucks my head under his chin. 'Your parents gave up a lot to make sure that you and Tabs found your way to me in one piece, and now it's payback time. That's all there is to it.'

'Thank you,' I whisper, snuggling in more closely against his chest.

Brendan Sullivan may adore his construction firm and his LEGO room, but it seems building a fairytale life for the two women he loves is his new favourite passion project.

And he's good at it.

He's really, really good at it.

BRENDAN

The water is crystal clear in Jost Van Dyck's White Bay, and the sand is white. We moved into our new home a fortnight before Christmas, just in time to get a tree up, but I've whisked the girls off to the British Virgin Islands for a week post-Christmas.

The trip is an opportunity to let the builders crack on with constructing Marlowe's new recording studio while we play with our newest toy, the Lagoon SEVENTY 8 catamaran, *Tabitha*. With everything that the summer held for us, I didn't get a chance to play with her in the Med, so I had her taken out here to the BVIs.

When we met, Marlowe was working so hard to survive that she had forgotten how to play and I was playing so hard that I had forgotten how to feel very much at all.

Now we're in a position of extreme privilege. We have love, health, wealth, and even a touch of wisdom, and we're damn well going to make the most of it. So at a time of year when we're lucky to get eight hours of daylight each day, the sensible thing seemed to give the bleak midwinter a huge Fuck You and jet off to somewhere where life is warmer and gentler.

Tabby's entire cardio-pulmonary system is operating perfectly these days, which is a polite way of saying she is fucking inexhaustible. She's already signed up for after-school clubs at her new school every day of the week *and* extra dance and trampoline classes on Saturdays. I thought I was in good shape, but my stamina is nowhere compared to that of a little girl with nine years of enforced downtime to make up for.

But it's cool. We've found a rhythm. We've been pottering around the BVIs for five days now. Tabs and I spend our mornings having diving and swimming competitions in the clear turquoise waters while Marlowe sunbathes on the cushioned tanning deck in various skimpy bikinis. It's a great eye-fucking setup for both of us. In the afternoons, we dock and explore the various islands, while our evenings are spent at beach bars—like last night at the iconic Soggy Dollar Bar—or eating quietly on the boat together.

Tabby's sleeping like a dream out here. No fucking wonder—she never takes a breather during the day. The slide I had added onto the catamaran is up there with the best purchases I've made. She must have done a hundred slides into the sea this morning. But it's all good, because when she's asleep, I can make love to my girlfriend as I gaze at the stars and thank them over and over for the incredible richness of my life.

This evening is just another blissfully chilled-out night as far as my girls are concerned. But for me, it's a big one. We're sitting out on the deck in our swimwear. We'll shower later, but we've promised Tabs a sunset swim before we get cleaned up. Tabby's wearing a sweet little custard-yellow skirt over her swimsuit, while her beautiful mother has wrapped a sarong we bought on one of the islands around herself and tied it behind her neck. Her blonde hair cascades in salty waves over shoulders that are bare and sun-kissed. She's never looked so stunning as she does here, carefree and tanned and utterly at ease.

Despite the fact that we're enjoying the view from a multi-million-pound catamaran, we're doing a pretty good job of demonstrating that the best things in life are free. Light beers —Orangina for Tabs—and crisps on deck as we watch the sky grow prettily pink is all we need to take the edge off as our chef prepares fish tacos below deck. It's a regular family moment, and it feels real enough for me to reach under the cushioned bench for the small bag I stashed earlier.

I adjust my baseball cap self-consciously. 'I wanted to talk to you both about something.'

They both look at me. Marlowe brushes her fingertips over the sand that's dried on my shoulder. 'What is it, honey?'

'Well, I wanted to say'—I clear my throat—'how much it means to me to have you both here. We've made a lot of memories already, and I can't wait to make more. And it feels like we're a proper... family, you know? Especially now that we're all living together properly.'

Tabby beams at me. I wink at her before catching Marlowe's eye. Thrilled as she seems with our new home, I know that giving up her independence to move her and her daughter in with me wasn't a straightforward decision for her. I'm painfully conscious that they've let me into their little family unit, that I'm a third wheel among two people with a stronger bond than any I've seen. That's why it was important for us all to move into a new home: neutral territory.

Still, I'm the one bankrolling it, and I know that makes Marlowe nervous. Her old place might have been a shithole, but she paid the rent. She called the shots. Now she's taking a huge chance by putting her and Tabby's eggs in my basket, and I know, much as she trusts me, that it leaves her feeling vulnerable.

Marlowe has been on the receiving end of far too much shitty circumstance over the past decade, whether that's come in the form of dickhead exes or Tabby's heart condition or the endless flaws in our healthcare system that make those dependent on it feel so vulnerable, and it ends here.

This is where I tie everything up with a great, big legal bow so that she and Tabby are protected for evermore in an iron-clad way.

Only my plan is to cloak it in more romantic terms than that.

And I'll probably wait until I've given her at least one orgasm before I come clean about the enormous trust fund I've set up for Tabby.

It's only prudent. Athena would try to give the whole lot away otherwise.

I put the fancy carrier bag on the table, and Marlowe arches an elegant eyebrow at the Cartier logo. God, I wasn't expecting to feel this nervous, but I guess splaying your heart wide open and slapping it onto the table in front of the two people whose love and acceptance you want most in the world is always going to feel raw.

'Like I said, we're a family.' I reach into the bag with a shaky hand and extract one small box and then a slightly larger one. 'But I'd like us to make it official, so that everyone understands that we belong to each other.'

It's still a weird-as-fuck concept in the best possible way: *we belong to each other.* These two have accepted me to be their person. My shakiness worsens as I open the smaller box and hold it out to Marlowe.

'Which is why I'm asking you to marry me,' I say, meeting her stunned gaze. In this light, her brown eyes are endless dark pools in which I'd happily drown. 'I want to be with you until the day I die, love. I don't ever, ever want to be apart from you.'

Tabby squeals, and Marlowe and I both laugh, as if we can use the tension-breaker. Marlowe opens her mouth but I hold up my free hand to cut her off. 'Hang on. Not quite done yet. You ladies need to confer before you give me your answers.'

I put the jewellery box down on the table in front of her so she can ogle the enormous fucking diamond Athena helped me choose on Bond Street before Christmas. To say the woman extorted me that day is an understatement, but I'm hoping it'll help me close the deal. Besides, I'm the one who'll get to enjoy the sight of my diamond sparkling on Marlowe's long, slender finger for the rest of my life.

'I think he's got one for you, too,' Marlowe tells Tabs, giving her a gentle nudge.

'I do.' I open the larger box and hold it out to Tabs. In it is nestled a gold charm bracelet that I hope she will take as a sign of my commitment to her. 'Tabitha Lily Winters, will you do me the honour of becoming my child in the eyes of the law?' At her blank look, I add, 'Will you let me adopt you, sunshine, so that I can be your legal dad?'

Marlowe, whose eyes did nothing more than grow moist during her own proposal, promptly bursts into tears. As usual, she's happier for her daughter than she is for herself, and I wouldn't have it any other way. I may have been bowled over by her looks initially, but it's her huge, selfless heart I've fallen in love with.

And honestly? I'm kind of relieved she's happy. Asking a kid to let you adopt them without consulting their actual parent first could easily take a bloke from Grand Gesture territory straight into Dick Move terrain.

Tabs clamps her hand over her mouth, her eyes enormous, as she looks from me to her bracelet and back to me again.

'Mummy, can we?' she whispers through her fingers. The innocent readiness of her answer fucking crucifies me, and I tear up like a great big idiot.

Marlowe gathers her up in a huge side hug while she hooks her free hand around my neck, tugging me towards her. The sea may be pink and sparkling and wondrous, but it has nothing on the sparkle in those brown eyes of hers.

'Is that a yes?' I whisper against her mouth before she kisses me hard.

She pulls away. 'Yes. Yes, yes, yes, a million times yes.'

I nod, screwing up my face against the godawful stinging in my sinuses. 'Good, love. That's very, very good.' I want to kiss her again, want to dive in and never come up for air. But I have one more answer to collect before I do.

'What about you, sunshine? Will you let me adopt you, too?'

'Yes please,' she whispers with a toothy grin before her face falls in confusion. 'But shouldn't *we* adopt *you*? 'Cause there's two of us and only one of you.'

'Get over here,' I growl, and she springs up from her seat to come around the table to my lap. She's light as a feather. I sit her across my legs and kiss her on the temple before tugging Marlowe more tightly into my side.

'That's a fair point, actually,' Marlowe says, attempting to wipe her cheeks with the back of her hand.

'He could be Daddy Winters,' Tabby suggests.

Marlowe instantly starts coughing. 'Oh my God, Tabs.'

'I don't know,' I say, leaning into her so I can brush my

lips over her hair. 'Daddy Winters. It has a nice ring to it.' I lower my mouth to her ear. 'Especially in the bedroom.'

She swats my thigh. *'Stop it.'*

'Let's get this jewellery on you ladies before a seagull comes and spirits it away,' I suggest.

'Good idea.' Marlowe reaches over and pulls both boxes towards us. 'Anyway, Tabs, Bren can't be a Winters. He literally has a whole company named after him.'

'I'm not so sure,' I say as I slide the symbol of my lifelong commitment onto my fiancée's finger. 'It could be a good call, actually. Maybe people will finally forget I'm a nepo baby.'

## THE END

Thank you for reading!

Get Marlowe, Brendan and Tabby's heartwarming Christmas
bonus epilogue here:
https://geni.us/duplicity_bonus

Ethan and Sophia are up next and these two will be HOT.
You can preorder Vivacity here:
https://geni.us/vivacity_seraph

# A Note from Elodie

Dear Reader,

There comes a time in every book when an author reaches a fork in the road. To the left lies the boring, sensible route of factual integrity, and to the right the dazzling temptations of artistic licence.

I turned right when depicting the final turn in Tabby's illness.

In real life, Brendan could never have flexed his billionaire muscles like that. Dr Elliott would not have been granted practising privileges and Tabby would have ended up getting emergency surgery on the NHS. Susie Tate, who is a GP (MD), enlisted the help of her paediatric consultant friend to confirm as much.

I considered this route, I really did. I thought that, actually, finding out that there was no financial wand he could wave would be a great life lesson for Brendan. Sometimes, you can't flex your way out of a crisis. You just have to give your time and your support.

*Sometimes, all you can do is show up.*

But here's the thing.

There was no way I was doing that to Marlowe.

*No fucking way.*

She prostituted herself and spent a fortune on getting her daughter across the Atlantic for surgery. She sacrificed everything for that trip. And there was no way on earth I was making her endure her worst nightmare after all that. I just couldn't inflict that on her.

Similarly, it's likely Tabby would have been in and out of hospital far more quickly than she was, given that her procedure was laparoscopic. But then Bren wouldn't have had his Encanto moment, would he? And we all needed that.

So thank you for humouring me. God damn, I loved every second of writing this book!

I'd like to say a huge thank you to the following:

Susie Tate and Rosa Lucas for not only beta reading but workshopping the heck out of this book. They low-key bullied me to ramp up both the betrayal and the grovelling (you can thank Susie for the Brendan-sleeping-on-the-floor scene) and talked through lots of tricky parts with me, as well as cheerleading and validating me along the way. They're the best, and if you haven't read their books yet, then I suggest you dive straight in. Having two of my favourite authors workshop this one was SO much fun!

Thank you also to Jennifer Brooks Brown for beta reading, Esther Kiburi for proof-reading, and to my wonderful ARC team for being just as skilled at picking up those last typos as they are at feeding my praise kink.

Last but not least, thank you to my lovely Nerds who continue to show up for me on Facebook.

Thank you for reading! This job is a blast, and you make it possible.

Elodie

xx

★★★★★ "∞ ☆ 🌶 🌶 🌶 🌶 YOU ARE NOT READY FOR AUDACITY!!! This book is straight-up FIRE  ." readbyS, Goodreads

I've always shot for the moon, but if you'd told me I'd be earning seven figures aged twenty-four, I would never have believed you.

And if you'd told me that I'd earn every penny of that success by selling my body and my soul, I'd have laughed in your face.

Still. Here I am at Seraph, an elite agency that recruits only the most well-educated, accomplished and discreet women.

Our area of expertise? "Full service" executive assistants to the most powerful men in the world.

Whatever our bosses need, we provide. Day or night, in the boardroom or the bedroom.

It's every bit the challenge I've longed for, and it's more fulfilling than I could ever have dreamt. My secret? Discipline. An open mind. And rock-solid boundaries.

None of which are a problem, until I cross paths with Gabriel Sullivan, a former Catholic priest turned billionaire CEO whose appetites are voracious as his demons are relentless.

In the midst of all his inner turmoil and outer pressures, I know it's my very impassiveness that he values the most.

Too bad he's the only man I've worked for who makes me want to burn every one of my boundaries to ash.

*Audacity is a scorching hot billionaire, age gap, workplace romance spun off from my Alchemy series. It's the story of Athena, Anton Wolff's "full service" executive assistant in Unveil.*

Read for free on KU:
https://geni.us/audacity_seraph

*Dive into the Alchemy*
*series with Unfurl...*

★★★★★ **"I knew it was going to be spicy, but DAMN. I was not prepared for this.** This may have been the most well done spicy read ever. We're talking crazy, INSANE levels of hot here." —Buttons and Books

An upbringing steeped in purity culture has saddled me with three things: an intact V-card, enough Catholic guilt to fill a cathedral... and a raging priest kink.

My religious extremist father is intent on preserving my virtue, but when I meet my magnetic older neighbour, Rafe, it seems the universe has other plans for my body... and my soul.

He's the precise opposite of me: a man who views sex as a commodity, whose club caters to the wealthiest, most debauched clientele in London.

But when I discover the club offers a programme to "unfurl" inexperienced women like me in a safe space, I'm in. Even the entry questionnaire has me clenching with desire. It seems I'm about to get schooled in every delight I've been missing.

Rafe makes it his mission to bring my wildest fantasies to life. When he and his friends don their dog collars, they put the *hot* into *hot priests.* He's so attentive, so *possessive,* and I have to remind myself that a boring little virgin like me could never make a man like him happy in the long run.

So when all the religious BS I've been battling comes to a head in the most horrifying way, what right do I have to think he'll stick by me?

*Unfurl is a super spicy romance featuring a 14yr age gap, an FMC intent on reclaiming ownership of her body and her belief system, and an MMC brought to his knees by the very woman he vowed to bring to* her *knees. Belle and Rafe enjoy some group fun along the way before they find their monogamous HEA.*

Read for free on KU:
https://geni.us/unfurl_alchemy

**Alchemy is a completed series of 7 books: 6 interconnected standalone and 1 extended epilogue.**

www.ingramcontent.com/pod-product-compliance
Lightning Source LLC
Chambersburg PA
CBHW031732180726
48283CB00005B/1474